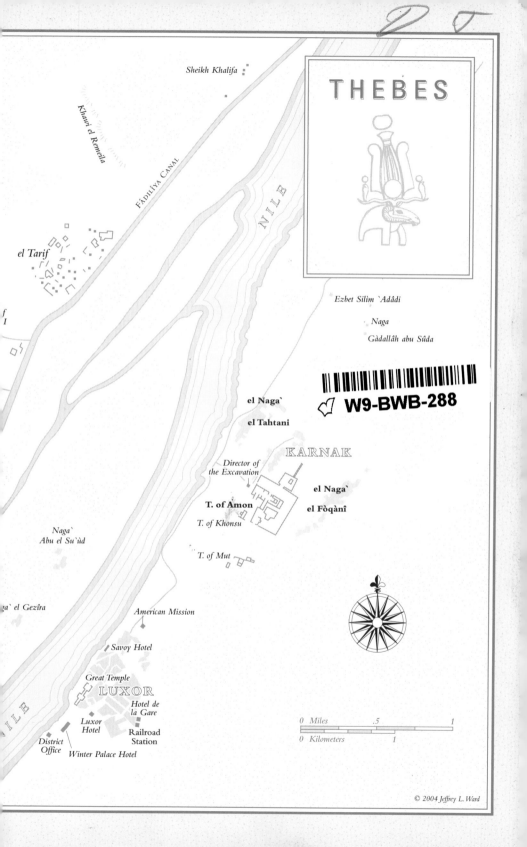

Sheikh Khalifa

Khaur el Remeila

FÂDILÎYA CANAL

NILE

el Tarif

f

Ezbet Silìm `Adâdi

Naga

Gâdallâh abu Sûda

el Naga`

el Tahtani

W9-BWB-288

KARNAK

Director of
the Excavation

el Naga`

T. of Amon

el Fòqànî

T. of Khonsu

Naga`
Abu el Su`ùd

T. of Mut

a` el Gezîra

American Mission

THEBES

Savoy Hotel

Great Temple

LUXOR

Hotel de
la Gare

NILE

Luxor
Hotel

Railroad
Station

District
Office

Winter Palace Hotel

0   Miles          .5              1

0   Kilometers          1

*In honor of volunteer*

**Kristi Moss**

*— April 2006 —*

# TOMB
## OF THE
# GOLDEN
# BIRD

# TOMB
## OF THE
# GOLDEN
# BIRD

# Elizabeth Peters

wm

WILLIAM MORROW

*An Imprint of* HarperCollins*Publishers*

TOMB OF THE GOLDEN BIRD. Copyright © 2006 by MPM Manor, Inc. All rights reserved. Printed in the United States of America. No part of this book may be used or reproduced in any manner whatsoever without written permission except in the case of brief quotations embodied in critical articles and reviews. For information address HarperCollins Publishers, 10 East 53rd Street, New York, NY 10022.

HarperCollins books may be purchased for educational, business, or sales promotional use. For information please write: Special Markets Department, HarperCollins Publishers, 10 East 53rd Street, New York, NY 10022.

FIRST EDITION

*Designed by Phil Mazzone*

Printed on acid-free paper

Library of Congress Cataloging-in-Publication Data

Peters, Elizabeth.
    Tomb of the golden bird / Elizabeth Peters.—1st ed.
      p. cm.
    ISBN-13: 978-0-06-059180-9 (alk. paper)
    ISBN-10: 0-06-059180-3 (alk. paper)
    1. Peabody, Amelia (Fictitious character)—Fiction. 2. Women archaeologists—Fiction. 3. Egyptologists—Fiction. 4. Tutankhamen, King of Egypt—Fiction. 5. Egypt—Fiction. I. Title.

PS3563.E747T66 2006
813'.54—dc22
                           2005057568

06  07  08  09  10  WBC/RRD  10  9  8  7  6  5  4  3  2  1

*To Phil and Kathe Gust*
*Members of the Fellowship*

# ACKNOWLEDGMENTS

Since I do not scruple to pick the brains of my friends, I must acknowledge the contributions of Joan Hess and Dennis Forbes. Joan suggested a new motive for Sethos (which turned out to be a cursed nuisance, but which is nonetheless appreciated) and Dennis reminded me that Emerson was, after all, the Father of Curses. Dennis's book, *Tombs. Treasures. Mummies.* gives one of the best accounts of the discovery and excavation of Tutankhamon's tomb. I would also like to thank him and my invaluable assistant, Kristen Whitbread, for reading the entire manuscript in search of errors. If they missed anything, the mistakes are my responsibility.

# LIST OF CHARACTERS

**The Emersons and their kin**

Professor Radcliffe Emerson, "the greatest Egyptologist of this or any other century"

Amelia Peabody Emerson, his wife

"Ramses," Walter Peabody Emerson, their son

Nefret Emerson, Ramses's wife

David John and Charlotte (Charla), their twin children

Walter Emerson, Radcliffe's younger brother

Evelyn Emerson, his wife

Seth, alias Sethos, alias Anthony Bissinghurst, Radcliffe's "other brother"; half-brother of Radcliffe and Walter

Sennia Emerson, child of Amelia's nephew (formally adopted)

David Todros, grandson of Abdullah (see below)

Lia Todros, née Emerson, his wife, daughter of Walter and Evelyn

Gargery, their butler, who considers himself a member of the family


**Their Egyptian family**

Abdullah, their former reis (foreman), now deceased (or is he?)

Selim, his youngest son, the present reis

Daoud, Abdullah's cousin, assistant reis

Kadija, his wife
Sabir, his son
Ali Yussuf, Hassan; his other sons
Fatima, the Emersons' housekeeper in Luxor

## Vandergelts and staff

Cyrus, American millionaire, longtime friend of the Emersons, and sponsor
    of excavations in Egypt
Katherine, his wife
Bertie, her son, adopted by Cyrus
Jumana, daughter of Abdullah's brother, first Egyptian woman trained in
    Egyptology
Suzanne Malraux, artist
Nadji Farid, excavator

## Luxorites

Inspector Ibrahim Aziz, chief of Luxor Police
Lieutenant Gabra, his assistant
Deib, Farhat and Aguil ibn Simsah, tomb robbers
Azmi, enterprising water boy
Wasim, a guard
Elia, the twins' nursemaid
Kareem, incompetent footman of the Emersons'
Badra, sous-chef
Jamad, stableman
Maaman, the Emersons' cook
Abdul, servant at Winter Palace Hotel
Ishak, guard in Valley of the Kings
Reis Girigar, Howard Carter's reis
Ali, suffragi at Shepheard's Hotel, Cairo
Ali Ibrahim, boatman

## Journalists

Margaret Minton, *Morning Mirror* (married to Sethos)
Kevin O'Connell, *Daily Yell*
Bradstreet, *Morning Post* (Cairo) *NY Times*
Bancroft, *Daily Mail*
Arthur Merton, *London Times*


## Archaeologists and hangers-on

Howard Carter, excavating in the Valley of the Kings
Lord Carnarvon, his patron, aka "Pups"
Lady Evelyn Herbert, Carnarvon's daughter
"Pecky" Callender, engineer and architect, friend of Carter
Herbert Winlock, head of the Metropolitan Museum staff at Deir el Bahri,
    Luxor
George Barton, one of his staff
Pierre Lacau, Director of the Service des Antiquités
Rex Engelbach, Chief Inspector for Upper Egypt
Ibrahim Effendi, his assistant
Theodore Davis, former American sponsor of excavations in the Valley
    of the Kings
Arthur Weigall, former Chief Inspector for Upper Egypt
Arthur Mace, member of Metropolitan Museum staff
Harry Burton, photographer, ditto
Hall and Hauser, draftsmen, ditto
Alfred Lucas, head of chemical laboratory of Survey Department, Egypt
Mr. and Mrs. Davies, artists, copyists of Egyptian tombs
Alan Gardiner, British philologist
James Henry Breasted, American Egyptologist
His wife; his son Charles


## Animals

Amira, dog
the Great Cat of Re

Risha, Ramses's Arabian stallion
Moonlight, Nefret's mare
Asfur, David's horse
Eva, Amelia's mare

## Ancient Egyptians and gods

Mertseger, "She Who Loves Silence"; cobra-headed goddess, name given to
    the pyramid-shaped mountain at Valley of the Kings
Amon, chief god of Thebes
Aton, the "sole god" of Akhenaton, below
Akhenaton, "the Heretic," pharaoh of late Eighteenth Dynasty
Nebkheperure Tutankhamon (Tutankhaton); possibly son of above
Ankhesenamon (Ankhesenpaaton); wife of above, daughter of Akhenaton
Nefertiti, wife of Akhenaton
Seti II, one of the "confusing pharaohs," Twentieth Dynasty
Ramses VI, one of the lesser Ramses, Twentieth Dynasty

## And

Sir Malcolm Page Henley de Montague, wealthy collector
Sir William Portmanteau, Suzanne's grandfather
Fuad, King of Egypt
Feisal, King of Iraq
Saad Zaghlul, head of Egyptian Nationalist Party
Gertrude Bell, English explorer, writer, king-maker
Ibn Saud, ruler of Arabia
Sayid Talib, Iraqi nationalist regarded by many as the most logical candidate
    to rule that country
Mohammed Fehmi, aka Bashir, Egyptian nationalist and ex-revolutionary
Bracegirdle-Boisdragon, aka Mr. Smith, head of a certain department that is
    unnamed
Wetherby, his assistant
Thomas Russell Pasha, Commandant of Cairo Police
Lord Edmund Allenby, British High Commissioner, Egypt

# TOMB
## OF THE
# GOLDEN
# BIRD

# CHAPTER ONE

"RAMSES!"

Seated on the terrace of Shepheard's Hotel, I watched with interest as a tall young man stopped and turned, as if in response to the calling of his name. Yet this was not the fourteenth century B.C., but the year of our Lord 1922; and the tall man was no ancient pharaoh. Though his bronzed skin and black hair resembled those of an Egyptian, his height and bearing proclaimed him for what he was—an English gentleman of the finest quality. He was also my son, "Ramses" Walter Peabody Emerson, who was better known in Egypt by his sobriquet.

He raised his hand to his brow, and realized that (as usual) he was not wearing a hat. In lieu of removing that which was not present he inclined his head in greeting, and one of his rare, attractive smiles warmed his thin face. I craned my neck and half rose from my chair in order to see the individual who had occasioned this response, but the crowds that filled the street blocked my view. Cairo traffic had grown worse since my early days in Egypt; motorcars now mingled with donkeys and camels, carts and carriages, and the disgusting effluvions their engines emitted offended the nostrils more than the odors of the above-mentioned beasts—to which, admittedly, I had become accustomed.

I deduced that the person my son addressed was of short stature, and most probably female (basing this latter assumption on Ramses's attempt to remove his hat and the affability of his smile). A portly person wearing a very large turban and mounted on a very small donkey passed in front of my son, and by the time he had gone by Ramses was wending his way toward the steps of the hotel and the table where I sat awaiting him.

"Who was that?" I demanded.

"Good afternoon to you too, Mother." Ramses bent to kiss my cheek.

"Good afternoon. Who was that?"

"Who was whom?"

"Ramses," I said warningly.

My son abandoned his teasing. "I believe you are not acquainted with her, Mother. Her name is Suzanne Malraux, and she studied with Mr. Petrie."

"Ah yes," I said. "You are mistaken, Ramses, I heard of her last year from Professor Petrie. He described her work as adequate."

"That sounds like Petrie." Ramses sat down and adjusted his long legs under the table. "But you must give him credit; he has always been willing to train women in archaeology."

"I have never denied Petrie any of the acclaim that is his due, Ramses."

Ramses's smile acknowledged the ambiguity of the statement. "Training is one thing, employment another. She has been unable to find a position."

I wondered if Ramses was implying that we take the young woman on to our staff. She might have approached him rather than his father or me. He was, I admit, more approachable, particularly by young ladies. Let me hasten to add that he did not invite the approaches. He was devoted to his beautiful wife Nefret, but it might be asking too much of a lady who is approaching a certain time of life to allow her husband close association with a younger female. Miss Malraux was half French. And she was bound to be attracted to Ramses. Women were. His gentle manners (my contribution) and athletic frame (his father's), his somewhat exotic good looks, and a certain *je ne sais quoi* (in fact I knew perfectly well what it was, but refused to employ the vulgar terms currently in use . . .).

No, despite our need for additional staff, it might not be advisable.

"Have you had any interesting encounters?" Ramses asked, looking over the people taking tea on the terrace. They were the usual sort—well dressed, well groomed, and almost all white—if that word can be used to describe complexions that ranged from pimply pale to sunburned crimson.

"Lord and Lady Allenby stopped to say hello," I replied. "He was most agreeable, but I understand why people refer to him as the Bull. He has that set to his jaw."

"He has to be forceful. As high commissioner he is under fire from the imperialists in the British government and the Nationalists in Egypt. On the whole, I can only commend his efforts."

I did not want to talk politics. The subject was too depressing.

"There is your father," I said. "Late as usual."

Ramses looked over his shoulder at the street. There was no mistaking Emerson. He is one of the finest-looking men I have ever beheld: raven locks and eyes of a penetrating sapphirine blue, a form as impressive as it had been when I first met him, he stood a head taller than those around him and his booming voice was audible some distance away. He was employing it freely, greeting acquaintances in a mixture of English and Arabic, the latter liberally salted with the expletives that have given him the Egyptian sobriquet of Father of Curses. Egyptians had become accustomed to this habit and replied with broad grins to remarks such as "How are you, Ibrahim, you old son of an incontinent camel?" My distinguished husband, the finest Egyptologist of this or any era, had earned the respect of the Egyptians with whom he had lived for so many years because he treated them as he did his fellow archaeologists. That is to say, he cursed all of them impartially when they did something that vexed him. It was not difficult to vex Emerson. Few people lived up to his rigid professional standards, and time had not mellowed his quick temper.

"He's got someone with him," said Ramses.

"Well, well," I said. "What a surprise."

The individual who followed in Emerson's mighty wake was none other than Howard Carter.

Perhaps I should explain the reason for my sarcasm, for such it was. Howard was one of our oldest friends, an archaeologist whose career had undergone several reversals and recoveries. He was presently employed by Lord Carnarvon to search for royal tombs in the Valley of the Kings. Searching for royal tombs in the Valley of the Kings was Emerson's great ambition—one he could not fulfill until Carnarvon gave up his concession. Rumor had it that his lordship was about to do so, having come to the conclusion—shared by most Egyptologists—that the Valley had yielded all it ever would.

Emerson did not share that conclusion. At the end of the previous season he had admitted to me that he believed there was at least one more royal tomb to be found—that of the little-known king Tutankhamon. He had done his best, without actually lying, to conceal this belief from Howard. One of the reasons why we had come to Egypt so much earlier than was our custom was to discover what plans Howard and his patron had made for the coming season.

One look at Emerson's expressive countenance told me what I wanted to know. Despite the heartiness of his vociferous greetings, his sapphirine eyes were dull, his well-cut lips set in a downward curve. Carnarvon had not abandoned his concession.

However, Howard Carter appeared no more cheerful. Nattily dressed as was his habit in a tweed suit and bow tie, a cigarette holder in his hand, he addressed me with a rather stiff bow before assuming the seat I indicated.

"How nice to see you, Howard," I said. "We tried several times this summer to communicate with you, but without success."

"Sorry," Howard muttered. "I was in and out, you know. Busy."

"I ran into him by accident at the office of the director," said Emerson, who had been haunting that spot for two days. He relapsed into gloomy silence. Ramses gave me a meaningful look and tried to revive the conversation.

"Like ourselves, you are out early this year, Carter."

"Had to be."

The waiter approached with a tray. He had, with the efficiency one expects at Shepheard's, noted our number and brought cups and biscuits for all.

"The area where I mean to excavate is very popular with tourists," Howard resumed. "Want to get it over before they arrive in full force."

"Ah," said Ramses. "So Lord Carnarvon has decided on another season. We had heard he was thinking of giving up the firman."

Emerson made a soft growling sound, but Howard perked up a trifle. "One more season, at least. I persuaded him we must examine that small triangle we left unexcavated near Ramses VI before we can claim we have finished the job we set out to do." He glanced at Emerson, and added, "I have the Professor to thank for that. Initially his lordship was of the opinion that another season in the Valley would be a waste of time, but when I told him that Professor Emerson had offered to take over the concession and my services, Carnarvon had second thoughts."

"Naturally," I said, managing not to look at Emerson. "Well, Howard, we wish you good fortune and good hunting. When are you off to Luxor?"

"Not for a while. I want to visit the antiquities dealers. Though I don't suppose I will come across anything as remarkable as that statuette you found last year."

"I doubt you will," said Emerson, cheering up a bit.

Howard asked about our own plans, and we thanked him for allowing us to continue working in the West Valley, which was properly part of his lordship's concession. After we had finished tea and Howard had taken his leave, I turned to Emerson.

"Don't say it," muttered my husband.

"Emerson, you know I would never reproach you for failing to follow my advice. I did warn you, however, that making that offer to Lord Carnarvon would have an effect contrary to what you had hoped. Given your reputation, your interest was bound to inspire a spirit of competition in—"

"I told you—" Emerson shouted. People at a nearby table turned to stare. Emerson glared at them, and they found other objects of interest. With a visible effort he turned the glare into a pained smile, directed at me. "I beg your pardon, my dear Peabody."

That brief moment of temper was the most encouraging thing I had seen for months. Ever since my near demise the previous spring Emerson had treated me as if I were still on my deathbed. He hadn't shouted at me once. It was very exasperating. Emerson is never more imposing than when he is in a rage, and I missed our animated discussions.

I smiled fondly at him. "Ah, well, it is water over the dam. We will not discuss it further. Ramses, when are Nefret and the children due back from Atiyeh?"

Ramses consulted his watch. "They ought to have been here by now, but you know how difficult it is to extract the twins from their admirers in the village."

"You ought to have gone with them," said Emerson, still looking for someone to quarrel with.

"Nonsense," I said briskly. "Selim and Daoud and Fatima went with them, which was only proper, since they wanted to visit with their friends and kinfolk. They ought to be able to keep two five-year-olds from taking harm."

"It would take more than three or four people to keep Charla from doing something harmful, to herself or others," said Emerson darkly.

In this assumption he was justified, since his granddaughter had a more adventurous spirit than her brother, and an explosive temper. However, it was not Charla who returned cradled in the muscular arms of Daoud. We had returned to our sitting room in the hotel, and when Emerson saw David John limp as a dead fish and green-faced as a pea, he sprang up from his chair with a resounding oath.

"Hell and damnation! What is wrong with the boy? Daoud, I trusted you to—"

"He's drunk," shouted David John's twin sister, her black eyes shining and her black curls bouncing as she jumped up and down with excitement. "The boys gave him beer and dared him to drink it." She added regretfully, "They wouldn't let me have any, they said it was only for men."

David John, who was as fair as his sister was dark, raised a languid head. "I wanted to know what it felt like."

"Well, now you know," I said, for of course I had immediately diagnosed the cause of the boy's malaise. "It doesn't feel very nice, does it? Put him to bed, Daoud, and let him sleep it off."

"I'll do it," said Ramses, taking the limp little body from Daoud, whose face was a picture of guilt. Daoud is a very large man with a very large face, so the guilt was extensive. Ramses gave him a slap on the back. "It wasn't your fault, Daoud." From the quirk at the corner of his mouth I knew he was remembering the time he had returned from the village after a similar debauch, though not in a similar condition. He had prudently rid himself of the liquor all over the floor of Selim's house before leaving the village.

"Are Selim and Fatima downstairs?" I asked. "They were afraid to come up, I suppose. Tell them it's all right, Daoud. I expect you were all busy watching Charla."

"But I was good," Charla informed us. She ran to her mother, who had sunk into a chair. "Wasn't I, Mama? Not like David John."

In a way I couldn't blame her for gloating a trifle. Usually she was the one who got in trouble.

Nefret patted the child's dusty curls. "No, you weren't. Climbing the palm tree was not a good plan. She got halfway up before Daoud plucked her down," she informed us.

"But I didn't get drunk, Mama."

"You must give her that," said Emerson, chuckling. "Come and give Grandpapa a kiss, you virtuous young creature."

"She is absolutely filthy, Emerson," I said, catching hold of Charla's collar as she started to comply. "Come along, Charla, we will have a nice long bath and then Grandpapa will come in to kiss you good night. No, Nefret, you sit still. You look exhausted."

The advantage of having the children spend the day with Selim and Daoud's kin at the nearby village of Atiyeh was that the enterprise usually left them so tired they went to bed without a fuss. David John was already asleep when I turned Charla over to Fatima, assured the latter that we did not consider she had neglected her duty, and returned to the sitting room to join my husband and son. Emerson was pouring the whiskey.

Owing in part to our early departure from England, we four were the only members of our staff in Egypt. In fact, we were currently the only members of the staff. Ramses's best friend David, our nephew by marriage, had finally admitted he would prefer to spend the winter in England with his wife, Lia, and their children, pursuing his successful career as an artist and illustrator. (He had admitted this under pressure from me, and over Emerson's plaintive objections.) Emerson's brother Walter and his wife, my dear friend Evelyn, who had been out with us before, had given up active careers in the field; Walter's chief interest was in linguistics, and Evelyn was fully occupied with grandmotherhood. She had quite a lot of grandchildren (to be honest, I had rather lost track of the exact number), from Lia and their other sons and daughters.

Other individuals whom we had hoped to employ the previous season had turned out to be murderers or victims of murder—a not uncommon occurrence with us, I must admit. Selim, our Egyptian foreman, was as skilled an excavator as most European scholars, and his crew had learned Emerson's methods. Still, in my opinion we needed more people, particularly since I was determined to carry out my scheme of allowing Ramses and Nefret to spend the winter in Cairo instead of joining us in Luxor. I hadn't proposed this to Emerson as yet, since I knew he would howl. Emerson is devoted to his son and daughter-in-law, as they are to him, but he tends to regard them as extensions of himself, with the same ambitions and interests. The dear children had given us loyal service for many years, and they were now entitled to pursue their own careers.

I assumed that Emerson and I would be going on to Luxor, though I wasn't certain of that. Emerson had reverted to his infuriating habit of keeping his plans secret, even from me, until the last possible moment.

That moment, in my opinion, had come.

"Very well, Emerson," I said, after a few refreshing sips of whiskey. "The moment has come. You have had several interviews with the director of the Antiquities Service, and since you did not return from them in a state of profane exasperation I presume M. Lacau was agreeable to your request. What site has he allotted to us?"

"You know," Emerson said. "I told you before."

"No, you did not."

"The West Valley?" inquired Ramses.

Emerson, who had been anticipating the prolongation of suspense, looked chagrined. "Er . . . yes. Quite right."

"What about Carter and Carnarvon?" I persisted. "If their dig in the East Valley comes up empty, won't they want to move to the West Valley? It is properly part of their firman."

"If—that is to say, when—they give up the East Valley, Carnarvon may decide to end the season," Emerson said. "If they do continue, it will most likely be in the tomb of Amenhotep III. Carter made a very cursory excavation there in 1919. It's at the far end of the West Valley from the area in which we would be working. There's room for half a dozen expeditions."

I seized my opening. "It would make better sense for us to join forces with Cyrus Vandergelt at the tomb of Ay. We are short on staff, and Cyrus has—"

A timid tap at the door interrupted me.

"Now who the devil can that be?" Emerson demanded. "I am ready for dinner. Where's Nefret?"

"She'll be here directly," Ramses said. "She wanted to bathe and change."

"Answer the door, Emerson," I said impatiently.

The suffragi on duty outside bowed low and handed Emerson a slip of pasteboard. "The gentleman is waiting, Father of Curses."

"He can damn well go on waiting," said Emerson, inspecting the card. "Of all the impertinence. It's that rascal Montague, Peabody. I won't see him."

Emerson seldom wants to see anyone, but he had a particular animus against Sir Malcolm Page Henley de Montague. He was a wealthy collector of antiquities, a category to which my spouse objects on principle, and a very irritating man in his own right. I doubted that he had called upon us from motives of friendship. However, it is advantageous to discover the motives of such persons in order to guard oneself against their machinations.

"Now, Emerson, don't be rude," I said. "We can't go down to dinner until Nefret is ready, so we may as well hear what he has to say. Show him in, Ali."

Sir Malcolm carried a silver-headed stick, not for support but for swatting at the unfortunate Egyptian servants he employed. Carefully doffing his hat so as not to disturb his coiffured mane of white hair, he bowed and greeted us all in turn.

"It is good to see you back in Egypt," he began.

"Bah," said Emerson. "What do you want?"

"Pray take a chair, Sir Malcolm," I said, frowning at Emerson. "We were about to go down to dinner, but we can spare you a few minutes."

The door, which Ali had closed behind Sir Malcolm, opened again to admit Nefret. Her eyes widened at the sight of our visitor, but she extended her hand and let him bow over it. His look of admiration was justified; she looked very lovely, although the styles of that year were not nearly so pretty as they had been in my youth. The frock, of a soft blue that matched her eyes, had no sleeves, only narrow straps supporting a beaded bodice, and the skirt reached just below her knees. At least she had not given in to the fad of cutting her hair short; its red-gold locks were swept into a knot atop her head.

"I apologize for coming at an inopportune time," said Sir Malcolm. "Since I know the Professor dislikes social conventions, I will come straight to the point. May I ask where you intend to work this season?"

"The West Valley of the Kings," said Emerson shortly.

"Not the East Valley?"

"No."

"Then Carnarvon has not abandoned the concession?"

"No."

I was surprised that Emerson had not informed Sir Malcolm at the outset that it was none of his (expletive) business where we intended to excavate. He can control his temper when it is to his advantage to do so, and I realized that, like myself, he was curious about the gentleman's motives.

"Ah," said Sir Malcolm. "I would give a great deal to have the firman for that area."

Emerson shrugged and took out his watch. Sir Malcolm persisted. "I believe you are of the same mind. You attempted to persuade Carnarvon to give up the concession to you, did you not?"

"Good Gad," said Emerson, his color rising. "Is there no end to gossip in this business? Where did you hear that?"

"From an unimpeachable but necessarily anonymous source," said Sir Malcolm smoothly. "Come, Professor, let us not fence. You believe Carter will find a tomb—specifically, that of Tutankhamon. So do I."

Emerson returned his watch to his pocket and stared fixedly at Sir Malcolm. After waiting in vain for a verbal reaction, Sir Malcolm was forced to continue.

"Evidence of such a tomb exists. You know it and I know it. Theodore Davis believed he had found it, but he was wrong; that cache of miscellaneous objects was clearly leftover materials from Tutankhamon's burial. The statuette that was in your possession last year obviously came from his tomb. Tomb 55, the only other East Valley tomb of the same period, is directly across the way from the area Carter means to investigate."

"I do know that," said Emerson impatiently. "But the evidence, such as it is, is irrelevant. Carnarvon has the concession, and that is that."

Sir Malcolm leaned forward. "What if Lacau could be persuaded to revoke it?"

There was a moment of silence. Then Emerson said softly, "By you?"

"There are ways," Sir Malcolm murmured. "He wouldn't award it to me, but he could hardly deny an excavator of your reputation."

"Supposing you could accomplish that," Emerson said, fingering the cleft in his chin. "What would you want in return?"

"Only the right to share the expenses and the . . . er . . . rewards," Sir Malcom said eagerly.

"Emerson," I cried, unable to contain myself. "You would not enter into such an immoral—"

"Hush, Peabody." Emerson raised a magisterial hand. "It seems to me, Sir Malcolm, that you are risking your influence on a very slim hope. Even if such a tomb exists, even if it is in the area in question, the likelihood is that it was looted in antiquity, like all the other royal tombs."

"It's not much of a financial risk," Sir Malcolm declared. He thought he had won his case; his eyes shone with poorly concealed excitement. "You, of all men, know it doesn't cost all that much to excavate here. Wages are low and one can manage quite well without expensive equipment. Carnarvon may complain about getting a low return on his investment, but the return can't be measured in terms of objects found. It's the thrill of the hunt, the gamble!"

For a moment Emerson's expressive countenance mirrored the enthusiasm that had transformed that of our visitor. Then he shook his head. "The return is in terms of knowledge gained. Your protestations would be more convincing, Sir Malcolm, if you were not known as a rabid collector. I cannot participate in such a scheme. I bid you good evening."

Sir Malcolm rose to his feet. "I am staying here at the hotel and I can be reached at any time."

"Good evening," said Emerson.

Sir Malcolm smiled and shrugged, and started for the door. "Oh," he said, turning. "It nearly slipped my mind. It is common knowledge that you are shorthanded this year. I know a well-qualified fellow who—"

"Good evening!" Emerson shouted.

"Well," I exclaimed, after Ali had shown the gentleman out. "What effrontery! Does the man never know when to give up?"

"He is a collector," said Emerson, in the same tone in which he might have said, "He is a murderer." "And he is still smarting about losing the statuette to Vandergelt."

The little golden statue, which had been temporarily in our hands the year before, was certainly enough to inspire the lust of any collector. An exquisitely fashioned image of a king, it had been identified (by us) as that of the young Tutankhamon, stolen from his tomb shortly after his burial by a thief whose confession had miraculously survived among the papyri found (by us) at the workmen's village of Deir el Medina. Tutankhamon's tomb was one of the few that had never been located, and Ramses's translation of the papyrus had led Emerson to believe it yet lay hidden in the royal valley. He was not the only one to think so, as Sir Malcolm's offer proved.

"Do you suppose Sir Malcolm really has that much influence?" I asked.

Ramses said thoughtfully, "It's possible. But of course any collaboration with a man like that is out of the question. It would ruin your reputation, Father."

"I am not such a fool as to be unaware of that," Emerson retorted.

"Besides," I added, "you said last spring that you would leave the matter in the hands of Fate. Fate appears to have made up her mind. It would be dishonorable to do anything more."

"I am not such a fool as to be unaware of that, either," said Emerson somewhat reproachfully. "As for taking on a staff member recommended by him, I would as soon hire a—a damned journalist. Where did he get the notion that we need more people?"

I was about to tell him when Nefret jumped up. "I'm ravenous! Shall we go down to dinner now?"

Emerson had had a trying day, what with one thing and another, so I attempted to keep the dinner conversation light and cheerful. (It is a well-known fact that acrimony at mealtime adversely affects the digestion.) Finding a neutral topic was not easy; any mention of archaeology would remind Emerson of his failure to obtain the concession for the Valley, and a discussion of family matters might start him complaining about David's absence.

After we retired to our room I assumed my most becoming dressing gown and settled myself at the toilet table to give my hair its usual one hundred strokes. Emerson likes to see my hair down, but even this did not rouse him from his melancholy mood. Instead of preparing for bed, he sat down in an armchair and took out his pipe.

"I wish you wouldn't smoke in our bedroom," I said. "The smell permeates my hair."

"What's wrong with that?" Emerson demanded. "I like the smell of pipe smoke."

But he laid the pipe aside without lighting it. I put down my brush and turned to face him. "I am sorry, my dear, that Lord Carnarvon refused to yield to you."

"Don't rub it in," Emerson grumbled.

The matter was more serious than I had supposed. More drastic methods were required. I went to him and sat down on his lap, my arms round his neck.

"Hmmm," said Emerson, his dour expression lightening. "That is very pleasant. What are you up to now, Peabody?"

"Must I always have an ulterior motive when I invite my husband's attentions? In fact I was about to thank you again for keeping your vow. You said last year, when I was so ill—"

"That I would give up every damned tomb in Egypt if you were spared to me." Emerson's strong arms enclosed me. "You are right to remind me, Peabody. I have been behaving badly. I shall not err in that fashion again."

I felt quite certain that he would, but I gave him credit for good intentions, and gave him a little something else besides.

## FROM MANUSCRIPT H

Insofar as Ramses was concerned, the sooner they left for Luxor, the better. Despite his claim of disinterest, Emerson was obviously up to no good. He spent more time than usual at the Museum and the office of the Directorate of Antiquities, and he cultivated Howard Carter in a highly suspicious manner. The city itself had an uneasy feel. The official declaration of independence in February had satisfied no one. The high commissioner, Lord Allenby, was vilified by the imperialists in the British government for giving too much power to Egypt; the Egyptian nationalists were furious with Britain for exiling their revered leader Saad Zaghlul; the king, Fuad, wanted to be an absolute monarch instead of being bound by the limits allowed him by the proposed constitution. Ramses was glad his friend David had not come out that year. David had been involved with one of the revolutionary groups before the war, and although his service to Britain since had won him a pardon, he was still devoted to the cause of independence. Some of his former associates held a grudge against him for what they considered his betrayal of their cause; others wanted nothing more than to involve him in their plots and counterplots.

His mother was plotting too. Ramses began to get an idea of what she was up to when she announced she meant to give "one of my popular little dinner parties." It had been a habit of hers to meet with their archaeological colleagues soon after their arrival in Egypt, to catch up on the news, as she put it. The war had interrupted this pleasant custom because so many of their friends were on the front lines or engaged in work for the War Office. When she announced her intentions Emerson grumbled but gave in without a struggle. Howard Carter was to be one of the guests.

When they gathered in the elegant dining salon at Shepheard's it was something of a shock to see so many new faces. The Quibells were friends from the old days, as was Carter, but many of the guests were of the new generation. Among them was Suzanne Malraux. She had come alone, and when he saw her standing in the doorway Ramses went to welcome her. She was a wispy-looking little thing, with large protuberant blue eyes and silvery fair hair so fine, the slightest breeze lifted it around her small head. She made Ramses think of an astonished dandelion. He presented her to his wife and parents. Nefret's greeting was warm; she must have taken Suzanne's hesitation for shyness, and she always went out of her way to encourage career-minded young women. She was only too well aware of the difficulties they faced, after the trouble she herself had had in obtaining her medical degree and in starting a woman's hospital in Cairo. His mother was pleasant but less effusive. After subjecting Suzanne to a searching stare she drew the girl aside and began to talk about her studies with Petrie.

She managed to have private conversations with some of the other younger guests as well, and Ramses began to wonder what she was up to. His father was too busy with old friends to notice. Emerson objected to his wife's social engagements as a matter of form, but he generally had a roaring good time once they were underway. All in all, it was a successful affair, with champagne flowing freely and tongues wagging just as freely.

Next day Ramses managed to get his mother alone. She had taken up embroidery again, and was stabbing at a grubby scrap of cloth when he joined her in the sitting room. Putting it aside with evident relief, she invited him to take a chair.

"A pleasant evening, was it not?" she inquired.

"Yes."

"Your father was impressed by Miss Malraux. I thought she stood up to his quizzing admirably."

"She's not the shrinking violet I had believed her to be," Ramses admitted. "Coming alone took some courage."

"It was a declaration of her desire to be judged for herself, without the support of a man. Nefret liked her too."

"Yes. Mother, you are scheming again. What is it this time?"

"There is a very nice house to let in Roda. It has a large walled garden, servants' quarters, even a nursery."

"I see." He only wondered why he hadn't foreseen it. Watching him, she picked up the embroidery again and waited.

"Have you taken the place?" he inquired.

"Goodness no, I would never venture to do that without Nefret's and your approval."

"Mother—"

"My dear boy." She leaned forward and fixed him with those steely gray eyes. "It is time the children were in school. Time for Nefret to carry on her work at the hospital. Time for you to have . . . er . . . time to concentrate on your interest in philology. Several of the young people we met last night are admirably qualified, including Miss Malraux. They can never replace you and Nefret, but they deserve a chance, and you two deserve the opportunity to pursue your own careers."

"Have you broached this scheme to Father?" Ramses's thoughts were in a whirl. He had a pretty fair idea of how Nefret would react. She missed the hospital and the chance to practice surgery, and although she adored his parents, their constant presence was bound to be a burden at times. As for himself . . .

"I don't know," he said slowly. "It would be such a change. I have to get used to the idea."

"Talk it over with Nefret. You needn't decide immediately. It is early in the year and there are always houses to let." She smoothed out the scrap of embroidery and frowned at it. "And it may take a while to convince your father."

"We can at least start out the season as usual," Ramses said.

"In Luxor, you mean?" She smiled with perfect understanding. "Of course. You will want to revisit your old haunts and see old friends."

"The children won't like living in Cairo."

"I don't suppose they will, not at first. They have become accustomed to being the centers of their little universe—not so little a universe at that," she amended. "For it includes most of Luxor. They are becoming spoiled. The change will be good for their characters."

Emerson might have lingered in Cairo had not two untoward events changed his mind. The first occurred when the entire family had gone to Giza for the day. The tourist season had barely begun, and the site was relatively uncrowded, but it offered innumerable opportunities for an adventurous child to get in trouble, with its open tomb pits and temptingly climbable pyramids. David John, who was developing a taste for Egyptology, stuck close to his grandfather, peppering him with questions, while the rest of them tried to keep close on Charla's heels. It took all three of them.

"We ought to have brought Fatima," Ramses said to his mother, after he had plucked Charla from the first step of the Great Pyramid. How she had got up there he couldn't imagine; he had only turned his back for a minute, and the steplike blocks were almost three feet high.

"Fatima is no longer a young woman," said his mother. "She cannot keep up with Charla. Charla, do not climb the pyramid. It is dangerous."

"Then you take me up," Charla pleaded, wrapping her arms round her father's waist. Her big black eyes, fringed with long lashes, were hard to resist, but Ramses shook his head. The idea of being responsible for his peripatetic daughter on that steep four-hundred-foot climb made his hair stand on end.

"When you are older, perhaps."

They returned in time for tea and handed the children over to Fatima for intensive washing. Ramses and Nefret were about to follow their example when his mother burst into the room without so much as a knock.

"I beg your pardon," she said, seeing him shirtless and Nefret unlacing her boots. "But this is important. Our rooms have been searched. What about yours?"

Ramses gazed helplessly round the room. Nefret stepped out of her boots and went to the bureau.

"He wouldn't notice unless his precious papers had been disturbed," she said. "I think . . . Yes, Mother, someone has been looking through this drawer. The paper lining is askew and my underwear isn't folded as neatly."

"Perhaps it was the maid," Ramses suggested. His mother was prone to melodramatic fantasies.

"The maids don't go into drawers," his mother said. "Is anything missing, Nefret?"

"I don't think so." She opened her jewelry case. "It's all here. What about you?"

His mother sat down and folded her hands. "Emerson of course claims he is missing several important papers, but he is always losing things."

Ramses had gone through the documents piled on his desk. "Nothing is missing. But you're right, someone has looked through them. Looking for what, do you suppose?"

"Something small enough to be concealed under the drawer lining or in among one's—er—personal garments. That suggests a letter or paper."

"I can't imagine what it could be," Nefret said. "You haven't received any strange messages or threatening letters, have you, Mother?"

"Not so much as a mysterious treasure map. Dear me, how odd. Could it have been Sir Malcolm?"

Ramses slipped back into his shirt. His mother clearly had no intention of leaving immediately; her eyes were bright and her brow furrowed with thought.

"There's no reason to assume that," Ramses said. "You only want to catch him doing something illegal."

"Yes, certainly. I know he was responsible for several dirty tricks last year, though I wasn't able to pin anything on him." She looked immensely pleased with herself for working in these bits of modern slang.

Ramses sympathized with her feelings—he didn't trust Sir Malcolm either—but he felt obliged to protest. "What could he hope to find? Father hasn't any secret information about . . ." A horrible thought struck him. "Has he?"

"If so, he has concealed it well." His mother didn't even look abashed at this implicit confession. In her opinion Emerson had no business concealing anything from her, so she was entitled to use any means possible to discover what he was hiding. "Let us see what information Ali can contribute."

The suffragi was unable to contribute anything. He had not seen anyone enter or leave their rooms. This proved only that the hypothetical intruder had been cautious enough to avoid him. Ali had a number of guests in his charge and was frequently absent from his post attending to their requests.

His "missing" papers having been located by his exasperated wife, Emerson was not inclined to take the matter seriously. It was the second incident that convinced him. At Nefret's strongly worded request, the party left for Luxor a few days later.

The request followed Charla's escape from the hotel in the company of Ali the suffragi. They had been seen leaving the hotel but no one knew where they had gone afterward. It was late afternoon before the guilty pair returned. Charla was indescribably dirty, smeared with sugary substances, and completely unrepentant. Ali, who had obviously begun to have second thoughts about his seduction, went into hiding in a broom closet, from which Ramses dragged him by the collar.

"She is not injured," said Charla's grandmother, holding her off at arm's length.

"Ali wouldn't let anyone hurt me," Charla shouted. "He only did what I told him. We went to the suk and a nice man gave me money and we bought whatever I wanted!"

"Nice man," Ramses repeated. "What was his name?"

"He said he was a friend of Grandpapa's."

She couldn't remember his name or what he looked like. Under questioning Ali could only say that he was dressed like a howadji, and that he had graying hair. "The Father of Curses has many friends," he insisted. "He knew you, he asked about all the family."

The repentant Ali was let off with a stern warning, since, as Nefret pointed out, it was primarily Charla's fault. "She took ruthless advantage of his fondness for children and his awe of a member of the Father of Curses's family. Let's go on to Luxor as soon as possible. It's easier to keep track of the twins when they're in their own home."

"Where the windows are barred and the entire household knows their little tricks," Ramses agreed.

Fatima, who hadn't let go of David John since his sister turned up missing, let out a heartfelt groan of agreement. Officially she was housekeeper, not nurserymaid, and although Ramses didn't know her precise age, she was no longer a young woman. It took several people in the prime of life to keep up with the twins.

•   •   •

Their house in Kent had been their English base for many years, its rose gardens lovingly tended by his mother, its grounds haunted by the descendants of the cats they had brought back from Egypt. Yet in a sense, returning to Luxor was coming home. It certainly was for his mother. If home is where the heart is, as she kept remarking, hers was in the ruins of the imperial city of ancient Egypt. Except for brief interludes at other sites, this was . . . he tried to remember . . . their twenty-third season at Thebes. Or was it longer? She had, he thought sentimentally, grown old here—though he would never have used that word to her. She had built a house, and another for Nefret and him, made friends and lost them, discovered treasure, and dug through tons of sand. It wasn't quite the same for him, but when they stepped out of the train he felt a surge of—well, call it satisfaction.

Their progress through the familiar streets of Luxor was slowed by hails from old friends and a few old foes. The sun was high in a cloudless sky when they reached the riverbank. The Nile flowed quick and swollen; it had reached maximum flood stage and would soon be subsiding, though, thanks to modern barrages and dams, its flow was now controlled so that water could be supplied during the formerly dry months of summer. The temperature was unpleasantly hot for October, and Emerson, who had the constitution of a camel, was the only one who didn't keep mopping perspiration from his face. The twins were beside themselves with excitement, and it took all the adults to keep them from falling overboard.

Leaving their baggage in the willing hands of men waiting on the west bank, they set out along the road that led through the cultivation and into the desert. The house his mother had caused to be built had a comfortable settled look, with green vines and blooming roses framing the arcaded windows of the veranda. The garden she had tended with such determination formed another patch of green behind and to one side; through the trees he could see the walls of his and Nefret's house. Every brick and every bloom was his mother's creation; it was no wonder she cherished it.

Cheers from the assembled household staff came to their ears, but the first to greet them was the dog Amira, who flung herself at the feet of the twins, howling rapturously. Ramses had believed (and hoped) she wouldn't get any bigger, but she had, and after a summer of pampering she was sleek and well fed and almost as large as a lioness. The Great Cat of Re did not believe in vulgar displays of emotion. He waited for them inside the house and showed his annoyance at their absence by sitting with his back turned, ostentatiously ignoring them for several hours, his plumy tail swishing. Their other cats had usually traveled back and forth with them, but the Great Cat of Re had made it clear that he did not care for travel, by sea or by land.

When the tea tray arrived he decided to overlook their transgressions and settled down at Ramses's feet. Sometimes there were fish-paste sandwiches.

They had gathered on the veranda, as was their usual habit, watching the soft glow of paling color on the eastern cliffs. Lights began to twinkle in Luxor, across the river, and the long stretch of sandy ground in front of the house was deserted except for a few shadowy forms of local villagers on their way home from the fields. Even the twins were subdued, having worn themselves out playing with the dog and rushing from room to room to make sure everything was where they had left it. The peace of Luxor, Ramses thought, and then smiled to himself. Their peace had been often disturbed, sometimes violently.

Reminded of one of the most flagrant disturbers of the peace, he asked, "Where's Father?"

His mother was pouring the tea. She handed him a cup before she replied. "He sneaked—I use the word intentionally—out of the house shortly after we arrived, ignoring my courteous request that he get his papers and books in order. I do not know where he went."

Ramses handed the cup to Nefret and went back to get one for himself. "You can guess, though," he said.

When Emerson turned up, half an hour late for tea, he didn't deny the charge. "Why yes," he said innocently. "I did go to the East Valley for a quick look round."

"What were you looking for?" his wife asked.

"Nothing in particular, Peabody. Nothing in particular."

"I suppose you will want to go to the West Valley tomorrow."

"What's the hurry?" inquired Emerson, who was always in a hurry. "Vandergelt won't be here for a few more days, and we ought to consult with him before we begin. It is his concession, after all." He shifted uneasily under his wife's steady stare, and went on, "I thought I would spend a little time getting the motorcar back in operation. Selim believes he has diagnosed the difficulty; he has brought several new parts from Cairo. That is—if you have no objections, my dear."

"What possible objection could I have? Aside from the fact that Selim is our reis, in charge of our excavations, not a mechanic, and the additional fact that a motorcar has limited utility here."

The motorcar had been a bone of contention between them from the first. Her point was well taken—there were few usable roads on the West Bank—but her chief objection was that Emerson knew absolutely nothing about the internal workings of the vehicle but was under the mistaken impression that he did. She was primed for an argument, cheeks flushed and eyes accusing, but Emerson refused to be provoked.

"I won't let it interfere with our work, Peabody. Come now, my love," he went on, with one of his most winning smiles, "you know we always spend a little time reacquainting ourselves with our favorite sites and determining what has gone on since we were last here. Aren't you the least bit curious about that final little triangle Carter proposes to excavate?"

"Idle curiosity is not one of my failings, Emerson. However, since you are so determined, who am I to stand in your way?"

Emerson's eyes twinkled. He recognized hypocrisy when he heard it. "We'll make a day of it," he declared. "Take the kiddies. You'd like to see the Valley of the Kings again, wouldn't you, my dears?"

He patted Charla's curly head—a familiarity she permitted from no one else. She nodded eagerly, visualizing, her father felt certain, a large picnic basket. David John was also pleased to indicate his agreement.

They made quite an imposing caravan when they started off the next morning, the children on their favorite donkeys and the adults on horseback. Leaving their mounts in the donkey park by the entrance, they passed the barrier into the archaeological zone. The East Valley was not a single canyon but a web of them, with smaller wadis leading off on either side of the main path. Bounded on all sides by towering cliffs and the hills of rocky debris washed down by rain or tossed out by excavators ancient and modern, it was a waterless waste that had once held treasure beyond imagining. On either side the rectangular openings of the royal tombs of the Empire gaped open and forlorn, robbed of the rich grave goods that had been meant to provide the dead kings with all the luxuries they had enjoyed in life. Only tantalizing scraps of their gilded and bejeweled equipment had survived.

For the convenience of tourists the once uneven floor of the wadis had been smoothed, and access to the most popular tombs made easier. Some were even illumined by electric lights, provided by a generator in one of the sepulchres. Tourists brought money, not only to the Department of Antiquities but to the dragomen and guides who earned their livings from them; but Ramses sometimes regretted the old days, when visitors had to scramble up the uneven rock surfaces and carry candles through the deep-cut passages of the tombs. One thing hadn't changed: above the valley rose the pyramid-shaped peak representing the goddess Mertseger, "she who loves silence." The mighty pyramids of the kings of old lay empty and violated when the monarchs of Thebes determined to abandon ostentation in favor of secrecy, hiding their burial places deep in the cliffs and building temples elsewhere to serve their funerary cults. Emerson believed the shape of the mountain served as a substitute for the pyramid, a symbol of the sun god and of survival after death.

"You see the advantage of coming out early in the season," Emerson declared. "Not so many cursed tourists. Charla, stay with me. I won't have you wandering off alone."

The tourists were less numerous than they would be later on, but there were a number of them. They observed our little procession with open curiosity and a buzz of whispered comments followed our progress. Dragomen and guards gathered round the twins, chuckling with pleasure as the children returned their greetings in Arabic as fluent as their own. Ramses didn't have to worry about carrying one or both of the twins; a dozen willing hands reached for Charla when she fluttered her lashes and declared she was tired.

"She isn't tired," said David John in disgust, watching his sister being hoisted onto the shoulder of a beaming dragoman. "She just likes being high above the rest of us."

Ramses deemed it wiser to ignore this accurate appraisal. David John, having made his point, did not pursue it. He slipped his hand into that of his father's.

"Just remind me, if you will, of the relative location of the tombs in this area," he requested. Amused by the contrast between the high-pitched voice and the pedantic speech, Ramses said, "Remind you? You haven't been here very often, David John. How much do you remember?"

"Naturally I have studied the maps and the books, Papa. There, I believe, is the entrance to Tomb 55, where you worked last season. A most frustrating excavation."

The entrance had been filled in, as was Emerson's custom when finishing an excavation. Only an uneven surface of sand and pebbles marked the spot. Obediently Ramses indicated the other nearby tombs—Ramses IX, and across the way, on the hillside, that of another obscure Ramses, awarded the number six by modern historians.

"There is certainly a great deal yet to be done here," said his son judiciously. "What is Grandpapa looking at so intently?"

"The remains of workmen's huts. Not very impressive, are they?"

They were nothing more than seemingly random heaps of rough stones. Only an expert eye would have recognized them as the temporary living quarters of men who had worked on the nearby royal tombs, or understood, as Ramses was beginning to do, why Emerson stared at them with such interest.

Charla had forged ahead of the others, urging her grinning bearer on with shouts of glee. Her grandmother clucked disapprovingly. "Ramses, she is becoming a positive little slave driver. Make her stop."

Emerson had also observed the situation, and by the time Ramses reached his daughter his father had already caught her up and was lecturing both Charla and the man who carried her.

"I told you you were not to get away from the rest of us," he said sternly. "And you . . . what is your name? I don't know you."

The man was a stranger to Ramses as well—a tall, well-set-up fellow with a narrow face and protruding jaw. "Mahmud, O Father of Curses," he said readily. "I came here from Medamud because I heard you would be hiring workers. I have two wives and thirteen children, and—"

"Yes, yes," said Emerson. "See my reis, Selim. You know him, of course."

"All men know Selim, Father of Curses. My thanks."

Charla propelled herself into Emerson's outstretched arms. He set her on her feet. "It won't do you any harm to walk awhile," he declared. "Take my hand."

"He was a nice man," said Charla, unrepentant. "He ran very fast when I told him to."

"You must not treat people like beasts of burden," Ramses said. "I hope you thanked him properly."

Charla looked round, but the nice Mahmud was no longer in sight.

They had their picnic lunch in the mouth of an empty tomb, and then returned to the house. David John's fair skin was turning pink, despite the hat his mother insisted he wear, and both children were drooping a little from the heat. They considered themselves far too old for afternoon naps, but they were receptive to the idea of a quiet hour in their room. Nefret went to her clinic; the news of her arrival had spread, and a number of patients had turned up. Hers was the only clinic on the West Bank, and Nur Misur, Light of Egypt, as Nefret was called, had earned the loving respect of the villagers. Some of the older men still preferred the medical (and magical) skills of her mother-in-law, who decided to accompany her. Ramses found himself alone on the veranda with his father.

"Odd, that," he said.

"The helpful Mahmud?" Emerson gestured him to a chair and took out his pipe.

"I might have known you'd wonder too."

"I am wondering about a number of things." Emerson turned to look down the road to the little guardhouse they had built the year before. It was a humble mud-brick shelter, designed to discourage uninvited visitors. Wasim, the man on duty that day, squatted in the open doorway, placidly smoking his water pipe.

"I had a word with Wasim," Emerson went on. "I thought he was looking pleased with himself, and he frankly admitted to having extracted a tidy amount of baksheesh from a fellow who was asking questions about recent visitors."

"A fellow named Mahmud?"

"The description didn't match. Wasim said he spoke Arabic fluently but with a strange accent."

"Odd," Ramses repeated. "What did Wasim tell him?"

" 'The truth, O Father of Curses.' That we have had no visitors since we arrived."

"We're being watched."

"It seems that way," Emerson agreed. "People hanging about the vicinity of the house at odd hours last night."

"You noticed too? I was tempted to go out and run them off, but . . ."

"But they weren't doing anything illegal," Emerson finished. "Quite. This sheds rather a new light on your mother's claim that our rooms in Cairo were searched."

"And on the amiable Mahmud?"

Emerson frowned. "He can't have hoped to carry the child off, not with so many people about."

"But he might have asked her the same questions the other man asked Wasim. She's a chatty little creature."

"Did she tell you what they chatted about?"

Ramses laughed. "That's the disadvantage of Charla's chattiness. She doesn't answer questions, or even hear them. She carries on a monologue. Anyhow, we haven't had any visitors."

"True."

"It's all very tenuous, Father. A possible search of our rooms, an un-

known person asking possibly harmless questions of Wasim, a postu-
lated but unproven attempt to question Charla."

"Two such attempts," Emerson corrected. "We never identified the
nice man who gave her money in the suk."

"We may be letting our imaginations run away with us."

"Possibly." Emerson chewed on the stem of his pipe. "Better safe
than sorry, though, as your mother would say. If there is any basis to
our suspicions, the suspects will have to try something more direct
sooner or later. At the moment we can only wait and see; there are too
many possibilities to allow speculation." Emerson chuckled. "Perhaps
it's Howard Carter, suspecting me of designs on his firman."

It wasn't until the following afternoon that Emerson's prediction
proved correct. The message wasn't from Howard Carter, however.

"The old familiar anonymous letter," Ramses said, perusing the paper his father handed him. "Does Mother know about this?"

"Good Gad, no. And she mustn't find out. She'd insist on coming
with us."

"You mean to respond? This is an open invitation to an ambush,
Father."

"It's an invitation to a solution," Emerson retorted. "I'm tired of
subterfuge and mystery. I cannot conceive of any danger the two of us
couldn't handle."

The implicit compliment was so flattering, Ramses abandoned his
half-hearted objections. Emerson was an army unto himself, but as the
saying went, "A friend does not leave a friend's back exposed." He said
only, "How do you propose to get away from Mother—and Nefret?"

"Hmmm." Emerson frowned. "That does present a difficulty. Have
you any suggestions?"

"We might try telling them the truth."

"Good Gad, are you serious?" Emerson thought it over. "It's a new
approach, at any rate."

Somewhat to Ramses's surprise, it succeeded. Emerson waited until
after dinner to break the news. His wife had also noticed the surveillance to which they had been subjected—or so she claimed. (She always

claimed to know everything, and who would have the temerity to call her a liar?) In this case it was a tactical error, of which Emerson took immediate advantage.

"The fellow didn't tell me to come alone, but we cannot suppose he will appear if the whole lot of us turn up. I take you into my confidence, Peabody—and you, Nefret—because you know that to be true. I trust in your good sense, as you must trust in mine."

"Bah," said his wife. She had taken out her embroidery, and in her agitation she stuck a needle into her finger. Sucking it, she said indistinctly, "Nefret, what do you think?"

"I don't like it one damned bit, Mother. But . . ."

Her voice trailed off. "Think of the children," Emerson said. "If we don't respond, these people may go after them next."

She had thought of it. Her eyes were wide and her cheeks a trifle paler than usual. It was the only argument that could have convinced her, but her distress was so obvious that Ramses couldn't refrain from protesting.

"That's a low, underhanded trick, Father. The children are amply protected."

"Any guard can be circumvented," his mother said. "And Charla is too inclined to trust a friendly face. Nefret, I believe we must let them go—and that we must remain, on the remote chance that this is a trick to get us all out of the house."

Emerson's jaw dropped. She was one step ahead of him, as usual.

"Now see here, Peabody," he began.

"Oh, I don't believe for a moment that any such thing will happen," she said soothingly. In fact, she was half hoping it would; her hands were clenched, as if around the handle of a weapon, and her lips were curved in a little smile. "Do you go on, then, you and Ramses. And for pity's sake don't behave foolishly."

"That didn't work out the way I expected," Emerson muttered, as he and Ramses started toward the riverbank. "You don't think there is a chance—"

"No, Father, I don't. Let's get this over with."

Daoud's son Sabir took them across to the East Bank. Emerson told him to wait, and they started for the rendezvous point, by the entrance to the Temple of Luxor. The gate was closed, but a nearby light showed the form of the man they had been told to expect, wearing a galabeeyah, with a distinctive red-striped scarf over his shoulders. As soon as he was sure they had spotted him he started walking away from the temple.

"Shall we take him?" Ramses asked.

"No, no. He can't be the only one involved. Wait till we can get our hands on the rest of them." Emerson's teeth closed with a snap.

They followed the flitting form of their guide through the streets of the tourist areas, past the Luxor Hotel, where colored lanterns swung from the trees of the garden, and into the back alleys of the city. Ramses moved closer to his father.

"This is beginning to look like a bad idea," he said softly.

"Quite the contrary." Emerson didn't bother to lower his voice. "The more insalubrious the surroundings, the greater the chance that something interesting will occur."

"Are you armed?"

"Me? Good Gad, no. Why should I be?"

He stumbled. Ramses caught him by the arm. His eyesight was better than his father's, and there was very little light here. The form ahead of them was as insubstantial as a shadow, vanishing and reappearing whenever a ray of moonlight found its way into the narrow alleyway. Then it seemed to fade into the darkness, and was gone.

Emerson came to a halt. "Where's he got to?"

Ramses took his torch from his pocket. Its beam failed to locate their guide, or anyone else. The buildings on either side were those of small shops, closed for the night. Some had living quarters above, but no lights showed. The windows and doors were barred. But just ahead a shape of blackness indicated an open door.

"Ah," said Emerson and plunged ahead before Ramses could stop him. He caught Emerson up at the door and pointed his torch into the room beyond. At first he saw nothing to cause alarm—a counter, shelves holding tinned and packaged food, boxes of wilting lettuce and dried lentils, open bags of staples such as flour and sugar, a few stools.

The door slammed into his back and propelled him against Emerson, who staggered forward into the room, knocking over a stool.

"Stop there," ordered a voice in Arabic. "Put out the light."

Ramses didn't bother to turn round. He could sense their presence behind him—two men—no, three. And the door had closed with a depressingly solid sound.

"Don't switch it off," Emerson ordered.

"No, sir," said Ramses, who had had no intention of doing so.

There were three more men behind the counter. They were muffled in long, enveloping robes, and the scarfs wound round their heads and faces concealed everything except their eyes. One of them flinched and raised a hand to his brow as the torch beam found him.

"Turn it off," he repeated. "Here is light enough."

He struck a match and lit a lamp—an earthenware bowl filled with oil with a floating wick. Carrying it, he came out from behind the counter, staying at a safe distance, and motioned them to one side.

"Now?" Ramses inquired in English.

"We may as well find out what this is all about. No sense in starting a row if we don't have to." Backing away, Emerson went on in Arabic. "Is it money you want?"

The leader spat on the floor. "We have been paid. We want information. No harm will come to you if you tell us."

The fellow wasn't a good strategist, Ramses thought. He and his father were in a better position with their backs against the wall—or rather, against the motley collection of goods that hung from hooks or filled various sacks. The six confronted them in a rough semicircle. No sign of a firearm, but all six had knives.

"How do I know I can trust you not to harm us?" Emerson asked. His voice quavered a little.

Ramses smiled to himself. The man must be a fool if he believed the Father of Curses could be so easily intimidated.

He wasn't a fool, nor were the others. They stood their ground and the leader's voice hardened.

"Do not play games with me. Where is he?"

"Who?" Emerson inquired curiously.

"You know! Speak or my knife will drink your heart's blood."

"Now that is nonsense," Emerson declared. "What good would that do you?"

The leader's laugh was probably meant to sound sinister. "He would come to avenge you, and then he would be at my mercy."

Emerson let out a snort of amusement. Feet apart, hands in his pockets, he seemed perfectly at ease. "You sound like my wife. I might consider an exchange of information. Who paid you to lure us here?"

One of the men plucked urgently at the sleeve of the leader. Ramses, whose hearing was excellent, understood a few words of the whispered comment. "He will not . . . fool's errand."

The other henchmen shared his doubts. They began backing away. They were all now between the Emersons and the door.

"One last chance," the leader said. "Will you speak?"

"Certainly not," said Emerson, tiring of the game. He took his hands out of his pockets. They were empty—but nonetheless lethal for that, as all men in Egypt knew. Ramses drew his knife, prepared to get between his father and the leader; before he could move, the man flung the lamp onto the floor. The pottery shell smashed, spraying oil. Flames leaped up, feeding on the spilled oil and the scraps of paper and other debris. Their assailants piled out the door, yelling in alarm. The leader was the last to go.

"Burn then!" he shouted, melodramatic to the last. "If you change your mind, call out and we will free you."

The door slammed.

# CHAPTER TWO

RAMSES JUMPED BACK AWAY FROM THE FLAMES LICKING AT HIS FEET. The fire was between them and the door. He didn't doubt it was locked or barred in some way and he didn't believe for a moment that their attackers would hang about long enough to reply to a call for help.

"Shall we go?" he asked.

"Hmph," said Emerson. His face was a devilish mask of black shadow and flickering red light. "Can't let the place burn, can we? Your mother would not approve of such irresponsible behavior."

As he spoke he picked up one of the half-filled sacks and upended its contents onto the fire. Ramses opened his mouth to protest, and then realized that—of course—Emerson had selected the one substance available that would smother the fire without feeding it. Salt.

A cloud of acrid-smelling smoke arose. A few last flickering flames awoke crystalline sparkles in the white heap. Coughing and swearing, Emerson stamped out the flames, leaving the room in darkness except for the beam of Ramses's torch.

"We must make certain the shopkeeper and his family haven't been harmed," he said, and led the way toward the back of the shop.

A curtained doorway behind the counter led to a storage room and a narrow flight of stairs. The rooms on the first floor were unoccupied except for one, whose door was held fast by a wooden wedge. Emerson pulled it out and opened the door, to be greeted by wails and shrieks from a group of people huddled together in the far corner.

"It is I, the Father of Curses," Emerson bellowed over the uproar. He took Ramses's hand and turned the torch onto his own face. "You are safe. The evil men have gone."

It took a while to calm the terrified family—man and wife, aged grandmother, and six children. Emerson had to take the old lady by the shoulders and shake her before she stopped screeching.

"Gently, Father," Ramses said in alarm.

"Ah," said Grandma, subsiding. "It is indeed the strong hands of the Father of Curses. Alhamdullilah, he has saved us."

They knew nothing of the men who had burst into the shop as it was closing and herded them upstairs. The intruders had threatened to cut their throats if they called out or tried to escape.

Relief changed to groans when they saw the mess in the shop. "A full bag of salt!" The owner groaned. "It was worth ten pounds!"

The bag had only been half full, and it wasn't worth a tenth of the price he had mentioned, but Emerson dispensed coins with a lavish hand. On the whole, the family had probably made a profit from the affair, as their smiling faces indicated.

As Ramses had expected, there was no sign of their attackers. Roused by the disturbance, the neighbors had turned out to help, and lingered to find out what was going on. Several of them claimed to have seen sinister figures, robed in black like afrits, running away from the shop. The descriptions included long fangs and burning red eyes.

In other words, no one had seen anyone. Emerson handed out more coins to the wide-eyed children in the crowd and patted a few on the head. They were unable to escape their admirers until the shopkeeper and Grandma had finished telling everyone about the hideous dangers from which they had been saved by the Father of Curses and the Brother of Demons. (Ramses had never been entirely certain whether this Egyptian epithet was meant as a compliment.) After assuring the audience that the evil men would not return, they made their way back to the river.

"Damn," said Emerson. "Did you get a good-enough look at any of them to be able to recognize him again?"

"One of them had a scar on his jaw. I saw it when the scarf slipped. But I doubt they'll stay around to be identified. They're a ruthless lot. D'you think they'd actually have let the place burn, with those poor devils locked in upstairs?"

"My dear boy, you exaggerate. The family could have got out the window at any time, and the fire was no more than a distraction to keep us from following them. If they had meant us harm they'd have jumped us as soon as we entered the room. Six to two are reasonably good odds. All in all, I would say they were among the less competent of the opponents we have encountered over the years."

"You know who they're after, don't you?"

"One name leaps to mind," Emerson admitted. "What the devil do you suppose he's been up to?"

***

Between concern for her husband and fear for the children, Nefret was understandably uneasy. I prescribed a glass of warm milk, and would have slipped a little laudanum into it if she had not been watching me closely.

"Really," I said, "it was too bad of Emerson to imply there was danger to the children."

"I should be with them," Nefret murmured.

"If you pop into their room at this hour you will alarm them unnecessarily. The dog is outside their window, and I sent Jamad to stand in the corridor. Now come to the sitting room. There is no use trying to sleep until they get back."

No one else was asleep. The servants knew what was going on, they always do; Fatima hovered, offering food and a variety of drinks. Nefret was finally persuaded to drink her milk, nicely seasoned with cardamom and nutmeg.

"Has Ramses discussed the idea of your spending the winter in Cairo?" I asked, in an attempt to turn her thoughts to a less worrisome subject.

Nefret nodded. She had, at my urging, assumed a comfortable dressing gown and slippers. I myself lifted her feet onto a hassock and put a pillow behind her. She smiled faintly and pushed a loosened lock of golden hair away from her face.

"Yes, we talked about it. He's torn, Mother. And so am I. We love Luxor and our house, and the family. But I begin to wonder whether we might be better off—"

"Safer, you mean. It is true that we seem to attract unprincipled persons." I sipped my whiskey. Warm milk is all very well for some, but there is nothing like a whiskey and soda for calming the nerves.

The minutes pass slowly when one is concerned for loved ones. I made an effort. We discussed various candidates for the staff, and agreed that two in particular stood out—Miss Malraux, and a young Egyptian, Nadji Farid. Nefret made an effort too, but as the slow seconds ticked by she fell silent, her golden head bowed. Fatima dozed in her chair. I was not at all drowsy. Having finished my whiskey, I rose and tiptoed out of the room. The veranda was dark, the door barred on the inside. I stood there for a time, looking out across the stretch of moon-silvered sand. Nothing moved along the road to the river. Then I became aware of an indistinct form just outside, half concealed by the twining roses. The sharp turn of my head brought an immediate response.

"It is I, Sitt Hakim."

"Selim?" I whispered. "What are you doing here?"

"Standing guard, Sitt. Why did you not send for me?"

"Fatima did, I suppose? Yes. I am sorry you were disturbed, it was unnecessary."

He replied with one of his father's favorite adages. "There is no harm in protecting oneself from that which does not exist, Sitt. It would bring shame upon us if we failed to keep you safe."

"You have never failed us. You may as well be comfortable, Selim. Come in and keep me company." I unbarred the door. He slipped soundlessly in. In the dim starlight I saw the gleam of the knife at his belt.

We sat in companionable silence, waiting, until a faint sound turned our eyes toward the door of the house. At the sight of the white form in the doorway, Selim let out a stifled cry.

"It's only Nefret," I said. "Dear girl, I had hoped you were asleep."

"Selim?" She peered at him through the darkness. "I might have expected you would be here. It's all right, they will be home soon."

I didn't ask how she knew. Dearly though I loved her, I found Nefret a bit uncanny at times. Since they were children she had always known when Ramses was in imminent danger—"a fear, a feeling, a nightmare," as she had once put it. So strong was that bond that it had never misled her, and I had seen it demonstrated often enough to believe in it, as I believed in my dreams of Abdullah.

She sat quietly, hands folded in her lap, and eyes turned to the screened window beside her. My eyes were not as keen as they once had been; I was the last to see the two tall forms coming with long strides along the road.

"They are unharmed," Selim said, with a sigh of relief.

"Ah, there you are," said Emerson, looking in. "Selim too? Excellent. Let us have some light, eh, and perhaps a refreshing drop of whiskey. We deserve it, I believe."

"You weren't worried, were you?" Ramses asked, putting his arm round his wife.

"Oh, not at all," she replied, and slipped away from him in order to help Fatima light the lamps. Ramses looked at her uncertainly, and then went into the house, returning with the drinks tray.

"Everything all right here?" Emerson asked, settling himself in a comfortable chair and stretching his legs.

"There is not a stranger within half a mile," Selim replied, stroking his beard. "We made certain of that. You had no trouble?"

"Oh, not at all," I said, echoing Nefret. "Emerson, what have you done to your new boots? And the bottoms of your trousers are scorched. And—"

"I'll tell you all about it if you will stop fussing, Peabody." He took the glass Ramses handed him, nodded his thanks, and launched into his tale. "No one was hurt," he finished. "And the damage was minimal. Not a bad night's work, take it all in all."

"You let them get away," I said.

Emerson gave me a reproachful look. "Now, Peabody, don't be critical. We couldn't go after the bastards until we were certain there was no danger to the place or its occupants."

"I beg your pardon, Emerson," I said. "You are quite right. It's a pity you didn't recognize any of them. I wouldn't say it was a good night's work."

"If you will forgive me," said my husband, with excessive politeness, "you are missing the point, Peabody. We learned something very important tonight. We now know what these fellows are after. Or should I say 'who'?"

"You should say 'whom,' Emerson."

No one spoke the name aloud, but we all knew whom he meant. Of all our acquaintances the one most likely to attract the attentions of unprincipled persons was Emerson's half brother Seth, better known by his nom de crime of Sethos. He had, before I reformed him, been in charge of a criminal network of antiquities thieves. He had assured me he had long since abandoned that profession, but he might not have been able to resist temptation if a prize fell in his way. Were the prize great enough, a rival might be after him. His current role as an agent of British intelligence might also have led him into danger. The secret service is part of a dark and murky underworld, whose occupants are not bound by the ordinary rules of society.

Selim was one of the few who knew Sethos's identity and occupation. He had encountered Emerson's renegade brother under circumstances that made it impossible to conceal the truth from him, even if we had not had complete confidence in his discretion. His handsome features set in a thoughtful frown, he said, "So. What has he done to anger these people, and who are they?"

"That is the matter in a nutshell, Selim," I agreed. "Unfortunately we don't know the answer to either question."

"There is another question," said Selim, pleased at my compliment. "Why would they think he had come here?"

"Now that is a point I had not considered," I admitted. "He has friends and bolt-holes all over the Middle East."

"He wouldn't lead enemies to us," Nefret said.

"Not unless he was desperate," Ramses muttered.

Nefret gave him a quick look. "It seems to me," she snapped, "that this discussion is getting out of hand. It's all conjecture, including the assumption that he is the man these people are after."

"It is the most reasonable assumption," Ramses said. He and his uncle had never got on. "Father is right, Nefret. Our encounter tonight made it clear these people are looking, not for an object, but for a man. Not one of us, nor one of our friends; their whereabouts are known. Who else could it be?"

Nefret bowed her head. She would have defended Sethos, for whom she had a certain weakness, but the reasoning was compelling.

"I was under the impression that you and he kept in touch, Emerson," I said. "Don't you know where he is?"

"I haven't heard from or about him for months," Emerson said.

"Then I suggest you endeavor to find what has become of him. A wire to his superior, that Mr. Smith—"

"Bracegirdle-Boisdragon," Ramses corrected.

"I can't be bothered to remember that absurd name," I said. "His alias is unimaginative, but easier to pronounce. You might also telegraph Margaret, Emerson. Surely Sethos's wife must know where he is."

"I don't know where she is either," Emerson grumbled. "It's the damnedest marriage I've ever seen, Margaret off to one corner of the world covering a news story and he in another corner doing God knows what. They've been married less than a year."

"They were—er—together for several years before their marriage," I said. "Margaret is deservedly proud of the success she has achieved in her journalistic career, and his present occupation is not one a wife can share."

"He wouldn't allow it," Nefret said. "It would be too dangerous for her—and for him. And wouldn't the Official Secrets Act prohibit him from confiding in her?"

"We can but try," I said, rising. "I will wire her and Mr. Smith first thing tomorrow. Go to bed, Fatima, we will tidy up in the morning. Good night, Selim, and thank you."

Sending the wires would serve another purpose—or at least I hoped it would. Those who were on the trail of Sethos would not hesitate to bribe the clerks at the telegraph office. If they learned we were ignorant of Sethos's whereabouts they might turn their attention elsewhere.

Emerson pooh-poohed this idea as soon as I mentioned it, which I did the following morning at breakfast.

"You underestimate their persistence and their intelligence, I believe," he said, cutting savagely into his bacon. "The men we encountered were ordinary thugs, but there is a cleverer mind behind this, there must be. We may be able to prove he has not communicated with us thus far, but what's to prevent him from doing so in the future? He certainly wouldn't be fool enough to telegraph us. He is fully aware of the fact that the clerks gossip with all of Luxor."

He had made a point, and I was prompt to admit it.

The replies to our wires were unsatisfactory. The telegram to Mr. Smith had been carefully couched, referring to Sethos as "our mutual friend." Smith's answer was brief and to the point. "Have no idea. Do you?" Margaret's newspaper, the *Morning Mirror,* informed us she was on assignment and could not be reached.

"That sounds ominous," I remarked. "You don't suppose she is running around with the Bolsheviks, do you?"

"It would be like her," Ramses said. "The woman will stop at nothing in pursuit of a story. Remember the time she sallied into Hayil and was taken prisoner by the Rashid?"

"I detect a certain note of vexation in Mr. Smith's reply," I said, studying the brief message.

"I don't detect anything except that he is unable or unwilling to give us information," Emerson growled. "We've come to a dead end, and I for one intend to forget the whole business." He tossed his napkin onto the table and rose. "Who is coming to the Valley with me?"

"No one, Emerson. The Vandergelts arrive this morning and we are going to meet the train. Yes, my dear, you too."

There was quite a crowd waiting at the station. Galabeeyahs flapped and turbans bobbed up and down. Cyrus was a generous employer and very popular. When the train stopped and his smiling face appeared at the window, a cheer arose. Cyrus swept off his fine Panama hat and bowed in response.

Winters spent in Egypt's sunny clime had turned our American friend's face lined and leathery, and his sandy hair and goatee were sprinkled with silver, but he jumped out of the train with the agility of a young man. Though without formal training in archaeology, unlike other wealthy individuals who sponsored excavations as a form of amusement, Cyrus was no dilettante. He had always worked side by side with his crew and listened respectfully to the advice of my distinguished spouse.

Turning, he offered his hand to his wife Katherine. I observed that she had gained a bit more weight; her cheeks were pink with heat and her green eyes looked tired. Her son Bertie followed her, his somewhat plain features transformed by the affability of his smile. He immediately offered an arm to Jumana, the other member of Cyrus's staff, but the girl hopped lithely out without giving him so much as a glance of thanks. A typical Egyptian beauty with melting dark eyes and delicate features, she was as ambitious as she was attractive. Bertie had been in love with her for years, but had not succeeded in winning her heart.

"Good to have you back," Emerson declared, wringing Cyrus's hand.

"Good to be back," said Cyrus, drawing a deep breath. "What have you been up to? Any fresh corpses, Amelia?"

"You will have your little joke, Cyrus. We don't have a murder every season."

"Name one," Cyrus countered with a grin.

"There have been a few odd occurrences—"

"Never mind," said Emerson sharply.

I declined Katherine's invitation to a late luncheon, wishing to give our friends time to rest after the long dusty train ride. "We will see you this evening, if you feel up to it," I proposed.

Emerson cleared his throat. "We are dining with Carter tonight, Peabody."

"Howard?" I turned to stare at him. "I didn't know he was in Luxor."

"Got in yesterday," Emerson said, looking off into the distance and shuffling his feet.

"I was unaware of that. He asked us to dine this evening?"

"Yes. Most kind. I accepted, of course." Emerson added hastily, "Subject to your approval, my dear."

"That's all right," Cyrus said, with a concerned look at his wife, who was leaning on his arm. "Cat could do with a day of rest. We'll see you tomorrow."

We escorted the Vandergelts to their carriage and waved them off. Emerson disdains any form of transport (except the motorcar), so we set off on foot toward the dock. The weather was cooler and the sky a trifle overcast. I regretted having assumed a proper morning frock instead of my comfortable trousers and coat. The styles of that year were lighter and less cumbersome than the garments of my youth, with their trailing skirts and awkward bustles, but my shoes pinched and the heels were too high for easy walking. However, I do not allow discomfort to distract me and I at once began to query Emerson.

"How is it that you were aware of Howard's arrival before I learned of it? Why didn't you tell me he had asked us to dine?"

"I just did," said Emerson. "Take my arm, my dear, those shoes are really not suitable for such rough surfaces. I like your frock, though. New, is it?"

It was, but Emerson would have said the same about any garment I assumed, since he never paid the least attention to what I was wearing. Before I could pursue my questioning, he turned his head and addressed a remark to Nefret, who was walking behind us arm in arm with Ramses.

"You are both included in the invitation. Carter was particularly insistent that you join us, Nefret. I believe he still admires you. In a perfectly gentlemanly manner, of course."

Nefret laughed. "Howard is a perfect gentleman, despite what certain British snobs say about him. I've heard that he has become attached to another lady, though."

"You refer to Lord Carnarvon's daughter, Lady Evelyn Herbert, I presume," I said. "From what I have heard, the attachment is rather more on her part. However, I never indulge in vulgar gossip of that nature."

Howard's house, which he called Castle Carter, was at the northern end of Dra Abu'l Naga, close to the road that led into the Valley of the Kings. I sometimes wondered whether the name was an attempt to imitate Cyrus Vandergelt, whose elegant and capacious home was known to all in Luxor as "the Castle." Howard did not get on well with Cyrus, who had often outbid him for the unusual antiquities he hoped to acquire for his patron, Lord Carnarvon. Ramses suggested that Howard was rather referring to the old saying about an Englishman's home being his castle. Ramses has a more kindly nature than I.

Howard had designed and built the house himself, with the financial assistance of Lord Carnarvon. The location was not attractive, being only barren ground without trees or grass, but the structure was pleasant enough, quite in the Arab style, with a domed hall in the center and high arched windows in the dining and sleeping rooms.

Howard greeted us warmly (which did not dispel my suspicion that the invitation had not been his idea, but Emerson's). We took drinks in the domed reception hall. It was simply but comfortably furnished, with low chairs and settees and brass tables. Howard introduced us to his new pet, a little yellow canary. Nefret, who shared Howard's fondness for animals, went at once to the cage and chirped at the pretty creature. It tilted its head and chirped back.

"Charming," I said.

Emerson grunted. "I hope it meets a happier fate than some of your other pets, Carter. What with feral cats and hawks—"

"Oh, I shan't let it out of its cage," Howard said. He put his finger into the cage. The canary hopped onto it and let out a melodious trill. He added, "The men say it is a bird of good omen. A golden bird foretells a golden discovery this season."

We went into the dining room and Emerson, who felt he had wasted enough time on the amenities, asked what luck Howard had had in the antiquities shops of Cairo. Howard shrugged. "Not much. I hope to do better here in Luxor."

He took a spoonful of soup and made a face. "I must apologize for my cook. He has not the skill of your Maaman."

The meal was in fact rather bad—the soup overseasoned, the beef tough, the vegetables stewed to mush. Naturally I did not say so.

After dinner Howard showed us his acquisitions. One was rather charming—a cosmetic pot consisting of seven joined cylinders, each of which had contained a different variety of paint for face and hands. Howard shrugged my admiration aside. "It isn't the sort of thing that will excite his lordship. Do you happen to know of any artifacts at the Luxor dealers? Anything Vandergelt hasn't already got his hands on," he added somewhat sourly.

"Mr. Vandergelt only arrived this morning, so you may be able to get in ahead of him," Ramses replied with a smile. "However, we haven't heard of anything unusual."

"I'll go round to Mohassib's first thing in the morning," Howard said.

"So you don't mean to start work immediately?" Emerson asked.

Howard didn't miss the implicit criticism. "I see no reason for haste. His lordship will not be out for several more weeks, and it won't take us long to clear that small section."

"And then what?" Emerson asked.

Howard motioned to the hovering attendant to refill his wineglass. "That will be up to his lordship."

Some persons might have accepted this evasion and not pursued the subject. Not Emerson. "Do you hope to persuade him into continuing in the East Valley?"

"If Tutankhamon isn't in my little triangle, he must be somewhere," Howard declared.

"Not necessarily," Emerson said. "That is—not necessarily in the East Valley." He immediately looked as if he regretted having said so much, adding, "His is not the only royal tomb we haven't located."

"But his is the one I'm after," Howard said. He leaned forward, planting his elbows on the table—a vulgar habit which, I am sorry to say, was shared by my husband, who did the same. "You know that, Emerson, old chap," Howard went on. "You told me last year—didn't you?—that I ought to keep on looking. 'Preciate your advice. Your help."

Emerson, who had done his best to send Howard to another part of the Valley, had the decency to look embarrassed.

"It'll be empty, like all the rest," Howard said sadly. "If it's there."

From the bird in the adjoining room came a ripple of song.


FROM MANUSCRIPT H


Ramses was not surprised that his father should dismiss the search for Sethos, to quote his mother. (She had a penchant for colorful phrases.) Emerson was obsessed. Why he believed that Carter would find a tomb in the unpromising little triangle of ground Ramses did not know. Perhaps he had no real evidence, only a feeling, a hunch; but as Ramses knew, the greatest excavators develop an instinct for discovery. It had happened over and over again, especially to the untrained but phenomenally successful tomb robbers of Luxor. Emerson's instincts were as great as theirs.

He had to control himself, fuming, while Howard Carter made the rounds of the Luxor dealers. At Cyrus's urging he agreed to open their own excavation in the West Valley, but his heart wasn't in it. Instead of badgering the men who were finishing the clearance of the tomb of Ay, where they had worked the year before, he wandered around the far end of the West Valley with Bertie and Jumana in tow. He was looking for new tomb entrances. He didn't find any.

They heard nothing more from the men who had lured them to the shop. The more Ramses thought about it, the more he was inclined to agree with his father. It had been a singularly inept and pointless ambush. The men must have been strangers, since no local man would believe the Father of Curses could be so easily intimidated. Selim had been unable to find any trace of them, and his contacts were extensive.

The gatekeeper reported no inquisitive strangers, the dog didn't bark in the nighttime. But then she wouldn't, Ramses thought, unless someone approached the children's window. Amira was the possessor of a very pretentious doghouse, designed by David. Charla had assisted him, so the house had a minaret, a veranda, and carpets throughout. The dog had refused to sleep in it, though, until they moved it under the children's window.

The apparent absence of activity didn't reassure Ramses. During his war years he had acquired a sort of sixth sense about being watched—it was a necessary survival trait—and he knew the watchers were out there, somewhere. The ambush might have been a feint, a crude attempt to distract them from more subtle methods.

He didn't like uncertainty, and there were too many unsettled problems. They were in the West Valley on sufferance, since technically it was part of Carnarvon's concession. If they did find any new tombs, Carnarvon was sure to take over, especially if his excavation in the East Valley came up empty. There had been no further discussion about Nefret and him moving to Cairo for the winter, but he knew his mother had not abandoned the scheme.

And where the devil was Sethos?

He didn't suppose his mother would put up with this state of affairs for long. She brought matters to a head one evening when the Vandergelts were dining with them. The cook had prepared all Emerson's favorite dishes and he had almost finished his postprandial whiskey and soda before his wife cleared her throat portentously.

"I have a few things to discuss with you, Emerson. No, my friends, don't go. We have nothing to hide from you."

"She believes I will behave better with you here," Emerson explained. Replete and relaxed, he was in an affable mood, his pipe in one hand and his glass in the other. "Very well, Peabody, have at me."

The affability lasted only until she mentioned her intention of hiring new staff. Emerson sputtered and glared. When she went on to inform him that the younger Emersons planned to spend the winter in Cairo, Ramses braced himself for an explosion. Emerson's reaction was worse. His massive form seemed to shrink.

"Is this what you want, my boy?" he asked in faltering tones.

"No, sir. That is—we haven't really . . . That is . . ." He gave Nefret a helpless look. She came to sit on the arm of Emerson's chair and put her arm round his bowed shoulders.

"We've talked of it, Father, but we haven't come to a decision."

"It's up to you, of course." Emerson fumbled for a handkerchief and blew his nose loudly. "I shall miss the kiddies."

Now that, Ramses thought, was a bit too much. Emerson's emotions were completely sincere, but instead of shouting he was using guile to get his own way.

"Shame on you, Emerson," said his wife coldly.

Cyrus, who hadn't ventured to speak until then, said tentatively, "If you want my opinion . . ."

"I don't," said Emerson, forgetting his role.

"I do," said his wife. "We are all in this together when it comes to our plans for the remainder of this season and for seasons to come. It is agreed, is it not, that we wish to continue the arrangement that has proved so successful—combining our forces into a single group?"

"Nothing would please me more," Cyrus exclaimed. "It would only be making it official. I'm no Egyptologist, and I would be more than happy to have Emerson take over as director."

"Hmph," said Emerson. "Well . . ."

"Excellent," said his wife briskly. "We cannot continue in the West Valley indefinitely. It was a temporary arrangement in any case. We must settle on another site and add to our staff."

"I tell you what we need," said Cyrus. "An artist. I don't suppose Mr. or Mrs. Davies would be available?"

"No, no," Emerson said. "Not a chance. They have other commitments. But David—"

"Also has other commitments," said his wife, in a tone that brooked no argument. "What about that young Frenchwoman, Mlle. Malraux?"

She had done it again. Emerson became so involved in arguing about details that he tacitly conceded her point. She made two of her little lists, one of sites they should consider, and another of potential staff members.

"I shall just pop up to Cairo tomorrow, then," she announced.

"What for?" Emerson demanded suspiciously.

In a tone of exaggerated patience, she replied, "To interview possible staff members, inform M. Lacau of our new arrangement, and ask his advice about another site. Unless you would prefer to go in my stead?"

Faced with several chores he detested plus abandoning his surveillance of Howard Carter, Emerson gave in without a struggle—as she had known he would.

Ramses managed to get a word alone with her after the Vandergelts had left. "You aren't going to look at houses for us, are you?"

"I doubt there will be time," she replied, studying her lists. "I don't want to be away too long. Try to prevent your father from bullying Howard."

"Yes, Mother. You've something else on your mental list, haven't you?"

She looked up at him, her face grave. "We are still under surveillance."

"I've been keeping an eye out. Haven't seen anything suspicious."

"But you have felt it. So have I. One develops certain instincts."

"One does," Ramses agreed. He couldn't help asking the question. "Have you dreamed of Abdullah lately?"

"You've always scoffed at those dreams."

"Now, Mother, I never have."

Nor had he, not in so many words. When she first spoke of those unusual, vivid dreams of their former reis, he had been happy she believed in their reality, for they comforted her. Abdullah had sacrificed his life to save hers, but the bond between them had already been strong. She and the old Egyptian had come to care for each other in a way he would once have believed impossible, considering the differences in their backgrounds and beliefs. Gratitude and strong affection, the denial of loss, might reasonably account for her need to believe the people she had loved were not gone from her forever. He couldn't say precisely when he had begun to share her faith in her dreams. Perhaps it was the sheer strength of her belief.

"I will certainly ask him about Sethos when next I see him," she said, straight-faced. "Until I do I will have to rely on less reliable sources. I mean to call on Mr. Smith while I am in Cairo. He wouldn't confide information in a telegram, but a face-to-face interview may be more productive."

Ramses didn't doubt that. She had her methods.

"Shall I give him your regards?" she asked.

She knew how he felt about Smith, who exemplified to him the faults of the intelligence services. They didn't give a damn about how many lives they destroyed in the pursuit of their self-defined duty. He had hated every second of the time he spent working for them. "No," he said.

I had a busy day in Cairo, one that taxed even my energy. I had not made an appointment with M. Lacau, but I did not anticipate any difficulty in seeing him, and so it proved. I think he was so relieved to find himself dealing with me instead of with Emerson that he would have agreed to anything I asked. But in fact, he and Emerson were on reasonably good terms these days. (Emerson could not be said to be on excellent terms with very many Egyptologists.) We had preserved for the Museum some of its greatest treasures, risking our own lives in the process, and Lacau was not ungrateful. He was a distinguished-looking man, with white hair and beard, so meticulous in his habits that people said he made lists of lists. (An excellent idea, in my opinion.) He bowed me into his office with the utmost courtesy, and for a while we chatted of generalities, including the director's recent statement about the partage (division) of artifacts discovered by foreign expeditions.

"Some arrogant excavators behave as if the entire land of Egypt were their own personal preserve," Lacau declared. His beard bristled. "I intend to tighten the laws so that the great majority of objects remain, as they should, in Egypt."

"Emerson is in full agreement with you, sir," I said truthfully. "You may count on his support. And mine, of course."

After that, M. Lacau would have acceded to my slightest wish.

My next appointments were with the young persons I was consider-

ing as potential staff members. I had selected two for further consideration. Having spoken at greater length with Mlle. Malraux, and observed
Nefret's warm reception of the girl, I had decided my initial reservations were unfounded. She was a vivacious little creature, bubbling with
enthusiasm, but one's initial impression of prettiness was based on her
manner rather than the regularity of her features, and there was something a little unnerving about her eyes; the blue pupils were entirely surrounded by milky white, so that she appeared to be in a permanent state
of surprise or alarm. However, physiognomy is not an accurate indica-
tor of character, and the portfolio she had brought impressed me. An
archaeological artist has different qualifications from those of a painter;
he or she must be capable not only of accurate copying, but of a certain
feeling for the techniques and beliefs of the culture. I was particularly
struck with a watercolor she had done of the head of a mummy in the
Louvre.

My other candidate was the opposite of mademoiselle in almost
every way, and a contradiction in himself. He had one of the jolliest
faces I had ever beheld, round-cheeked, smiling, eyes beaming goodwill.
One would have expected such a cheery-looking man to bubble as mademoiselle did; but Nadji Farid appeared to be very shy. He sat with
eyes lowered and spoke only when he was spoken to, in a soft, melodious voice. However, what he said when he did speak displayed his familiarity with the methods of excavation, and I did not object to
taciturnity. It would be a pleasant change.

By mid-afternoon I had completed all my tasks save one, and had
every expectation of being able to catch the evening express as I had
planned.

However, tracking down Mr. Bracegirdle-Boisdragon, aka Mr.
Smith, proved to be more difficult than I had expected. He had once
given me a private telephone number, but when I rang it, a woman's
voice informed me in Arabic that they did not accept lady customers.
Not being entirely certain what to make of that, I did not pursue the
matter. My next step was to go through the Ministry of Public Works,
which was Bracegirdle-Boisdragon's cover position. It took some time

to work my way through the bureaucratic muddle, and when I was finally connected with his assistant the hour was late and I had become exasperated.

"Inform him that Mrs. Emerson will be at the Turf Club at five o'clock, and that if he does not meet me he will deeply regret it."

I have always found that unspecific threats are the most effective; the victim's imagination supplies consequences more terrifying than any I could carry out. I was also fairly certain, from the assistant's occasional silences, that Bracegirdle-Boisdragon was in the office. However, he had not the courage to speak directly to me.

"Not the Turf Club, Mrs. Emerson." The young man sounded as if he were quoting. "They have not yet recovered from your last visit. Take tea at Groppi's at five."

I was ready for a refreshing cup of tea and one of Groppi's excellent pastries. The ambience was certainly more pleasant than the aggressive masculinity of the Turf Club; lamps with crimson shades cast a soft glow, and footsteps were muted by Persian rugs. Scarcely had I seated myself when a low voice greeted me by name. I looked up to see, not Smith's long nose and pointed chin, but the countenance of a younger man, with a forehead so high his features appeared to have been squeezed into the lower half of his face and miniaturized: a softly rounded chin, a button of a nose, and a mouth as sweetly curved as that of a pretty girl.

"Mrs. Emerson, is it not? My name is Wetherby. We spoke earlier today. May I join you?"

"By all means," I said. "And then you may explain why your superior sent you instead of coming himself."

Mr. Wetherby edged himself into a chair. "He thought it better that he not be seen tête-à-tête with you at the present time. I am completely in his confidence, ma'am, and will report directly to him."

"Hmmm," I said. "Very well. I must catch the evening express, so just listen and don't interrupt."

My description of Emerson and Ramses's encounter with the arsonists caused him to purse his lips. "Why were we not informed of this earlier?"

"I asked you to refrain from interrupting me. Why did your employer not respond more informatively to Emerson's telegram?"

"His reply was the simple truth, Mrs. Emerson. We have no idea where the individual in question may be, and we are as anxious as you to locate him."

"So you agree that the attackers were searching for—er—that individual?"

"It seems likely," Wetherby said cautiously. Lowering his voice and glancing over his shoulder, he went on. "It has been almost six weeks since his last report."

"And he was at that time where?"

It goes against the grain for anyone in the secret service to give up any information whatever. Reluctantly he murmured, "Syria."

"Doing what?"

"Now really, Mrs. Emerson, you cannot expect me to answer that."

"The Official Secrets Act? Such an unnecessary nuisance, these rules. Answer this, then. Who might his adversaries be?"

"God only knows," said Mr. Wetherby, in a burst of genuine feeling.

"You ought to be in a position to hazard a guess, since you know the nature of his mission," I persisted.

"I know what he was *supposed* to be doing, Mrs. Emerson."

"And you will say no more? I see." I glanced at my lapel watch. "I have not time to continue the conversation, Mr. Wetherby. You have been singularly unhelpful."

"Believe me, Mrs. Emerson—"

"Yes, yes. If it were up to you . . . Please remind Mr. Smith that he once offered to do anything possible to assist me or my family. We are in need of that assistance. I don't like to be spied on and harassed."

The rosebud mouth broadened into a smile. "I don't blame you," Wetherby said. "I believe I can safely promise that my superior will take steps to relieve you of that inconvenience. A few false trails . . . You will let us know if you should hear from the individual in question?"

"If you will do the same for me."

"You have my word."

For what that is worth, I thought. At least Mr. Wetherby had a sense of humor, which was more than I could say for Smith. Regretfully I abandoned the remains of my apricot tart, leaving Mr. Wetherby to pay the bill. I arrived at the railroad station in good time.

All in all, it had been a profitable day, and after a leisurely meal in the dining car I sought my swaying couch in the consciousness of duty well done.

I have never understood why I should dream of Abdullah at such irregular and seemingly unrelated occasions, nor why I always saw him as a young man, black-bearded and vigorous, instead of as the white-haired patriarch he had been at the time of his death. He scarcely ever turned up when I had a particular reason for wanting to consult him, and his remarks were, for the most part, enigmatic. Sometimes he reassured me when I was worried, sometimes he dropped vague hints that only made sense when it was too late to act on them; often he scolded me for behaving foolishly. It would have been nice to receive more practical advice; after all, when one has a close acquaintance on the Other Side, where all is known and understood, one has a right, in my opinion, to expect a helpful suggestion or two. However, it was enough just to see and hear him, to know that, in some way and in some dimension, he continued to exist.

He was waiting for me at the usual place and time, the cliffs above Deir el Bahri at Luxor, at sunrise. He seemed to be in an affable mood, for he greeted me with a smile instead of a scowl; and for a few moments we stood side by side looking out over the valley, watching the light flow across river and fields and desert until it brightened the colonnades of Hatshepsut's temple below us.

"So," I said. "No dead bodies this year, Abdullah."

It was an old joke between us. Abdullah grinned. "Not yet," he said. "Whose?"

I did not expect an answer, nor did I receive one.

"There is always a dead body." There was the faintest show of emotion, a suggestion of moisture in his dark eyes, when he added, "Last time it was almost yours, Sitt."

"Oh, that was months ago," I said dismissively. "Have you any news for me?"

Abdullah stroked his beard. "Hmmm. You will soon have a visitor whom you expect and do not wish to see. And Emerson will be proved right when he hoped he would be wrong."

It was a more informative answer than I usually got, even though it did sound as if Abdullah had been prompted by a spiritualist medium. I took it for granted that the unwanted visitor must be Sethos. The second tidbit could only refer to . . .

"Aha," I exclaimed. "So there *is* a new royal tomb in the Valley of the Kings?"

"I told you there was."

"You told me there were two."

"I did," said Abdullah agreeably.

"Where . . . Never mind, you won't tell me, will you? What about the attack on Ramses and Emerson? Are they still in danger from those people?"

"They were never in danger. It was a foolish gesture, made by foolish men."

"What men?"

"Their names would mean nothing to you. They have gone back whence they came."

"Who sent them? Will there be others like them?"

"I have told you," said Abdullah, with exaggerated patience, "that the future is not set in stone. Your actions affect events. The actions of others also do so."

"Ah," I said interestedly, "so we do have free will. That subject has been debated by philosophers down the ages."

"I will not debate it, Sitt."

"As I expected." I turned to face him. "Is all well with you, my dear old friend?"

"How could it be otherwise?" His broad chest rose as he drew a deep breath of the fresh morning air. "May it be well with you and those we love till we next meet, Sitt."

Without farewell he walked away, along the path that led to the Valley. It was always so.

Emerson was at the station when the train pulled into Luxor next morning. I did not see him at first, since he was sitting cross-legged on the platform engaged in animated conversation with several of the porters. Seeing me at the window, he hurried to help me down the steps.

"I came on the chance that you might be on this train," he explained.

"Chance indeed. I told you I would be. Dust off your trousers, Emerson. Where is your hat?"

Emerson brushed vaguely at the oily stains on his trousers and ignored the question, to which he probably did not know the answer. I had sometimes wondered whether it was his habit of going about bareheaded in the noonday sun that had kept his handsome black hair so thick and untouched by gray, except for two picturesque white streaks at the temples. I knew he didn't employ any variety of hair coloring, since I would have found it—and I kept my own little bottle well hidden.

Taking my arm, he said, "What luck?"

"Luck had nothing to do with it. Everything worked out as I anticipated."

"Hmph," said Emerson.

"What about you?"

Emerson took my valise from the porter and led me toward the carriages that waited for customers. "Carter starts work tomorrow."

"Good Gad, Emerson, is that all you can think of?"

Evidently it was. He asked no further questions and did not even protest when I said I would wait to make my full report to the assembled group that evening.

Travel by train leaves one dusty and rumpled. After Emerson had gone off to the West Valley I enjoyed a nice long soak in my tub, washed my hair (and applied just a bit of coloring) and assumed comfortable garments. I spent the rest of the day on the veranda putting my notes in order and watching, without appearing to do so, for unfamiliar persons. We were accustomed to seeing the villagers around and about the house, for Fatima and the others of our household staff had kin all over the West Bank, and these individuals were in the habit of dropping in for gossip and a meal. I had no objection to this arrangement, nor to Fatima's habit of feeding many of the local beggars. Like that of Islam, our faith tells us to share our bounty with those whom (for reasons of His own) the Almighty has not favored. And these individuals often possessed interesting information, which they passed on to Fatima and she passed on to me, thus verifying the undeniable fact that virtue has its rewards.

I had got to know most of the beggars, by sight at least; some were considered holy men. One of them wandered past the veranda that afternoon, a ragged fellow with a long gray beard and a stick that supported his bent frame. He gave me a vague smile and a murmured blessing, which I acknowledged with a bow, before he went on toward the kitchen.

He could not be considered unfamiliar, since I had seen him often before. The same applied to the child who came up the road sometime later. I kept an eye on him, since some of the lads tried to sneak into the stableyard to admire the motorcar (and remove bits of it), but he squatted down some distance away and stayed there.

I had asked Fatima to serve tea early. My intuition was correct. Ramses and Nefret were the first to arrive, with the rest close behind them: Cyrus, Bertie, Jumana, Selim and Daoud, and, after a brief interval, Emerson himself. I plunged at once into my report, since I knew I would not be able to make myself heard once the children joined us.

"I have seen Mlle. Malraux's portfolio, which was first-rate. Both she and Mr. Farid impressed me with their qualifications."

"So you hired them?" Cyrus inquired.

"Gracious no, I would never do that without your approval and that of Emerson."

"If they suit you, Amelia, they're fine with me," Cyrus declared.

"Emerson?"

Emerson started and spilled his tea. "What? Oh, yes, certainly, my dear."

I was pleased to hear this, since I had informed both young Egyptologists that we would take them on.

"M. Lacau has been most accommodating," I continued. "He offered us several sites: the royal mortuary temples along the cultivation, with the exception of Medinet Habu—"

"There's nothing left of them," Cyrus protested. "Just heaps of rubble."

"Kindly allow me to finish, Cyrus. The far western valleys, where the tombs of Hatshepsut and the three princesses were found, and the site of Tod, south of here."

"Too far away," Cyrus said promptly.

"There will be time to consider these possibilities," I concluded. "M. Lacau wishes us to finish this season in the West Valley."

From the gleam in Cyrus's eyes when I mentioned tombs, I knew what his choice would be. Emerson said vaguely, "Yes, yes, Peabody, well done. We will—er—consider the possibilities."

The appearance of the dear little children put an end to the discussion. They went straight for their grandfather, both talking at once. Under cover of their sweet but penetrating voices, Ramses said softly, "Did you see Smith?"

"He sent his assistant, Mr. Wetherby, to meet with me, instead of coming himself."

"Wetherby?" Ramses frowned slightly.

"Do you know him?"

"No. He must be new since my time. Did he explain why Smith snubbed you?"

"In the intellligence business, a snub is not a snub but excessive caution. According to Wetherby, his superior did not feel it advisable for us to be seen together. The Department still has not heard from Sethos."

Ramses's raised eyebrows indicated a strong degree of skepticism. "I believe he was telling the truth about that," I said. "He did say that

Sethos was in Syria when last heard from, but that is about all I got out of him. Except that he promised he—Smith, rather—would take steps to draw any possible watchers away from us. 'Laying a few false trails' was how he put it."

"Not very satisfactory," Ramses muttered.

"Oh, and he also said he would inform us if and when he heard from Sethos, providing we do the same. I agreed, of course."

"Of course," said Ramses.

He turned away to greet his son, who offered him a somewhat battered biscuit. "I brought you this, Father, since Charla is about to eat the rest of them."

"That was good of you," Ramses said. He sat down. The little boy leaned against his knee, and Ramses ate the biscuit, with appropriate murmurs of appreciation. Then David John said, "Remind me, if you will be so good, Father: Who was Tutankhamon?"

I smiled to myself. David John did not like to admit ignorance of archaeological matters. This was his oblique method of obtaining information on a subject he knew little or nothing about. His ignorance was not surprising, since he was only five years old, and Tutankhamon was one of the most obscure of all Egyptian pharaohs.

Ramses looked startled. "Why do you ask, David John?"

"Grandpapa believes his tomb is in the Valley of the Kings. He would like to find it."

"I'm sure he would," Ramses said. "It is true that Tutankhamon's is one of the few royal tombs that has never been found. But he was not an important king, David John. He ruled at the end of the Eighteenth Dynasty, succeeding his father-in-law, who may also have been his father. You have heard of Akhenaton?"

"The Heretic," said David John promptly. His blue eyes shone. "A fascinating figure. His wife was Nefertiti and he had six daughters. He forbade the worship of the old gods and founded a new city, Amarna, dedicated to his sole god, the Aton. One might call him the first monotheist."

"Well done," I said. "David John must have been reading Mr.

Breasted's *History*. Like his father, he was appallingly precocious in certain areas, and he had learned to read at a very young age.

"Akhenaton's reforms did not endure, however," I continued. "After his death the court went back to the worship of the old gods and abandoned Amarna. Tutankhaton, as he was originally called, changed his name to Tutankhamon. His wife, one of Akhenaton's daughters, changed hers as well, to incorporate the name of the god Amon, whose worship had been forbidden by her father."

David John nodded emphatically. "From Ankhesenpaaton to Ankhesenamon."

"Good Gad," I said involuntarily. "Er . . . again, well done. That is about all we know of Tutankhamon, David John. Few monuments of his have survived."

"Then if his tomb were to be found—"

"That is most unlikely," I said. "Your grandfather has got a bee in his . . . er . . ."

"Bonnet," said David John. "A metaphor. I understand. I shall ask him about it."

He returned to Emerson, and I said, "Really, Ramses, I am beginning to worry about the boy. He rattled off those polysyllabic names as readily as he does that of his sister."

"He can't be any worse than I was," Ramses said with a smile.

I could only hope he was right.

It was shortly after midnight in the early hours of November 4 (I have good reason to remember that date) that I awoke to find Emerson gone from my side. Emerson wakes with a great deal of grunting and tossing about. For him to vanish as silently as a spirit aroused the direst of forebodings. Without stopping to assume dressing gown and slippers, I snatched up my parasol and ran out of the room. The sound of low voices led me to the veranda. The moon had set, but the stars were bright enough to enable me to make out the stalwart form of my spouse in muttered conversation with a much smaller figure. I heard Emerson say, in Arabic, "You are certain?"

"Yes, Father of Curses!" The voice was a high-pitched treble, that of a young boy. The sight of me wrung a small scream from him, but he stood his ground. Emerson glanced over his shoulder. "Ah, Peabody. What are you doing with that parasol?"

I lowered the weapon, feeling a trifle foolish. "Is there news of . . . of him?" I cried.

"Quietly," Emerson hissed. "Who are you talking about? Oh, him. No." He went on in Arabic, "Good lad. Here."

He fished in the pocket of his trousers, his only garment, and the jingle of coins brought a flash of white teeth from the child. "Wait," Emerson said. "We will return together."

"Curse you, Emerson," I said, trotting after him as he hurried back to our sleeping chamber. "What is going on? If it is not about *him* . . ."

Emerson took me by the shoulders. "Peabody," he said in a low, strained voice, "they have found a stone-cut step."

A thrill of electrical intensity ran through my limbs. I understood, who better, what that phrase betokened. A step, carved out of the stone, could mean only one thing. A tomb. And where else could it be, but at the spot Emerson had been haunting for days?

I exclaimed, "I am coming with you."

"I cannot wait for you, Peabody."

However, his attempts to assume his garments were slowed by excitement and by his habit of strewing his clothing all over the room when he retires. It took him a while to find his boots, which were under the bed. By that time I had slipped into my trousers and shirt and coat, which were where I had neatly arranged them earlier.

"I am driving the motorcar," said Emerson, giving me a defiant look.

If he had thought that would deter me, he was mistaken. It is impossible to explain, to those who have not experienced it, the all-consuming passion of archaeological discovery. To be actually on the spot when such a discovery is made, to be among the first to behold with one's own eyes an unknown tomb . . . well, I could not blame Emerson for stealing a march on Howard Carter. It was not good form, but it was understandable.

However, I prefer not to drive in the motorcar with Emerson, particularly when he is in a hurry, so I said, "The car makes a frightful racket, Emerson. I presume this expedition is not one you wish to advertise."

"Hmph," said Emerson. He added, more emphatically, "Bah. Make haste, then."

He dashed out. I knew he would have to wake Jamad, who was not at his best in the middle of the night, and get the horses saddled, so I finished my toilette, fastening on my hat and buckling my belt of tools—canteen, brandy flask, sewing kit, torch, knife—round my waist. When I reached the stable Emerson's gelding was ready, and Emerson and Jamal were saddling my mare, a gentle creature I had named Eva after my gentle sister-in-law. (Some of the more spirited Arabians objected to the jangle of objects on my belt.) The child greeted me with a bow and a wide grin. I recognized him now, and my suspicions were confirmed. He was one of Howard's water boys, the same one I had seen waiting outside the house. Waiting, I did not doubt, for Emerson.

"This is really too bad of you, Emerson," I said. "What underhanded scheme have you got in mind?"

Emerson seized me round the waist and tossed me onto the mare. Mounting in his turn, he reached down and hauled the boy up onto the saddle in front of him.

"It was Azmi here who found the step," he said.

"At your instigation?"

"I cannot imagine," said Emerson, in a reproachful voice, "why you should leap to the conclusion that I am up to no good. I only want to have a quick look, to make sure Azmi hasn't let his imagination run away with him. It would be too bad to raise Carter's hopes and then see them dashed."

"Howard would be touched by your concern, Emerson."

Emerson did not reply.

Emerson would soon have forged ahead had I not kept shouting at him. Concern for me, I feel certain, encouraged him to moderate his pace; I am not the most skilled of horsewomen. At least there was no one abroad at that hour. When we turned onto the road that led into the Valley, the cliffs on either side cut off what little light there had been, and at my emphatic suggestion Emerson slowed his steed to a walk. Cyrus Vandergelt's Castle loomed up against the stars, illumined like a veritable palace by flickering torches at the doors and in the courtyard, for Cyrus was extravagant with lighting. Howard Carter's house had been a dark huddle on the hillside when we passed it, and I had heard a chortle of satisfaction from Emerson. Howard was not yet awake. Nor would he be, I expected, for several hours.

The entrance to the Valley was closed, naturally. We left the horses outside the barricade; Emerson jumped nimbly over it and lifted first me and then Azmi over.

The Valley is somewhat eerie at night, as silent and deserted as it must have been in the days when the pharaohs lay undisturbed in their deep-dug sepulchres, surrounded by uncounted wealth. High overhead the brilliant stars of Egypt shone diamond-bright against the black velvet sky, but we walked through shadows. There had been guards in ancient times, as there were now; when a reverberating snore broke the silence, I thought that those ancient guards probably had shirked their duties in favor of sleep as often as did their modern counterparts.

Rounding a curve in the path, we reached the area we sought, and I ventured to switch on my torch. Howard hadn't bothered to station a guard near his site. Why should he, when he had found nothing except some wretched workmen's huts?

"Well done, Peabody," said Emerson, taking the torch from me. "Now, Azmi, show me the step."

The remains of the huts had been removed the previous day, but there was a good three feet of soil and rubble remaining over the bedrock. Azmi indicated a depression less than two feet long and a foot wide.

"I put the sand back, Father of Curses," he said in a thrilling whisper. "So that you could be the one to find it."

Emerson handed me the torch, dropped to his hands and knees, and began digging like a mole, throwing the sand out behind him. His large callused hands were efficient tools; it was not long before he let out a muffled swear word and held up a bleeding finger. It was not a request for sympathy, but confirmation of Azmi's claim. He had scraped his finger on a hard rock surface, the same color as the sand that almost covered it. We all banged our heads together trying to see down into the hole. Sand kept trickling back into it, but before Emerson stopped we all saw the straight edge of what had to be a ledge or step.

Emerson sat back on his heels. I waited for him to speak but he remained silent.

"Dig it out, dig it out," the boy urged.

"No." Emerson rose slowly to his feet. "I have not the right to do so."

"Isn't it a little late for such scruples?" I inquired. Archaeological fever had gripped me, and I was as anxious as Azmi to enlarge that enticing hole.

"Refill it," Emerson ordered, in the same quiet, even voice. He took me by the elbow and raised me from the squatting position I had assumed.

Azmi groaned. "Again?"

"Again."

"But, Emerson," I cried. "It may be only a natural feature, or the start of an unfinished cutting. Don't you want to make sure?"

"I have not the right," Emerson repeated. "In fact," he went on, "I hadn't the right to do this much, and it would not be prudent to admit that I had. Azmi, you must allow Reis Girigar to take the credit for finding this, as he will do so in any case. I shall see you are properly rewarded. There, that will do."

Emerson sat down on the low retaining wall at the nearby entrance to the tomb of Ramses VI and invited me to join him. The predawn chill was bitter. Emerson drew me close and put an arm round my shoulders. "Have a sip of your brandy, Peabody, to ward off the cold."

"The brandy, as you well know, is for medicinal purposes only. If you had given me time I would have brought a Thermos of coffee."

"Perhaps I was unnecessarily hasty," Emerson admitted. "But you understand, Peabody—"

"Yes, my dear, I do. How did you know precisely where to look?"

"Yesterday, after the last of the huts was cleared away, I observed something that caught my attention. The soil lies differently over a concavity. Not much of a difference, unless one is looking for it, but I was looking for it, you see. I couldn't be absolutely certain," Emerson said modestly, "so I pointed the spot out to Azmi. He waited until the guards had settled down for the night before he began digging. He's small, and he knows every nook and cranny in the Valley. Nobody spotted him. He then reported to me."

A shiver ran through me—part excitement, part cold. "Curse it," said Emerson. "One would have supposed that by this time our presence would have been noted. Azmi, see if you can rouse one of the guards and tell him the Father of Curses wants coffee."

Azmi scampered off. The sky had begun to lighten before he returned with two men, whom Emerson hailed by name. "You sleep soundly, Ibrahim, Ishak. What sort of guards are you, to allow us to enter the Valley unchallenged?"

The older of the two, a wiry chap with a grizzled beard, salaamed. "We knew it was you and the Sitt Hakim, Father of Curses, so we left you to do as you wished."

"That shows excellent judgment," said Emerson, with a smug smile. "Haven't you made your morning coffee?"

"As we always do, Father of Curses," the younger man said. "Ali Mohammed will bring it when it is ready."

We had our—their—coffee, very black and sweet and hot. Neither of the men ventured to ask what the devil we were doing there at such an hour, although the younger of the two kept looking curiously at the half-filled hole. Conversation was general and somewhat scurrilous; Ali Mohammed expressed doubts as to the virtue of one of the village wives, and Ishak reported that Deib ibn Simsah was said to have found a new tomb back in the Wadi el Sikkeh. Nothing to do with him, Ishak, of course. Finally our hosts left, having been properly thanked by Emerson. They would never have accepted payment for their hospitality, but an exchange of gifts was only good manners.

The sky turned from soft gray to pale blue. The sun had risen above the eastern cliffs, but in the depths of the Valley the shadows clustered. Emerson waxed impatient, fidgeting and muttering. Eventually we heard voices, and along came Howard's crew, led by his reis. They greeted us without evidencing surprise; clearly they had been told of our presence. Reis Ahmed Girigar was one of the most respected foremen in Luxor, and was made of sterner stuff than the others. Fixing Emerson with a respectful but steady eye, he asked whether Carter Effendi was expecting us.

"No," said Emerson. "We want to surprise him. And you, I think, will have a greater surprise for him. Look there."

Howard did not turn up for another hour. (His procrastination prompted a number of caustic remarks from Emerson, who was always at the site as soon as his men; but to do Howard justice, the removal of the remaining debris was a task well within the skill of his experienced foreman.) The reis had finished clearing the first stair, and he and Emerson had arrived at an understanding by the time Howard arrived, swinging his stick. The men fell silent when they heard him approach. Howard didn't see us at first. We had tactfully retreated into the background.

"Why have you stopped work?" he demanded of Girigar.

The moment was one of high drama. Instead of replying, the reis made a sweeping gesture, directing Howard's attention to the step.

British phlegm went up in smoke, together with dignity. Howard turned pale, then red, and fell to his knees. I doubt he was praying, he only wanted a closer look; but for the first time I fully realized how much such a discovery would mean to him, and I remembered something he had once said about the excavations carried on by the American Theodore Davis. "It don't seem right that he should find one tomb after another when there's been nothing for his lordship." Or for Howard Carter, whose career was dependent on the goodwill of a patron.

"Good Lord," he gasped. "When . . . how . . ."

"We found it almost at once, Effendi, as soon as we began digging. Then we stopped and waited for you."

"Yes, yes." Howard got to his feet and dusted off the knees of his trousers. "Quite right. Get on with the job, then. It may not be anything."

"I think it is, though," said Emerson.

Howard jumped. "What the devil— Oh, good morning, Mrs. Emerson. Er . . . how long have you been here?"

"We decided on an early-morning ride, you see," said Emerson evasively. "When we arrived, Reis Girigar had just made his great discovery, so we were unable to resist hanging about to see what developed. Don't mind, do you? Here, Peabody, take a seat."

The seat was a campstool, gallantly produced by the reis. I took it and smiled at Howard, who had been left with no way of getting rid of us short of a blunt dismissal.

I really would not have blamed Howard for cursing Emerson, who stood at Howard's shoulder and kept giving orders to the men, but before long Howard was too absorbed to feel resentment. The usual debris still overlay the steps, however many there might be, and the cutting itself. The men worked with a will, as anxious as we to see what lay below, but the work seemed to progress with agonizing slowness. Howard was—I must do him credit—a careful excavator, and with Emerson looming over him he was not tempted to neglect proper standards. As the morning went on, the crowd round the excavation increased—most of the guards and dragomen, curious tourists. The latter did not linger, for there was nothing much to see, but some of the Egyptians remained to watch. They knew, as the tourists did not, what those stone-cut steps might mean, and I was sorry to see among the watchers the villainous countenance of Deib el Simsah, one of Gurneh's most notorious tomb robbers. The sun was high and we were all sticky with dust and perspiration when we were joined by another group—Cyrus and Bertie Vandergelt, Jumana, and Ramses and Nefret.

"We heard," said Cyrus. "Looking good, is it?"

"It's too early to say," Howard replied cautiously.

"We brought a luncheon basket," Nefret said. "Won't you stop and rest for a bit?"

Her sympathetic smile brought home to Howard how disheveled he looked, his tie at an angle and his garments covered with dust. It also prevented him from protesting our presence, but in fact there was nothing he could do about it.

The tomb of Ramses VI was the nearest shelter, but it was popular with tourists. Emerson soon took care of that difficulty. "The tomb is temporarily closed," he informed the guard on duty. "Get them out of there, Mahmud, and don't let anyone else in until we have left."

Cyrus had also brought refreshments, so we had a nice little private luncheon. Speculation was rife. Was it a finished tomb, or only the beginning of one? Was it royal, or the smaller sepulchre of a nobleman? Was the entrance still sealed, or had it been breached in ancient times? We all knew that the former possibility was too much to hope for, but hope, dear Reader, does not rest on logic. Only Ramses remained his usual silent self.

By the end of the workday we were still uncertain as to what we— Howard, I should say—had found. Lest the Reader wonder why, allow me to remind him or her of how such tombs were constructed. Steps were cut down into the bedrock at the base of the cliff, within a descending stairwell, and when the desired depth was reached, a squared-off doorway gave entrance to the corridors and chambers of the sepulchre itself. This doorway must be well below the level of the topmost steps, since there had been no sign of it as yet, and detritus lay deep over the area—almost thirteen feet down to bedrock in some places. Howard kept on until growing darkness made careful work impossible. Emerson would have gone on beyond that time, had I not tactfully reminded him that the decision was not his to make. He was extremely restless that night, mumbling and throwing himself from side to side until I threatened to expel him from our chamber.

If I had not protested, Emerson would have headed for the Valley at dawn next morning; when interrogated, he had to admit that by his calculations it would take another day of hard work to clear the entire cutting.

"We ought at least pretend to be casual visitors," I informed him. "Howard will not take it amiss if we drop by on our way home from the West Valley, but if you push him too far—"

"Curse it," Emerson shouted. "See here, Peabody—"

"Mother is right," Ramses said.

"What?" Emerson stared at him. "Oh. Well. If you think so."

I wished Ramses had not interfered. We had had the beginning of a nice little argument developing.

Our morning's work in the West Valley was a waste of time, though. Neither Emerson nor Cyrus could concentrate, and the former was, for once, the first to suggest that we stop for the day. Exhibiting the delicacy which was so characteristic of him, Cyrus refused Emerson's invitation to call on Howard. He did not, as he might have done, point out that it wasn't Emerson's tomb.

"I feel kind of funny about hanging around," he explained.

"Why?" Emerson asked, in honest bafflement.

"Well, Carter didn't ask me."

"He didn't ask us, either," I said. "But that will not deter my husband. Come to dinner this evening, Cyrus, and we will tell you what went on."

Nefret had decided to spend the morning at her clinic, so it was just the three of us, Emerson, Ramses, and I, who wended our way to the East Valley.

Emerson had underestimated the zeal of Howard's crew. We arrived on the scene in time to see that the rubbish above the steps had been removed. Howard gave us only an abstracted greeting before urging his men to proceed. There was no thought of stopping now, and no possibility of leaving. One by one the descending stairs were exposed as the cutting deepened. The sun was low in the west when the level of the twelfth step was reached, and there before us was the top of a doorway blocked with plastered stones.

Howard sat down suddenly on the ground and wiped his forehead with his sleeve, too overwrought to take out his handkerchief. "I can't stand the suspense." He groaned. "Is the blocking intact? Are there seals on the plaster?"

This was as good as an invitation to Emerson, who probably would not have waited for one anyhow. Howard tottered after him as he descended the steps.

"I can't see," Howard mutttered. "It's too dark down here. The exposed section seems to be solid—"

"Keep your hands off the plaster," said Emerson curtly. "Peabody, toss down a candle."

I handed Ramses my torch. He had courteously refrained from comment or suggestion, feeling, I suppose, that his father was doing enough of both, but I knew the dear lad was as eager as we to inspect the doorway. With a smile at me, he descended in his turn. The rest of us crowded round the opening, breathlessly awaiting a report.

It came at last, in the form of a groan from Howard. My heart sank; and then Ramses's even voice called up, "Plastered stone blocks. There are several seals stamped in the plaster—the seals of the necropolis, the jackal and the nine kneeling captives."

"No cartouche?" I asked.

"Not here. But the lower part of the doorway is still hidden by rubble."

"I must see," Howard cried. "I must see what is behind that door."

"It will take several more hours to finish clearing the rubble from the stairwell," Ramses said coolly. "And it's getting dark."

"I must see," Howard repeated. "I must!"

"Some of the plaster at the top has fallen away," said Emerson. It was the first time he had spoken since Ramses went down with a light, and it was clear to me that he was having some difficulty speaking calmly. "There appears to be a wooden lintel behind it. Peabody, I don't suppose you have such a thing as a drill on that belt of tools?"

"I regret to say I do not, Emerson. I will make certain to carry one in future."

"Good Gad," said Emerson, whether in response to my comment or in general, I cannot say.

With Ramses's knife and an awl provided by the crew, a small hole was drilled through the beam. The wood was old and dry but very thick, so it took a while. It was like being spectators at a play—sightless spectators, since we were dependent on the reports of the actors instead of our own eyes. The suspense was not lessened thereby. It had not occurred to anyone, even Emerson, to object to Howard's mutilation of the lintel; only a mind completely lacking in imagination could have resisted the temptation to look beyond that blocked doorway.

Ramses was the first to ascend the stairs. "Well?" I cried.

He gestured toward Howard, who had followed him, with Emerson close on Howard's heels. "Well, Howard?" I demanded. "What is there?"

"Rubble." Howard held the torch, which wavered about. "The space beyond the door is entirely filled with stones and chips, from floor to ceiling."

"But surely that is good news," I said. "If the passage beyond—it must be a passageway—is closed, the tomb has been all these years undisturbed!"

"Yes, I suppose so," Howard said flatly. "I—to tell you the truth, Mrs. Emerson, I am so worn down with suspense and excitement, I am incapable of thinking."

"It has been quite a day," I said sympathetically. "You ought to go home and rest."

Emerson said only, "Hmph."

Howard's bowed shoulders straightened. "Not before I have filled in the excavation."

"Filled it in! But surely—"

"In fairness to Lord Carnarvon I must do so. He will want to be present when we take down the door."

"But that will mean a delay of weeks," I cried. "How can you bear to wait?"

"In fairness to his lordship, I must," Howard repeated.

Emerson said, "Hmph." This grunt was particularly expressive. If Emerson had been allowed to take over the concession, there would have been no delay.

On the other hand, if Emerson had been in charge, Howard would have been relegated to a subordinate role, and the glory, if glory there should be, would be Emerson's. It may have been this realization that consoled Howard. He sounded almost cheerful when he directed his crew to begin filling in the stairwell.

"We will leave you to it, then," I said. "Congratulations, Howard."

"A bit premature, perhaps," said Emerson. "The necropolis seals indicate that it was the burial of a person of importance, but the dimensions of the stairwell are not those of a royal tomb."

"Never mind," I said, giving Emerson a little nudge with my elbow. "It is a tomb and it has not been entered for thousands of years. Just think, Howard, you have stolen a march on our tomb-robbing friends from Gurneh. They are only too often the first to find a new tomb."

"You are babbling, Peabody," said Emerson, taking me by the arm. "Time we went home. Didn't you ask the Vandergelts to dine this evening? Speaking of tomb robbers, Carter, two of the ibn Simsahs were among the spectators this afternoon. Hope springs eternal in the breasts of those bastards."

"I saw them too," said Howard somewhat huffily. "They can hope all they like, but there isn't a chance they can dig through the fill in the stairwell and the corridor without being caught in the act."

"Hmph." Thus Emerson conceded the point.

"Will you join us for dinner, Howard, after you have finished here?" I asked.

"No, thank you, ma'am, it is most kind, but I am going straight to bed. As you so neatly put it, this has been quite a day."

The tourists had departed and ours were the only horses left in the donkey park. Emerson helped me to mount, and as we rode slowly homeward, I said, "Emerson, you have done nothing except grunt today."

"Not true," said Emerson, stung. "I gave Carter a good deal of useful advice."

" 'Discouraging' is the adjective I would choose. Howard has made a remarkable discovery, and the signs are propitious. Why can't you admit it?"

"Hmph," said Emerson.

# CHAPTER THREE

BY THE FOLLOWING AFTERNOON THE CONTENTS OF THE CABLE CARTER
had dispatched to Lord Carnarvon was known to all the informed citizens of Luxor. Foremost among these was Daoud, who quoted the cable
to us verbatim. "At last have made wonderful discovery in the Valley. A
magnificent tomb with seals intact."

"How does he know it is magnificent?" Emerson grumbled, when
Daoud reported this to him.

"There will be much gold," said Daoud with complete conviction.
"The golden bird of Mr. Carter is an omen of good luck."

This was the common opinion in Luxor. Even Emerson admitted
there was no need to place extra guards at the tomb. Its entrance had
been filled in and the passage was still blocked.

"Even if they bribed the guards, they would have to finish the whole
job in a single night. Anyhow," he added morosely, "we still don't know
what is down there. The tomb may be empty."

"Quite right," I agreed. "Since there is nothing to be done until Lord
Carnarvon arrives, perhaps you will consider turning your attention to

our work. Shall I invite Mlle. Malraux and Mr. Farid to visit us here, or will you go to Cairo to interview them?"

Emerson gave me a blank look. "Who?"

I reminded him of the identity of the persons I had mentioned. His eyes narrowed suspiciously.

"A woman and an Egyptian," he said. "I was under the impression that we would seek the most qualified persons and not be influenced by your socialist theories."

"The word 'socialist' is ill chosen, Emerson. If you are referring to my sentiments on the subject of discrimination against females and non-Europeans, I got them from you."

"Hmph," said Emerson, stroking his chin.

"These young people are at least as well qualified as their competitors," I went on, warming to the subject. "And less likely to find employment in a profession which, like most, is dominated by arrogant men. I am only proposing to level the playing field, in whatever small—"

"Oh, bah." Emerson threw up his hands. "Have it your own way, Peabody. You always do. But," he added, frowning fiercely, "I insist upon the right to make the final decisions. I will go to Cairo myself."

I had known he would. There was nothing to be done with his—Howard's, I should say—precious tomb until Lord Carnarvon arrived, and Emerson could think of little else. He was a perfect nuisance on the dig, emerging from periods of frowning abstraction to shout contradictory orders at everyone. Furthermore, the mere fact of his interviewing the pair meant that he had agreed in principle to the enlargement of our staff. I had already arranged with Cyrus that they should be housed at the Castle.

## FROM MANUSCRIPT H

Insofar as Ramses was concerned, it was a relief to have his father out of the way for a few days. It wasn't easy to get on with one's own work even when Emerson was in a cooperative frame of mind, and for the past few days he had been hard to deal with. The French Institute staff would be arriving shortly to take over at the workmen's village of Deir el Medina, and Ramses wanted to finish the translation of the papyri they had found the year before. Cyrus amiably agreed that he wasn't needed in the West Valley. Ramses had already made copies of the texts in Ay's tomb. They would have to be collated with the photographs Nefret and Selim had taken, but that job could wait.

He was alone in the house that day, except for the servants, so it ought to have been easy to concentrate, but his mind wandered—from memories of the man who had been his amiable and murderous assistant, to the voices of his children playing in the garden, to the Great Cat of Re, who was determined to recline on the delicate papyrus scraps laid out on the table.

"Go and bully the dog," Ramses said, carrying the cat to the window.

Once there he lingered, enjoying the fresh air and the vivdly colored blossoms along the path that led from the main house to the one his family occupied. His mother had proceeded with the construction of the latter without bothering to consult them in advance, but he had to admit it suited their requirements and was far enough away so that they weren't often bothered by unannounced visits. The children had their own quarters, and a set of rooms had been set aside for Nefret's clinic. From where he stood he could see its entrance, shaded by tamarisk trees with a bench under them for waiting patients. He was about to force himself back to work when someone moved along the path. It was Fatima, wearing her self-decreed uniform of black robe and head veil; but she was acting oddly, moving at an undignified trot and glancing frequently over her shoulder. She reached the door of the clinic, cast a final comprehensive glance around, and went in.

Nefret was in the West Valley with Cyrus. Fatima knew that. If she was in need of medical attention, why hadn't she mentioned it to Nefret at breakfast? Nefret always kept the clinic door locked, but Fatima, as head housekeeper, had a full set of keys. Surely she had better sense than to dose herself.

More curious than concerned, Ramses decided he had better ascertain the reason for her extraordinary behavior. He walked along the edge of the path, stepping lightly. His mother's favorite roses, pink and white and crimson, had sprinkled the ground with a rain of petals. The tall spires of hollyhocks had been partially denuded by Charla, who made dollies out of the blossoms. The unopened bud, inserted into the base of an inverted blossom, did bear a faint resemblance to a turbaned lady in a full skirt. A long row of wilting ladies, pink, rose, yellow, and crimson, lay along the path.

The door of the clinic was closed. He opened it.

Fatima spun round with a little shriek, clutching something to her breast. She was standing in front of the open medicine cabinet.

"What's going on?" Ramses asked. "Are you ill?"

Fatima shook her head dumbly. Her round, plain face was the picture of guilt, mouth ajar and eyes staring.

"I'm sorry I startled you," Ramses said gently. "What are you looking for?"

Fatima burst into tears. He'd been afraid she would. He put his arm round her shaking shoulders, patted her, made soothing noises, and waited patiently until her sobs subsided into broken exclamations of self-reproach. She had deceived them, she had concealed the truth, she had done wrong. The object she clutched was a bottle containing pills of some sort.

All at once Ramses had what his mother would have called a foreboding or premonition. It was, in fact, a sudden coming together of miscellaneous bits of knowledge. Fatima did not resist when he took the bottle from her.

Quinine.

"It's all right," he said. "I understand. Where is he?"

They all knew Fatima fed the local beggars. Occasionally one of these unfortunates was given a bed for a night or two, in a room in the servants' wing. (They could always tell when this had happened because Fatima scrubbed and disinfected the room next day.) Still sniffing, she led him to a small chamber next to her own comfortable quarters.

She'd put him to bed and drawn the curtains over the single window. The room was dim and stuffy. It smelled of carbolic and lye soap.

Ramses stood by the bed looking down at the sleeping man. What he had looked like when he arrived at the house Ramses could only guess; Fatima must have cleaned him up, for he was now beardless and pale, his prominent nose jutting up between hollow cheeks. For only the second time in his life, Ramses saw the basic Sethos, stripped of disguise, his features undistorted. His resemblance to Emerson was unnerving—it was like seeing his father aged and ill and defenseless.

"How long has he been this way?" Ramses asked.

"Last night he came," Fatima whispered. She was crying again. "He was very sick with fever."

"Malaria," Ramses said. "He's had it before. Did he send you to get the pills?"

"When he woke this morning." She wiped her wet face. "He wrote the word so I would know what to look for. He did not want you to know he was here. I did not have a chance to get away before now. I am sorry, Ramses."

"He's the one who should be sorry. He had no right to put you in this position!"

"Oh, but he is my friend. And he needed my help."

That would do it, Ramses thought. Sethos had gone out of his way to ingratiate himself with Fatima, treating her with the same courtly charm he bestowed on "real" ladies, and paying her extravagant compliments. An appeal to her large sympathies would have tipped the scale of divided loyalties.

Malaria wasn't curable. Once infected, the victim was subject to recurrent bouts whose onsets were unpredictable. Ramses tried to remember what Nefret had told him about the disease when she had nursed Sethos through his first attack. In this form the sufferer was coherent and fairly comfortable in the morning. In late afternoon chills set in, to be followed by high fever and, sometimes, delirium.

"We'd better wake him up and get him to take this," Ramses said. He bent over Sethos, who was wearing one of Emerson's nightshirts, and shook him, none too gently.

Sethos opened his eyes. He showed no surprise at the sight of Ramses, though his expression was not welcoming.

"I didn't suppose she'd be able to hold out for long," he said resignedly.

"She didn't tell me. I caught her stealing your quinine." Ramses opened the bottle. "How much are you supposed to take?"

"One grain three times a day. I've been on the run for weeks. No chance to replenish my supplies."

"I will bring food," Fatima said, and bustled out.

"This was a filthy trick to play on her," Ramses said. "Why didn't you come to Father or me?"

A spark of unregenerate amusement lit the pale eyes in the sunken sockets. "I didn't want Nefret to get her hands on me when I was weak and helpless."

"I'm in no mood for humor."

"Give me credit for a faint residue of decency, then. I wouldn't have come near the place if I hadn't been laid low by this damned malaria. I heard— Oh, thank you, Fatima. That looks delicious."

He pulled himself to a sitting position and took the tray from her. His hands weren't too steady. Was the afternoon onset starting already? Ramses had no way of knowing for sure, but Sethos could even use weakness as a defense.

"You heard what?" Ramses asked.

With a little cluck of distress, Fatima took the bowl of soup from the tray and began feeding her patient. "Do not bother him, Ramses, he is falling sick again."

Sethos obediently opened his mouth when she pushed the spoon against his lips. After he had swallowed, he said, "I may as well wait to explain myself until my entire doting family is assembled. You will tell them I'm here, of course."

"Of course. You heard what?"

"Open," Fatima ordered.

Sethos grinned at Ramses. After he had finished most of the soup he said weakly, "I'm sorry, Fatima. It's very tasty, but I can't—I can't eat any more."

He sank back on the pillow and closed his eyes. Ramses couldn't re-sist a parting shot. "I'm going to fetch Nefret."

Even that threat didn't get a response. A long shiver ran through Sethos's body. Fatima pulled another blanket over him.

"I will sit with him, Ramses, until Nefret comes."

If not an order, it was a very strong suggestion. Ramses beat an ig-nominious retreat, swearing under his breath.

Work was out of the question. He did not carry out his threat of go-ing for Nefret; by the time he reached the West Valley she and the oth-ers would be getting ready to close down for the day. He decided to make a quick survey of the premises. Sethos had got to the house with-out being intercepted, but he might have been followed.

Jamad was enjoying his afternoon nap, stretched out on a pile of straw in one of the stalls. Ramses saddled Risha himself. He made a cir-cuit of the house, going some distance into the desert before returning toward the river and skirting the edge of the cultivation. The scene was disarmingly peaceful. The fields were lined with egrets, like a lacy white border; the farmers welcomed them, since they ate insects that might damage the crops. Ramses saw nothing to arouse misgivings. Maybe Smith had actually kept his promise to lead the watchers away.

He got back in time to greet his mother and Nefret, who were ac-companied by Selim and Daoud. They all settled down on the veranda and Ramses was trying to think how to break the news to them when the door of the house opened and Kareem staggered out, balancing a loaded tray. A round-faced, unquenchably cheerful youth, he was the only so-called footman to survive Fatima's nagging. Ramses got to him in time to keep a pile of cups from sliding to the floor. Unabashed, Ka-reem smiled proudly and managed to get the tray onto the table without further mishap.

"You see, we are ready for you, Sitt Hakim," he announced.

"Where is Fatima?" that lady inquired.

"You had better sit down," Ramses said.

"She's not ill, is she?" Nefret asked anxiously.

Her mother-in-law was quicker. Or perhaps, Ramses thought, she had got the news in a dream, from Abdullah. "He's come," she said. "Where is he?"

Ramses got rid of Kareem by sending him to fetch the napkins he had forgotten. "Sit down and have your tea first," he urged. "Everything is under control."

"Ha," said his mother. But she did as he asked, pouring with a steady hand, while he told them. The responses were varied. Selim's neat black beard parted in a white-toothed grin. He had enjoyed his earlier adventures with Sethos, whom he considered quite a dashing person. Daoud, holding his cup daintily in the palm of his big hand, only nodded. Very little surprised him.

"Malaria again?" Nefret put her cup down and started to rise. "Damn. I'd better go to him."

"He's had one dose of quinine," Ramses said. "Don't go rushing off, darling, you look tired. What are we going to do about this development?"

His mother selected an iced biscuit from the plate. "What can we do but accept it? Finish your tea, Nefret, and then we will have a little chat with . . . with our visitor."

"All of us?" Selim asked hopefully.

"Why not?"

When they crowded into the small, shadowy room, Sethos was awake. "Splendid." He gasped, trying to keep his teeth from chattering. "Daoud and Selim, too. Where's Emerson?"

"Cairo." Nefret sat down on the edge of the bed. "Open the curtains, Ramses, I need more light."

"Better not," Ramses said. "I'll get a lamp."

"I will do it," Fatima said. She slipped out.

"She is ashamed," Selim declared. "As she should be. To deceive the Sitt Hakim—"

"There was no damage done," said that lady coolly. "At least I hope there wasn't."

"No one followed me," Sethos muttered. "I wouldn't have come if I had thought . . ."

A violent fit of shivering ran through him.

Fatima crept in carrying a lamp and Nefret said, "Everybody out. You can't question him now."

"No," her mother-in-law agreed. "But you are not going to sit with him. I will do that. I beg you will not argue, Nefret. I know precisely what to do. Go and tidy up for tea with the children—and get Kareem to make a fresh pot."

"Kareem?" Fatima let out a gasp of horror. "Did he serve the tea? It is not time! Oh, oh, oh, it is my fault. Did he break any of the beautiful dishes?"

"Not yet," Ramses said.

"Go and take charge, Fatima," his mother said. "You can join me here later."

Fatima twisted her hands together. "You are not angry with me, Sitt Hakim?"

"Not very." A forgiving smile took the sting out of the words. "Run along."

Remembering the usual course of the disease, Ramses knew it would be morning before they could get any sense out of Sethos—even supposing he was inclined to tell the truth. If his mother had hoped Sethos would wax confidential while alone with her, she was disappointed. When Fatima relieved her and she joined the others on the veranda, her lips were tightly set and she indulged in an extra glass of whiskey.

"Remember," she said, when Daoud and Selim were ready to leave, "no one must know he is here."

"Yes, Sitt Hakim," said Daoud. He considered his reply, decided it was somewhat ambiguous, and to be on the safe side, added, "I hear and obey."

"He'll tell Kadija," Nefret said, after their friends had left.

Her mother-in-law smiled. Daoud's wife, a massively dignified woman of Nubian extraction, was one of their closest friends, and a natural-born healer. "He thinks of her as part of himself. She will understand the situation and keep her own counsel."

They spent the rest of the afternoon entertaining the twins and trying to keep the Great Cat of Re from abusing the dog. Over dinner they engaged in futile but irresistible speculation. How was Emerson going to react? How could they keep Sethos's presence a secret? Would Kareem manage to serve the soup without spilling it?

Nefret insisted on having another look at Sethos after dinner, but was then persuaded to go to bed and leave the nursing to Ramses and his mother. Sethos was in the next stage of malaria, burning with fever and semicomatose. When the fever broke later that night, they had to change the sheets. His mother modestly turned her back while Ramses got Sethos into a dry nightshirt.

"His arm is bandaged," he said. "Was he injured?"

His mother said, over her shoulder, "A bullet graze. It's become infected. I must change the bandage. Is he . . . er . . . covered?"

"Yes."

The bullet had ripped out a sizable strip of flesh. It looked ugly, inflamed, and oozing. Sethos twitched and muttered while she disinfected it and replaced the bandage, but did not waken.

Ramses succeeded in sending her off to bed once the patient was cool and comfortable. "Call me if there is any change" was her last order.

"There won't be. Good night, Mother."

He extinguished the lamp and made himself as comfortable as possible in an overstuffed chair brought from Fatima's room. As his eyes adjusted to the darkness, he kept his eyes on the shaded window. No movement, except for the swaying of the fabric in the night breeze.

He considered the afternoon's activities, wondering if there was anything else he could or should do. The trouble was that most of their questions could only be answered by Sethos. Should they notify "Smith," and if so, how? What about Margaret? Sethos might know how to reach her; they sure as hell didn't. Ramses had had a long heart-to-heart talk with Kareem, and he felt sure he had put the fear of God and the Father of Curses into that inveterate gossip. Daoud was also an expert gossip, but he was a man of his word and he had sworn not to speak of the presence of a stranger. Fatima wasn't likely to talk. None of the other servants was currently sleeping at the house. They would find out about Fatima's patient next day, though, and eventually one of them would mention that Fatima had taken in another beggar. He could only hope that Sethos's pursuers were off on another trail or that they would fail to put two and two together.

He slept lightly, knowing that any unusual noise would bring him to full wakefulness. Once a rustle of the bedclothes roused him; when he bent over his uncle, Sethos was sound alseep, or pretending to be, his breathing slow and even. Resisting the impulse to shake him, Ramses pulled the blankets up to his chin and returned to his cramped chair.

I woke just before dawn. The memory of the previous day's events rushed into my mind, dispelling any temptation to further slumber. Without pausing to dress, I assumed a comfortable dressing gown and went through the courtyard to the servants' wing.

Ramses woke when I opened the door. Seeing me, he relaxed, yawned, and rubbed his eyes.

"You look very uncomfortable, dear boy," I said.

"I am." He rose and stretched stiffened limbs. "He hasn't stirred."

"He is awake," I said. "Go and have a wash and some food, my dear. I heard Fatima moving about in the kitchen."

Sethos waited until Ramses had gone before he rolled over and addressed me.

"What, no chaperone? What would Emerson say if he found us like this, you in that very fetching dressing gown and me—"

"Not a sight to inspire amorous feelings in a female. You sound very chipper. Are you hungry?"

"That's the way malaria works, as you know." He stretched luxuriously. "Ah, there is Fatima with my breakfast."

"Enjoy it," I said.

"Why don't you go and enjoy yours?"

"I have a few questions."

"Amelia dear, I can't eat and talk at the same time. Ramses and Nefret will want to be present when you interrogate me, so why don't we wait until—"

"I only wanted to ask about your grandson. We haven't heard from Maryam for a while."

He hadn't expected such a harmless question. His eyes narrowed. Then he shrugged. "As you know, my daughter and I are not on the best of terms these days. I disapproved of her choice of a husband and was foolish enough to tell her so."

"I don't understand what you have against Mr. Bennett. He is a respectable man with an excellent reputation."

"You had him investigated, did you?"

"Naturally. I didn't trust you to do it without prejudice. Are you sure you aren't jealous?"

Sethos put his fork down. "You are spoiling my appetite, Amelia."

"Painful truths often have that effect. You feel you have been supplanted, with daughter and grandson. It is only natural that you should feel resentment."

"Are you always right?" Sethos said with sudden violence. "Maryam and I had become friends after years of estrangement, and I scarcely know the little boy."

"Whose fault is that?"

I had seldom seen his countenance so unguarded. It was not a pretty sight; anger tightened his mouth and lit sparks in the strange pale eyes that could be brown or green or gray. I had obviously struck, not one nerve, but a bundle of them.

"Well, we will leave that for a future time," I said, rising. "Have a good breakfast."

I cannot say that I enjoyed mine. Maaman's food was as good as always, but watching Kareem stumble in and out, dropping boiled eggs and spilling coffee, tried nerves already on edge. I hadn't realized relations between Sethos and his child had become so strained. It was primarily his fault, of course. He had made some attempt to look after the girl, but her mother, his former mistress, hated Sethos as much as he detested her, and after Bertha's death Maryam blamed her father and left him to join the group of criminals Bertha had founded. The birth of Maryam's son and her subsequent reformation had reconciled father and daughter. Now Sethos had made a mess of that too. It was just like him. I added another item to my mental list of Things to Do.

"Fatima is with her beggar," Kareem announced.

"I know," I said. "She has a good heart."

"Is he a holy man?" Kareem inquired.

Nefret took the coffeepot from him. "Very holy," she said. "He wishes to be left alone in order to meditate and recover."

We paid Sethos the courtesy of waiting until he had had time to breakfast and tidy up before we returned to his room, though in the opinion of several of us it was a courtesy he did not deserve. We found him sitting up in bed, pillows plumped and blankets smoothed, holding a coffee cup. Fatima and his breakfast tray had discreetly vanished.

As I might have expected, he went on the offensive before any of us could speak. "I feel naked without some sort of disguise," he grumbled. "Ramses, can you oblige?"

It was not an unreasonable request. Though unshaven and hollow-cheeked, without hirsute adornment he was the image of Emerson, even to the cleft in his chin.

"What were you wearing when you arrived?" I asked, sitting down on the side of the bed.

"A voluminous if somewhat wispy gray beard and a patchwork gal-abeeyah. Fatima wouldn't let me have them back."

"Ah, the old beggar disguise," I said. "She has probably burned it."

"There were a few insects inhabiting the beard," Sethos admitted. "Authenticity is very important in—"

"Never mind. Ramses will see to it," I said. "Later. Start talking, if you please."

"What about?"

Ramses emitted a growling noise, as his father was wont to do when exasperated. "What have you done? Who is after your blood?"

"Quite a lot of people, I expect" was the cheerful reply. He caught Nefret's eyes and looked a trifle shamefaced. "It's rather a long story . . ."

"We have all morning," I replied, settling myself in the overstuffed chair with a pad of paper on my knee and a pencil in my hand.

"You all know . . ." Sethos began. Then he stopped speaking and eyed me askance. "Amelia, what are you doing?"

"Taking notes, of course."

Thanks to those notes and my excellent memory, I am able to give the Reader an accurate account of his long and rather rambling explanation.

"You all know what the situation in the Middle East is like since the war. The Great Powers have carved up the parts of the Ottoman Empire to suit themselves. France won't give up her interests in Syria, Britain has a mandate over Palestine, and Gertie Bell and her crowd have cobbled together a new kingdom of Iraq from an unholy mixture of warring factions, with a king none of them wanted on the throne and a British commissioner in actual charge. The Kurds were promised independence, but Gertie won't let them have it, since Iraq without Mosul and its oil can't stand. That old fox Ibn Saud is arguing about borders and hoping for control over Syria. If that weren't bad enough, Britain, under pressure from the Zionists, has come out in favor of a Jewish homeland in Palestine. The Arabs are afraid the Zionists will take their land, the Jews are divided between Zionists and those who oppose a temporal state, the Arab League demands the independence Lawrence promised them, and Fuad of Egypt is playing backstairs politics in the old Ottoman style.

"There have been rumors about . . ." The hesitation was so brief, only one who knew Sethos well would have noticed it. "About a shadowy group that is bent on stirring up mischief, for reasons that remain obscure. Not a difficult task, given the situation. I was sent to Baghdad and Damascus to see what I could find out. By the way," he added with genuine feeling, "the archaeological sites are being torn to pieces. There's no control over illicit digging and some marvelous pieces are being sold to collectors."

Ramses's black eyebrows drew together. "So you decided to 'rescue' some of them? And you are being hunted by competitors?"

"If I had done, it *would* have been an act of rescue," Sethos retorted.

"But as it happens, the—er—object I made off with was not an antiquity. I found it in the private files of a certain official in Baghdad—"

"Don't be coy," Ramses said. "Who?"

"The name would mean nothing to you. He stays out of the public eye, and not many people know that he is a kind of deus ex machina, a player behind the scenes. I had to take the damned thing rather than copy it, because it was in code and my time was limited."

"If it was in code, how did you know it was worth stealing?"

"Because it was in code," Sethos said with exaggerated patience. "And in a locked file that required all my talents to open. One doesn't go to all that trouble with linen lists."

"Go on," Ramses said between his teeth.

"I knew its absence would be noted. In fact," Sethos admitted, "my departure from the scene was not without incident. So I wasn't surprised when I ran into a spot of trouble at the railway station the following day. What did surprise me was that I recognized the drunken coffee seller who tried to push me under the train. He works for the department that used to be headed by your old friend Cartwright."

"British intelligence!" Ramses exclaimed. "Why would they try to kill you?"

"Precisely what I asked myself. I had, like a loyal little spy, intended to take the damned thing back to Cairo and hand it over. That incident put a damper on my zeal. It was obvious I had been under surveillance the whole time, or they wouldn't have been able to get on my trail so quickly."

"That's a standard technique," Ramses said, his lip curling. "They don't trust anybody."

"I am well aware of that. Still, their assumption that I might put the confounded thing up for sale rather than turn it in struck me as a trifle unkind. Instead of taking the Cairo train, I slipped out and returned later, in time to catch a train to Damascus. It was there that the second attack occurred, and I barely got away from three ugly fellows with long knives, who were almost certainly not hired by our lot."

"You might have been followed from Baghdad," I suggested.

"Not by our chap." Sethos's smile was not pretty. "I left him under the train."

Nefret put her hand to her mouth. Sethos's smile vanished. "I didn't set out to kill him, Nefret. He'd have pitched me onto the track if I hadn't slipped out of his grasp. It put him off balance, and . . . well. To make a long story short, after several further incidents I was forced to the conclusion that I had become an object of interest to a number of different groups. I made it to Egypt, but I didn't dare go near headquarters. They might be after me too; or there might be a traitor in the organization. I thought I'd got everyone off my trail by the time I reached Luxor, and then I heard of Ramses and Emerson's encounter at the greengrocer's. So I went off again, as far as Aswan, and wandered conspicuously round town until I attracted attention. That's when I got this." He touched his arm. "Since then I've been moving rapidly, doubling back on my trail and keeping a wary eye out. For the past few days I've been holed up in the cellar of a ruined shack in Sebu al Karim; felt this coming on last night, and decided to come here."

"That's very touching," Ramses said. "That you should seek out your loved ones."

Nefret frowned at him. Sethos said coolly, "I had a more practical reason. I can't make plans, I can't trust anyone, until I know what's in that document. You're good at codes and ciphers." Ramses remained silent. Watching him, Sethos went on, "I hadn't intended to come to the house. That's the truth, whether you believe it or not. I was about to communicate with you indirectly and ask for a meeting in a neutral spot when I fell ill. I don't believe I was followed here, but . . . well, the damage is done. Whatever this document contains, some people want it very badly—badly enough to come after you again if they can't find me."

I cleared my throat. "If you will forgive me for saying so, that is the most preposterous story I have ever heard."

Sethos's haggard face broadened in a grin. "I take that as a compliment, Amelia. You have heard a good many preposterous stories over the years."

"But really," I exclaimed. "This one is straight out of sensational fiction. Secret societies, shadowy organizations, a mysterious document obtained from an individual you can't or won't name . . . You'll have to do better than that, my friend, if you want our cooperation."

Still smiling, Sethos looked from me to Ramses.

"Whether he meant to or not," the latter said slowly, "he has us over a barrel. Where is the damned document?"

"In the cellar I mentioned, hidden under a dead dog."

Nefret winced, and Sethos said, "It was already conveniently dead, Nefret."

"I'd better go after it then, before someone else does." Ramses rose.

"Take Daoud and Selim." Sethos leaned back and closed his eyes. "And try to think of a reasonable excuse for being there in case someone sees you."

## From Manuscript H

Offhand Ramses couldn't think of a reasonable excuse for visiting the poor little village, much less the ruined house. He was furious with his uncle, and Selim's delight at participating in the venture annoyed him even more. Was everyone except his father and him under Sethos's spell?

The village was one of several that bordered the cultivation south of the temple of Seti I. As they rode toward it Selim said, "We are looking for tombs, yes?"

"There aren't any in that area."

"Who can say?" Daoud inquired. He was riding Emerson's gelding, the only horse in the stable that was up to his weight.

"He speaks the truth," Selim said. "We heard a rumor, eh? That is not hard to believe. There are always rumors of tombs."

"I suppose so," Ramses said grudgingly. He ought to have thought of that excuse himself. It was Sethos's fault, for getting him too angry to think straight. But it was unfair of him to take out his ill humor on Selim.

"While we look for tombs, Daoud will go into the house and find the paper," Selim said.

"You'd leave the dead dog to him?" Ramses asked with a smile.

"I do not mind," Daoud said placidly. "What does it look like, this paper?"

Their arrival brought the villagers out in full force. Most of the men were working in the fields, so their audience consisted of women, small children, and the usual livestock, plus a few doddering old men. When Ramses asked about new tombs, they were deluged with information from everybody except the livestock. Ramses knew he was the chief attraction; this sad little place was seldom visited by foreigners, and the visit of a member of the family of the Father of Curses was an event that would be talked about for days.

He and Selim made their way through a tumble of toddlers and barking dogs, led by the old gentleman who had appointed himself guide, and trailed by the rest of the local citizens. The noise level was high. There were a few tombs in the rocky surroundings, all small and empty except for thick layers of trash. They spent more time examining them than the wretched places merited, and then started back. Daoud was waiting with the horses. His large amiable face wore a smile and his hand was in the breast of his robe.

Not until they were well away from the village did Ramses ask, "You found it?"

"Yes." Handing over a small packet sealed all round with heavy tape, he added, "It was buried deep. The dog was a joke, I think. There were only bones."

"Typical," Ramses muttered.

"Open it," Selim urged.

Ramses was curious too. Drawing his knife, he slit the tape and pulled back the rubberized fabric. Inside, between pieces of pasteboard, were two sheets of folded paper.

"There are no words on the paper," Selim said, leaning closer. "What does it mean? Is it what you wanted?"

"Want? Hell, no, I don't want the damned thing. But I guess I'm stuck with it."

The symbols were numbers, dozens of them. The only codes and ciphers with which he was familiar used letters of the alphabet.

"Bloody hell," Ramses said.

On the Wednesday we were in receipt of a telegram from Emerson announcing his arrival the following morning. That was all it said. I would have appreciated a trifle more information—something along the lines of "Have hired new staff" or "Have not hired new staff"—but I was only too familiar with Emerson's disinclination to spend good money on telegrams.

Sethos's condition had improved; according to Nefret, he would be out of the woods in another day or two. Ramses had supplied him with a rather raggedy grizzled beard and enough putty to sculpt a new nose. Sethos seemed to enjoy playing with the latter; over the course of the day the contours of his nose changed from retroussé to hooked to concave. I hadn't realized how drastically the shape of a nasal appendage can alter one's appearance. My own experiments with the putty were not successful. The cursed stuff wouldn't stick. I decided there must be some trick to it, and determined to ask Ramses at a later time.

I was unable to extract any additional information out of Sethos, even when I showed him the little list I had made. "You have absolutely no idea who is involved in this shadowy organization of yours?"

Smiling his irritating smile, he read the list aloud. "The French, the Zionists, the anti-Zionists, Ibn Saud, Feisal of Iraq, the British Secret Service, Sharif Hussein, Gertrude . . . Gertrude Bell? Come now, Amelia! I know you and she don't get on, but—"

"I do not approve of women who claim the privileges of men for themselves but deny them to other women. She is a confirmed antifeminist with a monumental ego. She fancies herself a king-maker. Such people consider that the end justifies the means."

"It could be any of them, or all of them, or none of them," Sethos said, tacitly accepting my judgment of Miss Bell.

"Not a very comforting conclusion, I must say."

"Did you discuss your list with Ramses?"

"I am thoroughly conversant with the present political situation," I replied. I never lie unless it is absolutely necessary. "It is even more volatile than your initial summary suggested. Since Ibn Saud defeated his chief rival, the Rashid, at Hayil—"

"I know, I know," Sethos said somewhat abstractedly.

"Hayil is where you and Margaret first met, isn't it? Where is she now?"

Sethos started. "You do have an unnerving habit of jumping from one subject to another," he complained. "I don't know where she is. What would you do with the address if you had it? You surely didn't intend to inform her I was with you, or issue an urgent summons to Luxor. You might as well stand in the suk and shout the news aloud."

"Would she not wish to be by your side when danger threatened?" I asked.

"My dear Amelia, you are such a romantic. I'll tell you what will fetch her, though. If that tomb of Carter's turns out to be big news, she'll be first on the spot."

He was playing the same trick on me, but I decided not to challenge the change of subject. "Who told you about the tomb? Ramses?"

"Ramses is avoiding me these days. Hadn't you noticed? No, it was Selim. He and Daoud believe the omens are propitious."

"The golden bird," I said with a sniff. "It is only Howard's canary."

"That was Daoud. Selim isn't superstitious. From his description I'd say Carter may have come upon something . . . interesting." He moved restlessly. "I'd love to have a look for myself. When can I get up?"

"Not until Emerson arrives."

"You aren't afraid I'll bolt, are you?"

"You aren't fool enough to try that. We must find a new identity for you and work out some explanation for your presence. The dying beggar won't serve much longer."

"I have a few ideas," Sethos said pensively.

"I'm sure you do. Try to control your extravagant imagination. Emerson will be here tomorrow and then we will have a council of war."

"I am afire with anticipation at the prospect."

• • •

Emerson had hired the two new staff members, and what is more, he had brought them with him. We were all at home that morning; Nefret had patients and Ramses was still struggling with Sethos's mystery document. I sent Fatima to summon Ramses, and greeted the newcomers.

"As I told you, Peabody, they suit our requirements admirably," said Emerson. "I trust their rooms are ready?"

"As *I* told *you*, Emerson, they will be staying with Cyrus," I replied. My temper was firmly under control. I did not even mention the fact that Emerson had neglected to tell me they were coming with him. "I will notify Katherine at once that they are here. If you would like to freshen up, Mademoiselle Malraux, Fatima will show you to the guest room and supply anything you need."

"Oh, please, Mrs. Emerson, do not be so formal." The girl's eyes widened alarmingly, but I decided she was only attempting to indicate goodwill. "I hope you—all of you—will call me Suzanne."

A murmur from Mr. Farid included a pair of syllables that sounded like a name. "Suzanne and Nadji, then," I said with a smile.

Having dealt with the immediate problems caused by Emerson's lack of consideration, I invited the young people to join us for luncheon, it being almost time for that meal. My motives were part hospitality, part cowardice. I had given some consideration as to how to break the news of his brother's presence to Emerson and had come to the conclusion that there really was no way of doing it tactfully. This enabled me to delay the revelation a little longer.

The young lady bubbled with Gallic enthusiasm about the house and its arrangements. "I had glimpses of a beautiful garden, Mrs. Emerson. May I hope for a stroll later? I am exceedingly fond of flowers."

"You will have ample time to enjoy the garden in the weeks to come," I replied. "I am sorry we were unable to ask you to stay with us, but we are constantly in and out of one another's houses, and Mr. Vandergelt's home is much more elegant than ours."

"What is the news from Cairo?" Ramses asked, knowing Emerson was about to tell us anyhow.

"Carter is there, and Carnarvon is on his way," said Emerson. As far as he was concerned, there was only one matter of interest in Cairo. "By chance I happened to run into Carter— What did you say, Peabody?"

"Nothing, my dear. Do go on."

"That's all," Emerson said grumpily. "Except that Carter has been calling on all his friends, dropping veiled hints and looking mysterious when they ask questions. Fine way to keep his discovery secret."

"Why should he?" I asked. "The wire he sent Lord Carnarvon was known to all of Luxor, and I expect his lordship has confided in a number of his friends, who have confided in their friends. There is no keeping such things secret."

"The archaeological community is abuzz with rumors," Suzanne said. "Is it true, Mrs. Emerson? That Mr. Carter has found a new unrobbed tomb? The Professor wouldn't tell us anything."

"Said I wouldn't," Emerson grunted, attacking his food with vigor. "I keep to my word."

Nadji, who had spoken very little, looked up. His English was excellent, with only the slightest trace of an Egyptian accent. "The word had got round before your arrival, sir. You have nothing with which to reproach yourself."

"But you have actually seen the tomb," Suzanne exclaimed, her eyes popping. "Please tell us. It can't be kept secret for long, can it?"

"I only hope Howard has not raised Lord Carnarvon's expectations too high," I replied. Then, seeing no reason to remain discreet when Howard and Carnarvon had not done so, I went on. "Thus far he has found a sealed doorway, with what appears to be a blocked passage behind it. The signs are hopeful, but one never knows, does one? I expect we won't have to wait long, though. Carnarvon will surely wish to press on to Luxor as soon as possible."

Ramses said to his father, "Callender is here."

"Pecky Callender? What the devil for? He's no Egyptologist."

"But he is a trusted friend of Carter's. I believe he has been instructed to prepare for Carnarvon's arrival."

Emerson scowled darkly. I knew what he was thinking; I always do. He had offered his services, which had not been accepted. It was a snub, and I felt for him. All the more since he was due for an even more painful shock.

We had just finished luncheon when the reply to my note to Katherine came, expressing her pleasure at receiving the two new members of our staff, and inviting us to dine that evening. She had sent the Vandergelts' carriage for them and their luggage.

"We will see you tonight at dinner," I said. "No, Emerson, there is no need for you to accompany them, they will want to have a little rest this afternoon."

"I thought we might go on to the Valley," said Emerson, trying to detach my grip on his arm. "They will want to see—"

"Not this afternoon, Emerson."

Hearing something in my tone, Emerson objected no further. After the carriage had driven off, he turned to me.

"You have all been behaving very oddly," he said, looking from one of us to the other. "What has happened?"

"Sit down, Father," Nefret said.

"Good Gad!" Emerson cried in anguished tones. "Not one of the kiddies!"

"Now stop that, Emerson," I said severely. "Do you suppose we would all be so calm if something had happened to one of the children? No. Guess again."

Emerson dropped into a chair. "The tomb has been robbed," he said in a hollow voice. "Pecky Callender is no more use than—"

"At least you put the children before the tomb," I snapped. "Allow me to remind you once again that it is not your tomb. Guess again."

Emerson's noble brow furrowed. "Give me a hint."

"Confound you, Emerson," I began. "How can you have forgotten—"

"Not so loud, Mother." Nefret, who had been struggling with laughter, sat on the arm of Emerson's chair and put a finger to his lips. "We have a guest, Father. The— Oh, dear, how can I put this? The person who inspired your adventure at the shop. The fire. The bag of salt. The—"

As comprehension gradually dawned, her dainty finger proved inadequate to the task. "Hell and damnation!" Emerson shouted. "Has that bas— Has he had the effrontery to come here?"

"He was ill," Nefret said. "Please, Father, don't fly off the handle."

"And keep your voice down," I added. "How successful we have been in concealing his presence I cannot say, but there is nothing to be gained by shouting it from the rooftops."

Emerson could not get up without dislodging Nefret. He squirmed a bit, but she stayed firmly in place. "Oh, bah," he said in a strangled voice. "Ramses, would you care to explain how this came about? No, Peabody, not you; you are inclined to digress, and I want a succinct, informative account, without commentary."

He got it. In my opinion Ramses might have elaborated a trifle more; however, my attempts to add color to the narrative were ignored by all parties. When Ramses had finished, Emerson sat in silence for a time, stroking his prominent chin.

"That is the most preposterous story I have ever heard," he said at last.

"That was my initial reaction," I admitted. "And I feel sure Sethos hasn't told us all he knows. However, this is a preposterous world, Emerson, and some persons will stick at nothing to gain their ends."

Emerson could not deny this. We had encountered a number of such persons, and history had preserved the names of many others.

"This mysterious paper," he said. "Have you succeeded in deciphering it?"

Ramses shook his head. "It's really not my field of expertise, Father."

"You need not apologize, my boy. Very well. You can get up now, Nefret; my temper is firmly under control. I want to see him. Now."

Naturally I went with Emerson. He appeared to be in a reasonable state of mind, but there was no telling how long it would last if his brother provoked him—which he was almost certain to do.

Sethos was sitting up in bed, reading. He greeted Emerson effusively, but without surprise. "I heard you were back," he explained. "Who are the two people who came with you?"

His attempt at insouciance did not deceive Emerson, for the beard and the silly nose failed to conceal the hollowness of his cheeks and his sickly complexion.

"Fatima told you, I suppose," Emerson said gruffly. "The two newcomers are members of our staff. Egyptologists, well known to me. Er—how are you feeling?"

"Much better. It is good of you to ask."

"Hmph," said Emerson. "What the devil are we to do with you, eh?"

"That sounds more like you," said Sethos. "I'll be out of here as soon as Nefret gives me leave."

Emerson sat down heavily on the side of the narrow bed. "Where will you go?"

"I'll stay in touch."

"Damned right you will!" said Emerson. "Curse it, you can't simply stroll out the front door. Your adversaries aren't all fools. If they discover you have been here they will assume we have your confounded secret message, or a copy of it."

Sethos's eyes fell. "What do you suggest?" he asked meekly.

Emerson studied him with suspicion. Meekness was not one of Sethos's normal traits. "You will need a new persona," he said. "The role that comes to mind is one you've played before. It is known that we are taking on additional staff."

"Brilliant," Sethos exclaimed. "Who shall I be, then? Petrie? Alan Gardiner?"

"Control yourself," I said firmly. "You cannot take on the identity of a well-known person. You had better be a philologist. You can spend your time with Ramses, ostensibly working on the papyri from Deir el Medina, and avoiding situations that could betray your ignorance of archaeological technique."

"I'm not all that ignorant," Sethos said indignantly.

"We can work out the details later," said Emerson. "The most important thing is that the elderly beggar must go."

Little did we know, but he already had—into a more distant realm.

## From Manuscript H

Cyrus was delighted with the additions to his staff. Some of the others were less enthusiastic. When they met at dinner that night, Jumana was unnaturally silent. Ramses couldn't decide which of the newcomers she resented; she was cool, verging on brusque, with both of them. Bertie flirted clumsily with Suzanne and Katherine smiled benignly upon them. She would have been delighted to see Bertie turn his attentions from Jumana to a "respectable" European girl. Bertie did have a gift for falling in love with women of whom his mother disapproved. For a while he had taken a fancy to Sethos's illegitimate daughter, whose criminal past did not recommend her as a daughter-in-law. Presumably Maryam's engagement, to a dull but respectable merchant, had put an end to that. They had all been surprised at the announcement: Bennett was middle-aged, plain, and dull; Maryam's background was not precisely respectable. However, as Ramses's mother was fond of saying, love is unpredictable. To dull Mr. Bennett Maryam must represent youth, charm, romance, and after her exotic life Maryam might look forward to a bit of boredom.

"Now we can make progress," Cyrus declared, motioning his butler to refill the wineglasses. "As soon as we finish clearing the burial chamber of Ay's tomb, Mam'selle can start copying the paintings and Bertie can draw up a final plan. First thing tomorrow morning, eh? Is that all right with you, Emerson?"

"What?" said Emerson, staring.

His wife frowned at him. "Emerson feels, as do I, that we ought to allow our new friends a day of sightseeing before they begin work. It has been some time since they were in Luxor, I believe."

"I've never been," said Suzanne. "And I would love to see the places I've read about. Deir el Bahri, the Valley of the Kings, Deir el Medina, and all the rest. If you don't mind, Mr. Vandergelt?"

"Fine, fine," said Cyrus. The Sitt Hakim's word was law to him.

"Good," said that lady. "Why don't you all join us for breakfast and we will decide upon an itinerary."

The Emersons did not keep a carriage. It was pure perversity on Emerson's part; he clung to the hope that his wife would accept the motorcar as a substitute—which Ramses doubted she ever would. When she nagged her husband, Emerson pointed out that Cyrus's carriage was always at their disposal, as was the case that night. On the return trip no one spoke for a time. Only the distant howl of a jackal broke the stillness. Ramses put his arm round his wife; the crisp night breeze blew a strand of her hair across his face and starlight turned the landscape into patterns of iron-gray and silver. He thought of Cairo—the stench of rubbish, the fetid air, the crowded noisy streets. Shut away in their walled compounds, the foreign residents avoided these discomforts. He wouldn't, though, and neither would Nefret. The hospital she had founded was in one of the foulest parts of the city, near the infamous Red Blind District. She had walked those vile streets many times, unafraid and unmolested; but he had always hated the thought of her doing so.

Nefret, half asleep against his shoulder, stirred and spoke. "I think the newcomers are going to work out well."

"Hmmm," said her mother-in-law, seated across from them. "I confess to having some misgivings."

"You were the one who wanted to take them on," Ramses said.

"Professionally they suit admirably. But I did not consider fully the social ramifications."

Nefret chuckled. "Bertie was only flirting with Suzanne to make Jumana jealous."

"Jumana *is* jealous, but not of Bertie," Ramses said. "She's afraid she will take second place to Suzanne. Cyrus really ought to give her an official title and position. She's earned it."

"I agree," his mother said. "You must speak to him about it, Emerson."

"What?"

It was still early when they reached the house, to find Selim on the veranda drinking coffee. "A bit late for a call, isn't it?" said Emerson.

"Don't be rude," said his wife. "It isn't late. I suggested we leave the Castle early because we have an important matter to settle tonight."

"What?" said Emerson.

For a moment Ramses thought his mother was going to fly at her oblivious husband. "Sethos," she hissed through her teeth. It was a name made for hissing.

"Oh," said Emerson, fingering his chin.

Selim, who usually enjoyed their exchanges, remained grave. "I have news, Sitt Hakim," he said.

"I knew something had happened," she exclaimed. "What?"

"The old man is dead. The beggar."

Emerson sat up straighter. "What beggar? How? When?"

The old man's body had been found that evening, behind a wall of the cemetery. How long it had been there no one knew; the spot was not often visited. Selim had been among the first to hear of it. He had gone at once to examine the body.

"There was no mark of violence, no wound. I could tell because he had been stripped of his clothing."

"Why would anyone do that?" Nefret asked in surprise. "He owned nothing, he had nothing of value."

"He might have done it himself," Ramses said. "Sometimes he did. He would walk about naked, talking to himself or to God, until a kind person took charge of him."

Selim nodded. "It is possible. His few pieces of clothing had not been taken away, they lay on the ground next to him." With a sidelong look at Nefret, he added, "I deduce he died in the night. The stiffness had gone from his feet and legs."

As experts know, the process of rigor mortis is affected by many variables, including the temperature and the victim's physical condition. However, it was a reasonable deduction for Selim to make. He rather fancied himself as a detective.

"An excellent deduction, Selim," Nefret said. "I suppose he has been buried?"

"No, Nur Misur. He is here."

They had laid him out, as reverently as possible, on a table in the garden shed, covered with a clean white sheet. Fatima sat by him. The lamplight reddened the tears on her cheeks.

"I wanted to wash the body, but Selim would not let me," she murmured.

"Good thinking, Selim," Ramses said. Nefret lowered the sheet. It was a scene straight out of Doré, or one of the illustrators who specialized in Gothic horrors—the shifting light and elusive shadows, and the naked body, skeletally thin and pallid. Ancient dirt lay encrusted in the wrinkled flesh; a louse crawled out of the wispy gray hair. Normally one of the most fastidious of women, Nefret went over the body with professional detachment. Fatima let out little cries of protest.

"He is filthy and covered with insects, Nur Misur. Let me do that."

"It's all right, Fatima," Nefret said. "Rigor is well advanced. No wounds on the face or skull. The poor man is covered with bruises and scrapes. Fatima, hand me that damp cloth. I want a better look at his throat."

"He was always falling and running into hard things, God be merciful to him," Fatima murmured.

"There are bruises on his neck, but no worse than the ones on the rest of his body," Nefret reported.

"It wouldn't take much to send a feeble old man like that into cardiac arrest," Ramses's mother remarked.

"Oh, bah," said her husband, now fully attentive. "You are always looking for signs of murder, Peabody."

She limited her response to an evil look, but Ramses knew exactly what she was thinking. The poor old man's death couldn't have come at a more fortuitous time for them and Sethos.

Selim cleared his throat. "I told the men who brought him here that he had run away from you, and that you could help him," he said.

Nefret, scrubbing her hands with the soap and water Fatima had supplied, turned to stare at him.

"Help him from being dead?" her mother-in-law inquired caustically. "He was ice-cold and stiff, wasn't he?"

"They believe you can do magic," said Selim, scratching his beard. "He should have been buried tonight, but they believed me when I said . . ." He stuck there, unnerved by her sarcasm, and Ramses came to his rescue.

"You did right, Selim. The precise time of death is open to question. By the time the news spreads, people will confuse Fatima's patient with the old holy man, who will be unquestionably dead. This is the perfect moment for our guest to reappear in a new identity."

"That is what I thought," Selim declared.

"Let's have a little chat with—er—him," said Emerson, heading for the door. Over his shoulder he added, "Ramses, fetch the whiskey."

When our guests arrived for breakfast, we introduced them to the latest member of the staff. Sethos had reverted to his Anthony Bissinghurst role. Ramses had supplied him with a dashing black mustache and dye to turn his pale face a healthy tan. He had also supplied him with clothes, for they were almost of a size. He was proving to be a cursed inconvenience in every way; we would have to order new garments for Ramses, since his wardrobe had not been extensive to begin with.

A slow grin spread across Cyrus's face when he recognized Bissinghurst. Bertie and Jumana were also acquainted with him and with his true identity, and had been sworn to secrecy; poor Bertie, not the cleverest of individuals, hardly spoke a word, so fearful was he of saying the wrong thing. His silence caused no remark, since he hardly ever got a word in when the rest of us were conversing.

Jumana's dark eyes shone with pleasure when "Tony" bent over her hand. She had obviously been attracted to him when they last met and, as was his habit, he had been at his most dashing and courtly. Perhaps she preferred older men. If that was the case, Bertie was doubly disadvantaged. No one could have called the poor boy dashing.

Cyrus managed to have a word alone with me as we prepared to leave the house. Concern had replaced his amusement.

"What's up, Amelia? That fellow never appears unless there is trouble brewing."

"I will tell you about it another time," I replied, wondering what the devil I could tell him.

"It better not be Carter's tomb he's after," Cyrus muttered. "Emerson will skin him alive if he tries any tricks."

We went first to Deir el Bahri, where the Metropolitan Museum crew was working, and then made the circuit of other temples before turning toward the Valley of the Kings. It was of necessity a cursory tour, but by the time we reached the entrance to the Valley, anticipation had mounted. The persuasive air of suppressed excitement (I am sensitive to such things) surprised me. Clearly the word of a great discovery had spread—not, as yet, to the general public, but among those who had a professional interest in such matters.

I glanced at Sethos, who was walking beside me. He looked tired but alert. A new and ugly suspicion had taken root, seeded by Cyrus's remark. What evidence had we of the truth of Sethos's story? Only a mysterious document, which could not be deciphered, and his own word. The attacks on him and on us might have been made by rivals in the antiquities game. If he had returned to his old profession, Carter's tomb would present . . . interesting possibilities.

The tomb itself was something of an anticlimax. There was nothing to see except a pile of rubble that filled the stairwell and concealed the steps. After a glance Suzanne raised her shoulders in an elegant Gallic shrug and joined the tourists entering the tomb of Ramses VI. Bertie trailed after her and Jumana offered to show Nadji some of the more interesting tombs. The rest of us stood staring as if hypnotized at the heaped-up debris.

"No signs of digging," Emerson muttered after a time.

"Even the experienced tomb robbers of Gurneh wouldn't tackle that," said Sethos, hands in his pockets and eyes intent. "If any of them have illegal intentions they'll wait until the stairs are clear and the passageway—if it is a passageway—is open."

"Is that what you would do?" Ramses inquired, his voice carefully neutral.

"It is what any sensible individual would do. Why go through all that hard manual labor, with very little chance of doing it unobserved, when you aren't certain that it would be worth the effort?"

The tomb robbers of Gurneh were not always sensible. But Sethos was.

. . .

Carnarvon and Lady Evelyn arrived in Luxor on the twenty-third. We were in the West Valley, completing the clearance of Ay's burial chamber—all of us except Sethos and Daoud. Sethos had shown signs of fatigue so I had insisted he rest. Daoud ought to have been with us; the fact that Emerson did not ask about him ought to have given me a hint about his activities. When he turned up we heard him coming long before he appeared, his large sandals rhythmically slapping the ground.

"They have gone to the tomb," he panted. "Straight from the train."

"Well, of course," said Emerson. "Who could blame them?"

"Is it Lord Carnarvon and his daughter of whom you speak?" I asked. "See here, Emerson, I won't have you haring off to the East Valley today."

"Would I do that?" Emerson gave me a look of injured innocence. After a moment he added, "Tomorrow will be soon enough. It will take several days to clear the steps again."

There was no restraining him. And I will admit, to the Reader, that my interest was almost as keen as his. After two weeks of uncertainty we were within a few days of learning the truth. I could only imagine the state Howard must be in. Really, we owed it to him to express our support and friendship, particularly if, as was likely, the tomb proved to be empty.

I did manage to convince Emerson he should wait until a reasonable hour next morning, pointing out that it would not be proper to anticipate the arrival of Lord Carnarvon, who would probably not be early. However, I had underestimated Carnarvon's zeal. When we arrived— Ramses and Nefret, Sethos, Emerson and I—he and Lady Evelyn were on the scene, watching the workmen remove the debris under Howard's direction.

George Edward Stanhope Molyneux Herbert, Fifth Earl of Carnarvon, was of medium height and slight build, with features which one could only call unmemorable. His eyes were pale and his complexion, marred by the scars of smallpox, unhealthy. He had not been a well man since a serious motor accident some years earlier, though wintering in

Egypt had improved his health (and aroused his interest in Egyptology).

I had met the young lady once before and found her somewhat silly and frivolous—a typical example of the young female aristocrat—but I had to admit she knew how to dress. Her skirt was mid-calf length and her laced shoes had low heels. However, they had been died saffron to match her sport suit and she wore a jaunty bow at her throat, of the same brown as her stylish toque.

"We dropped by to welcome you back to Luxor," said Emerson, wringing Carnarvon's hand. "And congratulate you."

"You think it looks promising, then?" Carnarvon asked eagerly.

"Too soon to tell," Emerson said. "You haven't uncovered the lower part of the door yet."

"Don't be such a killjoy, Professor Emerson," the young lady exclaimed. "It's all so frightfully thrilling! Pups is frightfully bucked up." She squeezed her father's arm. Emerson winced. He detests coy nicknames.

"That is right," I said. "Always look on the bright side. Is there anything we can do to assist? Our son, as you know, is expert in the Egyptian language."

Howard came forward and Lady Evelyn turned a bright, admiring smile on him. Howard swelled up like a pouter pigeon. "I believe I can claim to have the ability to carry out a proper excavation. However—er—if any more seals turn up, a second opinion would be useful."

He nodded at Ramses, who said gravely, "I would be happy to be of use, naturally."

Emerson was peering down into the pit. "You won't reach the bottom of the stairs before later this afternoon."

"How do you know how many steps there are?" Lady Evelyn inquired pertly.

Emerson shrugged away the question as he would have shrugged off a fly. Glancing at him, Howard said, "The Professor bases his appraisal on the apparent dimension of the doorway, Evelyn. It is standardized in tombs of this period. Isn't that right, sir?"

"Hmph," said Emerson. His hands flexed, as if aching to grasp a tool.

No one was rude enough to tell us to go away. Nothing short of a direct order could have accomplished it, and Emerson would have ignored even that. We had waited for weeks to learn whether the doorway had been breached, and what lay beyond it. We stood round the edge of the stairwell, watching with pent breath as step after step came into view. Down below, the shape of the doorway lengthened, but it was impossible to make out details owing to the lack of light. Finally Reis Girigar called out, "Sixteen steps, mudir. The door is clear."

Emerson was quivering like a hunting dog waiting to be released. He controlled himself, however, and so Howard was the first to descend. Carnarvon and Lady Evelyn were next. A mumble of conversation followed, broken by the young lady's cries of excitement. Then Howard came back up.

"Oh, dear," I said. "You don't look at all pleased, Howard. Don't tell me . . ."

"There are signs of forced entry. A hole. It was filled in afterward."

"But that is encouraging news, Carter," Ramses said. "If the tomb had been completely looted, the necropolis priests would not have bothered to close up the hole and stamp their seals all over the door. Are there any other seals?"

"Dozens of them." Carnarvon gasped. His daughter helped him up the stairs. "Hundreds. Carter couldn't read them . . ."

I should explain, in Howard's defense, that the seals to which Carnarvon referred had been stamped into the wet plaster after it was spread across the stones of the doorway. The passage of time, and perhaps the hastiness of the ancient workers, had wrought considerable damage on these impressions. Crumbling and broken, they were not easy to decipher, especially by a man in a considerable state of excitement.

Nefret hastened to Carnarvon and took his other arm. "Sit down here in the shade, sir."

"Yes, do, Pups." Lady Evelyn looked doubtfully at Nefret. "You're a doctor, they tell me? Is he all right?"

"It's just excitement, I think," Nefret said with a reassuring smile.

"I can't rest until I know what those seals read," Carnarvon insisted. "Is there a king's name? Whose name?"

"Ramses," said Emerson. "Relieve his lordship's mind, if you please."

"Yes, sir," Ramses said. "Unless Mr. Carter would rather—"

"No, no," Carter said. "That is . . . yes. Come along."

They went down together. Knowing his father was about to burst, Ramses reported his findings in a loud, clear voice. "There are signs of entry at the top of the doorway—an uneven, roughly oval gap, which has been blocked up again and resealed. There are more necropolis seals—the jackal and the nine kneeling captives—and a number of cartouches."

A cry from Lord Carnarvon was echoed by one from Emerson. "Whose?" they shouted.

"Most of them are illegible, or nearly so, but they appear to be the same name."

Carter said something in a low voice—a question, to judge by the inflection. "I agree," Ramses said loudly. "That is definitely a neb sign. And at the top, a sun disk."

"Nebkheperure," Emerson said.

"Possibly," Ramses said cautiously.

"Not Tutankhamon?" Lady Evelyn asked.

"Nebkheperure *is* Tutankhamon," I said.

# CHAPTER FOUR

FOR A FEW MINUTES THE SILENCE WAS ABSOLUTE. HAD WE INDEED found the missing tomb of that shadowy monarch, the last of his line, the successor of the great heretic Akhenaton? When Howard and Ramses came up the stairs, Carnarvon burst out, "The doorway must be dismantled. Immediately."

"That would be inadvisable, sir," Ramses said, for Howard seemed incapable of speech. "We must preserve the seals if we can, so that they can be studied in detail. That will take a while. Anyhow, according to protocol, an inspector of the Antiquities Department should be present. I presume you notified Mr. Engelbach that you would clear the stairwell today?"

Howard nodded dumbly.

"Then where is he?" Carnarvon demanded. "Why hasn't he had the courtesy to respond promptly to my message?"

"He is a very busy man," I said. "He has all of Upper Egypt in his jurisdiction. But I am sure he will be along soon."

The febrile color in his lordship's cheeks faded, leaving him pale and shaking. Nefret lifted his limp hand and placed her fingers on his wrist.

"I would advise you to get your father to bed, Lady Evelyn. He is somewhat agitated, but a good night's rest should set him right."

"No, no," Carnarvon said. "I'll wait for Engelbach."

We had to wait another half hour. I confess I began to share Lord Carnarvon's frustration. One would have supposed the mere existence of a hitheto unknown tomb would have aroused the interest of the Chief Inspector for Upper Egypt, which included the Valley of the Kings; but when Engelbach finally turned up, accompanied by Ibrahim Effendi, his lieutenant, he shook hands all round before even looking at the cleared stairs. He was at that time in his mid-thirties; we had known him since he began his career in archaeology and we had always been on good terms. He was not on such good terms with Howard, whom he greeted somewhat cavalierly.

"So what have we here?" he asked—of Emerson.

Glancing at Emerson as if for support, Howard said, "The lower strata of rubble from the stairwell contain potsherds and inscribed scraps. Ramses has—er—we have found the name of Tutankhamon, but also those of several other pharaohs, including Akhenaton."

"A cache, then," Engelbach said coolly. "Containing several burials."

"Or the remains of them," said Emerson. "Those broken pieces suggest the tomb was robbed in antiquity, and that a number of objects were removed before the necropolis priests resealed it."

Engelbach nodded thoughtfully. "Like KV55. Let's have a look, then."

He remained, watching, while the men cleared the last few feet of debris from the bottom of the stairwell. Additional scraps of funerary equipment were found—a certain sign that some objects had been removed from the tomb before the steps were filled in. After inspecting these, and the seals on the door, Engelbach glanced at his watch.

"I must be off. You will of course notify me as you proceed. Let us hope," he added, with a sharp look at Howard, "that this discovery won't be botched as was the excavation of KV55."

Botched it unquestionably had been, by the elderly American dilettante Theodore Davis, whose dictatorial control had made it virtually impossible for his archaeological assistant to follow the rules of proper excavation. We had been helpless observers of the havoc wrought by Davis, the mention of whose name still brought a snarl from Emerson. He was equally incensed with the inspector of the time, Arthur Weigall, who had been far less strict with the old American than he ought to have been. Rex Engelbach wouldn't make that mistake.

"You can count on Carter to do the job right," Emerson said fairly.

"I feel certain he appreciates your advice, Professor," said Engelbach.

I didn't feel at all certain about it. Emerson's compliment had left Howard unmoved; he bit his lip and looked daggers at the inspector. Engelbach tipped his hat politely to the ladies and went off.

"Well," said Emerson, rubbing his hands together, "there are several more hours of daylight left. Shall we get at it?"

"By all means," Carter cried, too excited to resent Emerson's bland assumption of participation.

"I am surprised at you," said I, having been in receipt of a pointed look from Ramses. "Both of you. There is not enough light for proper photography, and removing the blocks without damaging the seals will take time."

"Bah," exclaimed Emerson. "That is—er—quite right, Peabody. Curse it," he added morosely.

Accepting the fact that nothing more could be done that day, Carnarvon agreed to go home and was led off by Lady Evelyn. The rest of us followed his example.

"I am surprised at Rex Engelbach's disinterest," I said, as Emerson and I left the Valley. "He was rather rude to Howard, I thought."

"Snobbery," said Emerson. "He looks down on Carter because of his lower-class origins, and so do many other Egyptologists. He'd rather someone else made a great discovery." After a moment he added grudgingly, "The excavation couldn't be in better hands."

Except yours, I thought. I gave the arm I held an affectionate squeeze, in silent acknowledgment of his nobility of character.

•   •   •

Howard was something of an amateur photographer himself, but on this occasion he was happy to accept the services of Nefret and Selim. We were all on hand early the following morning, and the job was well underway when Lord Carnarvon and Lady Evelyn arrived.

Every square inch of the doorway was photographed and then the blocking stones were taken down one by one, with the greatest possible care. The men at once began removing the stone chips that filled the passage beyond. Its dimensions were obviously those of a passage, not a chamber, but since its length was unknown, it was impossible to determine how long this process would take. As the afternoon wore on, additional disquieting evidences of disturbance appeared—scraps of pottery and of leather (the remnants of bags brought by the thieves to carry away valuable oils) in the lowest levels. At sunset there was no end in sight and Howard decided to stop for the day.

We were all on hand the following morning, and so was Mr. Callender, Howard's friend. Whence he had acquired the name of Pecky I did not know; absurd nicknames would seem to be a British failing. He was an engineer and architect, not an Egyptologist, and Emerson greeted him with a certain reserve.

"If he is an example of the assistants Carter intends to employ, I do not approve," my husband muttered to me.

"Howard is not dependent on your approval," I reminded him. "Do not be premature, Emerson. We do not yet know what sort of assistance may be required."

Hour after hour the basket men carried up their loads. The corridor lengthened. Fifteen feet, twenty feet, twenty-five . . . At last, in midafternoon, the top of another sealed doorway appeared. The clearance was halted while Ramses and Howard examined what they could see of the door.

"It's like the outer door," Ramses reported. "It has been breached at least twice, and the openings refilled and resealed."

"Never mind," Howard said, wiping the dust from his perspiring face. "Let's get the entire door exposed."

The weary men went back to work. "What's he so cheerful about?" I asked Emerson.

Hands in his pockets, eyes intent on the cutting, Emerson said, "The contents of an unrobbed tomb belong in their entirety to the Antiquities Department. It took a while for that to dawn on him."

"Ah, I see. So if this tomb has been entered—"

"The discoverers may expect a division of the remaining contents."

The next hour dragged interminably. Howard stood by smoking one cigarette after another. At last the entire doorway was exposed. Carter and Carnarvon went down, accompanied by Lady Evelyn and Mr. Callender. No one else was invited, but I felt it my duty to follow; in my opinion Howard was on the verge of nervous collapse and Carnarvon was in even worse case. They might require immediate medical attention.

Beyond the light entering from the stairwell the descending corridor was extremely dark. I crept along, feeling my way with a hand resting on the wall. Ahead I could see the lights of electric torches moving to and fro. Then Howard's voice, soft, but amplified by echoes, reached me. "There's empty space beyond, as far as the iron testing rod reaches."

So he had drilled a hole in the door. I stopped, my hand resting on the wall, my heart beating fast. I hoped Howard would have sense enough to use a candle to test for noxious air before widening the hole. A mutter of conversation, of which I heard only a few words, indicated that he had. It was followed by the sound of metal rubbing against stone. He was enlarging the hole.

A period of silence followed. Then came Carnarvon's voice, sharpened by suspense. "Well? Can you see anything?"

I crept a little closer, trying to move quietly. I could make out their shapes, crowded close to the doorway. Callender's bulky form almost hid the slimmer frame of Lady Evelyn. The other men stood next to them, so close that they resembled the shape of a single, monstrous creature.

"Well?" Carnarvon repeated. "Here . . . let me look."

I think he gave Howard a shove. Howard fell back and Carnarvon took his place. A loud, wordless cry from Carnarvon finally aroused a response from Howard. "Wonderful! Marvelous things, wonderful things!"

I blush to admit that I so lost control of myself as to exclaim, "What?" However, my voice was drowned out by those of the others. Lady Evelyn had replaced her father and was emitting little shrieks; Callender kept bellowing, as I had, "What? What?" Carter and Carnarvon uttered broken ejaculations of disbelief.

Then came that magic word: "Gold!" It came from Lord Carnarvon. He was again looking in the hole, describing to the others in incoherent phrases what he saw. I listened for a few minutes and then crept quietly up the corridor. It was some time before Howard and the others returned to the top of the stairs.

All the world knows what they saw through that small hole; but the first impression was so overwhelming and, let me add, the view so limited, that it is no wonder their description was confused. Howard kept repeating, "Wonderful things! Marvelous things!" Lady Evelyn embraced her father and Howard alternately (and once hugged Ramses—I *think* by mistake). Eyes glazed, Carnarvon could only murmur the word "gold," over and over.

When Emerson asked politely if we might have a look for ourselves, I don't believe Lord Carnarvon heard him. Nor do I believe Emerson would have heard a refusal. Emerson and I, Nefret and Ramses therefore proceeded. We took it in turn to peer through the small opening, passing the torch from hand to hand.

At first glance it looked like Ali Baba's cave, filled with a bewildering jumble of gleaming objects. It took a while for the eye to sort them out and for the trained mind to interpret them. From that first look I remember only the huge funerary couch, with the head of some fabulous beast, gilded and painted, on which rested various objects. Under it were piled boxes and pots.

The others had their turns. When we went up, Howard turned to Emerson with an eager "Well?"

"Remarkable," said Emerson, stroking his chin. "You've months of work ahead of you, Carter. More, if there are other rooms beyond this one."

He was the calmest of us all. Even Ramses's normally composed countenance betrayed the wonder he felt. Lord Carnarvon had collapsed into a camp chair and was being fanned by his daughter.

"There must be other rooms," Howard exclaimed. "There is another doorway."

"I saw it," said Emerson. "Naturally you will notify Engelbach before you do anything more."

Howard's bow tie was askew, his shirt streaked with dust, his hair standing on end. "Yes," he said. "Yes. Notify. Tomorrow?"

"We will be happy to join you," said Emerson graciously.

At Howard's order, a wooden grille had been set in place at the beginning of the entrance corridor. We watched him close the padlock and then rode homeward. When we neared the house, to see its hospitable lights shining through the gathering dusk, Emerson roused himself from a brown study.

"I hope Fatima has put dinner back. I could do with a whiskey and soda."

"It isn't that late," I said. "So much has happened that the day seemed longer than usual."

We had missed tea. I deduced that the children had been taken off to bed, since the dog was not couchant in front of the door to the veranda. However, the seats in that room were occupied. Sethos was there, of course, his countenance bland as ever. Nor was I surprised to see Cyrus. With his customary delicacy he had refrained from intruding on Howard's activities, but I knew he would be burning with curiosity. The others were there too—Suzanne and Nadji, Bertie and Jumana.

"You'll have to excuse us," Cyrus said sheepishly. "We've been hearing rumors. About a room piled high with gold."

"Already?" Nefret exclaimed.

"You need not apologize," I said, clasping his hand warmly. "Emerson, will you serve the whiskey?"

I then launched into a tale that held my audience spellbound.

"He's found it, then," Nadji exclaimed. "Tutankhamon. Not a cache?"

"So it would appear," Ramses replied. He had taken a seat next to

Nefret, "I was able to make out a few cartouches on various objects. They were all those of Tutankhamon and his wife."

That was more than I had been able to make out, but Ramses's keen eyesight and remarkable memory were legendary in Egypt. At Cyrus's request he drew a rough sketch of what he had seen through the small opening, explaining as he went along. "Directly opposite the door was a funerary couch, in the shape of the Hathor cow. Piled on top of it were an ordinary bed with animal legs, a wicker chair, several stools, and a wooden box. Under it were a number of white-painted ovoid boxes, probably containing food offerings, and in front of them two rectangular wooden boxes and a pair of what seems to be footstools. To the right I made out the tail of what may be another funerary couch, and to the left the head of a third, in the shape of a hippopotamus. I'm not much of an artist," he finished modestly. "The place was in complete disarray."

Emerson had lit his pipe. Now he took it from between his teeth. "The tomb was robbed, right enough. The thieves tossed the objects about looking for small valuables. The priests who set the place in order afterward were in a hurry."

"We knew the tomb had been robbed at least once," I said. "The golden statuette we found last year and the confession of the thief prove that."

"Twice," Ramses said. "There is evidence of at least two breaches in the door."

"They couldn't have stolen any large objects, if the holes were the size you describe," Cyrus said shrewdly. "What an incredible find! Even if the tomb was robbed, most of the funerary goods are still there. When is Carter taking the inner door down?"

"Tomorrow, I believe," I said.

"I sure admire his patience," Cyrus said, shaking his head. "I'd have been at it all night."

"I would give anything to be there," Suzanne exclaimed.

The lamps swung in a sudden puff of wind, sending strange shadows across the intent faces. No one answered Suzanne's implied request; but Jumana turned her head to look at the other young woman. If

Suzanne got into that tomb before she did, there would be trouble, and to spare. Bertie cleared his throat and looked hopeful, but dared venture no further. After his first ejaculation of wonder, Nadji had relapsed into silence.

Fatima came to the doorway—or rather, since I knew she had been eavesdropping, she showed herself in the doorway. "Dinner is served," she announced.

"Will you stay?" I asked Cyrus.

"No, no, we've imposed enough already. Will we see you in the West Valley tomorrow? Emerson?"

"What?" said Emerson.

"I doubt it," I said. "But you may be sure we will keep you informed."

Dinner was a silent meal. We were all tired, even Emerson, who sat hunched over his plate and who had to be reminded from time to time to put food in his mouth. For once Sethos spoke very little. His abstracted expression reawakened suspicions I had tried to dismiss. There was something on his mind, something of which he preferred not to speak.

Instead of joining us for coffee in the sitting room, Nefret excused herself.

"I'm awfully tired, and I want to look in on the twins."

"Allow me to see you home," Ramses said, offering his arm.

She laughed a little, and yawned. "There's no need, darling. I'm going straight to bed."

Ramses said something in a low voice; she laughed again. "Thank you, kind sir."

I smiled to myself and thought how nice it was to see them so devoted. Ramses had not allowed the thrill of the tomb to let him forget his familial obligations. They went out arm in arm, his dark head bent devotedly toward her. The little byplay passed right by Emerson. He did not even respond to Nefret's soft good night. I attempted a few conversational advances, getting no more response than Nefret had, and then decided to abandon indirection.

"What is it now?" I demanded. "Your preoccupation arouses the direst of suspicions, Emerson. I do hope you are not planning something underhanded. If you have some idea of breaking into that tomb—"

Slowly, like a hunched vulture spreading folded wings, Emerson straightened his shoulders and got to his feet. The look he fixed on me was so dreadful, my tongue froze.

My unpredictable brother-in-law burst out laughing. "It took you long enough, I must say. I was afraid I would have to mention the possibility myself."

"You did," I cried, as realization dawned. "They will wait until the passage is cleared, you said. Good heavens!"

"Not a possibility," Emerson muttered. "A probability. They will. Of course they will. And they may not be the only ones."

"She did go straight to bed," said Ramses, in the doorway. "So I decided to come back for . . . Is something wrong?"

Emerson whirled on him. "Come with me. At once."

Accustomed though he was to his father's eccentricities, this order caused Ramses's dark eyes to widen and his heavy brows to rise. "Where?"

"The Valley, of course." Emerson pushed past him. "Hurry."

"Wait for me," I cried, dropping my embroidery. Grinning, Sethos rose to his feet.

"Wait for me," I repeated, this time to Ramses. Emerson had left.

I dashed down the corridor to my room. My belongings were in perfect order as always, so I was able to lay my hands on the objects I wanted without delay. My parasol, of course, and two electric torches; there was not time for a change of clothing, nor even for the assumption of my useful belt of tools. (It took a certain amount of adjustment because of the tendency of the objects hanging from it to become entangled.) Hoping I would not need it, I hastened back to the sitting room. Sethos and Ramses had obeyed my order to wait.

"Does this mean what I think it does?" Ramses demanded.

"Yes. Perhaps. Cursed if I know," I said, rendered incoherent by confusion. Sethos had spoken of robbers attacking the tomb. Had Emerson been referring to another group of intruders?

A distant bellow from Emerson propelled us into rapid motion. "He isn't planning to break into the tomb," I panted, trotting to keep up with Ramses's long strides. "At least I don't think so. I more or less accused him of it, and he said . . . He said something like, 'Of course they will, and so may others.'"

"Damnation," said Ramses. "Why didn't I think of that?"

Sethos cleared his throat in a pointed manner.

We were soon mounted and on our way. I must have made a pretty picture riding astride with the skirts of my frock hitched up to my knees and my hair coming loose from its pins. I did not allow these minor inconveniences to distract me, for I was preoccupied with what might lie ahead of us.

I hadn't thought of it either, and I ought to have done. Of course Carter and his patron would return to the tomb under the cloak of darkness and break into the enticing chamber. Whether they had the right to do so was questionable. By Emerson's rigid standards, no one would have set foot in that room until every angle of it had been photographed and every precaution taken to avoid damage to the artifacts. However, I could understand why Carter and Carnarvon might violate the spirit, if not the letter, of their concession. Few archaeologists could have resisted.

And they might not be the only ones. By now every man in Gurneh would have heard that magical word "gold"; indeed, Cyrus had said as much earlier that day. Tonight might be their best chance. There was nothing to prevent a break-in except the wooden grille and a single layer of stone blocks. An experienced tomb robber, of which there were many on the West Bank, could get through both in a quarter of an hour.

Ramses slowed Risha and fell back to ride beside me. "Are you all right, Mother?"

I spat out a mouthful of hair. "Surely Howard posted guards."

Ramses shrugged. His meaning was clear, at least to his mother, who was accustomed to his taciturnity. Offered a share of the treasure, few men could have remained faithful to their duty—especially men whose wage was a few piastres a day.

When the Valley was closed to tourists the barrier at the entrance was up. It now stood ajar, and the donkey park, which ought to have been empty, held several horses and donkeys. Emerson's theory was confirmed. With a vehement oath, he dashed through the opening.

The moon was a silver sliver but the bright stars of Egypt shed a ghostly radiance. I had removed my heeled evening slippers, so that my progress was silent (and cursed painful). Ramses, on my right, walked as silently as a cat, and Sethos, politely holding my left arm, made little more noise. Why we bothered to move quietly I do not know, for the running feet of Emerson, well in advance, crashed like the hooves of a charging bull. A louder crash followed, mingled with the inarticulate roars of Emerson and a higher-pitched scream.

My scream was louder. I had stepped on a sharp stone. Hopping and lurching, I pulled away from Ramses. "Hurry! Your father is in trouble."

"Go on," Sethos said calmly. "I've got her." His arm encircled my waist and guided me forward.

Rounding a spur of rock, we beheld a horrifying scene. The tomb of Tutankhamon lay before us, on the right side of the path. From its entrance came a dim glow. A squirming, shifting shape occupied the space in front of the steps. It resolved itself into the mighty form of Emerson, rising like Hercules from the fray and holding a slighter, still squirming form at arm's length.

"Sorry, Peabody, for taking so long," said my husband apologetically. "Bastard had a knife. I trust you were not worried?"

"Ramses!" I shouted. "Where are you?"

"Here, Mother." He emerged from the black shadows next to the tomb, with another wriggling miscreant in his grip. "I fear Deib has got away. He's a nimble chap."

"Ah," I said, relieved to see husband and son unscathed. "The ibn Simsahs."

"They were hiding in the rocks above the tomb," said Emerson, giving his captive a shake that made his head snap back.

"Where are the guards?" I asked.

"Never mind that," said Emerson. "What I want to know is—"

The glow from the mouth of the tomb strengthened, heralding the arrival of Howard Carter, torch in hand. Its wavering beam framed the former combatants in a theatrical glow: Emerson, disheveled and scowling; his captive even more disheveled, robe torn and turban askew. I recognized the scarred face of Farhat, the oldest and most unprincipled of the ibn Simsahs. He had realized who his captor was and he had stopped struggling.

Howard's face was a mask of bewilderment. "What the devil is going on here?" he demanded.

"Bluster will get you nowhere, Carter," Emerson growled. "What the devil are *you* doing here?"

"I have every right to be here," Howard said, drawing himself up.

"That remains to be seen," said Emerson. "I suppose the other co-conspirators are in the tomb chamber? Tell them to get up here. It's safe enough now. You damn fool, Carter, didn't it occur to you that you were risking not only your professional reputation but your patron's safety? These lads were lying in wait, and they are not known for patience."

Lord Carnarvon and Lady Evelyn came up in time to hear the end of this speech. They were followed by the other co-conspirator, Pecky Callender. "See here, Emerson . . ." he panted.

"No, you see here." Emerson rounded on him. "See Farhat ibn Simsah, to be precise. For all you know, there could be a hopeful thief behind every rock in the Valley. You ought not have come here without a dozen guards. But then there would have been witnesses to your illegal entry, wouldn't there?"

Lord Carnarvon had got his breath back. He drew himself up to his full height and looked down his nose at Emerson, every inch the British aristocrat. "I can't say I care for your tone, Professor Emerson," he drawled.

"I can't say I give a curse," said Emerson.

"Emerson," I murmured.

My gentle warning had no effect. Emerson had worked himself up into a state of righteous rage. "I presume you removed enough of the blocking stones to enter the tomb chamber? How much damage did you do—*and what did you take?*"

Carnarvon offered his arm to his daughter. "You have no right to question me, sir. I bid you good night."

Emerson pointed an accusing finger. His voice rolled like that of an outraged god. "Your pockets are bulging, Lord Carnarvon!"

Ramses and I managed to stop him before he went in pursuit of Carnarvon, who was retreating with as much haste as his dignity allowed. I verily believe Emerson would have searched the fellow, which would have led to serious trouble. The damage was bad enough. Once at a safe distance, Carnarvon turned. "You are persona non grata here, Professor. Stay away from the tomb. Do not presume on my goodwill again."

He walked off, followed by Carter and Callender and by Emerson's vehement curses.

"Now you've done it," I said, relaxing my hold. "We'll never be allowed in the tomb again."

His little outbursts generally refresh Emerson. Displaying his large white teeth in a jovial smile, he said, "In that case, we may as well make the most of the present opportunity."

We left the ibn Simsah brothers bound securely with strips cut from their garments, after relieving them of various sharp instruments. In his confusion (and, I believe, guilt) Howard had not even remembered to lock the wooden grille. As we made our way down the corridor I said to Emerson, "You ought not have cursed Lord Carnarvon, Emerson."

"Bah," said Emerson. "He was already out of temper with me."

"You threatened him with everything from dying of the pox to being devoured by demons in the afterlife."

Emerson emitted a loud groan. It was not caused by remorse, but by the sight visible in the beam of his torch: a gaping hole, several feet square, at the bottom of the blocked door.

"You were prepared for that, surely," said the cool voice of Sethos behind us.

"I hoped I was wrong," muttered Emerson.

"Be fair, Emerson," said his brother. "What Egyptologist could have resisted?"

"I do not require a lecture from you," said Emerson. He shone his torch into the opening and moved it slowly from side to side.

The full wonder of the chamber was disclosed, in a series of successive visions. It required some time for the eye to disentangle the strange shapes and sharp shadows: overlapping quartered circles that must be chariot wheels, three great gilded funerary couches with grotesque animal heads, laid end to end and piled with other objects. But what caught the eye and held it were two life-size statues that faced each other like guardians against the wall to the right. The exposed skin had been blackened with bitumen, the clothing and regal ornaments gleamed with gilt. On the brow of each figure the royal uraeus serpent reared its head, ready to strike any who threatened the king.

Even Sethos, the imperturbable, was shaken. On hands and knees, he said, "There's a drop of about two feet." He turned as if to lower himself down. Emerson caught him by the collar.

"There've been enough clumsy idiots tramping around in there. Go ahead, Ramses. Be careful where you step."

"It seems to me," I began, "that as the smallest person present—"

"Good Gad, Peabody, if I can restrain myself, so can you," growled my husband. "Ramses is light on his feet and agile as a cat."

"And not likely to pocket any small objects," said my brother-in-law, not quite sotto voce.

"Are you implying that I would?" I demanded.

"I was referring to someone else," said Sethos.

"Hmph," said Emerson. "Take the torch, Ramses."

Ramses slipped carefully down and stood still for a moment, gazing around. "There seems to be an opening on the far wall, under one of the funerary couches." We saw him stoop and look in. "Good God. It's another room, packed full of incredible objects, and in even greater disorder than this one."

"That blank stretch of wall between the two statues," Emerson said. "Have a closer look at it."

Ramses started in that direction and then paused, as the beam of the torch framed a painted chest covered with miniature scenes as bright and precise as those in an illustrated codex. Ramses moved carefully round it, emitting low murmurs of admiration.

"Curtail, if you please, your aesthetic instincts," Emerson growled. "Look at that stretch of wall."

The truth dawned. It made even the discovery of a second room filled with treasure pale by comparison. What else could the noble figures guard except the body of the god-king himself? Did his burial chamber lie beyond that seemingly blank wall?

"As usual, your instincts are correct, Father," Ramses reported. "There's a doorway, blocked and plastered, with seals stamped all over it. It hasn't been breached."

Emerson shot back, "Look behind the basket and the other objects piled against the wall."

The basket to which Emerson referred was of good size, a circular basin shape, atop a pile of withered reeds. Gently, using both hands, Ramses removed the basket and pushed the reeds aside.

There was no opening, but even at a distance one could see that an area several feet across, at the juncture of wall and floor, was of a different nature. The outer layer of plaster was missing. There was no mortar between the stones thus disclosed. It was clear that some of them had been removed and then hastily replaced.

"Blast and damn," said Emerson. "Carter."

"How do you know?" I asked. "It might have been the ancient thieves."

"The priests would have replastered the opening," Emerson said. "Since the damage has already been done, we may in good conscience repeat it. Take the loose stones out, Ramses, and have a look. What's in there?"

After a moment Ramses said in a hushed voice, "It looks like a wall of solid gold."

Emerson could contain himself no longer. Breathing hard, he lowered himself to the floor inside and picked his way to the north wall.

Since he had not specifically forbidden me to do so, I followed. Peering through the newly opened space, I saw what seemed indeed to be a wall of gold, reaching almost to the ceiling and leaving only a narrow corridor alongside.

"What is it?" I cried.

"A funerary shrine," said Emerson, on hands and knees, looking in. "See the doors? And the wretches have been here too," he added passionately. "There are footprints in the dust."

"Then we may also proceed," I exclaimed.

"The opening is too small for me," said Emerson. "I will not enlarge it."

"Emerson." My voice was scarcely louder than a whisper. Emerson turned his head and smiled at me. "All right, Peabody. Your turn."

With painstaking care I stepped down to the floor of the inner chamber, which was several feet lower than the other. Before me stood two great gilded doors, adorned with decorative hieroglyphs on a background of blue faience. They were closed by a wooden bolt.

I reported this to Emerson, who said, "Open it. I don't doubt Carter already has."

The bolt slid smoothly back and the doors parted enough to allow me to see within. "I can't make it out," I gasped. "A framework— gilded—bits of brown, rotten cloth, sewn with gold rosettes—"

"A canopy," said Emerson. "The cloth was a funerary pall. What else?"

"Another shrine, I think. Various objects on the floor—bows and sticks leaning against the walls . . . Someone has cleared a space in front of the doors of the second shrine."

"Carter," said Emerson, like a swear word. "Did he open those doors too?"

"I can't see . . . No, Emerson, he did not. The doors are closed in the usual way, with cords wound round the handles and a dab of mud over the knot. It's stamped with the necopolis seal—and it is intact."

"He does have some scruples left," said Emerson. "All right, come out of there, Peabody, and close the doors of the outer shrine. We will leave everything precisely as Carter left it."

"The walls are painted," said Ramses, also on hands and knees, his head twisted to see up. "A funerary procession, I think. And the cartouches of Tutankhamon."

"So he's there," Emerson muttered. "Still there. Inside his coffins and his sarcophagus and the shrines, alone in the dark, as he has been for over three thousand years . . ."

This flight of fancy was so unlike my pragmatic husband that I looked at him in surprise. But I ought not to have been surprised; the sensitive, poetic side of Emerson's nature is known to only a few—of which I am one.

"Perhaps he is with the gods he worshiped," I said softly.

"Hmph," said Emerson. "Which gods? The multitudinous pantheon of Egypt, or the sole god Aton in whose faith he was raised? Don't talk rubbish, Peabody."

Emerson's poetic moods do not last long.

The burial chamber contained one more surprise—a rectangular opening near the far corner, leading to a fourth room filled, like the two outer rooms, with a fabulous jumble of artifacts. Vision and brain were so overwhelmed that I remember only two objects: a reclining statue of Anubis and behind it a golden chest with an exquisite statue of a goddess extending protective arms across its side.

"It must be the canopic chest," I said, as Emerson helped me up. "I could only see one statue—the most beautiful thing, Emerson—"

I had completely forgotten about Sethos, but Ramses had not. He stood watching his uncle as the latter moved slowly round the outer chamber.

"Look here," Sethos said.

"Don't touch it," Ramses snapped.

"It's been opened." Sethos indicated a small gilded shrine. "Here's where your statuette came from."

"By God, I think you're right," Ramses said. The interior of the boxlike shape was empty, except for a wooden pedestal on whose base were the cartouches of Tutankhamon. "There's room for another statuette next to it," Ramses said. "Remember the thief's confession—that his friend took the image of the queen?"

"Enough," Emerson said in a subdued voice. His shoulders shifted uneasily.

Naturally I understood his feelings. I too had a sense of profanation, of intruding into a realm where we had no right to go. Framed by darkness, the monstrous heads of the funerary couches looked as if they might at any moment turn to stare accusingly at the invaders. Dust motes swam in the light, and from time to time we heard the smallest whisper of sound—an ominous sound, for it betokened the fall of a scrap of gold or bit of cloth disturbed by the entrance of air into the long-sealed chamber.

Following Emerson's orders, Ramses replaced the stones that had been taken from the entrance to the burial chamber. I held the torch, and I am not ashamed to admit my hand was a trifle unsteady. As I stood watching, the light caught the eyes of the uraeus serpents on the royal brows so that they seemed to blink and glare.

Slowly, in a state of dreamlike disbelief, we made our way back along the passage and up the stairs. I had not realized how dead and musty the air in the tomb had been until I felt a cool breeze against my face. No one spoke. The wonder of what we had seen left us without words. The tomb had been robbed in antiquity, but enough was left to make the find unique—the first royal burial with most of its rich grave goods intact.

Emerson was in the lead, Sethos and Ramses behind me. A sudden bellow from Emerson startled me, so that I toppled backward against Ramses, who let out a pained grunt but kept his balance. Cursing, Sethos shoved Ramses, who pushed me, and we stumbled to the top of the stairs.

"Now what?" I demanded breathlessly. "Have the ibn Simsahs got away?"

At first it appeared that they had attempted to do so, for Emerson gripped a dark form, which he was shaking as a terrier shakes a rat. Then I saw the miscreant brothers, still bound, and heard a plaintive voice gasp, "I give up. I give up. Please, Professor—"

He must have bit his tongue, for the plea ended in a sharp scream.

I recognized the voice, distorted though it was by pain and shortness of breath and by the absence of the brogue that ordinarily marked his speech.

"Kevin?" I cried. "Kevin O'Connell? What the devil are you doing here? I thought you were in London."

"Language, language, Mrs. E.," said Kevin, his brogue firmly back in place. Emerson had stopped shaking him and he was himself again. "Where else would a journalist be but at the scene of what may be the greatest story of the year, or the decade, or—"

Emerson gave his throat a final squeeze and dropped him. Kevin subsided onto the ground, and wisely decided to stay there. The ibn Simsah brothers rolled over to make room for him, staring wide-eyed. Emerson drew a deep breath; but before he could express his ire, Ramses's voice rang out. I turned. He was no longer behind me.

"Father. Here's another one."

"Another bloody journalist?" Emerson demanded.

"Better than that." Ramses rose into sight from behind the low retaining wall above the tomb, pulling another individual to his feet. Recognition was immediate. Starlight silvered a mane of white hair.

"Good Gad," I cried. "It is Sir Malcolm. What are you—"

"Don't ask," said Emerson in a strangled voice. "That question is becoming unbearably repetitive. How many others are lurking about? Come out, come out, wherever you are."

His tone of voice turned this into an unmistakable threat. It got immediate results, in the form of an apologetic cough in one voice and a bad word in another. Two forms emerged from the shadows near Tomb 55, across the way.

"Jumana," I exclaimed, having recognized that young person's voice. "And Bertie?"

"He followed me," Jumana said, giving Bertie a furious look.

"What," said Emerson, enunciating each word slowly, "Brought . . . You . . . Here?"

Bertie cringed. "I tried to stop her."

"Do be quiet," Jumana said impatiently. She threw her slim shoulders back and smiled at Emerson. "The same thing that brought you, Professor, I expect. Archaeological fever."

"You," said Emerson in the same ominous voice, "meant to creep into the tomb tonight?"

"I thought someone would," said Jumana, unabashed. "Tonight, while it lies open. I felt sure I could persuade one of the guards to let me in."

She brushed her dark hair away from her brow in an exaggerated gesture of coquetry. I didn't doubt her assurance. Bertie wasn't the only man in Luxor who was infatuated by her dainty form and pretty face.

"I didn't expect there would be no guards at all," Jumana went on. "That was a piece of luck. Or would have been, if Bertie hadn't held me back."

Goaded into speech, Bertie burst out, "And if I hadn't, you would have walked into the arms of the ibn Simsahs."

Sir Malcolm tried to free himself from Ramses's grasp. "Good evening, Miss . . . Jumana, is it? I have not had the pleasure of meeting you, but I hope to improve our—"

"Stop it," said Emerson, waving his fists. "Stop it at once. This is not a social occasion."

"Here's another one," said Sethos, appearing in his turn. He addressed the cringing figure next to him in his fluent Arabic. "Fear us not, my friend, you were here only because your master ordered it. We mean you no harm."

The unfortunate servant fell to his knees and tried to kiss Sethos's hand. Sethos snatched it away. "Kneel only to God. Certainly not to that piece of scum," he added in English, for Sir Malcolm's benefit.

Emerson was obviously in a quandary, trying to decide which intruder to curse first. Sir Malcolm saved him the trouble, pulling away from Ramses and straightening his rumpled garments. "I will overlook this gratuitous attack from your son," he began.

"Damned decent of you," said Emerson in the same well-bred drawl. "I trust you do not expect me to overlook your gratuitous act of trespass."

Kevin, who had been listening with interest, finished smoothing his hair and reached into the breast pocket of his coat.

"I wouldn't if I were you," I said to him.

Kevin grinned unrepentantly, but he put the little notebook back in his pocket.

"If I am trespassing, so are you," said Sir Malcolm. "I overheard what Lord Carnarvon said earlier. We are in the same boat now, Professor, and it would be to your advantage as well as mine to reach an agreement."

Emerson looked at me. In a conversational tone he asked, "Is the fellow determined to drive me to violence? Any lesser man would have lost his temper long before this. Everyone is here who ought not be here, no one is here who ought to be here. Curse it, the situation is turning to pure farce, and I feel myself beginning to—"

"Do not give way, Emerson, I beg you." I directed a severe look at Sethos, who had covered his mouth with his hand in an attempt to stifle his laughter. "Allow me to add a note of common sense. Kevin, you will come with us. Jumana and Bertie too."

"Oh, but I haven't seen the tomb," Jumana cried. "You wouldn't be so cruel, after all the trouble I went to? Please, Professor—"

"Er," said Emerson, deflating under the spell of her pleading voice. He is a perfect fool where women are concerned. "Well . . ."

"She doesn't deserve to be rewarded for her reckless behavior," Bertie exclaimed.

I had been about to say the same thing. "A quick look won't hurt," I said. "Go with her, Ramses. Just a look, and come straight back."

"In that case . . ." said Kevin eagerly.

"If she goes . . ." Sir Malcolm began.

"No!" I shouted. "Good Gad, of all the effrontery!"

"Now, Peabody, don't lose your temper," said Emerson. "I am the only one allowed to do that. Sir Malcolm, I advise you to leave at once. I cannot always control Mrs. Emerson when she is in this exasperated state of mind."

"Very well," said that gentleman with sudden meekness.

I took a deep breath, and then another. "Don't think you can linger until we have departed, Sir Malcolm. The tomb will be guarded now."

"I would be delighted to oblige," said Sethos quickly.

"I don't doubt it," muttered Emerson. "Stay if you like. With me."

Bertie had—of course—gone down the steps with Ramses and Jumana. They now returned, both men more or less dragging the girl between them.

"It wasn't long enough," she gasped. "There was so much . . . I want one more . . . Bertie, let me go at once!"

She pulled free from him, but not from Ramses.

"Oh, no, you don't," he said. "Jumana, don't try me too far. And," he added with an unwilling grin, as she leaned against him and gazed imploringly into his face, "don't try that either. You've got your own way, and gone one up on Suzanne. That should be enough."

Jumana chuckled.

Emerson sighed. "Jumana, go home at once. With Bertie. Don't argue with him, don't try to get away from him—"

"Don't call him bad names," I said.

"Don't call him bad names," said Emerson in some confusion. "Er—I have made myself clear, haven't I, Jumana?"

"Yes, sir. I will go straight back to the Castle and I will not call Bertie bad names."

"Good. Ramses, take your mother and that . . . that . . . journalist back to the house."

"What about them?" I asked, nudging one of the ibn Simsah brothers with my foot.

"Oh, please, Sitt," he moaned. "Let us go. We repent. We are reformed. Do not leave us for the jackals to eat."

"It's a tempting idea," said Emerson, scratching his chin. "But against our principles, eh? Untie them, Ramses. We know where to find them if we want them. At the moment they are only in the way. So are you, Sir Malcolm. Be off with you."

In the end it was Ramses who stayed with his father and Sethos who escorted Kevin and me back to the donkey park where we had left the horses. Sir Malcolm had already departed—with, I supposed, his unfortunate servant running along beside. Jumana and Bertie had come on foot and would return the same way. I had given the girl one of my little lectures, so I felt sure she would do as she was told. As we rode off I could hear her and Bertie bickering in loud voices, but, to give her credit, I did not hear any bad words.

Kevin had come without argument. He knew Emerson well enough to recognize the futility of learning more from him.

"A whiskey and soda would certainly hit the spot," he said cheerfully.

"Don't count on it," I said. "Over the years you and the *Daily Yell* have caused me considerable embarrassment, Kevin."

"But, ma'am, remember the times I proved a true friend in your times of need." His voice was as caressing as that of an Irish tenor.

"We will see," I said, "if friendship takes precedence over journalism on this occasion. Insofar as I am concerned, you are guilty until proven innocent."

I will confess to my Readers that I did not finish recording the events I have described until several days later. I stick to the accuracy of the account, however; it was a night to remember, one of the most unforgettable of my life. Earlier excavations of the royal tombs had turned up only broken bits and pieces of the funerary equipment, tantalizing hints of the exquisite originals. Tetisheri's tomb, which we had found, was a reburial. This was the first tomb that still contained the vast majority of the king's original equipment, more or less in situ. Imagination had conjured up glittering images of what once had been; *this* was the reality.

The only one of us who slept through the entire night was Nefret, and when she and Ramses joined us at the breakfast table her blue eyes were blazing with indignation. From his sheepish expression I deduced that Ramses had borne the initial brunt of her reproaches, but there were plenty left for me and Emerson. Instead of returning Kevin's cheery greeting, she fixed him with an inimical scowl.

"Why is that man still here?" she demanded. "Why haven't you sent him packing?"

Kevin attempted to look hurt. His carrot-red hair was sprinkled with gray and fine lines framed his blue eyes, but his freckles were as exuberant as ever. "I haven't done anything," he protested. "Our old friendship—"

"He will be sent packing as soon as he has repeated to the rest of you what he told me last night," I said. "It is of some importance, as I believe you will agree. How much has Ramses told you, Nefret?"

"Some of it." She transferred her frown from Kevin to the plate of eggs Fatima had placed before her. "I only woke half an hour ago."

"And half that time was spent calling me names," said Ramses. "As I told her, we did not know when we left the house what we might run into. There was no time to—"

"Let us not waste breath in futile recrimination and apology," I broke in. "We agree, I believe, on the following story: first, that we will mention Carter and Carnarvon's illicit entry into the tomb to no one. We went there because we feared an attempt at robbery, and discovered the ibn Simsah brothers. Emerson and Ramses remained on guard in order to prevent additional attempts until Reis Girigar arrived this morning."

"Lie, you mean?" Nefret demanded.

"I never prevaricate unless it is absolutely necessary, Nefret. In this case it is simply a matter of omitting certain details. Carter and Carnarvon had no right to enter that tomb, but Scripture tells us not to judge our fellowmen. Their own consciences must determine whether or not to confess."

"I hate it when you quote the cursed Bible," Emerson growled. "I don't intend to give Carter away, but what about him?" He gestured at Kevin with the fork on which he had impaled a piece of egg.

"He won't print anything," Ramses said. "He wants to stay in Carnarvon's good graces."

"Quite right," Kevin agreed, wiping egg yolk off his crumpled cravat. "Anyhow, I'd be risking a suit for libel if you lot refuse to back me up. They can't charge me with anything except being in the Valley after hours. I never got into the tomb."

"The same holds for Sir Malcolm, I fear," I said regretfully. "Whatever his intentions, he committed no act that could be considered trespass. Let us return to the point. Kevin has admitted that rumors of a great find have been circulating among his archaeological and journalistic connections for some weeks. Apparently Lord Carnarvon told various friends about Howard's telegram as soon as it arrived, and of course they told others. When Kevin learned that Arthur Merton of the *Times* had booked passage to Egypt, he took the next boat. You see what that means, don't you?"

"Other journalists will follow, if they are not already on the way," Nefret exclaimed.

"Including Margaret Minton," said Kevin, his pleasant countenance taking on quite a threatening aspect. "She's sharp as they come, and she'll stop at nothing to steal a march on me."

I was not the only one who looked involuntarily at Sethos. Not a muscle twitched in his face. He had, of course, anticipated this, and had realized what it might mean to him personally.

"She claims to be an old friend of yours," continued Kevin, who was, of course, unaware of the lady's relationship to "Anthony Bissinghurst." "See here, you won't let anything slip to her, will you? I've known you all longer than she has."

"I won't let anything slip to anyone, including you," said Emerson. "Have you finished breakfast? It is more than you deserve. Be off with you."

Kevin rose with alacrity. "The telegraph office should be open by now." He chortled. "I'll be the first, even ahead of Merton."

"If you quote me or Mrs. Emerson I will have your head on a platter," Emerson shouted after his retreating form.

"He won't dare," I said. "He's still counting on our goodwill. In fact, I don't see how he can find anything to write about. He didn't get inside the tomb."

"He doesn't need facts," Emerson grumbled. "He'll invent a pack of rubbish and fill it out with innuendo."

Sethos patted his lips with his napkin and put it neatly on the table. "I do hate to intrude on this discussion with my petty personal problems, but have any of you stopped to think what may ensue if Margaret comes here?"

"She'll be badgering us for information," Emerson growled. Then his face changed. "Oh. Good Gad. You mean—"

"Her arrival may reawaken the suspicions of those who know she is the wife of their quarry," I said. "We have been free of surveillance lately, but that may not last."

"Hell and damnation," said Nefret. She was thinking of the children. "Can't we head her off?"

"How?" Ramses demanded. "Any attempt to communicate with her will only arouse the interest we must avoid at all costs."

I was watching Sethos, whose eyes were fixed on Nefret's worried face. I knew, as surely as if he had spoken aloud, what he meant to do.


For the next few days I kept a close eye on my brother-in-law, though to be honest I had not decided what I would do if he made a conspicuous departure. He was torn too, I believe; having decided to throw himself to the wolves in order to lead them away from us, he was in no hurry to do so. There was, of course, the possibility that even that sacrifice would not save us if his pursuers believed we had a copy of the mysterious document. Ramses had gone back to work on it, realizing, as Sethos and I did, that its solution might offer the answer to our problems.

Everyone else was totally preoccupied with the new tomb. On the day following our little adventure there, the wall was removed and Carter entered the outer chamber for, as he claimed, the first time. Neither he nor Carnarvon admitted to their noctural trespass. Inexplicably, Rex Engelbach declined to attend, sending his assistant Ibrahim in his place. The boatmen were kept busy ferrying tourists across to the West Bank. We knew from our own experience that Howard would be besieged by requests from people wanting to see the tomb. First, of course, came the formal viewings for officials of the government and the Antiquities Department.

We were not included on either occasion. It was a deliberate snub, especially since Merton of the *Times* was among the second group of official visitors—the only journalist so favored. I fancied I could hear Kevin's curses all the way from the Valley.

We got all the news, fresh off the press as some might say, from Daoud. Emerson did not go near the East Valley. He was too proud to sue for favors. I was not, but he refused to allow me or anyone else to make overtures, not even Nefret, who had a way with gentlemen. Instead, Emerson put us all back to work in the West Valley, with a fervor that almost made up for his earlier disinterest.

"He's afraid Carnarvon will throw us out," said Cyrus. With Bertie and Jumana we were taking a little rest in the shade of the shelter I had caused to be erected. It was very warm, and we had been working hard that morning. Cyrus wrung out his goatee, which, like the rest of him, was soaked with perspiration, and then accepted a glass of cold tea. "What the dickens did Emerson say to his lordship? I've heard a dozen different versions, each worse than the last."

I sighed. "I was afraid of that. Goodness, what a hotbed of gossip this place is! It was one of Emerson's characteristic diatribes, Cyrus, complete with curses. One cannot blame Carnarvon for being angry—especially in view of the fact that Emerson's accusations were probably true."

"They are saying that the Professor accused Mr. Carter and the others of taking jewelry from the tomb," Jumana offered.

"They wouldn't do that," Bertie protested, his ingenuous face troubled.

Jumana shook her head. "You are soooo naive, Bertie."

Bertie flushed, but before he could respond, Emerson appeared in the mouth of Ay's tomb, arms akimbo and brow threatening.

"What are you doing there?" he shouted. "Get back to work. Bertie, you can start your measurements of the burial chamber now."

The other three jumped up. I had not finished my tea, so I remained seated. "Have you finished clearing the floor?" I called.

"Do you expect me to carry the sarcophagus lid out single-handed?"

It was an outrageous complaint, since he had himself sent the men away for a rest, but Cyrus called, "Coming. Coming right away," and trotted off.

I took a final sip of tea and with a nod of thanks handed the glass to Cyrus's excellent servant, who was in charge of the refreshments. I didn't believe Lord Carnarvon would actually go so far as to evict us—

M. Lacau had confirmed our right to remain in the West Valley—but I was very vexed to hear that someone had spread the word about Emerson's curses. Carter and Carnarvon would not have dared to do so, since they would have had to admit entering the tomb illicitly. We could not accuse them without admitting our own presence, even if we had been disposed to behave dishonorably. The only other persons who had overheard the exchange were the tomb robbers and Sir Malcolm, and perhaps Kevin O'Connell and Bertie and Jumana . . .

Some of them could not be trusted to hold their tongues, and for all we knew, other spectators had been there. At least the rumors were only that, unconfirmed and deniable.

We became for a time very popular with visitors, who assumed (as any reasonable person might) that we were among Howard's confidants. When we disavowed special knowledge or influence, some refused to believe us and a few tried to bribe us. Emerson sent Wasim to the guardhouse with his antique rifle.

Conspicuous among the ones who did not call were the members of the Metropolitan Museum crew at Deir el Bahri. They had all been friends of ours for many years, and I was unable to account for their absence until Ramses offered an explanation.

"Carter has approached them for help. He needs all the expert assistance he can get, and he's had special relations with the Met for years."

"Special relations, bah," said Emerson. "He's been selling them antiquities."

"They can afford to pay well," Ramses said equably. "And Carter is, after all, a dealer. No doubt the Metropolitan is hoping for a share of the artifacts in return for its help. It isn't surprising that they should avoid us now that we are in disfavor with Carnarvon."

He had come to tea straight from the workroom, where he had been closeted most of the afternoon. Emerson, who had been sulking most of the afternoon, nodded glumly.

"They've got the experts he needs," he admitted. "Burton for photography, Hauser and Hall as draftsmen. They say . . ." He grimaced painfully at the fact that he had been reduced to repeating rumors. "They say Breasted will be asked to assist with the translations."

"Your old mentor," I said, with a nod at Ramses. "We ought to ask him to tea, don't you think?"

"No," said Emerson.

"Don't you like him?" asked Charla, who had been occupied with the plate of biscuits.

"Your grandfather only means that Mr. Breasted will be very busy," I explained, before Emerson could reply with the truth. In his opinion Breasted had never given Ramses the credit he deserved. "Cheer up, Emerson, things will quiet down once Howard has closed the tomb again."

"Why will he do that?" asked Charla, leaning against her grandfather's knee. He patted her black curls, a familarity she permitted from no one else.

"He cannot leave it open while he collects supplies and assistants," I explained. "He will need film, packing materials, and a hundred other things. And people who are experienced in working with delicate objects."

"He should ask Papa and Grandpapa to help, then."

"Go and—and throw sticks for Amira, Charla. Outside, if you please."

The dog, lying athwart the threshold, jumped up, barking. Charla rushed out and they were soon locked in a fond embrace, which ended with both rolling about on the ground. David John's fair head was bent over a chessboard, with Sethos as his opponent. The boy had been taught the game the past summer by his uncle Walter. It was difficult to find reading material suitable for a juvenile mind; after finding David John immersed in *Dracula,* his blond hair virtually standing on end, Walter had proposed chess as an alternative. It had seemed like a good idea at the time.

Charla's talents lay in other areas. Intimidation, for instance.

"Any luck?" I asked of Ramses.

"Only in a negative sense." He came to take a cup from me and lowered his voice. Though apparently absorbed in the game, David John had an unnerving ability to overhear what he was not supposed to hear.

"The commonest codes consist of letters of the alphabet," Ramses explained. "Rearranged according to some preestablished system. *B* for *A, C* for *B,* and so on. That's the simplest variation, and the simplest to crack. Even more complex substitution ciphers can be decoded fairly easily, on the basis of letter frequency and repetition. In theory one could set up a system using numbers instead of letters, but . . . Confound it, Mother, I'm no expert. I played with simple codes like the ones I've described when I was a child, but it was only a game."

"So there is no hope of deciphering the message?" I asked.

Ramses ran his fingers through his disheveled locks. "I think—mind you, it's only a guess—that the numbers refer to a book or manuscript. The numbers can be broken into groups of threes, which would indicate the page of the book, the line on the page, and the word or letter in the line. Probably the word. Let's suppose that the manuscript Sethos found was the master copy. When other copies were dispatched to members of the organization, they already had the book in their possession. They would be able to read this message, and any other that might be sent. But we don't have it. How many millions of books do you suppose there are in this wide world?"

"Surely there are some obvious choices," I said. "Books one would find in most households."

"Oh, yes. The Bible and the Koran come to mind. Do you know how many different editions of each are in print? And before you can ask," he went on, in mounting exasperation, "it did occur to me that the numbers might be references to verses or suras or chapters. In what language? Arabic, Hebrew, English?" With a malevolent look at Sethos, he added, "You ought to have examined the gentleman's bookshelves."

There was no sensible reply to this unfair charge, and Sethos did not attempt to make one. With wrinkled brow he was studying the board. His queen seemed to be in imminent peril.

"It's late," Nefret said. "And Charla is filthy, she's been rolling round on the ground with Amira. Come, David John. You can finish your game tomorrow."

"I have finished," said David John, moving a piece. "Checkmate, sir."

After the children had been removed, I said to Sethos, "You shouldn't have let him win."

"I didn't let him win," said Sethos.

## From Manuscript H

It could not be said that many of their seasons in Egypt had lacked distraction, but to Ramses this was one of the worst. Not only did they have a wanted fugitive hiding out with them, but the discovery of Tutankhamon's tomb would bring half the world to the small town of Luxor. There was no question of keeping the find a secret. It had been known, and exaggerated, by the citizens of Luxor almost from the first moment. Arthur Merton, the *Times* correspondent, had been allowed into the tomb on November 30, and had wired his dispatch the same day. Representatives of the Cairo newspapers had begun to arrive. The hotels were full and some of the dragomen were wooing tourists by telling them about the great discovery and offering to show it to them. By December 3, there was nothing much to see, since Carter had refilled the tomb, but that didn't deter the curious. The sheer numbers of strangers provided perfect cover for assassins. If Sethos's adversaries hadn't become suspicious of "Anthony Bissinghurst" by now, they weren't the professionals Ramses believed them to be.

His premonitions turned out to be correct, but not in the way he expected. One night shortly after the tomb had been refilled, they were sitting on the veranda after dinner when they heard hoofbeats approaching.

"Someone's in a hurry," Ramses said, going to the door. "Good Lord, it's Bertie. What's wrong?"

"Can Nefret come? Right away?"

"Of course." Nefret rose without haste, her voice taking on its note of professional calm. "Who is ill, Bertie? Your mother?"

"No, thank God. That is . . ." He removed his hat. "Sorry. I'm afraid I rather lost my head. It's not a matter of life and death, I suppose, but he's an awful sight, covered with blood and—"

"Cyrus?" Emerson demanded.

"Nadji. He went over to Luxor this evening, and we were just starting to worry about him when he staggered in, covered with blood and—"

"Let me get my medical bag," Nefret said.

"I will start the motorcar," Emerson exclaimed.

"We will take the horses," his wife said, putting her embroidery back in its bag.

"Now, Peabody, the motorcar is in perfect condition. Selim and I had it out for a spin yesterday."

"The steering apparatus came loose."

"But the brakes worked," Emerson said triumphantly. "And Selim has repaired—"

"No, Emerson. Not in the dark and along that road."

Ramses slipped out. By the time the others reached the stables he had roused Jamad and saddled Risha and Nefret's Moonlight. Nefret hurried in, bag in hand, while, at his mother's insistence, several other mounts, including hers, were being saddled. He had known it was a forlorn hope that she would remain behind.

"We'll go on ahead," Nefret announced. "With Bertie."

"Aren't you coming?" Ramses asked Sethos.

Hands thrust into his pockets, he stared unenthusiastically at the mare Jamad was saddling, and then shrugged. "I suppose I ought."

Ramses left them to it, following his wife out the open gate and along the road. Nefret set a rapid pace. The Castle shone through the dark like a public monument, and the gates were open. Hastily dismounting, they hurried into the house, where Cyrus was waiting.

"Sorry if we scared you," he said. "Cat says it's not as bad as it looked, but Bertie got worked up and—"

"Don't apologize, Cyrus," Nefret said. "Where is he?"

Nadji had been put to bed in his own room. Though Katherine had sponged off his face and bared chest, he was still a nasty sight. When he saw Nefret he smiled apologetically.

"They should not have bothered you. Mrs. Vandergelt is a good nurse and I am not much hurt."

"You look like hell," Ramses said, studying the bruises and cuts and the blood matted in his hair. "What happened? Should he talk, Nefret?"

She had given the exposed parts of his body a quick inspection. Now she pulled down the sheet that covered him to the waist. He was wearing loose drawers, but he let out a cry of protest.

"I'll go," Katherine said tactfully. "You mustn't mind Dr. Emerson, Nadji, she is accustomed to—er—this."

Cyrus or one of the male servants must have helped him undress and change clothes, Ramses thought. Brick-red with embarrassment, Nadji looked even younger than his real age, which was probably in the early twenties, but he swallowed and tried to pretend he was accustomed to being examined by a woman. "Aywa. Yes. Of course, I understand."

Fortunately Nefret had finished checking the lower part of his body before the rest of the party burst in. Nefret smoothly raised the sheet as Nadji started convulsively.

"It could be worse," she reported, before her mother-in-law could demand details. "He got a nasty thump on the head, but there's no sign of concussion. Looks as if someone went at him with a club and another someone with a knife."

"What happened?" Emerson demanded, looming over the bed.

"Just a minute, Father." Nefret stirred drops into a glass of water and held it to Nadji's lips. "Drink this, it will help the pain while I disinfect these cuts."

"I will assist," said her mother-in-law eagerly.

"Not necessary, Mother."

Nadji let out a sigh of relief and let his head fall back on the pillow. Obviously the Sitt Hakim terrified him even more than her formidable husband.

"I will tell you, Father of Curses, what little I know. I had gone to a coffeeshop in Luxor, and when I started back toward the landing two men attacked me. I do not know who they were, their faces were covered, but I took them for ordinary thieves. At first I fought back, but I was losing and no one answered my calls for help, so then I thought, if it is my money they want, let them take it. I fell on the ground. They went on kicking and pulling at my clothing, and I had visions of Paradise and believed I would die. Then . . ." His brow furrowed. "Then I thought I heard a far-off voice say, 'Fools. A man may increase his height but not lessen it.' It must have a been a dream, for the words make no sense."

Not to him, perhaps. Ramses looked at his uncle, standing silently in the corner.

"What happened then?" Emerson asked.

"I fainted," Nadji said simply. "When I woke no one was there. So I came here. I am sorry, Mr. Vandergelt, that I was late."

Cyrus patted him on the shoulder. "Not your fault, my boy. How do you feel?"

"Sleepy." He flinched a little as Nefret dabbed antiseptic on the head wound.

"The worst is over," she said. "You should have been wearing your turban."

"They pulled it off." Nadji let out a weak giggle. "They pulled at my hair too. It hurt."

He had talked more that night than in the entire time they had known him, Ramses thought. Talked sensibly . . . even glibly. As if he had thought his story out in advance.

"Sleep now." Nefret pulled the sheet up to the patient's chin. "I will leave more medicine. You'll need it tomorrow morning, because you will be stiff and sore."

"How is he? What happened to him?" Suzanne was waiting outside the door. She had kept out of the way until then, and Ramses couldn't help thinking her inquiry sounded somewhat perfunctory. They assured her that the attack had been an ordinary attempt at robbery, and that Nadji had not been much hurt.

"Can I do anything to help?" The question was directed at Cyrus, and accompanied by one of her sweetest smiles.

Picturing Nadji's face if the girl was allowed to sit by his bedside, Ramses assured her that her assistance was not needed.

They refused Cyrus's invitation to stay for a drink. He was eager to discuss the revelations of the evening, but it couldn't be done in the presence of Katherine and Suzanne. Ramses knew they would have to take Cyrus into their confidence before long. His mother had told him what Cyrus had said about Sethos: "Whenever that fellow turns up it means trouble." Ramses couldn't have agreed more. They had managed to put their old friend off so far, but Cyrus was too shrewd to miss that revealing statement Nadji had overheard from his attackers. It could only mean that they had mistaken the young man for someone else. And, given his checkered past, Sethos was the logical suspect.

They held the horses to a walk so they could talk. Sethos edged close to his brother.

"Congratulations," said Emerson, who had observed this maneuver. "Once again an innocent took the beating meant for you."

Sethos didn't bother to deny it. "They're getting closer. Why did they pick on him?"

"Because not even you could disguise yourself as a petite French-woman," Nefret said.

"Then that only leaves Anthony Bissinghurst, doesn't it?"

"Not necessarily," Ramses said grudgingly. He didn't at all mind seeing his uncle in a state of nerves. "I wonder if attacks on male tourists have increased recently?"

"I wouldn't be at all surprised if they had," Sethos said, cheering up. "I could be anybody, even a tourist."

"Until Margaret turns up," Ramses said. "I can't imagine what's been keeping her."

"She may not have been in England when the rumors about the tomb began," Nefret said.

"She'll certainly have heard the news by now," Emerson said. "Merton's article was in the *Times* on the thirtieth. If she left right away she could be here any day now."

"Hmmm," said his wife.

"What's that supposed to mean?" Emerson demanded.

"It means that we will deal with Margaret when the time comes. Sufficient unto the day is the evil thereof."

The day wasn't over. Daoud and Selim were waiting on the veranda. The former's face was grave.

"Now what?" Emerson demanded. It took a great deal to wipe the smile from Daoud's face.

"Bad news, Father of Curses."

"We know about the attack on Nadji. We've just come from there," Ramses said. "He isn't much hurt."

Daoud shook his head. "Not that, Ramses. It is worse, much worse."

"You make it worse," Selim said emphatically. "It was an accident, meaningless—"

"For God's sake," Emerson shouted. "What has happened?"

"The golden bird," Daoud intoned. "It has been eaten by a cobra, the defender of the pharaoh. It means death to those who invade his tomb."

# CHAPTER FIVE

LORD CARNARVON AND HIS DAUGHTER LEFT FOR CAIRO AND ENGLAND on the fourth of December. Ramses happened to be in Luxor that day on business of his own, so he was privileged to see their procession sweep through town with all the fanfare of a royal progress, surrounded by admirers and followed by the press. Carnarvon passed him without a glance. Perhaps he didn't see me, Ramses thought charitably. Carter did see him. He raised one hand in a half-hearted salute before hurrying on.

Carter followed his patron to Cairo two days later. According to Daoud, he was saddened by the loss of his bird, but refused to understand the dire implications, which were evident to every sensible individual.

"Bah," said Emerson. "It was only a bird, and cobras are not uncommon."

"But the omen of the golden bird was true," Daoud replied. "The golden tomb was found. And is not the cobra the symbol of the pharaoh?"

"He has you there, Father," said Ramses.

"So you should be grateful to God that you are not the one who found the tomb," Daoud said earnestly. He bade them a ceremonial farewell and went off in something of a hurry. It was almost time for sunset prayers. Ramses didn't doubt the entire Emerson family would be featured in those prayers.

"We had better not tell him we've been inside the cursed—excuse me—place," he said.

"Not only the tomb, but the burial chamber itself," his mother remarked. "Don't underestimate Daoud. I'll wager he knows. He's hoping we weren't there long enough to arouse the royal wrath."

"If he knows, why didn't he say so?" Nefret asked. "It isn't like Daoud to keep secrets to himself."

"Don't underestimate him," her mother-in-law said again. "Daoud can keep a secret when he is persuaded it is necessary."

That afternoon they had a visit from Herbert Winlock and George Barton. Their friends were always welcome for tea, but it had been some time since any of the Metropolitan Museum crew had stopped by. Winlock was one of what Emerson called "the younger generation of Egyptologists," being approximately the same age as Ramses, though his rapidly receding hairline made him look older. He was a brilliant excavator and a genial host when the Americans entertained at their Luxor headquarters. He greeted them without self-consciousness, but Ramses thought Barton looked somewhat uncomfortable. A gawky, exuberant man, he had developed what Ramses's mother called a "crush" on Nefret, and had a tendency to stare admiringly and unnervingly at her.

After his mother had served the tea and Winlock had asked about their work in the West Valley, he got to the point.

"I understand you've fallen out with Carter and Carnarvon."

"Where did you hear that?" asked Emerson.

"From Carnarvon."

"Did he tell you that he was in the Valley that night?"

"He denies he was there. Says you invented the story in order to cover up your own illegal entry into the tomb and your theft of several valuable items."

*"Qui s'excuse, s'accuse,"* Ramses murmured.

His mother, stiff with indignation, said, "Or rather, he who accuses another seeks to excuse himself. How contemptible!"

Barton, who had been squirming, said, "We don't believe it, ma'am. I mean, it's known that you were in the Valley that night. The Gurnawis have been jeering at the ibn Simsah brothers for letting themselves be caught by the Professor, and Farhat has gone into hiding. But we all know you'd never have done anything wrong. I mean, confound it, you may have saved the tomb from being robbed. I think it's damned— er—darned ungrateful of his lordship not to thank you."

"Have another cup of tea," said Ramses's mother with a friendly smile. "And a biscuit or two, before the children arrive and finish them."

Barton helped himself. "*Were* they there?" he asked.

"Unlike his lordship, we do not accuse others," Emerson said loftily. "I will say no more."

"Admirable," Winlock said. "George has it right, Professor. No one would ever believe you had behaved in an underhanded manner. But—well—you folks understand the position we're in."

Emerson took out his pipe. "So it's true that Carter has asked you to join in the excavation?"

"Unofficially. I believe he is wiring Lythgoe in New York for official permission. So you see we can't afford to be drawn into your feud with Carnarvon. But," said Winlock emphatically, "no one, not even the President of the U.S. of A., tells me how to choose my friends."

Emerson appeared touched by this declaration, but after their guests had left he remarked, "Friendship is all very well, but Winlock won't let it interfere with business."

"I need to have a talk with Daoud," Emerson declared. "This is the third day in succession that he has been late."

We had concluded the excavation of Ay's tomb and moved most of the crew to the unfinished tombs, numbers 24 and 25. The only ones left behind were Suzanne, who had begun copying the paintings in the burial chamber, and Bertie, who was making his final plan. This arrangement pleased Jumana, for a staff artist was considered to be lower on the scale than an excavator. She was inclined to put on airs.

"Daoud is no shirker," I said. "And he is entitled to time off if he needs it."

"But he won't answer questions," Emerson complained. "That isn't like Daoud. Curse it, he is verging on insubordination."

"Perhaps he is taking steps to counter the curse of the golden bird," Nefret suggested.

"What steps?" Emerson demanded.

Nefret chuckled. "Praying."

"He prays too cursed much," grumbled Emerson.

Suzanne emerged from the entrance to the tomb, sketch pad in hand. Her blond curls hung limp around her face and her neat shirt-waist was soaked with perspiration. With a murmur of thanks she accepted the glass of tea Nefret handed her.

"You ought not stay inside so long," the latter said with a look of concern. "You aren't accustomed to the heat."

"I don't mind," Suzanne said valiantly. "The trouble is I drip perspiration onto the paper. The paint keeps smearing."

Disconsolately she studied her sketch pad. The drawing was indeed blurry.

"Have one of the men standing by to wipe your brow," I suggested.

Suzanne seemed to find the image amusing. "It would make me feel silly. I will just keep on trying."

"Come and see me if you feel unwell," Nefret said. "I'll prescribe a day of rest."

"That is kind. Perhaps when Mr. Carter returns I may be allowed to watch him reopen the tomb. What I have seen of it has not been exciting."

"None of us is going there," said Emerson.

"You may do as you like, Emerson, but you cannot dictate how others spend their leisure hours," I said.

"Did I hear you say something about the curse?" Suzanne asked, forestalling what would certainly have been a heated response from Emerson. "The men are all talking about it."

"There is no curse," said Emerson, like Jehovah issuing a commandment.

"*Mais non, certainement.* But it is a good story." She shivered in pretended alarm, and then laughed.

"What's so funny?" Cyrus asked, joining the group. "I could use a good laugh."

"It is only about the curse," Suzanne explained. "The curse of the golden bird." She broke into another peal of laughter. Cyrus smiled in sympathy, but shook his head. "Some people are going to take it seriously, my dear."

"I think the Professor does. He says we may not go near the tomb." She gave Emerson a sidelong glance, eyes widening even more. Emerson looked at her with the same expression as the Great Cat of Re when Amira makes playful approaches.

Daoud turned up at breakfast the following morning. He often did so, since he appreciated Maaman's cooking, but I could tell at once that he had a more compelling reason for being there. For one thing, his left cheek was green. I recognized Kadija's famous ointment, which she applied to injuries.

"Was there trouble?" I asked.

"Only from the lady," said Daoud, his honest face falling. "But do not fear, Sitt Hakim. I have her safe."

Margaret was safe, but, to judge from the scratches on Daoud's face, not in a pleasant frame of mind. Emerson's frame of mind was not much better. Thumping the table with such force that the crockery rattled, he shouted, "So that's what you've been up to. How dare you suborn my employees and plot against me, Peabody?"

"Someone had to," I replied, anticipating an enjoyable argument. "None of the rest of you seem to have given a curse about Margaret's safety."

Sethos ducked his head, avoiding my accusing look. Emerson looked almost as guilty. Nefret's eyes widened as enlightenment dawned. "Margaret is here? When? How? What's this all about?"

"It is very simple, my dear," I replied. "I knew Margaret would come as soon as she heard about the tomb, and that she would pass through Cairo without stopping. There was not much chance of her being intercepted, by us or anyone else, while she was there. Crediting our adversaries with intelligence approaching my own, I assumed they would be on the watch for her arrival in Luxor. So was Daoud. Following my instructions," I added, with a provocative glance at Emerson.

He was making bubbling noises, like a kettle on the boil. "Why didn't you tell me?" he sputtered.

"When one wishes to keep a secret, one confides in as few people as is possible, Emerson."

"Hmph," said Emerson. "Oh. Well."

I invited Daoud to sit down and tell us all about it. Nothing loath, he accepted a plate of eggs and toast from Fatima. "I knew her at once, Sitt Hakim, and she knew me and was pleased to see me. But then she said she would go to the hotel, and when I said no, she must come with me and wear the habara you told me to bring, and she said no, she would come to see you later, after she had got a room at the hotel. And I said there were no rooms, and she said she would find one, and what the—a bad word, Sitt—was I doing? And when I took hold of her, very gently, Sitt, she . . ." He raised his hand to his cheek.

"That's outrageous, Daoud," Nefret exclaimed. "What did you do, bind and gag her and wrap her in a habara and carry her off?"

"The Sitt Hakim said she must not be seen by anyone who might recognize her." Daoud's eyes filled with tears, like those of a chidden child. He was not accustomed to hearing harsh words from Nefret.

"Don't scold him, Nefret, he did exactly as I told him," I said. "I feared she might not take kindly to being ordered about."

"She never does," said Sethos. "Thank you, Daoud. You did right."

"One can only hope so," said Ramses grimly. "How many people saw you carrying a bundled-up woman, Daoud?"

"Many. When they asked I said what the Sitt Hakim told me to say.

That she was a young cousin who had run away from her father to make a foolish marriage."

"Not bad," Sethos admitted. "Where is she?"

Daoud had taken her to his house and delivered her into the kindly but powerful arms of Kadija. So there was no hurry. I finished my breakfast before I changed into my working costume.

Everyone wanted to come with me (though Sethos's offer was somewhat perfunctory), but it did not take long to convince them that a descent in force would only attract undesired attention. Ramses retreated to his workroom, Daoud went with the others to the West Valley, and I set off alone for Gurneh, leaving Sethos coolly drinking coffee.

Kadija was expecting me. "I am sorry to put you to this trouble," I began.

Arms folded, she shrugged her broad shoulders. "It is no trouble, Sitt Hakim. Though it was trouble for Daoud," she added with one of her rare smiles. Kadija admired strong women.

She had locked Margaret into one of the rooms reserved for visitors. It had only one small window, high in the wall, but it was pleasant enough, with a nice little bed, a basin of water for washing, and bottles of water and lemonade. I had supplied various items to make the prisoner more comfortable, including a reading lamp and several of the latest novels. Margaret was sitting on a pile of cushions when I entered. She looked up and then rose.

Many people, including my husband, claimed Margaret and I resembled each other. I could never see it myself, though her hair, like mine, was thick and black. She was a few inches taller than my meager five feet and a bit, and her figure was not so full, particularly around the chest. Her features were strongly marked, with dark brows and a prominent chin. It protruded even more than usual just then.

"Would you like a proper chair?" I asked, observing that she had had some difficulty getting to her feet.

"I would like an explanation." She sat down on the bed and folded her hands.

"You are taking it well," I said. "Daoud said you stopped struggling as soon as he put you over his shoulder."

"I accepted the futility of struggling with a man the size of Daoud."

"And you knew he was acting on my orders."

"I assumed so. But you cannot keep me a prisoner, Mrs. Emerson." Her dark eyes smoldered. "I'll get away by one means or another."

So I was no longer Amelia to her. I couldn't blame her.

"When I explain, you will understand why I had to act as I did. Are you aware that your husband is in mortal danger?"

"There is nothing new about that."

"Don't you care?"

Her eyes no longer smoldered. They blazed. "He promised me before we were married that he would give up his career, if you can call it that. He lied. It was his choice. I cannot spend the rest of my life in agony over a man who cares so little for me that he . . ."

Her voice cracked, and she bit her lip. So she did still care for him. I hadn't been certain. Their affair had been temptestuous. However, a lasting relationship is not based on passion alone but on mutual esteem as well. I had to admit Sethos hadn't shown much for her.

However, this was not the time to settle their marital difficulties. I would work on that later. Without further delay I told her about Sethos's present situation. I held nothing back, for there was a chance she might have a useful idea. "The danger to you cannot be dismissed," I concluded. "The people who are after him may know his true identity, in which case they will know you are his wife."

One quality of Margaret's that I believe I may claim to share was that she was quick to understand the ramifications. She at once realized that I had acted out of concern for her, and her face softened a trifle.

"It is an interesting problem," she conceded. "The attack on that unfortunate young man—Nadji?—and the comments he overheard certainly suggest that he was mistaken for my husband. His opponents can't be very clever, though, since the two do not have the same physical characteristics. Does that mean they don't have an accurate description?"

"That occurred to me, of course. It seems unlikely that they don't know what he looks like, but I confess I cannot explain the attack on Nadji."

Margaret shrugged. "I wish I could help, but I know nothing about his recent activities. Must I stay here until the matter is resolved—one way or another?"

I wasn't entirely certain what she meant by that, and I preferred not to ask. "Oh, it will be resolved. You certainly can't stay here indefinitely. I'll think of something."

"I must accept that, I suppose. In the meantime . . ."

"A chair," I promised, happy to find her so reasonable. "Whatever else you would like."

"All you know about the tomb of Tutankhamon."

"I beg your pardon?" I gasped.

"That scoundrel O'Connell is already here," Margaret said, taking pencil and notebook from the pocket of her coat. The smolder was back, about to burst into flames. "While I sit immured in this . . . this cell. The least you can do for me is give me a story."

The least I had done for her was, possibly, to have saved her life. Perhaps to a true journalist this meant less than an exclusive story. She and Kevin had been rivals for years, and as a woman she had had a hard struggle making a name for herself. A half promise would keep her quiet and give her something to do, but I attempted to temporize.

"If you have read the newspaper accounts, you probably know more than I do. We have not been invited to view the tomb."

"Why not?" The question came quick as a pistol shot.

"I would not care to speculate."

"But I would." The lines around her mouth folded into a grin. "Professional jealousy? Some personal disagreement? Did Lady Evelyn make eyes at Ramses and Nefret slap her face?"

"Really, Margaret, your imagination has got out of hand." I handed her the book I had brought with me. "Here is the second volume of Emerson's *History of Egypt*. Why don't you write a nice biography of Tutankhamon and his more famous father-in-law Akhenaton?"

"That will do to start." She took the book. "But I expect daily reports, Amelia, about what is going on in the Valley. And send Nefret to see me. She and Kadija are great chums, I understand, so a visit from her won't cause comment."

I left feeling as if I had got off fairly easily. "Sharp" was certainly the word for Margaret. One of the words.

She hadn't asked to see Sethos.

I didn't want to see him either, so instead of returning to the house I went straight to the West Valley. Emerson had been on the lookout for me; he hurried to meet me, with Nefret close on his heels.

"Well?" he demanded.

"How is she?" Nefret asked anxiously.

"I presume you are inquiring about her mental state, since you can hardly suppose Daoud or Kadija would have offered her bodily harm." I allowed Emerson to lift me down from the saddle. He set me on my feet with a thump.

"Don't equivocate, Peabody."

"I explained the situation and she has agreed to remain where she is for the time being." I took my handkerchief out and patted my damp forehead and cheeks before I added, "So long as I keep her informed about what is happening with the tomb."

Hands on hips, head tilted, Emerson considered this. The sun woke highlights in his raven locks, for he was, of course, without a hat. Finally he said, "I must give you credit, Peabody, for deviousness exceeding your usual talents in that direction. You have found the sole excuse I would have accepted for joining that lot in the East Valley."

"I assure you, Emerson, no such idea entered my mind until Margaret—"

"Hmph," said Emerson loudly.

"She also requested that Nefret visit her."

"Requested?"

"It was more along the lines of a demand," I admitted.

"I haven't been to see Kadija for some time," Nefret said. "Of course I will go. Margaret must be frightfully worried about him."

"On the surface she appears more angry than worried," I said. "However, anger is one sign of profound concern, according to—"

"She is hoping you will be more indiscreet than Peabody," said Emerson loudly. He was afraid I was about to utter the forbidden word "psychology." "You will have to watch what you say, Nefret."

Nefret looked alarmed. "What shouldn't I say?"

"Hmmm," I said. "We had better talk about that before you go."

Since I endeavor to be truthful whenever possible, I will admit to the Reader that Margaret's request/demand was like the answer to a prayer. I do not like being kept out of things. We had been excluded from interesting archaeological activities before (and, I must add, for the same reason), but this discovery was so extraordinary that it rankled to be treated like outsiders instead of the experts we were. In my opinion Lord Carnarvon was being petty-minded to react so vindictively to a few curses. Like Emerson, I had no intention of humbly suing for favors from him, but I had hopes of Howard—and there were others who owed us consideration.

However, I decided to postpone my visit till the following day. I had a number of other problems to deal with. Among them was what to tell Cyrus. He had been pestering me (his word, and a most expressive word too) about Sethos. I had managed to put him off so far, but I owed my old friend at least part of the truth, particularly in view of the fact that one of his staff had been affected. Sethos had to be dealt with, and so did Margaret. I had told her that the matter would be resolved, but just then I hadn't the faintest idea what to do about it.

Life was becoming complicated. I withdrew to a quiet corner and made one of my little lists.

## FROM MANUSCRIPT H

Ramses had given the others the impression that he had abandoned his attempt to decipher the message, but he hadn't been able to resist tinkering with it. The number groups were susceptible to several variations, and he had tried all of them without success.

What dangerous secret could the damned thing contain? A threatened coup, a secret alliance, plans for a war? Disclosure would presumably constitute a danger to those plans, which implied that they were of vital importance. However, he was only too familiar with the peculiar thinking of the intelligence services, and he had known men to massacre their fellowmen, and -women, for reasons that made no sense to a normal mind.

Tossing a Hebrew Old Testament aside in disgust, he went back to work on his hieratic translations and managed to concentrate on his work for a few hours before he realized that his ears were pricked, listening for sounds of his mother's return from Gurneh. Leaning back in his chair, he ran his fingers through his hair. She was getting out of hand. Kidnapping Margaret Minton was really beyond the pale. Her reasons for doing so had made sense at the time—those steely gray eyes and firm chin had a way of hypnotizing her listeners—but the more he thought about them the more he was inclined to think his mother had yielded to her fondness for melodrama.

He'd have to have a talk with her. What was taking her so long? Perhaps she had gone to the West Valley, leaving Sethos—and him— to stew.

A little chat with Sethos might not be a bad idea. Tossing his pen onto the table, he went in search of his uncle. After looking in the garden, where the children were playing, and on the veranda, he ran Sethos to earth in the courtyard behind the house. The women of the household were going about their business, preparing food, washing clothes; in a quiet corner where his mother's hibiscus flaunted crimson blossoms around a carved bench, Sethos sat with hands folded and head bent as if in profound meditation. He looked up with a start.

"Time for luncheon?"

"No." There was room on the bench, but Ramses was disinclined to give an impression of congeniality. He sat down on the ground, folding his legs under him with the ease of long habit. "Sorry to disturb your nap."

"I wasn't asleep." Sethos yawned, as if to give the lie to his statement.

He's trying to annoy me, Ramses thought. And he's succeeding.

"What are you going to do?" he asked.

"About what? Oh—Margaret? Your mother has her well in hand." Another gaping yawn.

"About the situation in general," Ramses said, holding on to his temper. "We can't go on like this indefinitely."

"Something is sure to happen sooner or later." He added pensively, "I have a plan."

"You wouldn't care to share it with me, I suppose."

Sethos scratched his chin. He hadn't shaved that morning, and now that Ramses took a closer look at him, he saw signs of strain—sunken eyes, new lines on his face. Then the old mocking smile curved his mouth. "It's not much of a plan yet. Stay out of it, Ramses."

"I'm already in it, thanks to you. And so are the rest of us."

"I made a mistake," Sethos admitted. "I should not have come here. But that's all water over the dam."

That was undeniably true, but, in Ramses's opinion, inadequate. He knew it was as close to an apology as he was likely to get, though. Sethos went on breezily, "I will tell you part of my plan. I shall come out of seclusion and make myself visible."

"In order to draw attention to you and away from us?" Ramses raised skeptical eyebrows. "How noble."

"Not at all. It's time I took an interest in that tomb."

Ramses duly reported this statement to his mother when she returned from the Valley. Her only response was a brief "We will discuss it later."

She was dusty and flushed and he knew she was anxious to get to the comfort of her "nice tin bathtub," but he held her back.

"Mother, has it occurred to you that we have only Sethos's word that he is in danger? Even the attacks, on Father and me, and on Nadji, bear his hallmarks—melodramatic but not life-threatening. Designed, perhaps, to bear out his claim of being in imminent danger. The only fatality has been the death of the old holy man, and that might not have been intended. Every incident could have been engineered by him, and the so-called code may be a fake."

She took off her hat and pushed the damp hair back from her face. "Why would he arrange such an elaborate scheme?"

"He's after Carter's tomb."

"Naturally the possibility had occurred to me."

Ramses managed not to swear. Observing his expression, she smiled. "Dear boy, I admit I have a tendency to claim the credit for prescience after the fact. In this case, however, I am not exaggerating. The conjunction of a rich find and an unexpected visit from a former antiquities thief could not but arouse suspicion. Certain facts do cast doubt on that theory, however—the timing, for one thing. The first attack, on you and your father, occurred long before Howard's discovery."

"Sethos has his sources," Ramses argued. "Father suspected the tomb was there, and so might Sethos have done."

"The bout of malaria could not have been planned."

"It was fortuitous, but if it hadn't happened he'd have found some other excuse for coming here."

"You make a compelling case." She patted his arm. "Now if you will excuse me, I must tidy up. Cyrus is coming for tea."

"Are you going to let him in on this?"

"High time I did, don't you think?"

When his father and Cyrus arrived, Suzanne was with them. Ramses had the distinct impression that his mother had not included the girl in her invitation, but she greeted the unexpected and unwanted guest with bland courtesy, and suggested Suzanne might want to "tidy herself" before tea.

"I could use a bit of tidying too," Nefret said with a rueful smile. "Come with me, Suzanne. You haven't seen our house yet, I believe."

"Bring the kiddies back with you," Emerson ordered. He settled himself in a cushioned chair and stretched his legs out. "Never mind tea, Peabody. I want a whiskey and soda."

She raised her eyebrows, but went to the door and called to Fatima. The housekeeper appeared with the tray so promptly that Ramses realized she must have been lurking. She often did when Sethos was among those present.

Seated modestly at a little distance from the others, he was the perfect picture of a humble subordinate, a propitiatory smile on his lips
and his eyes fixed on Emerson as if awaiting an order.

"I could do with something too," Cyrus declared. "Never mind the
soda. Now what about it, Amelia? You got rid of Suzanne very neatly;
she more or less invited herself. Start talking before she comes back."

She whisked one of her little lists from the pocket of her skirt. "How
to begin," she mused, perusing it.

"Perhaps you had better let me begin," Sethos said. He had abandoned his subservient pose. "Cyrus knows what I do. He won't be surprised to hear that I ran into a spot of trouble on my last assignment.
I . . . er . . . borrowed a certain document which seems to be of interest
to a number of people. They've been on my trail ever since."

Cyrus nodded. His pale blue eyes were fixed on Sethos, and his expression was not friendly. "They took poor Nadji for you. I thought so.
What's in the blamed document?"

"That's the trouble," Sethos said. "It's in code. I couldn't read it."

"So you came here, with a bunch of thugs at your heels." Cyrus took
the glass Emerson handed him. "A low-down trick to play on friends."

"He was ill with malaria," Ramses said, wondering why the hell he
was defending his uncle. "And they, whoever they are, would have come
looking for him here in any case."

His mother had been waiting for an opening. "Ramses is correct,
Cyrus. These people know Sethos's true identity, and that means they
know who his friends are. And," she added portentously, "who his
wife is."

"Good Lord," Cyrus exclaimed. "She'd be the perfect hostage,
wouldn't she? Where is the lady?"

As if drawn by a magnet, all eyes turned toward Ramses's mother.
She cleared her throat. "In a safe place, Cyrus. I saw her this morning—"

"She's here?" Cyrus was accustomed to the Emersons' unorthodox
habits, but this obviously took him aback. "Where? How? When did
she—"

"Please, Cyrus, allow me to continue. Some of the others haven't heard about my interview with Margaret either, so if you will permit me . . ."

Emerson let out a pained groan and emptied his glass. "This may take a while, Cyrus. You know Peabody's narrative style. Have another whiskey."

"Allow me." Sethos, who hadn't been offered one, went to the table and helped himself as well as Cyrus. "How is my beloved spouse, Amelia?"

"Perfectly comfortable and in a very bad temper."

"With me?" Sethos inquired.

"With everyone, especially you. However, she has agreed to remain where she is so long as I keep her informed about the excavation of Tut-ankhamon's tomb."

"So that's what brought her here," Sethos muttered.

"You expected it, didn't you? When have you ever known Margaret to miss an important story? She knows Kevin is in Luxor, and is count-ing on us to provide her with exclusive information."

"Hmph," said Emerson. "She's due to be disappointed, then. We haven't any exclusive information."

"That is what I hope to obtain tomorrow," said his wife smoothly. "Cyrus and I, Nefret and Ramses—"

"Here they come," Ramses interrupted. The others had heard them too; only a deaf person could have failed to do so: the dog's ecstatic barking, the shouts of the children, and mingling with them, Suzanne's high-pitched laughter.

"Never mind the dam—the darned tomb," Cyrus said quickly. "What are you gonna do to get out of this mess?"

"If you have any suggestions I would be happy to hear them," said Emerson.

"Get an expert to read that message," said Cyrus. "If I understand you rightly, that's what those fellows are trying to prevent."

Emerson's jaw dropped. It was such an obvious solution, none of them had thought of it—except Ramses. Painfully aware of his own lack of expertise, he had known better than to propose it; his mother and father would have scoffed at the idea that the family couldn't handle anything, up to and including murder, without outside help.

But there were a number of objections to the idea. Experts on codes weren't numerous, and most of the ones he knew worked for the Department. If his hypothesis was correct, even an expert couldn't read the message without knowing which book was referred to.

The twins burst in, demanding their tea and offering to share the biscuits with Suzanne. They had taken a fancy to her, which rather surprised their father. After an unfortunate incident a few years earlier, Charla had developed a suspicion of pretty yellow-haired ladies. Suzanne must have put herself out to win them over. Laughing, she allowed them to lead her to a chair and David John brought out his chess set.

"Let Mam'selle have her tea," his grandmother said sternly. "She may not wish to play chess."

"Oh, but I promised I would. I am sure he will win." She rounded her eyes at David John, who stared like a hypnotized rabbit. Unlike his sister, he had a weakness for pretty yellow-haired ladies.

Turning to Sethos, Suzanne said, "David John says you are a very good player."

"He wins every time," Sethos said, smoothing his mustache and leering. He had a tendency to overplay a role. Suzanne returned his smile. She wasn't really pretty, Ramses thought dispassionately; her cheekbones were flat and her chin weak. Admittedly he was prejudiced. As far as he was concerned, no woman in the world could compare with his wife.

Nefret had gone to Gurneh, to pay the promised visit to Kadija and her guest. At least she had had sense enough to go in daylight, instead of waiting till after dinner. There were lots of people around, and she had promised to ask Daoud to walk her home.

When he returned his attention to the others, he saw that Sethos had got Emerson out of his fit of the sulks by talking about the tomb. (The word no longer required a defining adjective; there was only one tomb in Egypt just then.)

"Where did you hear that?" Emerson demanded.

"I read the newspapers, Professor. Carnarvon sent a statement to the *Times* ten days ago asserting that the tomb had been robbed during the Twenty-first Dynasty."

"Stuff and nonsense," Emerson exclaimed. "If the existence of the tomb had been known at that time, it would have been emptied completely. And furthermore—"

"We know the other arguments, Emerson," his wife cut in. "The tomb can't have been entered after the Twentieth Dynasty; the workmen's huts from the time of Ramses VI covered the entrance and were not disturbed until Howard cleared them away. Why would Howard allow Carnarvon to make such a ludicrous claim?"

"It's obvious, isn't it?" Sethos inquired meekly. "An intact tomb belongs in its entirety to the Department of Antiquities. The definition of 'intact' is open to argument, but if the robbery occurred during the period when most of the other royal tombs were looted, the discoverers are entitled to a share of the contents."

Emerson growled in agreement. Suzanne gave Sethos an admiring smile. "How clever of you, Mr. Bissinghurst. You know a great deal about the subject."

"Enough to know that Carter and Carnarvon are heading for trouble," Sethos said, ducking his head in pretended modesty. "Thus far the *Times* is the only newspaper to get information directly from the excavators. The other papers resent having to get their news secondhand, and the Egyptian journalists are furious at being passed over. With nationalist sentiment on the rise . . ." He shook his head.

"And Lacau looking for an excuse to change the rules about the division of antiquities," Emerson added. "Carnarvon's concession stipulates that the museum is to keep royal mummies and coffins and all other objects of historical and archaeological importance. Every object in that tomb can be said to fall into the last category, and in totality they constitute a unique assemblage. The entire contents should go to the Cairo Museum. We didn't claim any of the objects from Tetisheri for ourselves."

"But we," said his wife, her chin protruding, "are not Lord Carnarvon. At heart he is nothing more than a collector."

"I guess maybe you could say the same about me," Cyrus said self-consciously. "I sure didn't refuse when Lacau offered me some of the artifacts from the tomb of the God's Wives."

"You have worked in Egypt for years," Emerson said. "Worked hard and conscientiously."

Compliments from Emerson were rare. Cyrus's lined face shone with pleasure. "Carnarvon thinks of archaeology as entertainment," Emerson went on. "And Carter deals in antiquities, for his patron and others. They expect to make money out of this one way or another."

"Now, Emerson, you don't know that," his wife said. "And you are being unfair to Howard; he has done excellent work in his time, but since he lost his position with the Department of Antiquities he has been dependent on the patronage of buyers and of wealthy men like Carnarvon. For pity's sake don't repeat your opinion elsewhere. And do not ask to accompany me to the East Valley tomorrow."

"I am not in the habit of asking you for permission, Peabody. Nor have I any intention of going within a hundred feet of the cursed tomb. I have lost interest in the matter," said Emerson, chin outthrust.

"How about me?" Cyrus asked hopefully.

"You will be very welcome, Cyrus. I am sorry I cannot include anyone else." She gave Suzanne a pleasant smile, and the girl closed her mouth.

"Hmph," said Emerson. "Ramses, are you going to let that child stuff herself with cake? She will spoil her dinner."

Ramses removed his daughter from the proximity of the tea table, and their guests, taking the hint, said good-bye.

His mother had one more bombshell for them. Gesturing at the mail basket, she said, "I received a wire from David today. He is coming out to Egypt, with Sennia and Gargery."

"Good Lord," Ramses said, taking a firmer hold on his squirming child.

Charla let out a shriek of delight. "Uncle David? And Sennia and Gargery too!"

"That will be very pleasant," said David John.

"No, it . . . Er. Yes," said Emerson in a strangled voice. "Very pleasant. Good Gad, Peabody, I told Gargery in no uncertain terms that he was not to come out to Egypt again. He's supposed to be a butler, for God's sake!"

"Language, Emerson," said his wife. "Gargery considers that his duties include defending us when the occasion demands; he has often wielded a cudgel on our behalf, and he has appointed himself Sennia's guard and defender."

"The old rascal can barely walk," Emerson groaned.

"He claims that his rheumatics improve in our dry hot climate. Medical opinion bears this out."

"David doesn't suffer from rheumatics," Emerson growled. "Confound it, I suppose it's the dam—er—confounded tomb."

"They are coming because they want to be with us at this season," said his wife. "Have you forgotten that Christmas is only a few weeks off?"

Speechless for once, Emerson got heavily to his feet and went for the decanter.

Cyrus turned up early next morning, ready and eager, as he put it. He joined us for coffee, and at my request Nefret repeated her report on her visit with Margaret. "She's hell-bent on getting an exclusive story," Nefret said with wrinkled brow. "She kept asking about our 'feud,' as she called it, with Lord Carnarvon. I made light of it, and denied all her allegations, but we had better come up with something important or she'll go for the scandal aspect."

"What scandal?" Ramses asked. "What allegations?"

"You don't want to know," Nefret said, with an amused glance at her husband.

"But there hasn't been—"

"Newspaper persons will invent scandal if none exists," I said. "I want you to accompany me to the East Valley this morning, Nefret. You get on well with gentlemen, and Carnarvon can't have anything against you. You weren't even with us that night. In fact, the only one who was warned off was Emerson."

"Is that right?" Cyrus asked. "Then why have we all been pussyfooting around as if we'd done something wrong?"

"Precisely," I agreed. "I allowed myself to be influenced by... Never mind. From now on we will behave as if nothing untoward had occurred. If his lordship makes a fuss, it won't be our fault."

Emerson had remained silent, pretending not to hear the hints or see the glances directed at him. He slammed his coffee cup into the saucer.

"I am going to the West Valley," he announced. "To work. There is an interesting area north of WV 25. I intend to have the crew excavate down to bedrock."

"Good luck," said Cyrus.

"Bah," said Emerson.

He stamped out. With a little cluck of disapproval, Fatima took the cracked cup and broken saucer away.

For the benefit of ignorant Readers I should perhaps explain that the system of numbering tombs in the Valleys had begun in the 1820s. Since then other tombs had been added in the order of discovery. Those in the main East Valley were distinguished by the initials KV, those in the main West Valley as WV. There were only four of the latter, and my distinguished spouse had always suspected other entrances were hidden in the rugged cliffs that enclosed the Valley.

Selim was in the stable, under the motorcar. Hearing our approach, he slid out, modestly adjusting his skirts. "I think I have repaired it, Sitt," he announced. "Shall I drive you to the Valley?"

"Where is Emerson?" I asked, surprised he was not assisting in the repairs.

"He saddled his horse and rode off in a great hurry, cursing," said Selim. "He would not wait."

"Just as well, I expect," I said. "He is not in a happy frame of mind. The rest of us are going to the East Valley, but you had better go to the West Valley with Emerson, Selim. *Not* in the motorcar."

Selim looked mutinous, but he knew better than to argue with me. "Is it true that David and the Little Bird are coming soon?"

Little Bird was Sennia's nickname. She was adored by our Egyptian family, as was David, who was related, through his grandfather, to most of them.

"Gargery too," I said.

"Ah," said Selim.

He helped Jamad saddle the horses and rode with us as far as the beginning of the road that led off to the West Valley, where he left us with a wave of farewell. We went on to the entrance to the East Valley and left the horses in the donkey park before we joined the stream of tourists. As we neared the tomb we were accosted by an individual I had hoped not to see. Jauntily attired in pith helmet and Norfolk jacket, Kevin O'Connell fell in step with me. "Good morning, Mrs. E. I thought you'd be coming round before this."

"Go away," I muttered, giving him a shove. Kevin put on a hurt expression, and then grinned.

"I wouldn't want to queer your pitch, ma'am. I'll see you later."

Rough retaining walls had been built around the entrance to the tomb, and a small shack, for storage and for the use of the guards, was under construction. Howard had learned something from that memorable night a few weeks earlier; the tomb entrance was now guarded by Egyptian soldiers and by Mr. Callender, perched on the wall with a rifle across his knees. When he saw us he sat up straight and burst into a fit of coughing. There was quite a lot of dust in the air.

I hailed him with my usual good humor.

"Good morning, Mr. Callender. You really should put on your hat, you know."

He looked warily from me to Ramses to Nefret to Cyrus to Sethos. Failing to see Emerson, he relaxed and replied with a courteous good morning.

The debris over the tomb entrance had been removed, but the stairwell was still half-filled. Square in the center of the rubble stood a large boulder painted with a coat of arms—that of Lord Carnarvon, I assumed, since no one else was armigerous.

"No trouble, I hope?" I inquired, edging closer.

"No, ma'am."

A loud cough from Sethos, at my elbow, made me add, "I believe you have not met our new staff member, Mr. Anthony Bissinghurst. His specialty is demotic, but he is something of an authority on the Amarna period."

"A pleasure, sir," said Sethos effusively. "Your dedication and ability have become a legend in Egypt."

Like myself, Sethos knew people will believe themselves worthy of even the most outrageous compliment. Callender beamed. No doubt he was pleased to have companionship in his boring job. He heaved himself to his feet. "Excuse me, ladies, for not rising at once. Will you take a—a piece of wall?"

"We mustn't disturb you," Nefret said, with a smile that brought her hidden dimples into play. "We only dropped by to say hello and bring you a bottle of Fatima's lemonade."

The lemonade had been her idea, and it met with an enthusiastic reception. Callender drank thirstily. "Very good of you," he said, wiping his mouth on a very dusty handkerchief. "And may I say, Mrs. Emerson, how well you are looking. It has been some time since I saw you."

The speech was not directed at me. Nefret said sweetly, "We have been remiss in not coming before. So many duties . . . But we are ready and willing to help in any way we can. If, heaven forbid, you should be in need of medical attention, I hope you will come to me."

This was another approach I hadn't thought of. Everyone knew that Nefret was the best physician in Luxor. Mr. Callender mopped the beads of perspiration off his balding head.

"Very kind of you, ma'am. I have been feeling a trifle seedy . . ."

"No wonder, sitting in the heat and dust all day," Nefret said.

"It must be done," Callender said nobly. "To keep vultures like that one away." He directed a scowl at one of the spectators who had pushed his pith helmet back to expose several locks of red hair.

"Has the press been annoying?" I asked sympathetically, congratulating myself for ordering Kevin to keep his distance.

"That fellow especially. He claims to be a friend of yours."

I laughed disdainfully. "He is no friend of mine, Mr. Callender.

You know these newspaper persons, they will say anything to gain an advantage."

"They are wasting their time," Callender said. "As you see, nothing of interest is going on."

"When is Mr. Carter due back from Cairo?" Cyrus asked.

Callender hesitated. "Any day now."

"So then you will be reopening the tomb?" Cyrus persisted.

I gave him a little poke with my parasol. Direct questions put people on the defensive.

"We must be getting on," I said. "Come to tea one day, Mr. Callender. You are always welcome. Here, take this." I opened the parasol and pressed it into his hand. "I have others."

"A pity we couldn't have got a photograph of Mr. Callender holding your parasol," said Nefret.

"He sure as heck didn't tell us anything," Cyrus said grumpily.

"Ah, but we have inserted a wedge," I replied. "Thanks in large measure to Nefret. Anyhow, I have other sources of information."

Ramses broke a long silence. "Were those the Carnarvon arms on that boulder?"

"I assume so," I replied.

"Rather arrogant, isn't it?"

"It won't go over well with the Egyptian government," I agreed. "Seth—Anthony is unfortunately correct. Carnarvon is heading for trouble if he continues to behave as if the tomb is his personal property."

"Davis always did," Ramses said fairly.

"Times have changed, Ramses. Resentment of foreigners has only increased since the negotiations for independence began. This find is precisely the sort of thing that could focus that resentment."

"May I quote you, Mrs. E.?"

"Certainly not," I replied. I did not need to look to identify the speaker, who was behind me. "Go away, Kevin."

"Now, Mrs. E., what harm can it do?"

"A great deal of harm, as you well know. Good Gad, Kevin, don't you have any other sources except us?"

.   .   .

Emerson hadn't really forgotten that Christmas was only a few weeks away. He had not been allowed to; David John had pinned a calendar to the wall of the playroom and was crossing off the days one by one. Charla kept presenting us with lists.

"A bo and arro," I read, after receiving one such document. "Your spelling is as reprehensible as your request, Charla. You cannot possibly suppose I would permit you to own a weapon."

"I will ask Grandpapa, then," said Miss Charla, scowling blackly.

"He won't let you have one either."

However, the lists reminded me that I had shopping to do. One more duty among many others. Some might say that a happy Christmas was less important than averting the danger to Sethos or deciding how to keep Margaret quiet, but since I hadn't figured out how to deal with either of those difficulties, I decided to concentrate on a more cheerful topic. My last visit to Margaret had been less than satisfactory. She was chafing at her imprisonment, as she called it, and she berated me for not providing her with information about the tomb.

When I announced my intention of running over to Luxor, Sethos was the first to offer to come with me. "Why?" I asked suspiciously.

"Presents for the children, of course," said Sethos, widening his eyes à la Suzanne Malraux. "And you should have an escort, Amelia dear. Who knows what enemies may be waiting to find you alone?"

"You'd run at the first sign of trouble," said Emerson.

"I don't require an escort," I said firmly. "But I will be happy to have company. What about you, Nefret?"

"I suppose I'd better. I haven't anything for the twins, and I'd like to find gifts for Aunt Evelyn and Uncle Walter and David."

So it was only the three of us. Sethos looked very dapper in flannel trousers and a brown tweed coat I recognized as coming from Ramses's wardrobe. While Daoud's son Sabir was occupied with starting the engine of his boat, I said to my brother-in-law, "Do you plan to continue wearing Ramses's clothes? He hasn't that many extras."

"You can hardly expect me to place an order with my haberdasher in Cairo," Sethos said reproachfully.

"Under which of your names? Oh, never mind. I will have to place the order in Ramses's name, I suppose. Fortunately Davies, Bryan and Company has his measurements."

I hadn't been to Luxor for some time, and my spirits rose as Sabir's boat took us smoothly across the sun-rippled water. Earlier Ramses had taken me aside and asked me not to leave Nefret's side, and to stay in safe areas, which I had intended to do anyhow. I was prepared to insist that Sethos remain with us, should he declare his intention of going off alone, but he made no such attempt, strolling along like any casual tourist, with Nefret on one arm and me on the other.

If he intended to make his presence known, he succeeded. We were always running into people we knew, and most of them wanted to stop and chat. So did a number of people we did not know. Unavoidable conversations with the latter ran along the same lines: "Ah, Mrs. Emerson, I am sure you remember me. Miss Jones of the Joneses of Berkshire. May I hope you and your family will dine with us one evening soon?"

I gave them all to understand that they might not hope.

We made the round of the shops. Sethos was at his most gregarious, introducing himself to all and sundry, and bargaining expertly for silver bangles and woven scarves. There was not a great deal of variety to be found in the shops of Luxor—mostly souvenirs and fake antiquities— but some of the good ladies at the school had begun encouraging local handicrafts such as woodwork, weaving, and alabaster carving. We finished our expedition at the Winter Palace Hotel, where a few establishments carrying European goods were to be found, just in time for luncheon.

"Let us lunch on the terrace," Sethos suggested. "It is too nice a day to be inside."

"If we can get a table," said Nefret, for the terrace was full.

"Amelia can always get a table," said Sethos.

And so it proved. After we had settled ourselves, Nefret began rummaging through her purchases. "Paints and pencils for David John . . . silver chains for Charla . . . I couldn't find anything for Uncle Walter."

"Men are always difficult," I agreed.

Half-turned in his chair, looking out over the street, Sethos said, "I've been thinking of going up to Cairo to meet them. Give me a list, and I'll see what I can do."

"Do you think that is a good idea?" I inquired.

"Why not?"

"You know perfectly well why not. Could it be that you want to avoid Margaret? You haven't once been to see her."

"It was you, I believe, who pointed out we ought to stay away from her. Perhaps I can—"

He broke off abruptly. A man had come to stand beside us. He removed his hat and inclined his head.

"Ah, Sir Malcolm," I said, wondering how much he had overheard. "Where have you been keeping yourself? I haven't seen you since we met unexpectedly in the Valley of the Kings."

The hair had to be a wig. It was too snowy white, too smooth.

Sir Malcolm acknowledged my hit with a smile. "An interesting evening, was it not? May I join you for a few minutes?"

"Certainly," I said. "Do you remember Anthony Bissinghurst? You met him last year, but briefly."

"A pleasure to see you again, Mr. Bissinghurst." Sir Malcolm bowed again, very cautiously, and subjected Sethos to an intense stare. "I heard you had joined the Emersons' crew. An excavator, are you?"

"My specialty is demotic," said Sethos. "I am privileged to further my acquaintance with the subject with an expert like Ramses."

The waiter came to take our orders and I asked him to fetch another chair. Sethos studied Sir Malcolm with what I could only regard as professional interest, taking note of every detail. I hoped he didn't intend to impersonate Sir Malcolm again. He had done so briefly the year before, and had been thoroughly confounded when Sir Malcolm arrived on our doorstep without warning. Sethos's hasty retreat had barely avoided a confrontation. Almost I could have wished that the confrontation had taken place—two Sir Malcolms, face-to-face, equally aghast. Even Sethos could not have talked his way out of that.

"Mother," said Nefret. I realized the charm of that image had made me lose track of the conversation. Sir Malcolm had addressed a remark to me.

"I beg your pardon?" I said.

"Let me put it more directly," said Sir Malcolm, mistaking my momentary abstraction for surprise. "I believe we can be of use to one another, Mrs. Emerson. Your distinguished husband would still like to get his hands on that tomb. I can help him to do so."

"Impossible," I said.

"Not at all. Carnarvon's folly in entering the tomb illegally puts him in a dubious position. If M. Lacau were convinced he and Carter had removed valuable artifacts, the Department of Antiquities would have grounds to cancel the concession."

Nefret let out a stifled exclamation, but she left it to me to reply. Pondering the outrageous suggestion, I remained silent and Sir Malcolm went on, with mounting passion. "The rumors are spreading, but so far they are no more than that. If you—those of you who were witnesses that night—and I were to go to Lacau and corroborate one another's testimony, he could not ignore it. If he were tempted to do so, a threat of public exposure would do the job. You have friends in the newspaper world; one of them was another witness to Carnarvon's actions. He would be delighted to publish the story."

"I see you have thought it out carefully," I said.

"The Professor's evidence is crucial," Sir Malcolm said. "His reputation is unimpeachable. And no one could believe he and I are—er—"

"In cahoots," I murmured. "Very true. His dislike of you is well known. I presume that should this scheme come to fruition you would expect something in return."

Sir Malcolm's pale cheeks took on a feverish glow. "You have seen the contents of that tomb. Any one of the objects would be the prize of a collection."

Nefret could contain herself no longer. She burst out, "How dare you suggest—"

"Now, now," I said. "Without wishing to be rude, Sir Malcolm, I think you had better go, before my daughter loses her temper. She is a person of integrity, you see."

The subtle insult was lost on Sir Malcolm. He was a true collector, a fanatic whose principles, assuming he had any, would always yield to the lust for possession. He was a clever-enough strategist to know better than to pursue the argument, however. Rising to his feet, he beckoned his attendant, who hastened to his side and handed him his stick.

"Think it over, Mrs. Emerson, and consult your husband. I hope to hear from you in due course."

He snapped his fingers. His servant opened a parasol; canopied like a potentate, Sir Malcolm stalked off.

"Mother," said Nefret in ominous tones. "You wouldn't. You couldn't."

The waiter presented me with a platter of chicken and rice. "That looks very good," I said. "Eat, Nefret. You need to keep up your strength. Naturally I have no intention of collaborating in such a reprehensible scheme."

"It's an ingenious idea, though," Sethos murmured. "It might even work."

"Emerson would howl at the very suggestion," I informed him. "So don't you get any ideas of your own. I allowed Sir Malcolm to think we might yet be persuaded, because I believe in keeping all avenues of information open. He is determined to obtain some of the objects from that tomb. He will stop at nothing. If this scheme does not work, he will try something else, up to and including murder. We owe it to Lord Carnarvon to watch Sir Malcolm closely."

"Surely you exaggerate," Nefret protested. "He is an unscrupulous man, but murder—"

"You don't understand the collector's mania, Nefret. The artifacts in Tutankhamon's tomb would drive many a man to mayhem."

"She's right," Sethos said, nodding at Nefret. "That painted chest, for example—"

"Ask the man who knows," I said, with a hard look at my brother-in-law.

•  •  •

I had hoped Mr. Callender would drop in for tea, but six o'clock came and went with no sign of him. "Ah, well," I said to Nefret. "Perhaps tomorrow. He wasn't looking at all well."

Emerson, who had been badgered into playing chess with David John, looked up from the board. "You didn't slip a little something into that lemonade, did you, Peabody?"

"I didn't know Nefret was bringing it."

Sethos burst out laughing, and Nefret said severely, "Don't encourage her."

She was out of temper with Sethos these days. I felt sure that Margaret had been regaling her with tales of his failings as a husband. As a professional woman in her own right, Nefret sympathized with other strong, professional women, and as a spouse Sethos cut a poor figure compared with Ramses.

Daoud had come by earlier with a demand from Margaret that I attend upon her that evening. I decided I had better go, though I couldn't think of anything that would satisfy her desire for an exclusive story. Obviously I could not mention Sir Malcolm's preposterous scheme, though that was certainly news of import, and if Kevin got hold of the story first, Margaret would be impossible to control.

However, I told myself, Kevin wouldn't dare print anything without our cooperation, and he was not going to get that. It had required two whiskey and sodas to calm Emerson after I told him about Sir Malcolm's proposition. Having admitted the reasonableness of my behavior, he turned his wrath on his brother.

"You ought to have given him a good thrashing!"

"On the terrace of the Winter Palace in front of fifty people?" Sethos raised his eyebrows.

"Hmph," said Emerson. After a moment he added, "Bah!"

Rising, I said, "I am going to run over to Gurneh for a while."

"Take your parasol," Emerson said.

"Give my love to my wife," said Sethos.

"Checkmate," said David John.

•   •   •

Kadija stood in the open door of the house, arms folded, chatting with her neighbors.

"I brought the medicine you asked for," I said, for the benefit of the audience that always gathered when I visited the village.

"Thank you, Sitt Hakim." She took the bottle I handed her and led the way into the house. An appetizing odor of roast lamb made my nostrils twitch. Observing this, Kadija asked, "Will you stay to eat, Sitt?"

"I had better not, Kadija. Some other night. Where is Daoud?"

"The lady sent him to Luxor to get the newspapers. Is that all right, Sitt Hakim? If you say no, I will not give them to her."

"You may as well. How is she?"

"All day she has been writing in her little book. She thanked me very politely for being so kind to her."

"Good," I said. Perhaps I might look forward to a peaceful interview.

"I feel sorry for her," Kadija said. "Today she asked me to bring her flowers. Only a few, she said, to remind her of the beautiful world outside."

Because my own conscience was troubling me just a trifle, I said firmly, "It is necessary for her own safety—and it won't be much longer." I hope, I added to myself.

Margaret was curled up in the comfortable armchair Kadija had supplied, reading. Daoud had smuggled her suitcase to her, and she was wearing a loose dressing gown in a drab shade of mauve. (She really could use some hints on the subject of dress.) On the table beside her were Kadija's flowers, roses and hibiscus and daisies, nicely arranged in a vase.

"I see you have found something to amuse you," I said, closing the door. Kadija's ponderous footsteps retreated kitchenward.

"It's a marvelous piece of rubbish," Margaret said. "Really, Amelia, I am surprised to find you reading such stuff."

"I was curious," I admitted. "The book was so popular last winter. It sold an extraordinary number of copies. I—er—only skimmed parts of it. That bad, is it?"

"Dear me, yes. Even better than my own efforts along the lines of romantic adventure." Glancing down at the page, she read aloud, " 'He seized my hand, his black eyes blazing with passion. "For days your glo-rious face has filled my dreams," he panted, his breath hot on my face. "I cannot sleep, I cannot eat. You are mine, alone in the desert with me. No one will hear you cry for help!" ' "

I laughed with her, pleased to find her in such a merry mood. "As I recall, your only venture into romance was the description of your first meeting with Sethos—and that, in fact, was not fiction."

"But it was very romantic," Margaret murmured pensively. "How is he?"

"Unharmed, so far," I said, taking a seat on the bed. "We are keeping a close watch over him. As we are over you."

Margaret started and turned her head. "There is someone at the window!"

I hadn't heard or seen anything, but she appeared so alarmed that I went to look out. The window was so high I had to stand on tiptoe. Palm branches, the walls of nearby houses, warmed to umber by the light of the setting sun . . .

The light went out.

# CHAPTER SIX

WHEN THE LIGHTS CAME ON AGAIN I SAW A TERRIFYING IMAGE: KADIJA'S face, distorted by horror, within inches of my eyes. "Alhamdullilah!" she exclaimed. "God be praised, you are alive. You are not dying."

"So it would seem," I replied, surprised to find that, in fact, I felt almost myself. My head ached, but my senses were functioning with their normal efficiency.

The sense of sight informed me that I was in the same room, reclining on the bed. Advancing dusk darkened the window. The lamp on the table burned bright, but the vase lay on the floor, the flowers scattered in a pool of water. Daoud stood in the doorway, gaping. Observing that my eyes were open, he retreated in haste, and I realized I was clad only in my undergarments. Fortunately I had never succumbed to modern fashion in that respect; my combinations, trimmed with lace and little pink bows, covered me from chest to knees.

Reason, putting these facts together, presented me with an unpalatable conclusion. "Curse it," I cried. "She stole my clothes! How long has she been gone? Did you see her leave the house?"

"Not long, not long," Kadija said, still agitated. "I did see her, Sitt, but she was walking quickly and did not stop when I called out. I took her for you! It was a while—not long, but a while—before I thought it was strange you did not say good-bye. So I came here, and found you. She had tied your hands and feet and put a cloth over your mouth, and you did not stir or open your eyes until I untied you, and I was afraid . . ."

"Never mind that," I cried, pushing away the firm brown hands that tried to hold me down. "Go after her! Bring her back!"

I would have gone myself, but Kadija would not let me, nor would she leave my side. She sent Daoud instead. By the time he returned, empty-handed and apologetic, I had been forced to the realization that the search was hopeless. Margaret had taken the black, all-concealing habara—with which I had supplied her! Once she had put it on over my distinctive clothing, she became another anonymous Egyptian woman. No one would recognize, or even notice her if she kept her face covered. She had also taken her purse, with its ample supply of money, and her notebook. And my parasol!

Sipping the hot, sweet tea Kadija had brought me, I tried to console the disconsolate Daoud. "She needed only a few minutes, Daoud. I fear our chances of tracing her are slim. She knows her way about Egypt, and a few words of Arabic, enough to supply her immediate needs."

"It was my fault," Kadija muttered. "I should have known her."

"In my clothing and in a dim light, her hair and figure resembling mine? No, Kadija, it was my fault. I know the lady well, and I ought to have been on my guard—especially after that pathetic appeal for a few little flowers! She had it all worked out before I got here: a heavy object to use as a weapon, strips torn from the bedsheet with which to tie me, a few essential possessions already packed. Oh dear. I suppose I had better go home and tell the family."

In my effort to console my friends I had made light of my own feelings. To say that I was seething with repressed rage is to understate the case. Margaret had made a fool of me. I am not accustomed to being made a fool of.

Kadija insisted on going over me inch by inch. Once she was forced to admit I was uninjured except for a bump on the head, I got myself into one of Margaret's unbecoming dresses and slipped my feet into a pair of her shoes, for she had, in order to make her disguise complete, taken my boots. Her shoes were too big for me. I sincerely hoped my boots would pinch and raise blisters.

I gathered up the rest of Margaret's possessions and tossed them into her suitcase, together with the books I had been good enough to lend her. Carrying it, Daoud escorted me home. He left me near the door of the veranda and vanished into the darkness. I couldn't blame him for not wanting to face Emerson. I was not keen on doing so either. Overconfidence (a quality of which I am often accused) and unwarranted trust had caused me to err.

He had heard us coming and was holding the door open. "Was that Daoud?" he demanded. "Why didn't he come in? Why the devil have you been so long? You are late for dinner. Maaman will—"

"Something has happened," Nefret exclaimed, hurrying to the door. "Mother, where are your clothes?"

Emerson hadn't noticed that. He wouldn't, of course. I swayed and put my hand to my head. Alarm replaced the anger on Emerson's face. He caught me up in his arms.

"Are you hurt? Peabody, speak to me!"

I couldn't, because he was squeezing me so tightly. The others gathered round, and Fatima came trotting out of the house, uttering squeaks of distress. Touched by their concern, I managed to loosen Emerson's grip and gave him a reassuring smile.

"A whiskey and soda will set me right."

"Put her on the settee, Father," Ramses said, removing the Great Cat of Re from that object of furniture.

Emerson lowered me onto the settee. I began to feel a trifle guilty for causing the dear fellow such distress, so I sat up and took the glass Ramses handed me.

"Thank you, my boy. I suffered a momentary faintness, nothing more."

Sethos spoke for the first time. "Am I correct in assuming Margaret has something to do with your—er—momentary faintness?"

The moment of truth could not be delayed. Nefret was about to drag me off to the clinic for another needless examination, and Emerson was still pale with alarm. I took a refreshing sip of whiskey and squared my shoulders.

"Margaret has got away. She knocked me unconscious, stole my clothes, and slipped out of the house. By the time Kadija found me, Margaret had disappeared. Daoud searched for her, but in vain."

"Good Gad," said Emerson. "Good Gad! She hit you?"

"Not very hard," I said. "I have a little bump . . . Ouch."

Nefret's skilled hands ran over my head. "Just here. The skin isn't broken. How many fingers am I holding up?"

"Four," I said. "I do not have concussion. Don't fuss over me. We must without delay consider what steps to take to find her. We will discuss it at dinner. All this excitement has given me quite an appetite."

Once reassured as to my state of health, Emerson was inclined to be critical. "Really, Peabody, I am surprised at you. How could you be so careless?"

He stabbed viciously at the inoffensive fish on his plate. Flakes flew.

"Let us not waste time in recriminations," said Ramses, with an amused glance at me. He was of course concerned about Margaret, but as he had pointed out earlier, she had only herself to blame if she ran into trouble. We had done our best to protect her.

Sethos, eating with good appetite, appeared even less concerned. I had described my encounter and our subsequent search in some detail.

"Where could she go?" Nefret asked, her brow furrowed. "She must have concealed her—Mother's—distinctive clothing under the woman's robe, which would have enabled her to leave Gurneh undetected. But after that? She can't maintain her disguise as an Egyptian woman for long, and she has no acquaintances on the West Bank. Perhaps she'll come here."

"No," Sethos said. Fatima removed his fish—or rather, the bones thereof—and replaced it with a platter of sliced beef. Sethos picked up his knife and fork. "There's only one place she could go. Only one place she *would* go."

Ramses's heavy black eyebrows tilted. "Straight into the thick of things. The Winter Palace."

"Or one of the other hotels," said Sethos.

"She wouldn't be so foolish," Nefret exclaimed.

"Oh, yes, she would."

"You are right," I said, remembering some of Margaret's other escapades. "But this is the height of the season. She won't be able to get a room."

"Dressed like the Sitt Hakim and bearing a strong resemblance to that famous lady?" Sethos popped a bit of meat into his mouth and left us to think it over while he chewed and swallowed.

"Then what are we waiting for?" I cried, pushing my plate away. "We must go after her at once."

Emerson's eyes narrowed to slits of sapphirine blue and his lips drew back, baring his large white teeth. "Not you, Peabody. I am not letting you out of my sight."

"Not she," Sethos agreed coolly. "It is time I assumed my responsibilities as a husband. I may be able to talk some sense into her."

Acknowledging the truth of his assertion, I said, "You aren't planning to go alone, I hope."

"Any volunteers?" Sethos looked round the table. "No, not you, Nefret, you're too soft-hearted. Nor you, Emerson, you would lose your temper."

After a moment, "That leaves me, then," Ramses said.

"So it would seem," said Sethos.

## FROM MANUSCRIPT H

They took two of the horses. Ramses had resigned himself to the job of mounting guard over his uncle—rather he than any of the others—but he intended to minimize the risks as much as possible. They were less vulnerable on horseback.

"You will bring Margaret here with you, of course," said his mother. "Perhaps you had better take another horse."

Sethos looked even more dashing on horseback. "I'll just toss her across the saddle," he said. "She loved it the last time."

He was an excellent rider, and he set so rapid a pace there was no opportunity for Ramses to question him. The fields were still and dark under a canopy of stars; no lighted windows showed in the sleeping villages, and the steady pound of the horses' hooves was the only sound that broke the silence.

It was late for the West Bank, but the lights of Luxor blazed bright across the dark river. A yawning boatman, ever hopeful for passengers despite the time, roused himself and put out the gangplank.

"No one would dare touch them," Ramses said, in response to his uncle's question about leaving the horses. "And they'll wait until we come back."

"You're armed, I hope," Sethos said.

"Just my knife. Why me?"

"I beg your pardon?" said Sethos politely.

"You meant me to come along. Why me?"

He didn't expect a direct answer; when he got one, surprise almost made him fall off the bench.

"You're as good in a fight as your father, and not as hotheaded."

"It isn't likely that we'll have to fight anyone except Margaret," Ramses said. "I am not likely to have much influence with her. She doesn't like me."

"And you don't care much for her. That's all to the good. You mustn't let her off lightly."

"No fear of that," Ramses said, remembering his mother's sore head. "If we find her."

"I could be wrong," Sethos admitted. "She may have contacts in Luxor about whom I know nothing."

"You don't confide in each other, do you?"

"No." Sethos's mouth clamped shut.

When they reached the opposite shore the boatman promised to wait for them, and settled down for another nap. They climbed the steps to the top of the embankment.

"We may as well try the Winter Palace first," Sethos said, indicating the lighted facade of the hotel. "She's arrogant enough to have gone to the most obvious place."

Ramses doubted this, but as it turned out, Sethos knew his wife well. The concierge informed them that although she had been late in arriving, and without luggage, he had been able to accommodate Mrs. Emerson's cousin. It was not one of the most desirable rooms, but the hotel was full and—

"My mother is indebted to you," Ramses said, cutting him short. "What is her room number?"

Their knock on the door went unanswered. "Maybe she's gone out again," Ramses said.

"She's there." Sethos knocked again. "Open up, Margaret," he called. "Or we'll get the key from the manager."

The response was slow in coming. "Who is with you?"

"Only me," Ramses said. "Ramses."

"Not your father?"

"No. But I assure you, the manager will give me the key if I ask for it."

"Damn," said Margaret loudly and clearly. The key turned in the lock and the door opened.

She retreated at once to the far end of the room and stood at bay, her hands clenched. Except for the boots, which she had removed, she was still wearing the stolen garments. Not that she had any choice; she had had to leave her own clothing behind. There was room for only a few toilet articles, and her notebook, in the handbag that rested on the table. Her hair hung loose, below her shoulders. She does look like Mother, Ramses thought. Even to the set of her jaw.

"Don't try anything," she warned. "I'll scream my head off if either of you lays a hand on me."

"Now why would we do a thing like that?" Sethos asked.

She glared at him. Some women might have felt at a disadvantage wearing ill-fitting clothes and with bare feet. But not Margaret. The sight of her, defiant and unrepentant, did nothing to calm Ramses's temper.

"We brought your suitcase," he said, dropping it on the floor. "I see Mother's boots have raised blisters. I hope they hurt."

He sat down, without waiting to be invited, and Sethos followed suit. Margaret relaxed a little, but she kept her distance. "How did you find me so quickly?"

"Ratiocination," Sethos drawled. "Sit down, why don't you?"

"I prefer to stand. What do you want?"

"An apology, to begin with," Ramses said.

"She's all right, isn't she? I didn't hit her very hard."

For sheer effrontery, Sethos had nothing on his wife. Trying to match her coolness, Ramses said, "That was a filthy trick. You took advantage of her goodwill and trust."

"All's fair in love, war, and journalism—isn't that one of her favorite sayings?"

"Damn you," Sethos said with sudden violence. "Do you ever think of anything except your bloody career?"

"Unlike you," she shot back with matching passion. "You're the one who is responsible for putting your beloved Amelia in danger. You're responsible for this whole mess! And what are you doing about it? Hiding out in the bosom of the family, putting them at risk, letting me walk into trouble without so much as a word of warning!"

She had some justice on her side. Ramses was tempted to say so, but he decided to keep his mouth shut. It was between the two of them now. Neither so much as looked at him. Sethos had risen to his feet. He returned her glare with interest.

"I am doing something about it. I had matters well under way when you pulled this idiotic stunt. Change your clothes. You're coming back with us."

"Like hell I am!"

He took a step toward her. Eyes widening, she retreated till her back was against the wall. "Ramses," she exclaimed. "You won't let him strike me?"

"Er—well, no," Ramses said feebly.

Sethos gave Ramses an astonished look, as if he had forgotten he was there. "For God's sake," he stammered. "I've never raised my hand to her. Though heaven knows I've been sorely tried."

"Maybe I'd better go," Ramses said. Her appeal had been pure play-acting; Sethos wasn't a wife-beater, and Margaret wouldn't have put up with physical abuse for a single second. The emotional temperature was so high he wanted to crawl away.

Sethos threw up his hands. "Have it your way," he said. "I'm not going to drag you out of here kicking and screaming. You'd love that, wouldn't you? Just try . . ." He hesitated, and when he went on his voice was several decibels softer. "Try to stay out of trouble. You know what to do, and what not to do."

"How touching." Margaret rolled her eyes heavenward. "I'm better at taking care of myself than you are."

Breathing hard, Sethos flung the door open and stalked out without another word.

"Good night," Ramses said. "Lock the door."

"But of course," said Margaret. Her smile was infuriatingly smug.

Ramses caught his uncle up at the foot of the stairs. Sethos didn't stop or speak until they were seated in the boat.

Ramses was absorbed in his own thoughts. He had seen a new and fascinating side of his impertubable uncle. He had no doubts as to the meaning of the encounter between Margaret and Sethos; he had seen a number of such confrontations, and been in the thick of a few himself. He wondered how this one would have ended if he hadn't been present.

Something told him the subject was not one he could safely raise.

"You said you had taken steps to clear up the—er—mess," he ventured. "Was that true, or were you only trying to keep Margaret quiet?"

Still brooding, Sethos continued to stare at his clasped hands. Then he said, "What about him?" and gestured at the boatman.

"He doesn't understand much English, and wouldn't know what we were talking about if he did. Are you going to come clean, or must I drag Father into this?"

"Good God, no. That's the last thing I want. The truth is that I have entered into negotiations."

"With them? How? When?"

Sethos turned to face him. "I had intended to tell you, sooner or later."

"I'm flattered by your confidence."

"My dear fellow, it's a question of common sense. One doesn't deal with such people without someone to back one up. You are the logical candidate, for the reasons I have mentioned."

And because I'm more expendable, Ramses thought wryly. His parents, the children, Nefret meant more to Sethos than he did. He had no quarrel with that.

"I received a communication a few days ago," Sethos said. "Delivered directly to me by the gatekeeper, as he had been instructed to do."

"Not another invitation to a secret meeting, I trust."

"They know I'm not that stupid. I was directed to reply to what you might call a poste restante. My correspondent was refreshingly candid. As he pointed out, it wouldn't do them any good to murder me; they have concluded that I wouldn't carry the document on my person. He proposed an exchange. If I return the document, he and his lot will leave us alone."

"That's ridiculous," Ramses exclaimed. "How do they know we haven't made copies?"

"Which you have done?"

"Yes. I've been working from one of them, since the original is somewhat fragile."

"The offer was disingenuous," Sethos agreed. "One may draw certain reasonable conclusions from it, however. They know we haven't deciphered the message, for the simple reason that we haven't acted upon it. One may also hypothesize that there is a time element involved. After a certain date the message loses its importance."

"That's obvious," Ramses said impatiently. "It will become irrelevant because the event referred to has occurred, or the information has been disclosed."

"If it was so damned obvious, why didn't you mention it earlier?"

"Nobody asked me," Ramses said, and grinned in the darkness as he heard Sethos's teeth grind together. He really oughtn't be baiting his uncle when the situation was so serious, but it was a rare pleasure to see Sethos lose his temper.

"So what did you tell them?" Ramses asked.

"I agreed to their terms."

"Ah. But you don't intend to return it just yet, do you?"

Sethos pushed his windblown hair back from his face. "You've thought of that too?" he asked sourly. "I don't know why I bother explaining when you know everything already."

"It didn't occur to me until just now," Ramses said. "If they're so keen on having the original back, is there something about it that would not be present in a copy, however accurate?"

"Is there?"

"I didn't see anything. But you may be sure I'll have another look."

Ramses and Sethos returned earlier than I had expected, without Margaret. In answer to our questions Sethos snapped, "She refused to come," and went off, declaring his intention of going straight to bed. Ramses announced that he had work to do, and would have followed Sethos, but of course I had no intention of allowing that.

"So our deductions were correct," I said. "She was at the hotel. Which one?"

Ramses sat down, resigned to answering our questions. Even his father was listening interestedly.

"The Winter Palace. She managed to get a room by invoking you."

"I hope she didn't claim to be my younger sister." This was a dig at Emerson, who had once asked if I was sure Papa had not misbehaved in his later years. Emerson's sense of humor is not always that of a gentleman.

"Cousin," said Ramses. Unable to repress a smile, he added, "She was barefoot."

"A petty-enough revenge," I muttered. "Go on. She refused your invitation to return with you? I suppose that is not surprising."

"Not considering the way the 'invitation' was couched." Ramses drew his chair closer to mine. "They had a flaming row," he said in a low voice. "He ordered her to change clothes and come with him, and she refused, flat-out, and a loud exchange followed, in which they accused each other of callousness, selfishness, and so on. She implied he was about to strike her."

"What nonsense," I said. "Margaret would have hit him back and sued for divorce next day. What else did they say?"

Nefret had also pulled her chair closer. Seeing our absorbed faces, Ramses looked a trifle self-conscious. "I shouldn't have told you. It's no more than meaningless and impertinent gossip."

"Not at all," I assured him. "One never knows what seemingly meaningless bit of gossip may prove relevant. Did he express concern for her safety?"

"I suppose one could say that," Ramses said, a self-conscious smile replacing his self-conscious frown. "She knows how to get past his defenses, all right. If a furious quarrel is an indication of caring . . ."

Nefret laughed softly and took his hand.

"Hmmm," said Emerson.

I was painfully reminded of Margaret's perfidy when I brushed my hair. According to Ramses, she hadn't even had the decency to apologize. I was tempted to go to the hotel next morning and have it out with her, but reason (and Emerson) prevailed. "Let her take her chances, if she is determined to play the fool," he said, removing the brush from my hand. "Come to bed, my love. And—er—leave your hair loose, eh?"

I allowed him to persuade me.

I had a number of other matters to deal with. Our dear ones were due to arrive in Cairo on the Thursday. Fatima was in a frenzy of cleaning, preparing Sennia's little suite of rooms for her and Gargery. David would occupy his old room, from which I intended to evict Sethos. He could stay with Cyrus, or in the servants' quarters, or find his own accommodations. The *Amelia* was at Qena, with Reis Hassan. Emerson had recently proposed we sell her, but I couldn't bring myself to do it; there were too many memories attached to the dear old boat, and one never knew when we might want to go sailing again.

So that was settled. The only question was whether one or more of us should go to Cairo to meet them. I announced my decision at breakfast the following morning.

"David must be warned to stay away from the revolutionaries," I said.

"If you are referring to the Wafdists, they are a legitimate political party," Ramses said mildly.

"I don't care what they call themselves. He is too innocent to become involved in politics."

The word might have struck some people as unapplicable to a man of David's age and experience. Heaven knew he had seen enough of the world to make a cynic of him—war, prejudice, betrayal, cruelty—but somehow he had come through it all with his shining idealism intact. Idealists are admirable persons, but their trust in the goodwill of others may put them and those around them in peril.

Fatima had taken away the toast rack and refilled it. "He must come straight on to Luxor," she said firmly. "And the Little Bird too."

"We all agree on that," I said, reaching for the marmalade. "Well, Emerson?"

"You mean to go, don't you?"

"I believe I ought."

"Then I am going with you."

He had his own reasons for wishing to go, of course. Howard Carter was in Cairo. I had my reasons too. We had received no communication from Mr. Smith. I found his lack of curiosity highly suspicious.

"Back to work," said Emerson, emptying his cup of coffee.

"If you don't need me today, Father, I would like to get on with my translations," Ramses said.

"What? Oh. Er—well, yes, that's all right. God knows we haven't found anything in the West Valley that requires your expertise," he added gloomily.

"I will join you later," I said, indicating to Fatima that she might clear away the breakfast things.

"You aren't going to see that woman, are you?" Emerson demanded.

"No, my dear. With guests coming and our trip to Cairo, I must make a few lists."

Sethos was still in an evil mood. Even Fatima's blandishments aroused only a few forced smiles and automatic compliments. He went off with Ramses, thus confirming certain suspicions of mine. I gave them time to settle down, and then went to the workroom. Both rose hastily to their feet and Sethos reached for an object on the table in front of them.

"Don't bother trying to hide it," I said, taking one of the vacated chairs. "I thought you had given up on the mystery message. What prompted you to return to it now?"

Ramses and his uncle exchanged glances. "I told you we hadn't a prayer of keeping it from her," the former said.

"You did." Sethos took the other chair, leaving Ramses standing. Then they both spoke at once.

By interrupting from time to time to get them back on track, I got a coherent statement. In my opinion the latest development cast no light whatsoever upon the matter, and I said so.

"This business becomes more illogical every day. You have, I presume, tested the document to see if there is a hidden message?"

"I've tried most of the common reagents," Ramses said, delicately lifting the document. "Heat, lemon juice, several other chemicals. Nothing."

"We mustn't return it until we are absolutely sure."

Sethos leaned back. "See here, Amelia, I'm fed up with the whole affair. Let them have their precious document back. It has nothing to do with us."

"I'm inclined to agree," Ramses said. Sethos put on a look of mock astonishment.

"Despite the fact that it may mean danger to a party or parties unknown?" I asked.

"We don't know that," Ramses argued. "Diplomats get the wind up over the most idiotic things. If a government falls, or a top official is disgraced, why should we care? We've done everything we can and taken risks in the process. If this will end the matter—"

"We don't know that either," I retorted. "Their demand for its return may be a trick." I directed a stern look at my brother-in-law. "Were you planning to go round to the address they gave you and watch to see who picked up your response?"

"Not on your life," Sethos said promptly. "It isn't in a very nice neighborhood."

"Well, then, I suggest we wait a day or two. I expect to see Mr. Smith when I am in Cairo. Can you stall them that long?"

Sethos stroked his mustache. "I can but try."

"Tell them we are considering their offer and are inclined to accept it, but we need a few more days."

"You needn't dictate my response, Amelia," said Sethos, with a flash of temper.

"I will leave it to you, then." I rose and straightened my skirt. "Continue your research, Ramses. I will have a look at the cursed thing myself later."

Ramses's eyebrows drew together. "With all respect, Mother, what do you expect to learn that I cannot?"

I gave him an affectionate pat on the shoulder. "One never knows, my dear. One never knows."

After collecting my parasol and my belt of tools, I ordered Jamad to saddle my gentle little mare. It was a pleasant day for a canter, with a bright sun and a hint of freshness in the air, but my thoughts kept wandering to the news Sethos had given me. Peculiar indeed, I thought, as Eva gave way to a cart loaded with sugarcane. The whole business was inexplicable. I could make no sense of it.

When I reached the West Valley, Emerson was talking with Daoud, who had arrived just before me. He at once addressed me, wishing to be the one to deliver his news.

"The dahabeeyah of the Breasted professor and his family is at Luxor."

"How nice," I said, glancing at Emerson's scowling countenance. "I will send a little note inviting them to tea this afternoon."

"You do so against my wishes," said Emerson, sticking out his chin.

"Yes, yes, my dear, I understand. Run along now and look for tombs."

The objects I carry on my belt include pen and paper. I seated myself on a nice flat rock and inscribed a brief message, which I handed to Daoud.

"Have that delivered at once, if you please. One more thing, Daoud. Did you make inquiries about Miss Minton?"

"As you ordered me, Sitt Hakim." Reminded of what he considered his failure, Daoud frowned. "Sabir said she left the hotel early this morning and went across the river. He offered to take her, but she said (a bad word), 'No, not you.' She has hired Rashid ibn Ibrahim as her dragoman."

"He is an honest man," I said, relieved. "And very strong, I understand."

"Not so strong." Daoud's countenance remained dour. "I can take her again, Sitt, if you say so."

"The idea has its appeal," I said musingly. "It would serve her right, after what she did to me. But no. She wouldn't let you within arm's length, not again. I suppose she has gone to the East Valley. Yes, I feel certain she has. Did Sabir observe anyone following her?"

Daoud looked puzzled, so I elaborated. "Anyone suspicious?"

"He did not say so."

Well, it had been a foolish question. To ask Sabir to note suspicious behavior, when I might not have been able to do so myself, was unreasonable. The boat landing was always crowded in the morning.

I thanked Daoud and sent him off to work. His massive strength was particularly useful when there was a great deal of rubble to be carried away, and that was all Emerson had found.

As the morning wore on, I wished I had worn a soft straw hat instead of my pith helmet. I didn't want to go about in the sun without it, but it pressed painfully on my sore head. The work was boring in the extreme. Cyrus had finished with Ay's tomb, finding very little of interest in the hardened mud of the burial chamber, except for the lid of the sarcophagus. As soon as Bertie finished the final plan, the entrance would be filled in. Not that there was anything valuable left, but the tomb robbers of Luxor were always on the lookout for something they could sell, including pieces of painted relief from tomb walls.

The two unfinished tombs had yielded very little. As a rule Emerson would have taken meticulous notes on these scraps; however, he had left that job to Selim and Nefret and was ranging around the cliffs, digging here and digging there. Poor dear, he wanted a tomb—any tomb, finished or unfinished, robbed or not—that could be added to the list of tomb numbers. It was not treasure Emerson sought, but knowledge. I wished I could give it to him, but I could not. And the work was not interesting enough to keep my thoughts from wandering.

To be sure, Margaret had behaved badly to me, but that did not relieve me of my responsibility toward her. By offering the olive branch of forgiveness I might be able to win her confidence again, and offer useful advice. I therefore sought a shady spot (which was not easy to come by, in that desolate cliff-enclosed valley) and wrote a few more little notes.

I persuaded Emerson to stop work early, which he was not unwilling to do because of the frustration of his search. When he joined me on the veranda after we had both bathed and changed, he studied my arrangements suspiciously. Fatima was trotting to and fro with platters of sandwiches and tea cakes, and she had put little crocheted doilies on the tables.

"What is this?" Emerson demanded. "Are you giving a party? You didn't tell me."

I was tempted to whisk the doilies away, but that would have hurt Fatima's feelings. She considered them the ultimate in elegance and had spent hours starching and ironing them.

"I invited a number of people, but I doubt some of them will come." I showed him a note that had been waiting for me when I got back from the West Valley. "Mrs. Breasted sends her regrets. They are engaged elsewhere."

"Thank God," said Emerson sincerely. "She always sends regrets, doesn't she? Why did you bother asking her?"

"As a matter of common courtesy, my dear. I don't know why she insists on accompanying her husband to Egypt. She has no interest in Egyptology and spends most of the time complaining about the inconveniences."

"Unlike you, my love," said Emerson, giving me a quick kiss. "Whom else are you expecting?"

"Cyrus and his group, of course; I invited them before we left today. I asked Miss Minton as well. And . . . But there he is now. Early, as I expected."

Emerson let out a resounding oath. "It's that blackguard O'Connell! Why—why—WHY—"

"Because I want to know what he has been up to," I replied. "He has stayed away from us, as I requested, and has published nothing scurrilous about us. That is highly suspicious."

Emerson's flush of wrath subsided. "And you want to see him and Miss Minton in mortal combat. Not a bad idea, Peabody."

"Oh, I doubt she will come, Emerson. That is another reason why I asked Kevin. I want to know what *she* has been up to."

I went to the door. Kevin was approaching slowly, in little fits and starts. When he saw me he came on more quickly, whipping off his hat.

"Ah, Mrs. E. Is it safe to come in?"

"Unless you've done something I don't know about." I held the door open. Catching sight of Emerson, Kevin gave him an ingratiating smile and smoothed his windblown red locks.

"I am innocent as a newborn babe, ma'am. I haven't had a chance to be anything else," he added despondently.

"Hmph," said Emerson. "Well, you may as well sit down, I suppose."

Kevin knew Emerson well enough to recognize this as a fairly genial welcome. "Thank you, sir. I kept at a distance, as Mrs. Emerson asked. May I inquire as to why she has changed her mind?"

I had given up any hope of worming my way back into Carnarvon's favor; Mr. Callender had not called on us, nor had the Metropolitan people after that initial visit. Mrs. Breasted had never accepted my invitations, but Breasted himself had been our guest on a number of occasions. Carnarvon or Howard must have got at him too. Nothing I could do would make matters worse, and if truth be told, I had come round to Emerson's viewpoint. I would not pander to persons I despised. The devil with them!

I did not express myself so forcibly to Kevin. Instead I contented myself with a vague reference to friendship, which brought a twinkle to Kevin's keen blue eyes.

Next to arrive were Cyrus and his crew. I was delighted to see that Katherine was among them. I took her hands and squeezed them.

"You are looking much better, Katherine. I was worried about you."

"I believe Egypt revives me," Katherine declared. "Egypt and you, Amelia. You never change. Whereas I"—she smiled, her cheeks rounding—"I have become too stout and lazy. I want to consult Nefret about proper diet and exercise. But don't offer me any of Fatima's tea cakes, because my willpower is still low!"

Nefret came in, with Ramses in tow. "I had to drag him away from his scraps," she announced.

"She wouldn't give me time to change," Ramses said, trying in vain to smooth his curly locks. "Excuse my appearance. Katherine! How good it is to see you."

"You look very handsome, as always," Katherine said with a fond smile. "Nefret, come and sit with me. I want your advice."

Emerson broke off his conversation with Cyrus to demand, "Where are the kiddies?"

"In temporary detention," Ramses replied. "Somehow they got wind of the fact that Mother had invited a number of guests, and they became so rambunctious I told them they would have to settle down before they could join us."

I looked round for Sethos, and saw him hovering in the doorway. "She hasn't come," I said softly.

"Ah." He had taken the time to change and looked quite dapper in one of Ramses's tweed suits. The ends of his mustache had a definite curl. After greeting the others, he went to the side of the veranda that opened onto the path, and stood there looking out—making certain, I felt sure, that Margaret wouldn't creep up on him unobserved. He was, therefore, the first to spot another of my guests. His exclamation brought me to his side.

"Did you invite him?"

"You can hardly suppose he would have ventured here without an invitation."

Sir Malcolm was followed by his servant, who held a huge parasol over his head. Like Kevin's, his approach was somewhat tentative, and he kept looking nervously from side to side.

As Fate would have it, at that precise moment the twins appeared, accompanied, as they always were, by Amira. Catching sight of Sir Malcolm, she ran toward him, baying like the hound of the Baskervilles. The twins broke into a run, shouting at the dog to stop; Sir Malcolm tried to get behind the servant and the parasol; the servant promptly turned tail and fled, still holding the parasol, which bobbed up and down as he ran.

It was quite an amusing sight, but I resisted the temptation to see what would ensue. Opening the door, I shouted at the top of my lungs.

"Amira! Stay!"

The dog at once obeyed, dropping to the ground practically at the feet of Sir Malcolm, who was flailing ineffectually at her with his stick.

"I do beg your pardon, Sir Malcolm," I called. "Please come in. She is perfectly harmless, you see."

Emerson, doubled up with laughter, moved aside as Sir Malcolm ran pell-mell toward the door. "Most refreshing," he said. "You've put together a real witch's brew, Peabody. What are you up to now, eh?"

"Wait and see," I murmured. Emerson grinned and held out his arms to the children. "There you are, my darlings. Come and say hello to our friends."

Sir Malcolm was no fonder of children than he was of dogs. Eyeing Charla askance—she had once tried to bite him after he patted her on the head—he sank panting into a chair. I took him a cup of tea.

"Did you plan that, Mrs. Emerson?" he said in a whisper.

"I assure you, I did not. You know most of the others, I believe? Cyrus and Katherine Vandergelt, their son Bertie, their assistant Jumana. May I present Suzanne Malraux and Mr. Nadji Farid, who recently joined our staff. Oh, and Mr. Kevin O'Connell, of the *Daily Yell*."

The courtesies gave Sir Malcolm time to compose himself. His dignity had been sadly damaged, however; Bertie was still grinning, and some of the others were trying not to laugh. The malevolent look he gave me assured me he would not soon forget the indignity.

All in all, it was a merry, noisy meeting. I moved from group to group as a good hostess should, offering refreshments and overhearing bits of conversation. Margaret did not put in an appearance.

Sir Malcolm succeeded in getting Emerson aside. The few words I managed to hear indicated that he was still attempting to persuade Emerson to join with him in a complaint to M. Lacau. This proved to be a serious error on his part. Emerson gave him a contemptuous look and turned his back.

"That was a serious error on your part," I said to Sir Malcolm. "I could have told you Emerson would refuse."

"Time is running out," Sir Malcolm said, clutching his stick as if he yearned to strike someone with it. "The Professor did not refuse—not point-blank. He implied that he would consider my proposal."

"Did he really?"

"I choose to interpret it thus, Mrs. Emerson, because the alternative—"

He stopped with a snap of his teeth, and I said, "Dear me. Is that a threat, Sir Malcolm?"

"Not at all." He glanced at the door, where Amira lay staring in. Her tongue hung out and most of her teeth were visible. "If you will be good enough to remove that creature, I will bid you good afternoon."

I did, and he did. After looking about and realizing his servant had not returned, Sir Malcolm set off on foot, at a pace that betokened ill for the poor fellow. I hoped he would have the good sense to keep on running and not return.

Naturally, the moment Sir Malcolm was out of earshot we all began talking about him.

"He would not play chess," said David John critically.

"I wouldn't trust him any farther than I could throw him," Cyrus declared. "What did he say to you, Emerson?"

"Same old thing. Wanted me to join with him in exposing to Lacau what he called Carnarvon's illicit activities. I said I would think about it." Emerson tried to look crafty.

"Well done, my dear," I exclaimed. "How far will he go, I wonder? He spoke of time running out, and of assuming you would cooperate with him, because the alternative—"

After a breathless interval, Emerson said, "The alternative was what?"

"He broke off at that point."

"How delightfully ominous." Nefret laughed.

"Bah," Emerson declared. "There is no alternative. If Carter and Carnarvon meant to confess they would have done so by now; but I will not have it on my conscience that I exposed them."

Kevin's hands were twitching. He knew better than to reach for his notebook, however.

"If you print anything about that, we will deny it," I said, thanking heaven that Kevin was unaware of the most damaging part of that incident. For Carter and Carnarvon to have entered the antechamber in secret was reprehensible but might be overlooked. For them to have broken into the sealed burial chamber and then concealed their action was a serious breach of their firman.

"Yes, ma'am," Kevin said gloomily. "I've got the material for a scoop to end all scoops, and you won't let me run with it. And there's Minton, hanging round the Valley, poking her nose into every corner and interviewing every ragged guard."

"Have you spoken with her?" I asked.

"I greeted her as a gentleman should," said Kevin, his nostrils flaring. "Would you believe it, Mrs. E.? She tried to get information out of me! We fenced for a while, and when I asked her point-blank if she had found out anything of interest, she grinned in that offensive way of hers and told me I would find out when her next dispatch was published."

Emerson began coughing violently. "Take a sip of tea, my dear," I said.

Would Margaret have the audacity to write about her "kidnapping" and "imprisonment," as she would term them? Such a story would cause a sensation, given our reputation with the newspaper-reading public. It would also infuriate Kevin, who wouldn't at all have minded being "kidnapped" if he could have got an exclusive out of it.

And, depending on how Margaret explained the reason for her detention, such a story might attract the attention of the very individuals from whom we had attempted to protect her. Would she really risk her husband's safety for the sake of a story?

Catching the eye of Sethos, I saw that he was thinking the same thing—and that he had arrived at the same conclusion.


Everyone wanted to go with me to greet our dear David and Sennia (and Gargery). There was no question of the twins going, naturally, although David John declared I was unfair and Charla raged like a miniature Medea. Nefret decided to remain with them, and after some discussion it was agreed that Ramses would accompany me instead of Emerson. This suited me very well. Emerson was not the most restful of traveling companions, and it was only right that Ramses should be among the first to greet his best friend.

Emerson insisted on going to the station with us, and so did Daoud. Despite the lateness of the hour the platform was very busy. Many people preferred taking the night express, which started from Aswan and made only a few stops after Luxor. The enterprising merchants of Luxor were out in force, in a last-ditch effort to peddle their fake scarabs and ushebtis. A juggler kept a circle of brightly colored balls whirling, and a snake charmer squatted before the basket in which his creatures were confined. Daoud was not at all sure about railway trains and pressed various amulets into our hands to ensure our safety. Emerson (who was not at all sure about me) looked as if he were having second thoughts about accompanying me.

"Don't let her out of your sight," he ordered Ramses, who had come back from seeing our luggage bestowed in our compartments. "Not for a second."

Rather than point out the inconvenience (not to mention impropriety) of this, I nudged Ramses, kissed Emerson, and got into the carriage. As soon as the train was underway we went to the bar for a whiskey and soda.

"You are looking very smart, Mother," said Ramses, raising his glass in salute. "Is that, by chance, intended to impress our friend Smith?"

"I had thought of calling on him." I acknowledged the compliment with a smile and adjusted my hat—a broad-brimmed white straw to which I had added a few red silk roses. "We promised to keep him informed, and we haven't reported Sethos's arrival."

"Do you think we ought?"

It was his way of saying he didn't think we ought.

"I share your doubts, Ramses, and I am glad to have this opportunity to discuss the matter with you."

Frowning, Ramses opened his cigarette case and offered it to me. In order to establish an atmosphere of congeniality, I took one and allowed him to light it for me.

"Have you thought about the theory we discussed the other day?" he asked.

I had to search my memory. "Oh, you mean the theory that—er—your uncle has deliberately misled us?"

"I would put it more strongly than that," Ramses said.

"Don't put it more strongly just now. We could be overheard." The waiter approached to ask if we were dining soon; if so, he would save a table for us. "We may as well go in now," I said. "We will continue the discussion over dinner."

"It isn't a discussion so much as an unprovable theory," Ramses said, after we had taken our places. "I agree that there are holes in my original proposal . . ."

There were holes in all the others we came up with as well: that Sethos had turned traitor and was being pursued by the British Secret Service; that Smith had turned traitor and was trying to keep Sethos from betraying him; that instead of a state secret Sethos had made off with a priceless artifact from a looted site in Syria or Palestine. In the end, I was forced to agree with Ramses that we ought not confide in Mr. Smith until we knew more. My suggestion that I have a little chat with the gentleman was not received with enthusiasm.

"You may give away more than you get," Ramses said. "What if he asks directly whether you have heard from Sethos? You never lie——"

"Unless it is absolutely necessary."

Ramses laughed. "Yes, I know. Well, we will leave it at that for now. You look tired, Mother. Do you want coffee?"

"No, thank you. I am not at all tired, but I believe I will retire."

We parted at the doors of our respective compartments. During dinner the porter had made up one of the berths. The bed looked very inviting, despite the fact that the sheets showed signs of wear. Though the room was stuffy I did not open the window; along with cool air came dust and windblown sand. I also cut my ablutions short, since to be honest I was somewhat tired. After assuming my nightdress I got into bed and lay looking up at the ceiling, which was painted in someone's notion of ancient Egyptian art. The jackal god Anubis glared down at me from amid a clump of violent purple lotuses. He was not a reassuring sight, but I fell asleep almost at once and did not stir until I woke to hear the conductor announcing our imminent arrival in Cairo.

It was almost midday when we reached Alexandria, to learn that the ship was in port and tenders were transporting passengers ashore. We went at once to the customs shed, where amid the milling arrivals I beheld David. He caught sight of us—or rather, of Ramses, who was, like David himself, a head taller than those nearby—and began waving. A flood of affection filled me at the sight of his lean brown face and black curls, so like those of my son.

"Where are Sennia and Gargery?" I asked, standing on tiptoe.

Like a small up-to-date version of Venus rising from the sea, Sennia was lifted high above David's head. She too was waving and calling out, though I could not hear her through the noise.

I did not see Gargery until after the trio had passed through customs. Leaning heavily upon his cane, he tottered up to me. "I brought them, madam."

"So I see," I replied, turning to receive the affectionate embrace of a son from David, and a breath-expelling hug from Sennia.

She seemed to have grown several inches in the past few months, and at thirteen was quite the little lady—white gloves, parasol and all. Half-English, half-Egyptian, she had the smooth brown skin and long-lashed dark eyes of her mother and, heaven be thanked, little resemblance to her father.

"Where are the others?" she demanded. "The Professor and Aunt Nefret and the twins and Selim and Daoud and Fatima?"

"You will see them tomorrow," I replied, straightening her hair bow. "We are taking the evening train to Luxor."

Gargery groaned. "Oh, madam, I had hoped we might have a day of rest, after that dreadful voyage."

"You were seasick, I suppose," I said. "Well, Gargery, I am sorry, but you brought it on yourself. No one asked you to come."

I did feel sorry for the poor old fellow, but as I had learned, sympathy only made Gargery groan louder. Gargery didn't like trains either; by the time we reached Cairo he was so pale and shaky I took the group straight to Shepheard's and settled Gargery in a comfortable chair in the lobby.

"We will take tea here instead of on the terrace," I said, torn between concern and exasperation. "The train doesn't leave for several hours, so have a little nap, Gargery."

"I am not at all tired, madam," Gargery said haughtily. His eyes closed and his white head drooped onto his chest. He didn't stir, even when the waiter brought tea and a mouth-watering assortment of biscuits. Forgetting her dignity, Sennia took the sweetest.

"Curse the old rascal, he doesn't look at all well," I said in a low voice. "He can have a compartment to himself. Sennia will share mine and you and Ramses another, David. You will probably sit up all night talking."

"I will take care of Gargery," Sennia said. She picked up the cup of tea I poured for her, her little finger elegantly extended. "Oh, it is wonderful to be back! Can we go to the Museum? Can we go to the suk?"

"I don't want to miss the train," I said, wavering under the appeal of a pair of big black eyes.

"It will probably be late," Ramses said. "You want to shop, I suppose, Sennia. Would you settle for a short stroll along the Muski?"

Sennia, her mouth full of cake, nodded eagerly.

"I could stand to do a little shopping myself," I admitted.

Ramses looked at his watch. "I have a call to make. I shall be back in good time. David, will you go with the ladies?"

David gave him an odd look, and agreed so readily that I wondered how much Ramses had told him. They hadn't had much chance to speak privately.

"What about Gargery?" I asked.

"He'll sleep for hours," David said. He put a gentle hand on the old man's shoulder and got a faint snore in response. "We won't be gone long. You had better write a note for him, Aunt Amelia."

I did so, and asked the headwaiter to look after our friend.

With Sennia dancing along at my side, talking incessantly, I had no opportunity to ask David anything. He stood by with that annoying patient look men have on such occasions while Sennia and I purchased Christmas presents. She was a generous little soul and would have emptied her small purse buying gifts for the twins if I hadn't prevented her. I cannot say the gifts were always in good taste. In one shop she made David turn his back while she negotiated with the owner for a hideous necktie printed with blue and purple scarabs.

Not until her arms were loaded with parcels, which she would allow no one else to carry, did I manage to persuade her to return to the hotel. Ramses arrived, by cab, at the same time we did and we entered the lobby together, Sennia chattering nonstop.

"We had better get ourselves to the station," I said. "The train may be on time for once. Wake Gargery."

But the chair he had occupied was empty, and there was no sign of him.

David went to look for him, in the obvious place. When he returned, his face was troubled. "The attendant said no one of his description had been there."

Seeing us, the headwaiter hurried up. "Are you looking for your friend, Mrs. Emerson? He has gone on."

"Good Gad," I exclaimed. "Gone where?"

"He mumbled something about the railway station, madam."

"How long ago did he leave the hotel?" I asked.

"Shortly after you did, madam. I kept an eye on the old gentleman, as you requested, but—well, we are very busy this afternoon, and I didn't notice he was gone from his chair until he tapped me with his cane and said to tell you he had gone on. He was mumbling to himself, madam. Complaining, I believe."

We stared at one another in consternation, but none of us voiced the alarm we felt because of Sennia. She chuckled. "He gets confused sometimes," she explained.

"Perhaps that is what happened," Ramses said. "We had better look for him at the station."

"We have no other choice," I said uneasily. "We must leave at once. Barkins, if the old idiot—the old gentleman—should come back, hang on to him and send someone to the station to inform us."

Our luggage had been sent on, so we got ourselves and our purchases into a cab without delay. Dusk advanced as the cab wound its way along the busy streets. The gathering darkness increased my uneasiness. The note I had left on the table for Gargery was missing too. He must have taken it with him. How could he have misconstrued my instructions?

My spirits sank further when we reached the main railway station. Supposing Gargery had found his way here, how were we to locate him amid the shoving, shouting crowds? We found the platform where the express to Luxor and Aswan was waiting. There was still half an hour before it was due to leave. Some people were boarding, others stood chatting with friends. Gargery could not have got on board, we had his ticket. He was not among the passengers still on the platform.

"Find your compartment," Ramses ordered. "And stay there. We'll look for him."

He waited until we had boarded before he and David went off in different directions. Porters were sorting out the luggage; I identified ours and had it brought to our compartments. I stood at the open window scanning the passersby, replying absently to Sennia's bright chatter. A quarter of an hour passed. Most of the passengers were boarding.

Then I saw Ramses and David, converging on the train. Seeing me at the window, they hurried up. I did not need to ask whether they had found him. Obviously they had not.

"I'm staying," Ramses said, before I could speak. "David, hop on and toss my bag out, will you?"

"We can't go without Gargery," Sennia exclaimed. "Where is he?"

"He's got lost, I expect," Ramses said with a forced smile. "The rest of you may as well go on; I'll track him down and bring him with me tomorrow."

I could not contain myself. "Ramses, do you think—"

"I think he's lost," Ramses said loudly. "Don't worry, Sennia, I'll—"

She interrupted him with a shriek of delight. "No, he's not! There he is now!"

David, in the next compartment, dropped the suitcase he was holding out to Ramses and stared. Ramses turned and stared. I stared. There he was indeed, hatless, white hair standing on end, pushing through the crowd, which gave way to him with good-natured grins. Old age is respected in Egypt.

Ramses kept his head. He usually does. Shoving his suitcase back at David, he reached Gargery in a matter of seconds, caught hold of him, and towed him toward the train. Gargery was talking and waving his cane, but I couldn't hear what he was saying. The pair made their way to the end of the carriage. I closed the window and went to the door of the compartment. My thoughts were in a whirl. Evidently my worst fears had been unfounded. The old rascal had got himself lost, and that was all. He had scared the wits out of me, though, and had made it only just in time. A jolt and a whistle from the engine betokened the train's departure. Coming toward us along the corridor were Gargery and Ramses.

Sennia wriggled past me, squeezed by a large lady enveloped in a feather-trimmed cloak, and flung herself at Gargery. "That was too bad of you, Gargery. We were afraid you would be late."

"It wasn't my fault, Miss Sennia. Wait till I tell you—" Another lurch of the carriage made him stagger. Ramses shoved him into the outstretched arms of David, who stood at the door of their compartment. "Get in there, Gargery. Sit down and keep quiet."

We all piled into the compartment. The two long couches which could be made into beds had seating for six. Gargery dropped, wheezing, into his seat, but he looked a good deal livelier than he had before. His lips parted in a grin, displaying an elegant set of false teeth we had had made for him. "I got away from them," he declared. "Clean away! They made a big mistake, I tell you, thinking they could hold a chap like me prisoner."

Sennia's eyes were as large as saucers. (Small saucers.) She clutched at his arm. "You were a prisoner? Oh, Gargery, are you hurt?"

"Hell," said Ramses. He took off his hat, threw it across the compartment, and ran distracted fingers through his hair.

The cat was out of the bag and the fat was in the fire, and short of gagging him there was no way of keeping Gargery from bragging about his heroic escape—or preventing Sennia from hearing him. He wasn't as keen about admitting how he had been hoodwinked, but by dint of pointed questions (and, once the train was well underway, the application of whiskey and soda), we got a coherent account out of him.

He had been awakened (roused from deep thought, as he put it) by a messenger who handed him a note which read, "Meet us at the railway station." At the suggestion of this helpful individual, he had informed the head waiter of his intention and followed the messenger out of the hotel, where a closed carriage was waiting. Considering that we had sent it for him (as was only his due), he felt no alarm until he found himself seated between two very sturdy strangers wearing masks. They fell upon him, and in a twinkling had him bound and gagged. The prick of a knife at his throat warned him to stop struggling—for, as he assured us, he had put up a valiant fight.

"Where did they take you?" I asked, when Gargery paused to refresh himself.

"Nowhere, madam." Forgetting his manners for a moment, Gargery wiped his mouth on his sleeve. "We drove round and round for hours, madam. Every second I thought one of the bas— one of them would cut my throat, but I was not afraid, madam, I was only biding my time. Finally the carriage stopped . . ."

Gargery took another sip of whiskey and appeared to be thinking deeply.

"And then?" I prompted.

"And then . . ." Inspiration came to him. "I had worked my hands free, you see, madam. One of the chaps got out of the carriage, leaving the door open, and I—er—gave the second fellow a hard whack with my cane, untied my feet, and leaped out. It wouldn't have done to stay and fight, madam, there were three of them, including the driver, and—and—and then I saw the railway station just ahead and ran as fast as I could till Mr. Ramses found me."

This remarkable account left us speechless, except for Sennia, who threw her arms round Gargery and informed him that he was a hero.

"Yes, quite," said Ramses. He had his voice under control, but not his eyebrows; they formed a black V over his narrowed orbs. "Gargery, why don't you take Miss Sennia to the dining car? It must be almost time for first service. We will join you shortly."

"I am a bit peckish," Gargery admitted. "As you know, sir, combat has that effect." With the assistance of his cane, he hauled himself to his feet and treated us to another glimpse of his expensive teeth.

"It is good to be back in Egypt, madam!"

David watched the pair reel off along the swaying corridor, and then closed the door. His lips were twitching.

"David, are you laughing?" I demanded.

"I can't help it. The old rascal is enjoying this. He looks ten years younger."

"He certainly has a gift for fantastic fiction," I said sarcastically. "Can you visualize him immobilizing a thug with one blow of his cane? He hasn't a muscle left in his body."

"But he hasn't lost the spirit of adventure," Ramses said. He was smiling too, that rare, carefree smile that lit up his entire face. "He didn't fight his way free, though. They let him go. After driving him around for—what?—two hours, they brought him to the station in time for the train, and walked away. They must have taken the note we left for him before he woke up."

David sat down and took out his pipe. "They being the anonymous individuals who have been bothering you?"

"Yes, they have been a bit of a bother," I said.

"Ramses gave me a quick outline of what you've been going through," David said. "I'm not surprised to hear that Sethos is up to his old tricks, but I can't believe he would invent such an outrageous story, or arrange even nonlethal attacks on any of you."

"You have more confidence in his goodwill than I do," Ramses said.

"You're letting your doubts of the man influence your judgment," David argued. "You haven't a scrap of evidence against him. He's devoted to all of you."

"So what's your explanation?" Ramses asked.

David shrugged. "I haven't one."

"Neither have we," I said. "What happened to Gargery only makes it more confusing. What was the point of carrying him off and then returning him without so much as a bruise on him?"

"It's obvious, isn't it?" Ramses was no longer smiling. "Another warning. This time it was Gargery. Next time it may be someone else."


FROM MANUSCRIPT H


Ramses and David did sit up half the night talking. After Sennia and Gargery had been tucked into bed, Ramses's mother joined them. She was wearing a voluminous dressing gown and her neatly braided hair was covered by a ruffled cap. Ramses always found these demonstrations of feminine vanity amusing; but her eyes were hard and alert, and she did not waste time.

"I don't want to leave Sennia alone too long. Where did you go this afternoon?"

"I was just about to tell David," Ramses said.

"And not me?" She sat down on the foot of his bed.

"I expected you'd turn up," Ramses said, smiling at her. "Anyhow, there's not much to tell. We decided, didn't we, that we wouldn't contact Smith directly. I made the rounds—the Turf Club, the Gezira, and a few of his other haunts—saw a few familiar faces, but not his. It's rather odd. None of his acquaintances has seen him for some time."

"Perhaps he's ill. Did you go round to his office?"

"No. That would have been too direct. I dropped in on Russell instead."

"Not a bad notion," she said, looking chagrined that she hadn't thought of it herself. "He is a man of integrity—unlike some of your acquaintances in the intelligence services—and as commandant of the police he has informants all over Egypt. I trust you were discreet in your questions?"

"I didn't mention Sethos, or cryptic messages, if that's what you mean. But he did give me a rather grim picture of the current political situation. Assassinations of British officials have increased, and even Russell doesn't know who is behind them. Most of the attacks occur when the target is on his way to his office, and though his car is preceded and followed by other vehicles containing armed guards, the killers sometimes manage to draw up alongside and fire several rounds before speeding away. Russell's not concerned with the broader picture except as it affects his work, but the entire Middle East is boiling with discontent."

"That isn't much help."

"It was the best I could do without giving away information."

"Yes, my dear, I know; I didn't mean to criticize." Murmuring discontentedly and shaking her handsome head, she bade them good night and went out. Ramses stood at the door until her door closed and he heard the bolt being drawn.

"So what about the famous tomb?" David asked.

"Was that what fetched you? I know you dote on us, but we can't really compete with Lia and the children."

David laughed. "How cynical! The *Illustrated London News* has offered me a substantial sum for drawings of the objects."

"I hate to be discouraging, but your chances are none too good. Father had a falling-out with Carnarvon, and we've been banned from the tomb."

"I heard about that. Did the Professor really curse him?"

"It's no laughing matter," Ramses said, shaking his head. "The prohibition includes the whole family, and many of our friends. It's a pity, really. You'd lose your head over some of those artifacts. However, I don't know that Carnarvon would admit you even if he weren't angry with father. There's a rumor that he intends to give exclusive rights to the *Times*."

"Tell me about the tomb." David knocked out his pipe and stretched out on the bed, hands under his head.

It was like old times, when they had talked the night away, discussing tombs, treasures, and mummies, or planning some wild adventure. In the early days, before David and he had become involved in darker plots, Nefret had often been a party to their schemes. Sometimes he wondered if she ever missed those days. They had been so young! Young enough to believe they would survive unscathed, however dangerous the scrapes they got themselves into.

He could talk to David as to no one else, and he spilled the whole story, from Emerson's initial discovery of the buried step to the cursing of Carnarvon and their own illicit entry into the treasure chamber. Some parts of the tale sent David into spasms of laughter, but he sobered when Ramses described what they had seen on that memorable night. He kept pressing Ramses for more details about the great funerary couches, the golden goddess his mother had seen, the sealed funerary shrine, the black-and-gold statues of the king guarding the burial chamber. When an ear-splitting yawn interrupted Ramses's description of the chariot, he said, "You can tell me more tomorrow. We'd better get some rest before the family descends on us in the morning."

David was asleep within minutes, breathing evenly. Ramses had a number of things on his mind, but he was not long in following his friend's example. It was good to have David back.

# CHAPTER SEVEN

"THAT RASCAL CARTER HAS PURCHASED A MOTORCAR," EMERSON shouted. "Can you believe it?"

Imposing as the statue of a Roman emperor, he stood with feet apart and arms akimbo, his bare black head dulled by a film of dust. Emerson's commanding presence always attracts attention; this shout, delivered at the top of his lungs, made everyone on the station platform stare.

"What sort of greeting is that?" I demanded, descending from the carriage with the help of Ramses. "Here we are, safely back with our dear guests, and you cannot even say you are glad to see them."

"Oh," said Emerson. "Curse it, of course I am glad to see them. David, my boy! Sennia, my love, give me a kiss. Hallo, Gargery."

Everyone had come to meet us, including the twins. Like the little gentleman he was, David John gravely offered his hand to David, but Charla, held aloft in the strong arms of Daoud, was squirming and screaming like a banshee.

"Emerson ought not have brought her," I said to Ramses.

"Charla can always talk him round," Ramses said.

"She can talk Daoud round too. Get hold of her, Ramses, and don't let her wriggle away."

It wasn't the easiest job in the world. After hugging her father passionately, as if he'd been away for a month instead of two days, Charla demanded to be put down. It was like trying to hold on to a large, undisciplined puppy. I considered, not for the first time, of equipping Charla with a leash and harness. Emerson had been outraged at the suggestion (and David John had smirked in a provocative fashion). Anyhow, Charla could probably unbuckle herself from any contrivance we could construct. Constant vigilance was the only defense. I certainly did not intend to let her run loose on the station platform, among the lemonade sellers and porters balancing heavy loads and a train on the verge of departure.

I took the child from Ramses so that he could greet his wife. I was pleased to see him hold her close and whisper something that brought a smile to her face.

"So what do you think of that?" Emerson demanded, hoisting Sennia onto his broad shoulders. "That villain Carter—"

"You make it sound as if his sole motive was to annoy you," I said.

"What other reason could he have? Blatant imitation, that is what it is. A motorcar is of no use here."

Realizing he had left himself open to a caustic comment, he went on before I could deliver it. "Well, well, let's get out of this crush, shall we? I don't know why you want to stand round gossiping, Peabody, when our guests are anxious to get home."

Someone—probably Selim—had had the forethought to order several carriages for us and our luggage. We sorted ourselves out, and I found myself seated with Emerson and Daoud.

Turning to the latter, I said, "I suppose it was you who found out about the motorcar."

Daoud beamed with pride. "It came on the train, and also a steel gate for the tomb."

The driver's head was half-turned, listening avidly. Our old friend's reputation as an all-knowing oracle had, if it was possible, increased over the past weeks. Some of the more superstitious workers believe he had supernatural means of information, but as we knew, he got most of his news from his son Sabir, who operated a successful boat service between the east and west banks. One might say that Sabir was an oracle in training, who made use of Daoud's connections on both sides of the river.

"Mr. Carter has returned, then?" I asked.

"Oh, yes. He went from the station to the dahabeeyah of the Breasted professor."

"So that is why they refused my invitation to tea," I said thoughtfully. "Howard must have written Breasted telling him about the tomb and offering him a chance to participate—and warning him about us."

"I forbid you to repeat the invitation," said Emerson fiercely.

"I am not accustomed to putting myself forward, Emerson."

"I have noticed that, Peabody."

"When will Carter reopen the tomb?" I inquired.

Daoud knew, of course. "Tomorrow, it is said. Callender Effendi has already begun removing the fill."

"Well, I don't give a curse," Emerson declared.

Sabir's boat was waiting at the riverfront; he had decorated it with fresh flowers and the ornate hangings usually reserved for festivals, and several other members of the family had accompanied him. Another round of salutations followed; the family thought highly of David, who was related to most of them, and they hadn't seen him for some time. The celebration continued until we reached the house.

By the time the newcomers had been welcomed by the household staff and the dog, Emerson was stamping with impatience. "Enough!" he shouted. "Fatima, stop fussing over Sennia and get luncheon started. By Gad, it has taken us two hours to get here from Luxor. Ridiculous. I haven't had a chance to talk with David. My boy, you won't believe what Howard Carter—"

"Later," I cut in. "They will want to tidy up and rest."

"I don't want to rest," Sennia said. "I want to see my rooms, and the Great Cat of Re."

She didn't seem to be at all worried about Gargery's melodramatic story. We had made light of it, and as I knew from my study of juvenile psychology (and years of painful experience), young persons are inclined to dismiss anything that does not affect them directly.

"Take Gargery with you," I ordered.

"But, madam, I haven't told the Professor about—"

"Later! Get along with you, Gargery. David John, will you lend him your strong arm? Charla, see if you can find the cat. He is probably hiding under some article of furniture."

David John gravely extended a slender arm, and Gargery had tact enough to take it. It was amazing how much quieter it was with the four of them no longer present. Fatima had gone off with the children, so it was Kareem who brought the coffee tray. I managed to catch hold of it before he spilled much, and we settled down to a comfortable chat.

"That was a painless way of removing the children, Mother," Ramses said, laughing.

"I believe I can claim to have a good understanding of juvenile psychol—juvenile human nature."

"The old rascal seems to have held up well," Emerson said. "What was he talking about?"

"In a nutshell," said Ramses, "he disappeared from the hotel where we had told him to stay, and turned up at the railway station barely in time to catch the express."

"He's becoming senile," Emerson said, scowling darkly. "Curse it! We'll have to watch over him as we would a child."

That certainly was the explanation that leaped to mind. Gargery's tale sounded even more improbable when it was reduced to bare statements, which Ramses proceeded to do. "He said he'd been lured away by a false message, thrust into a carriage, and been held prisoner by two desperadoes. He was able to get away from them and made it to the station in the nick of time."

"What nonsense!" Emerson exclaimed. "He invented the story to excuse his lapse of memory and make himself look like a hero."

"That's possible," David said. "We have only his word."

"Quite," said Emerson triumphantly. "What would have been the point of abducting him and then letting him go? As I was saying, David, Carter . . ."

It was easy for Emerson to doubt Gargery's tale. He hadn't been there. I had. Certain of the details were probably untrue, such as his escape from several armed men, but it was unlikely that he had suffered a temporary lapse of memory and recovered from it just in time to reach the station before the train departed.

Sethos finished his coffee and rose. "I'm sure David will find that fascinating. Ramses, may I have a word with you?"

He gestured toward the door. Ramses followed him into the house. I followed Ramses, leaving Emerson complaining to David about Howard Carter, the tomb, and the motorcar.

As I had expected, Sethos led the way to Ramses's workroom. "We must have a council of war," I announced.

"Ah, Amelia," said Sethos, attempting to appear surprised at my presence. "Do sit down. I presume you do not agree with Emerson that Gargery wandered off in a fit of senile dementia?"

I waved my hand in dismissal. "Like so many of the others, this event was alarming but not really dangerous. I am becoming weary of these demonstrations. It is time we took action instead of reacting to the acts of others."

"As a general theory, it has a great deal to recommend it," said Sethos. "What do you propose we do?"

"Return the message," Ramses said.

"It certainly goes against the grain to do so," I murmured. "And we dare not assume that it will satisfy their demands. Our vigilance must be increased, particularly with regard to the more vulnerable members of the family."

"So you think they took Gargery simply to prove that they could?" Sethos asked.

"If they want to ensure our silence, they will need a hostage," Ramses said. "Someone they think we value more than Gargery. In their eyes he is 'only' a servant. But then why bother demanding the return of the original message when they must have known we would have made copies?"

I sniffed. "Distraction and confusion. Putting us off our guard. Forcing us to waste time looking for a clue that doesn't exist. Who knows? At least we agree on one thing—we, all of us, must take extra care. I shall warn Cyrus to look after his family."

Leaning against the table, arms folded, Sethos shifted from one foot to the other. "What about Margaret?"

"She's been warned," Ramses said. "She'll have to take her chances."

"Now, my dear, you mustn't be so harsh," I said. "Perhaps I ought to have another little chat with Margaret."

"Invite her to tea," Sethos said sarcastically.

"I shall."

I did—but not at the house. Instead I suggested neutral ground, at one of the hotels. She accepted by return messenger.

The next item in my (constantly) revised list of Things to Do involved Selim, so I was pleased to find him on the veranda with David and Emerson, who had invited him to luncheon. They were all smoking and drinking coffee and talking about Tutankhamon. It took me a while to cut into the conversation; in fact, I had to interrupt Emerson in order to do so.

"Have you told Selim about what happened to Gargery?" I asked.

Cut off in mid-lecture, Emerson did not immediately catch my meaning. "What about him?"

I proceeded to tell Selim, who stroked his beard and looked bewildered. "I do not understand, Sitt Hakim. What does it mean?"

"It means that from now on any one of us may be in similar danger. I want extra guards round the house. I want the children watched closely at all times, by one of our own men."

Emerson's mouth had opened in protest when I began—for this meant the diminution of his work force—but when the children were mentioned he looked alarmed.

"Between Elia and the dog—" he began.

"Amira hasn't proved to be a very efficient watchdog, and Elia, though devoted, is the twins' nursemaid, not a bodyguard."

"Hmph," said Emerson. "Good thinking, Peabody. See to it, will you, Selim?"

"Yes, Emerson. Though I do not believe any man in Egypt would harm a child, especially a child of the family of the Father of Curses. The men of Gurneh would track him down and tear him to pieces."

His quiet, even voice held more conviction than shouts and curses. A weight seemed to lift from my heart. "It is true," I said. "Thank you, Selim."

Poor David paid the penalty for his popularity, being beleaguered by demands from all sides. The twins, who had been allowed, as a special treat, to join us for luncheon, insisted that he assist them in decorating the house for Christmas. Emerson suggested a tour of the sites Lacau had offered us for the following season—all in the same afternoon—and Cyrus sent a message inviting us to dinner that evening and asking whether we intended to bring David to the West Valley after luncheon. Daoud wanted to know when David would visit Kadija and his other kin at Gurneh; and Sennia, eating with exaggerated delicacy (to show up the twins) informed us that she intended to accompany us to all the places we had mentioned. Since David was too good-natured to refuse anyone, I took it upon myself to make the decision for him.

"We are taking tea at the Winter Palace this afternoon—yes, Emerson, we are—and dining with the Vandergelts tonight—I have already accepted—so there won't be time for much else. Sennia, I want you to rest and settle into your room; ask Fatima to iron your best frock, since you were included in Mr. Vandergelt's invitation."

"Me too, me too," Charla cried.

"No, not you."

Charla's face turned bright red and she bared her little teeth in a shriek. "When you learn to behave like a lady, you will be allowed to join the adults," I said, over her cries.

Charla was removed by Ramses—he was the only one except myself who could control her when she was in one of her rages—and I went with Sennia to see how Gargery was getting on. Since I had flatly refused his offer to serve at luncheon and since he would not sit down at table with us, I had had a luncheon tray sent to him. He sat hunched over it like an aging vulture and growled at me when I asked how he felt, but I noticed he had eaten everything.

I then joined the others in Ramses's workroom, where I had instructed them to meet me. "We must settle this business of the document," I informed them, taking the chair Sethos held for me. "I have looked it over and failed to find anything. I suggest we send it off immediately to the address Sethos was given."

Frowning, Emerson picked up the papers. They were somewhat the worse for wear, tattered and stained (and scorched in several places where I had held them too close to the candle flame). "I can't see any reason why we should not," he admitted. "Sethos?"

"I see a number of reasons why we should" was the reply. "In fact, I am in favor of enclosing a conciliatory note stating that we will refrain from further action if they will do the same."

Nefret said, "Will they take our word?"

"Possibly not," Sethos said. "But it's worth a try. What do you think, David?"

"I agree," David said briefly.

"We will leave it to you, then," I said, with a nod at my brother-in-law.


The tearoom at the Winter Palace is a spacious chamber with tall windows looking out over the famous gardens and handsomely furnished with oriental rugs and plush furniture. Ordinarily only the murmur of well-bred conversation and the muted clatter of crockery are heard. It was very crowded that afternoon, and the noise level was higher than usual.

"Not many journalists present," I remarked to Ramses.

"They prefer the bars," said Ramses. "Except that one."

He indicated Margaret, who had risen and was waving to us.

She watched us approach with a somewhat derisive smile. "I am reminded of the late Queen," she said. "A—er—petite, dignified lady, surrounded by very tall guards and accompanied by a pretty little lady-in-waiting. Consider me intimidated."

The description did not sit well with Nefret, whose sympathy for Margaret had faded after the latter's attack on me. Lips tight, she took the chair Ramses held for her and I took another. The small table was set for four people, and flanked by a velvet settee and two chairs. Margaret resumed her seat on the settee. "I wasn't expecting so many," she said with a look of mock chagrin.

"Well, we aren't going away," said Emerson, waving at one of the waiters. "Abdul, three more chairs here, if you please."

Abdul produced not only the chairs but another table, which he managed to fit in, to the great inconvenience of persons nearby. Once we had settled ourselves, I asked, "Whom were you expecting?"

"Not David." Margaret offered her hand to him and favored him with a friendly smile. "I didn't know he was here. How are Lia and the children?"

"Never mind the amenities," said Emerson. "Miss Minton, we have reason to believe that our adversaries are still active. You would be wise to take extra precautions."

He drained his cup, slammed it back into the saucer, and rose.

"I do admire your style, Professor," Margaret said. "Brief and to the point. Is that all?"

"Certainly not," I said. "Sit down, Emerson, do."

Abdul, who was well acquainted with Emerson's manners, brought another cup. I filled it.

"What else is there to say?" demanded Emerson. However, he sat down and took the cup from me.

"Have you had any—er—unusual encounters, Miss Minton?" I asked.

"Don't let us be so formal," said that lady. "Our little disagreement is forgotten and forgiven, I hope?"

"By you?" I inquired.

"Ah, well," said Margaret pensively. "Forgiveness is a conscious act. One cannot so easily forget an incident of such import, can one?"

I rather enjoyed fencing with a skillful opponent, but Emerson and his brother were showing signs of annoyance. Sethos, who had been pointedly ignored by his wife, expressed his sentiments without reserve.

"You refuse to take Amelia's warning seriously?"

Margaret's chin protruded. "I am quite capable of taking care of myself."

"As you did in Hayil," Sethos snapped. "If I hadn't got you out of there—"

"Nothing would have happened to me." She turned on him, eyes flashing. "You told me that yourself."

"Perhaps I was lying."

"It is a habit of yours."

"Now, now," I said.

"She only cares about her damned story," Sethos said violently. "Didn't you understand that she was threatening to accuse you, in print, of abducting her? Margaret, if you dare—"

"Then give me something else to write about!"

"Kindly lower your voices," I ordered. "People are staring."

Among the starers was Kevin O'Connell, red hair rampant, face sunburned, freckles blazing. He hadn't been in the room when we arrived, so he must have followed us. Catching my eye, he raised his cup in salute.

"You see?" Margaret demanded. "He's been on my trail all day. You promised you would keep me informed."

His countenance almost as flushed as that of Kevin, Emerson rose in all his majesty. "And you, madam, were the first to break that agreement by perpetrating a physical attack against my wife—your friend. Come, Peabody. She has been warned. If she fails to heed that warning, on her own head be it."

"Now, Emerson, don't be so hasty," I said. "I feel certain Margaret would never print such a story."

"Not without inviting a lawsuit for slander," Ramses said. "Everyone involved would deny the accusation."

Margaret's lips moved, as if she were silently going down the list of persons involved. "Hmmm," she said. "Including you, Nefret?"

"You cannot possibly suppose otherwise," Nefret said coolly.

"No harm in asking, was there?" Margaret said.

Her bland smile was too much for Emerson. His inherent chivalry even under such extreme provocation protected Margaret from his wrath; instead he turned on his brother. "Only a poor excuse for a man cannot control his own wife," he hissed, and he would have said a good deal more, I expect, had I not interrupted with a loud "Good afternoon, Miss Minton. Come, Emerson."

The reminder was sufficient. Silent and subdued, Emerson allowed himself to be led away. "Honestly," I whispered. "You might as well have made a public announcement introducing your brother and his wife."

"No one except ourselves heard me," Emerson muttered. "And it was a—er—a generalization."

"A very rude and improper generalization," I said. "An insult to all womankind, especially *your* wife."

"Come now, Peabody," Emerson protested. "I didn't mean anything by it. I was only—"

"Striking out at him," I said, looking back at Sethos. "Well, I forgive you this time, Emerson. I must admit that Miss Minton is an exasperating woman, and I cannot say we accomplished anything this afternoon. Ah well, we have done our duty."

We were followed into the lobby by Kevin. "What was that all about?" he asked.

"None of your damned business," growled Emerson.

I poked him with my parasol. "Miss Minton asked us to tea, and we accepted, in the belief that she intended it as a friendly gesture. As it turned out, she was only hoping to gain information from us."

"You didn't tell her about your secret visit to the tomb?" Kevin asked, trotting to keep up with Emerson's long strides.

"As you observed, we parted acrimoniously," I replied.

"Carter is reopening the tomb tomorrow." Kevin offered this like a dog wagging its tail in the hope of reward.

Emerson stopped. "I know that. How do *you* know?"

"I have my sources." Kevin winked. "Will you be there, sir?"

"No," said Emerson. "Come along, Peabody."

When we reached the house the twins were waiting for us, brushed and scrubbed within an inch of their lives. Looking as if no naughty thought had ever entered her pretty head, Charla begged all our pardons for her outburst of temper. The picture the two made was quite charming: hand in hand, blue eyes and dark raised imploringly; black curls and golden locks mingling, so close did they stand. They had missed tea with the family, which was one of the worst punishments we could devise, so I decided no further action was necessary. Making David John suffer for his sister's bad manners was unfair, but he preferred it that way. As different as they were in appearance and behavior, they shared that strong bond one often finds between twins, and joined ranks when either was in trouble. They went off, still hand in hand, and I heard David John say, "If you like, I will read more to you from the fairy book, Charla, since you apologized so nicely." She did like, as her vehement response made evident. Perhaps David John's influence would be more effective than my lectures—if he could learn to be less patronizing.

At my insistence we all assumed proper attire for dinner with the Vandergelts. It is virtually impossible to force Emerson into formal evening garb, but he looked very handsome in the nice tweed suit I had selected (flecked with blue to match his eyes). The garments I had ordered, ostensibly for Ramses, had arrived, and Sethos was formally attired in a dinner jacket and black tie. I assumed he had done so in order to annoy Emerson. Nefret's frock glittered with gold and silver beads from neck to hem. Sennia studied it enviously. "I wish I could have a dress like that," she said.

Nefret gave her a hug. "Not until you are a little older. That frock becomes you very well."

It had, in my opinion, too many ruffles. Sennia favored ruffles. However, it was suitable for a young girl, and the pale pink set off her black hair and brown cheeks.

In honor of the newcomers, Cyrus and Katherine had gone to some effort; porcelain and crystal, flowers in silver vases graced the table. This was Sennia's first outing as a grown-up, and Bertie himself led her in to dinner. Spreading her skirts, she seated herself and surveyed the glittering rows of utensils with an air of great complacency.

"I know which fork to use," she said to Bertie, in what my old nurse referred to as a pig's whisper—the reference being, I supposed, to the pig's manners rather than its vocalization.

"Then you can show me," Bertie said. They were great friends, for she had nursed him during his postwar illness. Observing her smiles and flirtatious looks, I wondered if she had transferred her youthful affections to him. She had at one time been determined to marry Ramses when she grew up, but that had only been a childish fantasy, born of her great affection and gratitude. Now she was thirteen, the age at which a young person's fancy turns to thoughts of the opposite gender.

"And you can show me," said Jumana, across the table. She and Sennia both laughed heartily. They hadn't always got on well, but they were now united in their common dislike of Suzanne. The French girl had made the fatal error of treating Sennia as if she were six years old, asking her about her dollies and laughing when Sennia said she preferred ushebtis.

Nadji had made a better impression. He greeted Sennia as he did the rest of us, with a bow and a handshake, and then retreated to a corner as was his habit. Whenever I glanced in his direction I saw that he was listening and looking, and his fixed, amiable smile reminded me of that perceptive observation of Mr. Robert Burns: "A chiel's amang you takin' notes." I couldn't make him out. Was he as shy as he appeared, or was he hiding something? According to Cyrus, he was working with skill and efficiency. Even Emerson had been unable to find fault with him.

As might have been expected, conversation centered on the latest news about Tutankhamon's tomb. Everybody had a snippet of news or a surmise.

"He'll have to start letting people in," Cyrus said. "There have been a lot of complaints from local dignitaries."

"Including you?" Nefret asked.

Cyrus coughed self-consciously. "To tell the truth, I did write a nice letter of congratulation to Carter. I sort of expected a response, if not an invitation, but I haven't heard from him. Course he's been away . . ."

"Don't hold your breath," Sethos advised. "I fear you've been tarred with the same brush as the rest of us. The rest of Luxor and Cairo society, come to that. They say he's behaving as if the tomb is his and Carnarvon's personal property. A number of people have complained, and the Egyptian press is up in arms."

"He is under considerable stress," Ramses said. "You know from our own experience how maddening it is to have one's work interrupted by idle curiosity seekers."

"I believe it is more complex than that," I said. "Now, Emerson, don't grumble, I am not talking psychology, only plain common sense—based, I should add, on my profound study of human nature. After all these years of being scorned and patronized, Howard is suddenly in the catbird seat. It has gone to his head. I am not surprised. The people who jeered at his common background and mocked his manners are now suing humbly for his favors. Subconsciously—er—that is, I mean to say, without realizing it himself, Howard may even have resented our attempts to assist him."

"He's got nothing against me," Cyrus protested. "I never jeered at him and I'm no idle curiosity seeker."

"But you are a rival of Lord Carnarvon's in the collecting game," Sethos pointed out. "He was green with envy when you acquired the Tutankhamon statuette last year."

"That's no reason to keep me out of the tomb," Cyrus said stubbornly. "Doggone it, I'd give anything to get a look. I'm not after any of the artifacts, I just want a look."

Suzanne, on Bertie's other side, had sat in sullen silence while he and Sennia chatted and laughed. She had gone to great pains to get herself up in a silken gown that spelled money to my experienced eyes; her face was painted and her hair confined by a silver fillet. Being supplanted in Bertie's favor by a little girl of thirteen did not sit well with her.

"Perhaps I can help," she said unexpectedly.

She got everyone's attention. Incredulity was the common reaction. Jumana rolled her eyes and Emerson blurted out, *"You?"*

Suzanne smiled a little cat smile. "My grandfather—my mother's father—is a neighbor of Lord Carnarvon's. They are old friends. I had a wire from him last week, to say that he is coming out to spend Christmas with me. And see the tomb, of course."

Katherine was the first to recover from her surprise. "We would be happy to have him stay with us."

"Oh, no, no, he would never invite himself; I have taken rooms for him at the Luxor. He looks forward to meeting you all. I have written much about you, especially, Mr. and Mrs. Vandergelt, about your kindness to me."

"Who the dev— Who is your grandfather?" Emerson demanded, expressing in his blunt fashion a question some of us might have put more politely.

"Sir William Portmanteau. Perhaps you know him, sir?"

The question was addressed to Cyrus. Frowning thoughtfully, he said, "I had business dealings with him some years ago, before I retired. Railroads and coal, those were his interests. He hadn't been knighted then."

"His Majesty honored him in reward for his services to England during the war," Suzanne said proudly.

"That's right," said Cyrus. "Well, my dear, perhaps he will join us here for our Christmas celebration." He didn't want to ask, but he couldn't help himself. "And if he has any influence with Lord Carnarvon . . ."

"He would be delighted to exert it on your behalf," Suzanne said.

"I say," Bertie exclaimed. "That's kind of you, Miss Malraux."

"Please." She turned her wide-eyed gaze upon him. "I have asked you to call me by my first name."

Jumana and Sennia exchanged pointed glances.

Emerson seldom sulks (he prefers more direct methods of expressing his feelings). He would have resented Suzanne's offer to include him, but he was equally resentful at not being asked. Loudly declaring he had heard enough about bloo—blooming Tutankhamon, he began describing to David our work in the West Valley.

"Perhaps you can give Miss Malraux a hand with her paintings of the scenes in Ay's tomb," he said, with a malignant look at the young Frenchwoman. "She appears to be having some difficulties."

"It is difficult working under such conditions," David said, with a friendly smile at Suzanne.

"But there are few artists with your talent," Suzanne replied, lowering her eyes and blushing prettily. "Never could I claim to equal it, Mr. Todros. I would be humbly grateful for any advice."

"Tomorrow morning," said Emerson. "Six A.M."

When Emerson speaks, the gods obey, much less mere mortals. We were all up before dawn and ready to go at the hour Emerson had decreed. We were able to get out of the house without Sennia; wearied by her first excursion into society, followed by a long chat with Gargery, who wanted to hear all about it, she slept late. Fatima had declared her intention of beginning preparations for her holiday baking, so I hoped that would keep the children and Sennia occupied until we returned. I had plans for the day.

The only one missing from Cyrus's crew was Suzanne. "I told her she could meet her granddad's train," Cyrus explained.

"He arrives today?" I asked in surprise. "I wonder why she didn't mention before last night that he was coming."

"Didn't want to make us feel obliged to entertain him, I suppose," Cyrus said.

"Who gives a curse?" Emerson demanded. "We are wasting time. David, I want to show you the areas we have investigated. Perhaps you will spot something I missed."

He strode off, with the others following like ducklings after their mother.

I waited until the luncheon baskets had been opened before announcing my plans. I could tell they came as no surprise to Emerson. His protests were somewhat half-hearted.

"You needn't come," I said, selecting a cucumber sandwich. "But David hasn't even seen the famous tomb. By tomorrow the word of its being reopened will have spread and everyone in Luxor will be there."

"May I go, sir?" Jumana asked.

"Sure," said Cyrus. "I'd kind of like to have a look myself."

"Oh, go on, the lot of you," Emerson shouted. "You're no use any-how. Selim and I can manage quite well without you."

Selim, who had hoped to join us, looked crestfallen. I gave him a wink and a pat on the shoulder.

Ordinarily the tourists left the Valley around midday, returning to their hotels across the river or to the Cook's rest house near Deir el Bahri. I delayed until later in the afternoon in the hope of avoiding the crowds. We made quite a large party in ourselves, for in the end every-one, with the exception of Emerson, had declared their intention of ac-companying me, and he had grumpily given Selim permission. He rode with us as far as the end of the path from the West Valley and galloped away with his nose in the air. I suspected he would not go far.

Lounging near the entrance was Kevin O'Connell. "I expected you before this, ma'am," he said, removing his pith helmet.

"Go away, Kevin," I said automatically.

"Why?" He fell in step with me, nodding pleasantly at David, on my other side. "You are persona non grata in any case. Be nice, Mrs. E., and I will return the favor. Carter has most of the entrance cleared."

"Where is Miss Minton?"

"Hovering over the tomb," said Kevin, scowling. "She has tried twice to approach Carter, but she had no more success than I did. I must say, his manners leave a great deal to be desired."

Some persons find the Valley of the Kings stark and forbidding, its monochromatic buff cliffs unrelieved by greenery or rippling water. Yet it has a beauty of its own. Shaped by wind and weather, the walls of the narrow wadis have assumed fantastic shapes and the shadows exhibit subtle changes in color, from soft lavender to gray-blue, as the direction of the sun's rays changes. In my opinion it was not as impressive as it had been before Howard Carter and his successors tidied the place, smoothing the paths, bringing electric lights into the most popular tombs and erecting walls round their entrances. It had to be done, not only to make access easier for the tourists who provided income to the local people, but to prevent rainwater from rushing down the cliffs into the tombs. Rainstorms in Luxor are infrequent, but formidable; I had beheld several myself, and knew how damaging they could be. And yet, and yet . . . the sheer romance of clambering over fallen rubble, of creeping down the narrow bat-filled passages with only a flickering candle to light the way, of being among the first to behold a burial chamber littered with the broken remnants of the treasures its occupant had taken to the tomb—and the remnants of the occupant himself—a snapped-off arm, its fingers extended like claws, a face whose withered lids were half open, showing slits of white, seeming to blink in the wavering flame . . .

How fortunate I had been to experience such delights! My deep sigh made David look curiously at me. "All right, are you, Aunt Amelia?"

"I was remembering the old days. Did you know," I said dreamily, "that sometimes onions were inserted under the eyelids of the mummy to give a lifelike appearance?"

David's sympathetic imagination understood the seeming irrelevance. He laughed a little, and slipped my arm through his. "That must have been a wonderful sight."

The stairwell leading to the tomb entrance lay in a pit approximately twenty feet below ground level. More tidying, I thought sadly, observing the cleared space before the stairwell, the rough shed that had been constructed, the electric cable snaking its way across the ground. Several tents had been erected, presumably for the use of the guards; I doubted very much that Lord Carnarvon or Howard would settle for such rude accommodations. Just above and behind the pit lay the rectangular opening to the tomb of Ramses VI. A low retaining wall of unmortared stone surrounded the declivity.

David and I joined the rest of our party near the entrance to the tomb. Howard's activities had not gone unobserved, and a few of the more dedicated sightseers lingered, leaning over the wall. They might be said to brighten the drab hues of the Valley, though not in an appropriate manner; some of the ladies wore frocks of saffron and nile green and the gentlemen, gaudily striped flannels. Many held cameras. Mingling with them and squatting on the paths that led like a spiderweb over the hills of debris on either side were representatives of the local villagers wearing turbans and galabeeyahs. Margaret Minton, close to the wall, raised her arm and waved. I did not wave back.

Mr. Callender, trying to ignore the cameras that clicked every time he appeared, was directing a group of workmen who were filling baskets with the last of the rubble and carrying them away.

"So that's it," David said softly.

"Not very exciting."

"You know better than that," David said. "Can we get any closer?"

"Several of your distant cousins are among the guards," I said, with a meaningful smile.

His arrival had been noted, and when he approached one of the men the others gathered round, embracing and greeting him. Hearing their raised voices, Callender popped his head up and demanded to know why they had left their posts.

"Allow me to introduce my nephew by marriage, Mr. David Todros," I said, stepping forward. "You are no doubt familiar with his work. Where is Howard?"

"He has left for the day," Callender said. "And I am about to do so. Er—Todros. A journalist?"

"No, sir," David replied.

"An Egyptologist," I said, stressing the word. "And an artist of some standing. He was greeting some of his kinsmen, as you saw."

"Yes. I have heard of him. Related to your former reis, Abdullah, I believe." Having established David's status as a "native," he nodded brusquely and then called out to the spectators: "The Valley is closing. Everyone must leave."

"How rude," Nefret said indignantly. Callender gave her a harried look and set off along the path toward the entrance, moving quite briskly for a stout man. In the same carrying voice Nefret announced, "That order does not apply to us."

Once Callender was out of sight, everyone relaxed. The workers put down their tools and lit cigarettes, and Reis Girigar began chatting with David. Some of the spectators left; the guards extracted baksheesh from those who wanted to stay on; and Miss Minton sat down on the wall and scribbled in her notebook, ostentatiously ignoring both Kevin and Sethos. Except for Cyrus, who stood staring hungrily at the stone-cut steps, the others lost interest and wandered off. Jumana attached herself to Nadji and led him off in the opposite direction.

"I am having a severe attack of déjà vu," I said softly to Ramses. "There are too many people lurking, and the tomb is accessible again. Why hasn't Carter installed the gate?"

"It isn't a simple procedure," Ramses replied in equally soft tones. "There will have to be a framework, bolted into solid rock. All the same . . ."

He broke off, frowning at Kevin, who was eavesdropping shamelessly. "You anticipate trouble?" the latter asked eagerly.

"Go away, Kevin," I said.

Ramses strolled off along the path, his eyes moving from side to side. I hastened to catch him up. We had not gone far when the air was rent by a horrific burst of sound—not from behind us, near Tutankhamon's tomb, but farther ahead, at the entrance to one of the side wadis. A cloud of pale dust rose heavenward. Ramses broke into a run. "Stay back," he shouted.

Naturally I proceeded, at the quickest pace I could manage. When I reached him the dust was still settling. A ragged gap had been blown out of the path and the hillside next to it. Fallen stone littered the ground. Fallen stone and . . .

I looked away. "Who?" I gasped.

Ramses turned something over with his foot. It left a hideous smear on the dust. "Farhat ibn Simsah."

"Are you sure?"

"Yes. Don't look, Mother."

I tried not to, but there is a ghastly compulsion that draws the eyes to scenes of horror. Ramses interposed his person between me and the torn, bloody remains, and seized me as I swayed. I heard voices and running footsteps, heard Ramses call out to the others to stay away; then I was lifted into a pair of strong arms that could belong to only one individual.

"Oh, Emerson," I cried. "You came. I knew you would!"

"Curse it," said Emerson. Strong emotion robbed him of further speech, but I knew what he would have said had he been able, and the comfort of his embrace restored me.

"I am not harmed, Emerson. I am quite myself again. You can put me down."

"Not on your life," said Emerson, and bore me away.

## FROM MANUSCRIPT H

As Ramses had known she would, Nefret insisted on having a look at Farhat, or what remained of him. One look was enough to satisfy her physician's conscience that nothing could be done for the man. Ramses stood by while she inspected the ruined body, hating what she was doing but knowing he couldn't have prevented her.

"He must have been bending over the . . . whatever it was . . . when it exploded," she said, rising to her feet. "The blast caught him full in the chest and head. Dynamite?"

"I don't think so. We mustn't disturb anything before the police arrive." He took her arm. "Come away, sweetheart. Mother may need you."

Nefret's face was paler than usual, but she managed a smile. "Not Mother. She'll be swigging brandy and telling them all about it."

In the shadow of the western cliff the rest of their party was gathered round his mother. Seated on the wall by the entrance to the tomb of Ramses III, she was talking and gesticulating with the hand that held her flask of brandy. Jumana held Bertie tightly by the arm. Reassured as to his wife's well-being, Emerson had planted himself in the middle of the path and was holding the curious back with shouts and a few shoves.

"No one is to approach. The police have been sent for."

"Aziz?" Ramses asked his father.

"You don't suppose the British authorities would be concerned about the death of a native?" his father replied with heavy sarcasm.

"I would suppose Howard Carter might be concerned about this one."

Ramses's father spared him a narrow-eyed glance. "You are thinking along those lines, are you? Well, well, we will discuss it later. O'Connell, stay where you are."

One of Emerson's more moderate shoves sent Kevin staggering back. His hat fell off. Someone laughed, and O'Connell lost his temper. "You are interfering with the freedom of the press, Professor," he shouted.

"Quite right," said Margaret Minton, notebook in hand. It was she who had laughed. She slid neatly past Emerson, evaded Sethos's outstretched hand, and trotted toward the scene of the . . . accident? Sethos started after her, but stopped after a few steps and stood with arms folded, his expression indecipherable.

Kevin tried to pull away from Emerson, who held him off with one hand. "You let her pass," Kevin panted. "Blatant discrimination! Mrs. Emerson, I appeal to you!"

"Let him go, Emerson" was her calm reply. "As he will see, there is no news in this. Only the unfortunate death of a local fellah."

"Don't you want to have a look?" Ramses asked his uncle.

"Unlike my . . . unlike Miss Minton I do not revel in bloody corpses," said Sethos. "Amelia's description was quite enough for me. Is anyone watching the tomb? Most of the guards seem to be here."

Margaret came into view, a little green in the face but quite composed. "What was his name?" she demanded.

"What do you care?" Sethos replied. "He was only a native."

"What happened to him?" Margaret addressed the question to Ramses.

Sounds of retching reached them, and after a moment Kevin appeared. He was wiping his mouth on his sleeve, but his journalist's instincts were unaffected. "What happened to him?" he gurgled.

Emerson turned. "Obviously the unfortunate man came upon some explosive device and accidentally set it off. That's all there is to it. The police are on their way. Now get away from here, all of you."

Margaret stood her ground until Emerson advanced upon her. "You are interfering with the press, Professor," she exclaimed, backing away.

"Damn right," said Emerson. "Leave of your own accord or be carried away. I want everyone out of the Valley immediately."

His wife leaped to her feet. "Witnesses, Emerson. Suspects! We must interrogate all who were present."

"Now?" Emerson exclaimed. "See here, Peabody—"

"At least take all their names and addresses." She replaced the brandy flask and whipped out paper and pencil.

This comment cleared the scene more effectively than Emerson's shouts. Ramses felt certain she had expected this; as a "profound student of human nature," she knew most people prefer not to be involved with the police. Most of the spectators melted away. Cursing, Emerson dragged a few diehards out from their hiding places and pursued them along the path to the entrance. When everyone had left except their own party, he addressed Girigar. "Everything all right here?"

"Yes, Father of Curses." The reis was obviously shaken. "Is there danger to the tomb, do you think? Shall I send word to Carter Effendi?"

"There will be no danger if you and your men remain true to their duty," Emerson said sternly. "Yes, Carter should be notified. Send one of your men at once."

"I'll stay until Aziz gets here," Ramses said.

His father nodded. "Quite right. The rest of us may as well go. I prescribe stiff whiskeys all round, especially for you, Peabody."

"They will be welcome, though not necessary, my dear." She patted her forehead delicately with a folded handkerchief. "Should not the other ibn Simsah brothers be told of Farhat's demise?"

"I suspect they know already," Emerson said grimly. "Come along. Cyrus, Jumana, Bertie . . . Nefret?"

"I'm staying too." Nefret moved closer to Ramses. "Mr. Aziz may want to consult me."

"Ah," said her mother-in-law, giving her a thoughtful look. "Quite. À bientôt, then, my dears."

Left alone with his wife (except for Reis Girigar and a dozen soldiers), Ramses said, "You needn't stay to protect me, darling. Everything is under control."

"Like hell it is. Was that an accident?"

"I don't suppose he deliberately blew himself up," Ramses said.

"Here's a nice flat stretch. We may as well be comfortable; it will take Aziz a while to get here."

The nice flat stretch was just out of sight of the tomb and the guards. Ramses put his arm round his wife, who nestled into his embrace.

"Alone at last," she murmured. "We don't get many such chances."

"And in such romantic surroundings," Ramses said sardonically. "With a mutilated corpse nearby."

She turned her face toward him. In the dusk her hair shimmered silvery gold. " 'Every year another dead body,' as Abdullah used to say. I don't mean to sound callous, but one does become accustomed to it."

"I'm the luckiest man in the world," Ramses said.

Nefret laughed. "What brought that on?"

"I don't say it often enough. Not many women could adapt to the bizarre life this family leads—and seem even to enjoy it."

" 'Enjoy' isn't precisely the word. I think I might miss it, though, if it ended." Smiling, the contours of her face softened by shadows, she looked like the girl he had fallen in love with in the caves of the Holy Mountain. He tightened his grasp and she leaned against him.

She was right—too right. They had few moments of quiet, without the demands of children or parents. Someone was always around, or about to be. There never seemed to be time enough to tell her how much she meant to him. Their relationship had its ups and downs, but that only made it more precious. Nothing is perfect except the works of God. An old woodworker of his acquaintance had said that once; he always left a little flaw in each piece of furniture.

All at once Ramses came to a decision he had been putting off for weeks. He'd talk to Nefret about it—but not now, not when her warm weight pressed against his body and her soft breathing rose and fell. He was almost sorry when a hail from Girigar betokened the arrival of the police.

Aziz ran a tight ship. His men, immaculate in white uniforms, made the soldiers in their dusty, ill-fitting black look even shabbier. The area in front of Tutankhamon's tomb was brightly lit, a security measure Ramses could only approve. He shook hands with Aziz, whose bearded brown face held a certain suppressed satisfaction. The job of guarding the tomb had been given to the army, not to him. He was on the job now, and meant to display his superior efficiency.

Nefret and Aziz were well acquainted; she had assisted the police on a number of occasions. She had a high regard for him, and Ramses had always suspected Aziz's feelings for her were a trifle stronger than admiration. Always the gentleman, he bowed over her hand before getting down to business.

"Tell me what you heard and saw. The facts only, please."

Ramses had had time to organize his thoughts. When he had finished his brief account, Aziz nodded approvingly. "Now show me."

The cliffs of the narrow side wadi cut off light from the stars and rising moon. Illumined by the light of torches, the scene of death looked even worse, a kaleidoscope of grisly images.

After a quick, comprehensive survey, Aziz stroked his neatly trimmed beard and said, "I fear it will be difficult to take photographs. We will try, however."

Nefret let out a little exclamation of dismay. "I am sorry, Mr. Aziz. I ought to have done that earlier."

"Do not apologize, madam. No doubt you have made an examination of the remains?"

"Only a superficial examination. I didn't want to disturb the scene. He was beyond help, and there can be no question as to what killed him. The explosion struck him in the chest and face."

"So he was holding it or bending over it. Unusual, to say the least," Aziz said dryly. "These people know how to use dynamite. He wouldn't stand by after he had lit the fuse."

"It wasn't dynamite," Ramses said. He directed the beam of his torch to one side. A spark flared. "That's glass. Part of a small glass bottle. And there, and there . . . Scraps of a pipe."

"A pipe?" Aziz exclaimed. "A bomb? I have heard of such things . . ."

"A very primitive bomb," Ramses said. "And horribly easy to make. You start with a piece of iron piping with screw end-caps. Inside, there's a metal container filled with picric acid. You suspend a small glass bottle from one end of the pipe. It holds nitric acid and is closed with a loose plug of cotton wool. The device is completely harmless as long as the pipe is held upright; but when it is tipped, the nitric acid oozes through the cotton wool and mixes with the picric acid and . . ."

"And detonates it," Aziz finished. "How do you know of this device?"

He sounded suspicious, but then Aziz always did. "Explosives aren't one of my major interests," Ramses said dryly, "but I heard of it a few weeks ago from Thomas Russell, the Cairo Commandant of Police."

Aziz's tight lips relaxed. Thomas Russell Pasha was admired, if not liked, by every dedicated police officer in Egypt. It was no disgrace to him, Aziz, to learn from Russell.

"Where did Farhat hear of it?" Nefret asked. "Easy to make, you say, and the materials wouldn't be hard to come by, but how would a man like that, illiterate and uninformed, know how to put them together?"

"You underestimate the criminal mind, madam," Aziz said. "These villains communicate with one another, passing on information by word of mouth or by example, from Cairo to the remotest villages. Unlike his brothers, who are as cowardly as they are unscrupulous, Farhat was a hardened criminal. But not a very intelligent one. Either he did not heed the warning about how to handle the device, or in his arrogance he disregarded it. He is no loss," Aziz finished, with a ceremonial dusting of his hands.

"Except, perhaps, to his mother," Nefret said.

Aziz's stern face softened. "You are a mother, madam, and good of heart. Do not distress yourself. You may safely leave this to me."

It was a dismissal, however kindly meant. As they walked along the path toward the entrance of the Valley and their waiting horses, Ramses wondered why Aziz hadn't asked the obvious question. What had Farhat intended to do with his homemade bomb?

"So Carter never bothered to come round?" Emerson asked, handing Ramses a whiskey and soda.

"Not while we were there." Ramses shoved the Great Cat of Re aside and joined his wife on the settee. "He knew the tomb was safe. Girigar and the others are on the job and Aziz is there with several of his men."

"I know, my dear Emerson," I said, in response to Emerson's wordless grumbles. "You would have marched up and down before the tomb all night. However, there is no reason to suppose that Farhat meant to use his handy little bomb in an assault on the tomb. A most useful device, I must say. Amazingly easy to construct . . ."

"Don't get any ideas, Peabody." Emerson's grumbles took on speech.

"Why on earth would I want to make a bomb, Emerson?"

"God only knows," said Emerson with feeling.

The Vandergelt gang, as Cyrus had taken to calling it, had declined my invitation to tea. Even Jumana had appeared upset, and I myself was in no proper state of mind to entertain. We got the children off to bed and persuaded Sennia to spend the evening with Gargery, so that by the time Ramses and Nefret arrived we were able to talk freely.

"What did he mean to do with it?" asked Sethos.

"Who?" Emerson roused himself from a train of thought which, to judge by his expression, had aroused certain forebodings.

Slumped in an armchair with his legs stretched out and his hands folded on his waist, Sethos said, "Farhat. What was he intending to blow up?"

I had revised my initial theory after hearing Ramses's description of the bomb. "You, perhaps," I said. "That sort of device is more characteristic of revolutionaries than tomb robbers."

Sethos let out a snort of derision, and Ramses said, "Farhat was no revolutionary, nor, in my opinion, was he likely to have been hired by such persons. However, I think someone other than Farhat constructed that bomb."

"Sir Malcolm was in the Valley today," I said. "I saw him looking on. He has acquired a new dragoman. The other fellow must have had enough of him."

"He's always in the Valley," said Emerson. "You only want to make him guilty of something, Peabody. What good would it do him to have a bomb tossed into the entrance of Tutankhamon's tomb?"

"It might risk damage to the antiquities," I admitted.

"Or block the entrance," Ramses said. "I agree with Mother's original suggestion. This smacks of politics, not theft."

"Dinner is served," said Fatima, in the doorway.

As we filed in, she plucked at my sleeve. "Is he in danger, Sitt? Was the bomb meant for him?"

"We don't know, Fatima. We must trust to God."

Her worried face brightened. "Yes, Sitt, it is true. Allah would not let harm come to such a good man. I have placed charms in his room."

Sethos may have overheard the exchange. He was an accomplished eavesdropper. Fatima served the soup course, and he said, almost casually, "I've been having second thoughts about the other business. Has it occurred to any of you that the mad pursuit and furious attacks don't really amount to much? No one has been killed or seriously injured, except for the old holy man, whose death might not have been intended. We agree, do we not, that Farhat's—er—accident had nothing to do with us?"

He had used almost the same words I had used when discussing the business with Ramses earlier—with Sethos as the suspect. "Then what was the point of it all?" I asked.

Sethos finished his soup before replying. "I don't know. But it may be that our fears of violence were groundless. Take the cases one by one. Ramses and Emerson were never in serious danger; the fire was easily extinguished and there were other means of egress. The old man might have passed away from sheer terror while being searched. Nadji was left relatively unharmed after they realized he wasn't me, and Gargery was delivered unscathed to the station in time to catch the train."

I didn't want to worry Fatima—she seemed to be more concerned about him than about the rest of us!—but I was curious to see what other facile explanations he could come up with. "You were shot at and wounded," I pointed out. "And someone tried to push you under a train."

"Oh, that was a long time ago. An initial burst of enthusiasm, let us say. The point is that no one else has been threatened, and I don't believe they will be. Certainly not the children. Anyone who knows your lot knows you would tear the Middle East apart if either was harmed."

He looked round the table, awaiting an objection. None was offered. Oh, well done, I thought. He *is* good at this sort of thing. Even Ramses looked impressed by the argument; Nefret's blue eyes smiled, and David nodded slowly, as if in agreeement.

"So," said Sethos breezily, "the logical conclusion is that our 'friends' know we haven't deciphered the message, since we would have acted upon it. They have decided, correctly, that we can't decipher it or we would have done so by now."

"You aren't suggesting that we relax our guard, are you?" Emerson asked.

"Not at all. All I'm suggesting is that we avoid stirring up trouble, and hope they will do the same. What's this? Ah, Maaman's famous stuffed lamb. Thank you, Fatima. I trust your concerns are relieved."

"Oh, yes. So long as you wear the charm."

"Wear? Charm?" Ramses asked.

I had not observed the thin silk cord round Sethos's neck. Feeling all eyes upon him, he fished the little object out from under his shirt. It was a silver hegab, of the sort usually worn by women, cylindrical in shape and containing a small scroll with a written protective charm or religious verse.

"Very nice," I said. Emerson chewed vigorously on his lower lip, repressing the rude comment that would have hurt Fatima's feelings; and David said gently, "Yes, Fatima. What about us, though?"

"You are not in danger," said Fatima with perfect composure, and finished serving the stuffed lamb.

It was very good, but my appetite was not at its best. Was Sethos so complacent that he failed to realize his reasoning pointed the finger of guilt straight at him? Every point he had made could be applied to him. He might even have shot himself. As he had once said to me, he was violently averse to pain, but the wound was not serious in itself. I could visualize him, eyes screwed shut and hand shaking, as he aimed and squeezed the trigger.

It had been a while since I dreamed of Abdullah; when I saw him coming toward me from the Valley of the Kings, looking from side to side as if enjoying the view, I was sufficiently vexed to say something silly.

"Where have you been?"

"Here," said Abdullah, stroking his silky black beard.

It was not such a bad place to spend eternity. Bleak as a lunar landscape, the rocky plateau stretched out behind him, but the wind blew fresh from the river and the valley below lay unrolled like a woven carpet—silvery sand bordered by emerald-green fields and sparkling water, patterned with little villages and the tumbled stones of the ruined temples along the cultivation. We always met there, where we had so often stood together in life.

"Hmph," I said.

Abdullah chuckled. "As Emerson would say. Have you ever wondered, Sitt, why I come to you and not to him, who was as close as a brother?"

"No."

There was no need to say more. We stood in silence for a moment, looking into each other's eyes.

"I didn't mean to reproach you," I said. "But I am in desperate need of advice. We have had our share of trouble, heaven knows, but never have I been in such a state of confusion. I don't know whom to trust or what to do."

"You want ME to tell YOU what to do?" Abdullah asked in exaggerated astonishment.

The moment had passed. It was just as well; such spiritual intimacy cannot be sustained.

I sat down on the ground and tucked my feet under me, hoping I would be able to rise without awkwardness. I didn't want any more pointed remarks about my age and infirmities from Abdullah.

"I will tell you, then," said Abdullah, dropping easily to a sitting position near me. "Celebrate your Christmas and make the little ones happy. But do not give Charla a bow and arrow."

"As if I would. But—"

"Bring them to visit my tomb on Issa's Day. They may each leave an offering," said Abdullah smugly. "A portrait of me by the little artist, a silver bangle from Charla—she is becoming too fond of possessions— and from Sennia, one of the pretty bows she wears in her hair. And money for the poor, in my name."

I looked at him in surprised disapproval. "Your sainthood has gone to your head, Abdullah. Or are you trying to get me off the track?"

"It is important to please the little ones, Sitt, and also to teach them charity and love. The Holy Koran and your own Holy Book tell us that we must share with those who have not our good fortune."

He looked so sanctimonious, lips pursed and eyes raised, that I was tempted to laugh. He had been a worldly man, following the precepts of his faith but not allowing them—how shall I put it—to interfere with his enjoyment of life. Perhaps becoming a saint had enlightened him.

"That is very true, Abdullah, and I will see that your wishes are carried out. Now what about some practical advice?"

"You are meddling in matters that do not concern you, Sitt. Leave them be."

"That has a familiar ring," I said dryly. "Perhaps you would care to be more specific. What matters should concern me?"

"Two matters only. The happiness of the little ones and the tomb of the pharaoh."

"I have taken steps to guard the children."

"That is not what I mean. No one threatens the children. No man in Egypt would dare touch them for fear of the wrath of the Father of Curses."

"That is what Selim said."

"Selim is right—for once," said Selim's father. "Make them happy and guard the tomb."

He got to his feet in a single flowing motion. Seeing that he was about to walk away in his usual abrupt fashion, I scrambled up.

"Wait! The tomb of Tutankhamon is not ours to guard, Abdullah. It is Lord Carnarvon's."

Abdullah turned in a whirl of white skirts. His face was set in a scowl and he spoke with unusual vehemence. "It is not his. It is not yours. It belongs to Egypt and to the world. Sitt, you are not usually so slow to understand. Guard the tomb, not only from petty thieves like the ibn Simsahs but from the greedy men who would seize its treasures for themselves."

# CHAPTER EIGHT

"HE WAS REFERRING TO CARTER AND CARNARVON," I EXPLAINED.

I had described my dream of Abdullah to the assembled family at breakfast. I had kept the dreams secret at first, but by now everyone, including every villager on the West Bank, knew about them, and expressions of doubt or derision no longer bothered me. Not that I received many of either. The Gurnawis believed firmly in Abdullah's status as a saint. Ramses and Nefret were neutral—open-minded, I should say. Emerson had learned to confine his doubts to raised eyebrows and inarticulate grumbles. For the most part.

"Not only them," Ramses said, accepting a bowl of porridge from Fatima. "The Metropolitan Museum will get its share, as such institutions have done in the past."

Nefret chuckled. "Who would have supposed dear old Abdullah would have nationalist sympathies?"

"Strangely similar to those held by Peabody," said Emerson.

"Make up your mind, my dear," I said pleasantly. "Either my visions of Abdullah are true or they are the product of my unconscious mind."

"I don't believe in the unconscious mind," Emerson grumbled.

"There you are, then," I said.

"We have almost finished the middle of bacon," said Fatima. "And I will use the rest of the raisins with my holiday baking. Will you order more, Sitt?"

"Make a list," I said. "I will send it off to Cairo."

Her effort to change the subject did not succeed. Smarting under my irrefutable riposte, Emerson inquired sarcastically, "Why not order direct from Fortnum and Mason? That is where Carnarvon gets his supplies. Tinned salmon and tongue and curried guinea fowl, good Gad."

"The expense is unwarranted, Emerson," I replied. "To return, if I may, to my conversation with Abdullah. His other recommendation was that we make this a joyous season for the children. We have only a week left in which to prepare, and there is a good deal to do. I must start David John on the portrait. Abdullah specifically requested that."

"How can he paint a portrait of a man he never met?" Emerson demanded.

"We have photographs," I said patiently. "And David will help him. Won't you, David?"

"Of course. He's becoming quite a talented little artist."

We had almost finished when Sennia came running in. I observed that she was wearing one of her "working suits," which resembled those of mine and Nefret's, except that it had a divided skirt instead of trousers.

"Why didn't you wake me?" she demanded, slipping into the chair Ramses held for her. "I am going with you today."

"A growing girl needs her sleep," I replied. "Aren't you going to help Fatima decorate the house and bake the Christmas cake?"

"The children can do that," said Miss Sennia loftily. "I want to see the tomb of Tutankhamon."

"We aren't going there," said Emerson—but he said it less emphatically than usual. We had taken Sennia into our home when she was barely two years of age, and she had found a permanent place in Emerson's heart.

"Perhaps we ought, Father," Nefret said. She finished a piece of toast and reached for another. "I expected to hear from Mr. Aziz this morning, but there has been no message."

"He is a man of great delicacy," I said. "No doubt he is waiting for you to offer your services."

"What can she do?" Emerson demanded. "There was nothing left of the fellow except pieces of . . . er . . ."

"He was blown to bits," Sennia said, tucking into her porridge with hearty appetite.

"Good Gad," Emerson cried. "Who told you that? Was it you, Fatima? I trust you have not shared that delightful description with the twins."

"Goodness, but you are in a combative mood this morning, Emerson," I said. "Fatima would never do such a thing. I expect it was Kareem or one of the others."

"Thank you, Sitt Hakim," said Fatima, giving Emerson a reproachful look. With great dignity she swept from the room—taking the coffeepot with her.

"She always takes the coffeepot when she is annoyed with me," Emerson muttered, looking sadly at his empty cup.

Fatima was persuaded to accept his apology and refill his cup. Emerson was then persuaded to accept my suggestion that we ought to return to the East Valley.

"Sennia deserves a look," he admitted. "Anyhow, I had better make certain Carter installs that gate of his today. Fellow can't be trusted."

This was unfair to Howard, but I did not say so. I was becoming less inclined to be fair to him, considering his treatment of us.

David declined to accompany us, explaining that he had promised Cyrus he would make a few sketches in Ay's tomb. "Mlle. Malraux is on leave for a few days, entertaining her grandfather, you see. It would not be . . . that is, I would rather not . . ."

"Suggest that her work was not good enough," I finished, giving him an affectionate pat on the shoulder. "It is like you, David, to be so sensitive to her feelings."

"Bah," said Emerson, pushing his chair back. "The girl is barely competent. I cannot imagine why you took her on, Peabody."

"It was you who took her on, Emerson."

"At your recommendation."

He probably hadn't even bothered to look at her portfolio. All the same, the responsibility was mine, so I felt obliged to defend myself. "It is difficult to find outstanding artists, Emerson. Howard and the Davies, and David, are becoming supplanted by photographers. Before long there will be color photography, and then—"

"But we haven't it yet," said Emerson. "And it will never replace the trained eyes of a human observer like David. Speaking of that, my boy, if you could stay on for a few—"

Knowing what he was about to ask, and determined to prevent him from asking it, I inquired of my brother-in-law, "What about you?"

Sethos leaned back in his chair with a sigh of repletion. "I am going to help Fatima mix the Christmas cake."

We weren't the only ones who found it impossible to stay away from Tutankhamon's tomb. After weeks of being inaccessible, it was now re-opened, and soon the removal of the antiquities would begin. Hopeful spectators, cameras at the ready, lined the wall. They expected to see golden treasures being carried out and down the path to the tomb of Seti II, which had been selected to serve as a storage room and conservation laboratory. They were doomed to disappointment, at least for a few days. If Howard followed the proper methodology, the objects would have to be photographed in situ and a detailed sketch of their locations made. The jumble of objects in the first room resembled a game of spillikin; they would have to be cautiously disentangled, piece by piece, and some were in fragile condition. The slightest touch could damage them.

My heart went out to my dear Emerson, who stood watching the activity round the tomb with a look of purest agony.

"He'll need to devise a system of recording," he said, as if to himself. "Every scrap, every object, numbered, sketched, photographed, and listed. He'll muck it up, Peabody, I know he will."

"Not with you looking over his shoulder," I said, taking his arm and squeezing it.

"If he had an ounce of sense he would consult Father," Nefret said indignantly.

"He has had the sense to acquire the best of assistants," Ramses said, adding, with a wry smile, "ourselves excepted. Hall and Hauser are excellent draftsmen, and they say Mr. Lucas has offered his services."

"I wonder if Mr. Lucas knows about paraffin wax," I mused.

"Considering that he is the head of the government's chemical department, and has had considerable experience in dealing with fragile antiquities, I expect he does," Ramses said. "But you will of course mention it to him."

"Naturally," I said.

"Callender has the steel gate up," Ramses said, in a further attempt to console Emerson, who replied with a growl.

"I don't see Howard," I remarked. "Didn't he come today?"

"There he is," Nefret said, pointing. "He must have been examining the scene of the . . . accident."

His face set in a frown, Howard approached us, pushing past various persons who tried to address him. I fully expected he would ignore us as well; instead he stopped, and after a moment removed his hat.

"I understand you were present last evening when the incident occurred," he said, after the slightest of nods.

"That is right," I said.

"One of the ibn Simsahs, I am told?"

"That is right."

"And this man is here at your invitation?" He gestured at Mr. Aziz, who had followed him at a little distance.

"He is here because a violent death occurred and he is chief inspector of the Luxor police," I said, poking my husband to keep him quiet.

"Yes, quite. Well, the body has been removed, and I see no reason for him to remain. He refuses to obey my orders," Howard went on, with a hard stare at Aziz. "Perhaps he will listen to you."

"Confound it, Carter, you have not the authority to give him orders," Emerson burst out. "If you would only employ a little tact—"

I poked Emerson harder, and he broke off with a pained grunt. He was in the right, but for Emerson to lecture someone else about tact was, to say the least, inappropriate.

"We will speak to the inspector," I said. "Are you sure you don't want some of his men to remain on guard?"

"No," said Howard shortly. Grudgingly he added, "Er—thank you."

"Mr. Carter," said a too-familiar voice. "A question, if I may?"

Howard made a growling sound reminiscent of Emerson at his best, and trotted down the slope into the pit. I turned to Kevin O'Connell.

"Put your hat on," I said. "Your nose is peeling. No luck?"

"Not for meself nor for any of me kind," said the irrepressible O'Connell in his best—or worst—brogue. He sighed and rubbed his itching nose. "Nor would the worthy officer of the law tell me anything of interest. I'll just have to go for the curse."

"What on earth are you talking about?" I demanded, observing that Ramses and Nefret were conversing with Aziz. The inspector's face was a trifle flushed and he was gesticulating emphatically.

"Oh, 'twill make a pretty tale," O'Connell crooned. "First the demise of Carter's golden bird, at the hands—er—jaws—of a royal cobra; now the mysterious death of a native—his name doesn't matter—on the day the tomb is reopened and the pharaoh's treasures are about to be removed from his last resting place by the impious hands of foreign infidels."

I waited for him to go on, but after one look at Emerson's darkening countenance and Sennia's round black eyes he decided not to mention specific curses against specific persons. "A pack of nonsense," I said.

"That is what such stories are, Mrs. E. Meaningless facts and a great deal of imagination. I ought to know, I've written several of them."

"I like stories about curses," said Sennia, looking very businesslike in her neat coat and skirt. "But they *are* nonsense, Mr. O'Connell."

"Go away, Kevin," I said.

Naturally Kevin did nothing of the sort. Remaining at a safe distance from Emerson, he followed us to the spot where Aziz and my children were chatting.

"Were you here all night?" I asked, observing that Aziz's cheeks were dark with stubble. Like most Moslems he was bearded, but he was always meticulous about shaving the areas that weren't part of the beard.

"As was my duty, madam. Mr. Carter has informed me that I and my men are no longer wanted."

"Nor am I, it seems," Nefret said pleasantly. "Mr. Aziz has removed poor Farhat's remains to the zabtiyeh, and he believes there is no need for an additional examination."

"The cause of death is obvious even to an ignorant native like myself," said Aziz. Regretting his snappish tone, he inclined his head to Nefret in tacit apology. "He is an ugly sight, even to such an experienced physician as yourself."

"Then he will be buried today?" I asked. "I wonder if we ought to attend the obsequies."

Emerson growled, Ramses raised his eyebrows, and even Aziz's controlled countenance expressed astonishment.

"Perhaps not," I said.

"Attendance will not be large," said Aziz, with a touch of irony. "He was greatly disliked, for he brought shame on his family. I myself will be present in case his rascally brothers are there. Thus far I have not been able to lay my hands on them."

"You think they were involved in his death?" Ramses asked.

"They were always involved with Farhat's evil deeds. I want to question them. Now if you will excuse me, I must remove my unwanted presence."

He summoned his men with a brusque command and led them away.

"Dear me," I said. "Howard does seem to be intent on offending everyone he can. Emerson, why don't you show Sennia the tomb and tell her what is going on?"

Make no mistake about it, dear Reader; children are fascinated by horrid events and gruesome sights. I have never met a child who did not delight in mummies. However, in my opinion, little Miss Sennia had heard enough of horrors; I had no intention of allowing her to view what might be left of Farhat. Emerson indicated his agreement with my opinion and took Sennia back to the tomb. I proceeded, as had been my intention, toward the scene of the . . . accident.

After all, there was not much to see. Aziz had done a thorough job of clearing away the mess. Every scrap had been removed, including the broken fragments of glass. Only darkened bloodstains remained.

"The blast was what killed him," I said to Nefret. "If he had been dead before it went off, there wouldn't be so much blood."

"Not if he had died only moments before," Nefret argued. "Struck down by a mortal wound."

"I yield to your medical expertise, of course," I said. "But on logical grounds such a scenario is most unlikely. We would have heard the sound of a shot or a struggle. And if I understand how the infernal device works, it would explode immediately after one sort of acid mixed with the other."

I looked questioningly at Ramses, who pondered the question and then said, "It would take a few seconds for the nitric acid to penetrate the cotton wool. That would begin as soon as the pipe was laid flat. I doubt that a killer would risk its being dropped."

"Not to mention the absence of motive for a murderous attack," I said. "At least I can't think of one."

"Do I detect a certain note of regret?" Ramses asked gravely.

It was just one of his little jokes. "I would prefer a nice simple murder to our present state of confusion," I replied, only half in jest.

I had forgotten about Kevin, who had the trained journalist's ability to creep up on a victim unobserved. Reminded of his presence by a faint scratching sound, I turned to see him scribbling away in his beastly notebook.

"You may not quote me, Kevin," I said sternly.

"If you say so, Mrs. E."

(I should add, in justice to Kevin, that he did not. When his story appeared, it said, "Mrs. Emerson is known to prefer murder to other forms of crime. She is also known to be an expert on ancient Egyptian curses." My solicitor has informed me that no action can be taken.)

## FROM MANUSCRIPT H

"I am becoming bored watching Mr. Carter swanking about," Nefret declared. "Why do we give him the satisfaction of snubbing us?"

Ramses was in full agreement, though he understood better than most the difficulties Carter faced. It had taken them more than a year to clear the tomb of Tetisheri, and that had been only a single room. Carter had at least four chambers to contend with, each jammed full of irreplaceable, delicate objects—including, perhaps, the mummy of the king. The eyes of the world, not to mention those of Emerson, would be fixed upon him, ready to criticize every move. He would also be harassed by visitors, journalists, and dignitaries, some of them too important to be turned away. Emerson had dealt with these infuriating interruptions— which also threatened the safety of the antiquities—by refusing to permit entry to anyone. Carter couldn't do that. He had to keep on good terms with his patron, and Carnarvon would want to show off "his" discovery.

Though he sympathized with his father's yearning to be in charge of the most challenging task any Egyptologist had faced, Ramses felt certain that Carter could be depended upon to do a good job. He was a responsible excavator, and he had assembled a team of unquestioned experts. Emerson and his family had been deliberately passed over; there was nothing they could do. Watching the busy bustle of men coming in and out of the tomb, Ramses felt a stab of anger—on his father's behalf, he told himself.

"We may as well go," he said to Nefret.

Sennia was easily drawn away. "There is nothing exciting happening," she complained. "And I'm hungry."

"I fear I neglected to bring a picnic basket," his mother said, fanning herself with a folded paper.

Neglected, my foot, Ramses thought. She wouldn't have overlooked that if she had intended to spend the whole day.

As they headed for the donkey park, they met another member of the staff of the Metropolitan Museum—Harry Burton, a slender, handsome man who was unquestionably the best archaeological photographer in Egypt. Burton had worked with them before, but Emerson, anticipating another rebuff, would have passed him with no more than a nod if Burton hadn't stopped, whipped off his hat, and extended his hand.

"You couldn't keep away either, I see," he said with a friendly smile. "I am not supposed to begin work until tomorrow, but I couldn't resist having a look."

"You have quite a job ahead of you," Emerson said.

"From what we have heard," his wife added smoothly.

"I look forward to it. I plan to take a few moving pictures and perhaps try some of the new color films."

"Fascinating," said Nefret.

Her attempt at enthusiasm didn't deceive Burton. The general air of reserve was palpable. Looking from one of them to the other, he said, "I hope I may be favored by an invitation to tea one day."

"Haven't you been warned to stay away from us?" Emerson demanded.

As was so often the case, Emerson's bluntness cut through the discomfort like a blast of fresh air. Burton's formal manners dissolved in a grin. "Carter did mention that Carnarvon had taken it into his head to bear a grudge of some sort. His lordship can be—er—unreasonable at times."

"If you are willing to risk his displeasure, you are always welcome," Ramses's mother said, thawing.

"It is no risk, Mrs. Emerson. Finding another photographer would take some time, and he cannot begin clearing the outer chamber until photographs have been taken of all the objects in situ."

"He couldn't find another one of your caliber," Nefret said sincerely. "I've never forgotten what you did in that cramped chamber of the God's Wives."

Burton placed his hand over his heart and bowed. "In any case, I do not allow Lord Carnarvon or Howard Carter to manage my social affairs. Vulgar sort of fellow, Carter," he added, wrinkling his aristocratic nose. "Well, I mustn't detain you. I hope to see you again soon. I trust there will be plum cake for tea?"

He winked at Sennia, who assured him that she would make certain there was, and strolled off along the path.

"What a nice man," Sennia said.

"Not such a bad chap," Emerson agreed. "But Winlock said much the same thing, and we haven't seen hide nor hair of him."

"We haven't seen hide nor hair of Margaret Minton today either," said his wife. "That isn't like her. I do hope she hasn't run into trouble."

"It's more likely she is in pursuit of another story," Nefret said. "Which is not a reassuring thought."

Sethos hadn't come to the Valley either. Perhaps, Ramses thought, he was doing his uncle an injustice by wondering whether he had really spent the morning baking cakes.

The enticing smell of sugar and spices wafted to our nostrils as we approached the house. For once the children did not come running to meet us. Everyone was in the kitchen with Fatima; the heat and the noise level were both outrageously high. Someone—I thought I knew who—had let the dog in, and Fatima was smacking it with a large wooden spoon. Amira cowered, but the way she kept licking her chops did not indicate genuine repentance.

Though Fatima did not share our faith, this was her favorite time of year. The Lord Issa was a revered prophet, after all, and Fatima loved making other people happy. She was the admitted queen of the oven, and Maaman gave way to her with good grace.

"Good Gad," said Emerson. "What an uproar! Having a happy time, are you, my dears?"

Charla embraced him round the waist, leaving floury handprints on his shirt. "You must stir the Christmas cake," she shouted. "For good luck."

"I have already stirred it," said Sethos, looking as if butter wouldn't melt in his mouth. Gargery was sitting next to him at the table, stoning raisins.

There was a good deal of flour on the floor, the table, and the dog; but everyone seemed to be having a jolly time, to say nothing of the dog. Even Fatima laughed as I escorted Amira out of the room.

"She ate all the biscuits I had cooling on the table. She burned her tongue, I think."

We all had the obligatory stir of the cake, including David, who had returned from the West Valley and come to see what was going on.

"I trust there is something for luncheon," said Emerson, licking the spoon he had dipped into the batter.

"Salads," said Maaman. "I have been helping Fatima."

"I will serve them," said Kareem eagerly.

I expected Gargery to offer, but either he and Fatima had come to an understanding or he was enjoying the pandemonium. The children always perked him up; he was chuckling like a thin beardless Father Christmas.

Fatima declined Kareem in favor of one of her sous-chefs, a sturdy young woman named Badra, and shooed us out of the kitchen.

Her pleasure was infectious. While we waited on the veranda for luncheon to be served, every face wore a smile and Emerson did not refer, even in passing, to the confounded tomb.

"It is time we turned our attention to celebrating the blessed season," he declared, with a provocative look at me. "What do you say, Peabody?"

Blessed season indeed, I thought. Emerson considered Christmas a survival of pagan celebrations of the midwinter solstice. He was something of a pagan himself. At my request he had not expressed his opinions to the children, and since they were present I did not allow him to provoke me.

"As you have observed, Emerson, those preparations are underway," I replied.

"We need a tree," said Emerson.

"And presents," Charla offered.

"Perhaps we should go to Luxor and do some shopping," said Emerson, with the air of a man who had just made a major discovery.

A general cry of approval greeted the idea. Even Sennia forgot her dignity and clapped her hands.

Emerson's good humor was only slightly dimmed when Gargery insisted on coming with us. The old fellow had informed me that he had brought gifts with him; however, it was his duty to watch over Miss Sennia, particularly in view of what had happened to him in Cairo. "She is a defenseless child, sir and madam," he said.

"And you think you can protect her?" Emerson demanded. "If you are so keen on your duty, why did you let her go to the Valley without you?"

"That was an entirely different situation, sir," said Gargery, squaring his narrow shoulders.

"Oh, bah," said Emerson. "Very well, very well." After Gargery had gone off, smirking, he added, "We'll have to keep a close eye on him."

Despite Emerson's forebodings (which he would have described as "simple common sense, Peabody") we had no difficulty keeping track of Gargery. Exhilarated and rejuvenated, he kept pace with Sennia, who never left his side. The rest of us divided forces, but there were enough of us to ride herd on the twins and watch over one another. We agreed to meet at the Winter Palace for tea, and I went off with the group that included Charla, Ramses, and David.

Charla appeared uncharacteristically subdued. Clutching her little purse, she examined the wares on sale in the shops along the corniche without interest. "I wanted to get a book for David John," she whispered. "But there is nothing he hasn't read."

Laughing, I gave her a little hug. "He isn't here. You need not whisper."

"We brought a number of books for him," David said. "And I expect there are more in that parcel your other grandparents sent."

"But they are not from me," Charla said, unconsoled. "And I don't have enough money to buy nice presents for Grandpapa and Mama and Sennia and Selim and Fatima and Kareem and—"

"Perhaps you have too many friends," I suggested.

Charla was not amused. Shaking her curly head, she put me in my place. "You keep saying a person cannot have too many friends, Grandmama."

"That is true." I regretted my little joke, for I knew her distress was genuine. For all her faults she was a loving little soul.

"Your friends don't care about expensive presents," Ramses said gently. "Why don't you write a nice letter to each of them telling them that you love them?"

"What an excellent idea," I said. It would keep her occupied for hours.

"I can't draw pictures or write very well," Charla murmured. "I am not as clever as David John."

I met Ramses's eyes and saw in them the same sense of remorse that had seized me. Why hadn't I realized that our constant scoldings (though often deserved) of Charla and our praise of David John had made his sister feel less loved than he? As a student of psychology I should have known her tantrums might be caused in part by frustration and resentment.

"Yes, you are," I said firmly. "You have different talents, but yours are as worthy as his."

Ramses echoed this statement, but without visible effect on his disconsolate daughter.

"I'll tell you what," David said. "Supposing you and I put our heads together and think of something. I understand you are very nimble with a pair of scissors. Perhaps your grandmama has some old magazines she can spare. We will cut out pretty pictures and make little books for everyone."

"We will all help," I said, with a grateful look at David.

"Not too much," said Charla, her face brightening. "Or it won't be my present."

With Charla's enthusiastic assistance we acquired the materials for the little books—colored paper and crayons and bright ribbons to tie the pages together—and made a quick call on my friend Marjorie Fisher to see if she had any old magazines to spare. She gave us several and promised to collect more from the ladies of Luxor. Her reward was a huge hug from Charla, which she returned with interest.

By the time we reached the Winter Palace, Charla was her old self, skipping along with her hand in that of her father and speculating loudly about the variety of sweets that might be available. David and I followed them, carrying Charla's purchases so that no one would suspect they belonged to her. (Thanks to private negotiations with the shopkeepers, the meager contents of her little purse had proved adequate.)

"Thank you, David," I said in a low voice. "I am ashamed I haven't taken more pains to commend Charla. David John gets most of the compliments."

"I am an expert at walking the tightrope between competitive children," David said with a laugh. "It's more demanding even than excavation."

The others had not yet arrived, so we commandeered a table on the terrace and settled down to wait for them. Luxor was at its most festive, since the hotels catering to foreign visitors put up Christmas decorations, and the Coptic shopkeepers had taken up the custom of celebrating the season with crèches and candles and fairly dreadful holy statues. It is amazing how, once an idea catches on, everyone tries to emulate and outdo his neighbors, in quantity if not quality.

I always enjoy watching people, particularly when they are unaware of being observed. The couple standing on the steps below, she in a fashionable flannel suit and he in the best of Bond Street tailoring, both extremely red in the face, appeared to be arguing. Was their marriage at risk, or were they only temporarily out of sorts after a long day in the sun and dust? The dignified bearded Egyptian enveloped in fine robes and crowned with a green turban was laughing and talking with the woman in black who trotted along beside and a little behind him. Carriages drawn by smartly trotting horses passed; the drivers were not using their whips, though some of the passengers shouted to them to do so. Our efforts on behalf of animal welfare had had some positive results. As one driver had remarked to me, "One does not know when the Father of Curses or the Sitt Hakim may be watching."

After a while I excused myself and entered the hotel. When I inquired at the desk for Miss Minton, the clerk told me she had left early that morning and had not yet returned. No, she had not said where she was going or when she would be back.

"Do you wish to leave a message for the lady, Mrs. Emerson?" he asked.

"No, thank you." I presented the clerk with a substantial baksheesh. "I would like to be informed when she does return. And—er—you need not mention it to the lady."

When I returned, the rest of our party had arrived. After a little bustle arranging tables and chairs, we ordered tea and then everyone began talking, comparing the day's activities and dropping veiled hints about their purchases. Even Gargery had a few parcels, closely wrapped in newspaper. He was in fine form, declaring that he had fended off at least one potential abductor. Emerson shouted him down and asked Charla what she had bought for him.

I found myself seated next to Sethos. "No potential abductors, I presume?" I asked.

"A miserable old man trying to sell Sennia fake ushebtis. Gargery would have wrestled him to the ground if I hadn't stepped in." He stirred sugar into his tea. "Is she back yet?"

He had seen me emerge from the hotel and drawn the obvious conclusion. "No," I said. "She wasn't in the Valley, at least not while we were there."

"So I heard."

"Where do you suppose she went?"

"How should I know?"

David John tugged at my sleeve. "Charla won't tell me what she bought, Grandmama."

"Christmas is a time for secrets," I said.


For the next few days we devoted ourselves to the merriments of the season. Abdullah had been right; what did mundane distractions such as royal tombs and shadowy plotters matter? In future years they would take their places in the long list of adventures in which we had triumphed. We had much to be thankful for.

When I expressed these sentiments to Emerson, he said only, "Kindly do not repeat yourself, Peabody. I can only endure a certain amount of such bloody optimism."

Since fir trees were at a premium in Egypt (nonexistent, in fact), we employed a feathery tamarisk, filling out its skimpy branches with a profusion of ornaments. In some families, I believe, the tree is not decorated until Christmas Eve. We do not follow that custom, since the children enjoyed hanging the ornaments and setting fire to the tree.

"It makes for an exciting interlude," Ramses said philosophically, after he had extinguished one such blaze and strictly forbidden Charla to light the candles unless he gave permission.

"That applies to you as well," I said, with a stern look at David John.

"But Grandmama, I did not—"

"You suggested it, though, didn't you?"

David John never lied. Like his father, he usually employed equivocation to avoid doing so. In this case the direct question allowed of only one truthful answer. Blue eyes wide and candid, he nodded his head. "Yes, Grandmama."

"And you provided the matches?" I knew Charla could not have taken them from the kitchen without being seen. Fatima watched her like a hawk, whereas David John was less suspect.

"Yes, Grandmama."

"Where are the rest of them?"

David John dug into his pocket and produced a handful of questionable objects, including several nails, a dead mouse tenderly wrapped in tissue paper, several broken crayons, and the box of matches. I confiscated the matches, the nails (on general principles), and the mouse, and delivered a stern lecture on the dangers of fire. David John hung his head.

"I didn't have to do what he told me," said Charla, throwing her arms round her brother.

"That is true," I said. "And I hope David John appreciates your coming to his defense. You are both culpable. However, in view of the season, we will let you off with a warning this time, so long as the offense is not repeated."

"Thank you, Grandmama," David John said. "I assure you it will not. May we give the mouse a proper burial?"

"Not in my flower beds," I said, handing over the deceased.

They went off, cheerfully discussing the funeral arrangements, and Ramses, who had listened in astonished silence, said, "Mother, you never cease to amaze me. How did you know?"

"Psychology, my dear."


The hand-crafted ornaments David had made many years before were ceremonially put in place, the children taking turns to hang the little tin and ceramic animals. Paper chains filled in the empty spaces. Charla proved to be expert at making them, and I praised her accordingly. She spent much of her time with David, presumably working on her little books. Many of the surfaces in the house were sticky with paste, and Fatima had to buy more flour.

Sethos took an active part in the proceedings, hobnobbing with Fatima and assisting her by tasting various products, helping make paper chains, and even bursting into song from time to time. He had a pleasant baritone voice, and, unlike his brother, he could carry a tune.

Naturally I wondered what he was up to. Apparently he had decided not to make a Judas goat of himself. As he informed me when I asked him point-blank, he had concluded there was no need. The return of the document seemed to have satisfied our unknown adversaries; there had been no activity on their part. Margaret had returned unscathed from wherever she had been, and had taken up her routine in the Valley.

"Shall we ask her here for Christmas?" I inquired of Sethos, who was helping me write out invitations.

"I see no reason why you should. She hasn't even apologized for banging you on the head."

"It is too sad to spend Christmas alone. I have forgiven her, as Scripture requires."

"The more fool you, then," said Sethos, dropping a blot of ink on the paper he was inscribing.

"Kevin O'Connell, too," I said, consulting my list. "I suppose there is no use asking Howard or any of the Metropolitan Museum people."

Sethos crumpled the spoiled paper and tossed it into the wastepaper receptacle. "According to Daoud, they are having their own celebration at Metropolitan House. We won't be asked."

"Nevertheless, I shall invite them," I said, writing busily. "In a spirit of Christian love. If they choose not to reciprocate, that is their decision."

Sethos blotted another sheet of paper and threw it away.

The only member of the "other camp" who had demonstrated Christian love (or simple good manners) was Harry Burton. He had come to tea one day, as promised, and described without reserve what the excavators had been doing. This occurred just in time to prevent a fit of bad temper from Emerson, whose enjoyment of the Christmas preparations did not entirely succeed in keeping his mind off Howard's proceedings. We knew, from Daoud, that Professor Breasted had been allowed inside the tomb, together with Mr. Winlock and a few others; that Mr. Burton had begun photographing; and that Lucas had arrived from Cairo. Mr. Burton was able and willing to provide more detailed information.

"We've cleared out KV55 to use as a darkroom," he explained to his absorbed audience. "Most convenient, being just across the way."

"Quite," said Emerson. "I trust that, in addition to photographs, Carter will make detailed sketches before removing any objects?"

"He has begun doing so. He's a good draftsman, you know, and he has Hall and Hauser to help." Burton sipped his tea. "He hopes to remove the first of the artifacts shortly after Christmas. It will be taken to the tomb of Seti II, which is to serve as a conservation and storage place."

"Not too convenient, that," said Emerson, who was looking for something to criticize.

"It is some distance away, but it has several advantages, including a large open area in front. To judge from what I've seen thus far, Lucas is going to need a bit of fresh air; the chemicals he uses for conservation can be pervasive."

"I trust he knows about paraffin wax," I said. "Do have another slice of plum cake, Mr. Burton."

"Paraffin wax has always been your mainstay, hasn't it?" Burton accepted the offering with a smiling nod at Sennia.

"There is nothing like it," I declared. "Especially for beads and loose bits of inlay."

Burton was ready to take the hint. "There's plenty of that sort of thing. Most of the storage chests are packed full of everything from jewelry to clothing. Sandals, beaded robes, wadded up and jammed in."

No one interrupted him as he went on with his description. Howard had applied numbers to each object in the first room, which he had termed the Antechamber. These were large enough to show in the photographs and would be listed and described in Howard's official index. The objects were to be removed one by one, working from north to south. The huge funerary couches would have to be taken apart, since they were too large to pass through the entrance corridor; they must have been assembled inside the tomb, after having been brought in piece by piece. The chariot parts would be left until last; they presented a particularly difficult job, since they were all in a jumble and bits of the gold and inlay were precariously attached. In the meantime, Mr. Lucas would unpack the storage chests. I knew—who better?—what a formidable task lay before him. According to Mr. Burton (and our own observations, which of course I did not mention), the contents of the chests were not in their original order. Tomb robbers are not noted for neatness; working in haste and fear of discovery, they had emptied the chests looking for gold, and when the priests entered to put things in order, they had acted in equal haste, tossing scattered objects into the nearest container and forcing the lid down.

Sethos listened with the same absorbed expression as the rest of us. I knew he was thinking of his "restorer," a member of his criminal organization, who had assisted us so ably with the fragile objects found in the tomb of the God's Wives before he was murdered. People who assist us often meet that fate, but Signor Martinelli had only himself to blame; he had allowed himself to be lured away by a female on whom he had designs of an improper nature.

Mr. Lucas had no such weakness. I could only hope he was as good at his job. It is a sad fact of life that honest persons sometimes lack the experience of the more unprincipled.

Mr. Burton accepted a third slice of plum cake before declaring he must be getting back to Metropolitan House. "By the way," he added, "Breasted has read the cartouches and confirmed that they are those of Tutankhamon."

"Reread them, you mean," snapped Emerson.

"Ah," Burton said. "I wondered about that."

He said no more, but shook the hand of Ramses with particular warmth.

"At least one person recognizes our contributions," I said.

"Oh, I expect there will be others," Sethos said, with an evil smile. "Carter doesn't work and play well with others. Mark my words, before he's through he'll have a good many people furious with him, from journalists and the Antiquities Department to certain of his colleagues."

I will confess, in the pages of this private journal, that I was not charitable enough to hope Sethos was wrong. We were among the few—the only ones, except for Cyrus—who had not received a formal invitation to view the tomb. The Breasteds, including their son Charles, Mrs. Burton, and even one of Winlock's children had been allowed to putter about in the Antechamber. It was small consolation to know that we had had a private look of our own, since we couldn't tell anyone about it. I felt for David, who would have had a keen appreciation of the wonderful artifacts. How he was going to carry out his assignment for the *Illustrated London News* I could not imagine. Howard was guarding the photographic and reproduction rights jealously. The ever-poisonous tongue of rumor had it that Carnarvon intended to sell them to the highest bidder, but I could not believe that, even of an individual who had treated us so shabbily.

Cyrus felt the slight as deeply as we. We hadn't seen a great deal of the Vandergelts recently; they were busy with their own holiday preparations, as we had been with ours. It was to escape the increasing strain of these that Cyrus dropped in one afternoon two days before Christmas.

"Cat has the whole place torn apart," he explained, "and the rest of them are aiding and abetting her, even Nadji. Sometimes I wish the blessed Savior had been found in the bulrushes, like Moses, date of birth unknown."

Emerson whooped with laughter. I refrained from comment, since the children were not present. "How many guests are you expecting?" I asked.

"Cat's in charge of that. Half the town of Luxor, from what I can make out, plus every tourist we ever met on the street. You folks will be there, of course?"

"We wouldn't miss it," Sethos said.

Cyrus favored him with a brusque nod. We had explained to our friend that Sethos was in the process of coming to terms with his adversaries, and that we anticipated no further difficulty with them, but Cyrus clearly had reservations.

"And you, I trust, will attend our Christmas Eve gathering," I said. "Katherine asked if she might bring Suzanne's grandfather, and naturally I said she might. What is he like?"

"Sweetest old gent you would ever want to meet," Cyrus replied somewhat sourly. "He loves everything and everybody. He's even polite to Nadji."

"Even?" Ramses asked.

"Well, he's a man of his generation and nation," said Cyrus poetically. "And from what I've heard, a real shark at business. But he's on his best behavior; only slips now and then, with some generalization about the great British Empire and her civilizing mission."

"It will be interesting to see how he treats Selim and Daoud," Nefret said, pursing her lips. "If he is rude I will show him the door."

Insofar as Emerson was concerned, this went without saying. He turned to a more interesting topic. "I take it he hasn't been able to get you admitted to the tomb?"

"Not so far. He had a letter from Carnarvon, which he duly sent on to Carter. Hasn't had an answer."

"There's one way you may be able to gain entry," said Emerson, chewing on his pipe. "Grovel to Carter and tell him you have broken off relations with us."

Cyrus paused in the act of lighting his cheroot. "As if I'd stoop so low!" he cried.

"Emerson was only making a little joke, Cyrus," I assured him. "Not a very amusing one."

"Hmmm, yes," muttered Emerson.

"All right, then." Cyrus applied the match and puffed. "I wouldn't mind so much," he said, in a burst of candor, "if Carnarvon wasn't going to get some of the artifacts."

"To say nothing of the Metropolitan Museum," said Ramses. "You don't suppose the board is donating the services of their staff members out of sheer altruism, do you? They've come to an understanding with Carnarvon and Carter."

"At any rate, Sir Malcolm won't get anything," I said in an effort to console Cyrus.

"I wouldn't be so sure," Emerson said darkly. "He's been hanging round the tomb with an increasingly lean and hungry look. Yesterday his wig fell off. He must have been so preoccupied he forgot to glue it on. When that miserable servant of his handed it back to him, Sir Malcolm gave him a thrashing."

My amusement at Sir Malcom's discomfiture was tempered by indignation. "Shameful," I said. "I must have a word with the fellow. He shouldn't have to put up with such treatment. How do you know that, Emerson? Not from Daoud, he would have told all of us. Oh, dear— have you been bribing that child, Azmi, to report to you? I saw him yesterday near the kitchen, but assumed he had come round for some of Fatima's sugar biscuits. She feeds everyone."

"What's wrong with that?" Emerson demanded.

"I have no objection to her giving treats to the children, but you should not encourage them to spy and eavesdrop."

"It is on Carter's account that I employ Azmi," Emerson said virtuously. "Montague hasn't given up. He may have another try at the tomb."

"Ha," I said.

"I wouldn't put it past him," Cyrus said. "But Carter has taken all possible precautions. He's got three different sets of guards on duty day and night, each reporting to a different authority so they won't be tempted to collaborate. The keys to the gates are held by him or another member of the staff."

Sethos put down the paper chain he had been working on and cleared his throat in a pointed manner.

"I suppose you think you could get at those keys," Emerson said.

"I can think of at least three different methods offhand," Sethos said with a faraway look. "And two ways of distracting the guards."

"Then it is a good thing you have reformed," I said.

Cyrus looked as if he was not so sure it was a good thing.

I had several private errands of my own to carry out. They had nothing to do with our holiday preparations, but I made certain they did not mar the spirit of the season by not telling anyone about them. Running back and forth to Luxor on various errands provided sufficient excuse for my occasional absences. I did not lie to Emerson about the reason for them. While in Luxor I did do errands and call on friends. I saw no reason to mention what else I did.

Unfortunately I was seen leaving the zabtiyeh, and the word duly reached Emerson. He waited until we were alone, preparing for bed, before he went on the attack.

"Can't you stay away from corpses even at this time of year?" he demanded.

"There were no corpses in which I took an interest, Emerson."

"I cannot believe there is a corpse in which you do not take an interest. What did you go there for?"

I decided not to lie. Emerson had just returned from the bath chamber. His hair waved about his brow and his admirable form had a slight sheen of dampness.

"I prefer not to tell you, Emerson."

"You prefer? You *prefer?*" Emerson drew a deep breath. His muscles swelled. So did the veins in his neck. I waited for the burst of outrage I had every reason to expect.

Alas, my expectations were not fulfilled. Emerson let his breath out. He placed a heavy but gentle hand on my shoulder.

"Peabody, my darling girl, I came close to losing you last year. I wish you would allow me to protect and cherish you. I wish you would not do this sort of thing."

I wished he would not do *that* sort of thing. When Emerson stoops to appeal he makes me feel that I have taken unfair advantage. Turning into his outstretched arms, I murmured, "I give you my word, my dear, that I did nothing that requires me to be protected."

"Hmph," said Emerson—and spoke no more.


## From Manuscript H

The children were accustomed to visiting Abdullah's tomb. Ramses's mother had been right (as usual) when she claimed there was nothing morbid about remembering the honored dead. The twins and Sennia had heard the stories about his heroism and devotion; to them he was a distant figure of legend, like Charlemagne and King Arthur. They anticipated this particular visit with delight, since the whole family was going and they would be allowed to make a special offering.

Attired in their best, they set out for the small cemetery of which Abdullah's tomb was the most prominent feature. It was a beautiful little structure, designed by David, with graceful columns supporting its domed roof. The servant of the tomb roused himself from his prayers and came forth to meet them. Having heard of their plans, a number of the villagers had turned up, not only to honor their local saint but to enjoy the spectacle. The Emersons could be depended upon to do things in style.

Daoud outshone all others in a new caftan and elaborately wound turban. Cyrus had brought Jumana and Nadji, and, to Ramses's surprise, Suzanne.

Across the open entrance hung the usual offerings—trinkets and beads and bits of cloth. Ramses lifted Charla up so she could attach her gift of a little book, which she had decided Abdullah would prefer to an offering anyone might make. David had tactfully pointed out that Abdullah might not appreciate pictures of ladies in low-cut frocks, so the pages contained photographs of the family. David John was next. Strictly speaking, his portrait violated the law against representations of the human form, and it bore a strong resemblance to M. Lacau (except for the turban), but the spectators only smiled approvingly, as they did when Sennia added a particularly large, colorful ribbon. After the servant had led the proper prayers, they made their contributions to the fund for the maintenance of the tomb and its attendant, and prepared to depart.

Emerson blew out his breath in a sigh of relief. He considered religious ceremonies of all kinds to be gross superstition, but he had learned to keep his opinions to himself around the children.

"Well, now, that was fine," said Cyrus, who had contributed largely to the fund. He replaced his hat. "I hope Abdullah was pleased."

They had all become accustomed to speaking of him as if he were still among them. Ramses's mother was responsible for that, of course. She had followed the proceedings with a smile, and from time to time she had nodded, her smile broadening, as if she were listening to words no one else could hear.

"Oh, yes," she said.

"He was a great man," said Nadji seriously. "I have heard much about him."

"Did you know that he saved Grandmama's life by giving his own?" David John asked. "If you have not heard the story, I will tell you."

Nadji smiled down at the little boy. "I would like to hear it."

Emerson edged away. To say he was jealous of his wife's attachment to Abdullah would have been absurd, but there was something . . .

The excitement reached its peak on the morning of Christmas Eve. One would have supposed that after days of preparation there was nothing left to be done, but Charla had thought of several other friends who required little books and Fatima was convinced she had not prepared enough food for the party. Shrieks and curses came from the kitchen, mingled with the sobs of Maaman, for Fatima in a frenzy tried the nerves of those around her. When Kareem spilled an entire pot of coffee across the breakfast table, Emerson leaped to his feet with a roar.

"I am going to—to the Valley," he announced, mopping at the stains on his shirt and trousers with a napkin.

"An excellent idea," said his wife, exchanging glances with Nefret.

"Yes, go away, all you men," said Nefret. "None of you is up to this sort of thing."

"Does that include me, madam?" asked Gargery, who had finally been persuaded to take meals with them—but only if guests were not present.

"Yes," Nefret said.

"No," said Emerson.

Eventually the women got all the men out of the house, except for Gargery. Emerson had pointed out that he would have to ride a donkey. Gargery did not care for donkeys.

"That was an excellent idea, Father," Ramses said feelingly, as they rode out of the stable.

"Don't know why women get in such a pother about holidays," Emerson grumbled.

"Where are we going?" Sethos asked. He had resisted coming at first, but had been shoved out with the rest of them. "Cyrus won't be working in the West Valley today."

"Does it matter?" David adjusted his pith helmet and buckled the strap under his chin. There was a stiff breeze that morning, and the sun was veiled by light clouds.

Emerson mumbled something, and Ramses said, "I doubt Carter will be working either."

"I don't give a curse what he's doing," said Emerson.

So it was to be the East Valley. Emerson had probably had that in mind from the first. He had stayed away for several days, and curiosity was eating at him.

They rode single file in order not to impede the traffic, which included local villagers as well as tourists. The latter were not so considerate; their hired carriages yielded the way to no one except the camels, who yielded the way to nothing. The donkey riders spread out across the road, and some of them stopped to photograph anything that moved: camels, rude carts loaded with produce, a man perched on a donkey with his wife walking alongside, women balancing heavy water jars on their heads.

When they were able to do so, Emerson went ahead with David, and Ramses drew up beside his uncle. Sethos hadn't spoken since they left the house. He rode with his usual ease, but his mouth was set and his forehead furrowed. Tinted glasses darkened his eyes to hazel.

"You received another private communication yesterday," Ramses said.

"Hassan was bribed to tell no one," Sethos said.

"I bribed him to tell me."

"Dear me," said Sethos, with a fair show of insouciance. "Don't you trust me?"

"Should I?"

Sethos reached into his breast pocket and took out a folded paper, which he handed to Ramses.

The message was short and to the point. "Yours received. Do nothing more."

"English," Ramses said.

Sethos sneezed and swabbed his nose with a handkerchief. "Brilliant."

"Don't be rude," Ramses said equably. "What's put you in such a bad humor? The response was what we expected."

"Precisely." Another, louder sneeze was muffled by the folds of the handkerchief.

"Have you caught cold?"

"It would appear so."

"You could give it to Margaret," Ramses suggested.

His uncle turned the tinted spectacles toward him, and then, unexpectedly, burst into laughter. "What a charming idea. Will you aid and abet me when I catch her in a close embrace and breathe heavily on her?"

"She'll probably be there this morning."

"I know." Sethos sighed and dabbed at his nose. "You are omniscient, so you have anticipated that I'm not looking forward to encountering her. As for the message, I would have liked something more positive. Something along the lines of 'count on us to behave ourselves.'"

"Or a simple 'Happy Christmas'?"

His uncle's mouth twitched. "Point taken. I'll do my best not to shed gloom over the proceedings. After all, we've no reason to assume our unknown acquaintances (who do write excellent English) mean to bother us. As for Margaret, why should I give a damn about her? She doesn't give a damn about . . . about anything except her bloody newspaper."

Ramses had been mistaken about Carter. He was at work, and so were several others of his crew. His nose in the air, Emerson strode past the tomb without so much as a sidelong look, but Ramses and the others joined the spectators, of whom there were quite a number. There wasn't much to see; most of the activity was being carried on in the tomb chamber, deep underground.

"Yes, they are drawing pictures and taking photographs," said one of the guards, in response to a question from David. Leaning on his rifle, he yawned.

"There is nothing much to do," Ramses said. "It is a boring job."

"Boring?" The man scratched his beard. "There are worse tasks, Brother of Demons. As soon as the gentlemen leave we can lie down and talk and smoke and have a sleep. Tomorrow is your holiday, yes? So we will have another day of rest."

"Possibly two days," David said.

"It is so?"

"On the day after Christmas the English take a holiday and give presents to those who have served them well," David explained.

"So I have been told. But there will be none for us, I think."

"I think he's right," Ramses said, as he and David turned away.

"One can hardly expect Carter to reward this entire lot," David said.

There were certainly a large number of guards. They lined the wall around the tomb, wearing a variety of uniforms and headgear. Ramses recognized the khaki of local troops and the fezzes of the men from the

Ministry. Margaret and Kevin O'Connell were not in evidence. Looking around, he realized Sethos and his father were also missing.

"Where's Father got to?" he asked.

He got an immediate answer, though not from David. Sounds of a loud altercation reached his ears. It was safe to assume that whenever voices were raised, Emerson's would be one of them.

He and David hurried toward the spot, which turned out to be the area in front of the remote tomb of Seti II. It was some distance away, at the far end of a path that branched off to the right from the more traveled route that led to the tomb of Thutmose III.

Only his father's voice would have carried that far, Ramses thought. Of course the echoes helped.

Emerson's adversary was none other than Sir Malcolm Page Henley de Montague. Holding his stick like a dueling sword, he shouted back whenever Emerson paused for breath. "No right!" and "How dare you?" formed the refrain of his remarks. His rage was so enormous it overcame his fear of Emerson—and perhaps he counted on the three other people present to step in if Emerson was moved to violence. In that, Ramses thought, he deceived himself. Margaret Minton to the right and O'Connell to the left of the furious pair were busily taking notes.

Seeing Ramses and David, Montague's servant dropped to his knees and clasped his hands. "Brother of Demons, help my master! Todros Effendi, speak to the Father of Curses!"

Emerson whirled round. "Oh, it's you," he said. "Do you know what this bastard is doing?"

"No," Ramses said. "What?"

"Er . . . Hmph." Emerson rubbed his chin.

"I have every right to be here," Sir Malcolm said shrilly.

His appearance had deteriorated since Ramses had last seen him. Goatee and wig had taken on a grayish hue, and his cravat was unpressed. Evidently his latest servant, a youngish man, well-set-up and broad-shouldered, had not been trained for valet duties. His robe was shabby and his sandals patched.

"This is the tomb that will be used as a storage room and laboratory," Emerson said. "Don't tell me his presence here is a coincidence!"

"Of course not." Sir Malcolm brushed dust from his sleeve. "Any more than yours is. I was curious. There is no law against that, I believe?"

In the silence that followed, Ramses heard O'Connell muttering as he continued to write. ". . . presence a coincidence . . ."

"Stop taking notes, O'Connell," Ramses said. "There's no news in this."

"But readers love hearing about Professor Emerson's little encounters," Margaret said innocently. "Isn't that right, O'Connell?"

"Indeed but it is. And the *Times* won't have this exclusive!"

Belatedly aware of what he had done—and what his wife would say about it—Emerson attempted to redress his error. The forced smile he directed at Sir Malcolm made him look as if his jaw would crack.

"Just a friendly discussion between—er—old acquaintances," he declared. "Isn't that right—er—old chap?"

Montague was no more anxious than Emerson to be featured in the pages of the *Daily Yell* or its competitor. "Quite, quite—er—old chap. We will continue our—er—discussion another time, eh?"

He made good his escape, followed by his servant, who gave Ramses an ingratiating smile. The fellow's face was familiar, but Ramses couldn't remember where he had seen him.

"Sorry," Ramses said to Margaret. "There won't be an encounter. Or a story."

"One can't make a story out of a friendly argument between archaeologists," David added. "They do it all the time."

O'Connell uttered a fulsome Irish curse but Margaret only smiled. "What about this tomb, then?" she asked. "What's so interesting about it?"

Since he could see no reason not to answer, Ramses explained. Margaret's face took on its journalist's stare. "So they will be carrying the objects along this path, all the way from Tut's tomb?"

"They will be guarded every step of the way," Ramses said.

"Oh, I wasn't planning to steal them," Margaret said. "Which reminds me—I haven't seen my—Mr. Bissinghurst today. Didn't he come with you?"

"He's not feeling well," Ramses said.

"Something lingering, with boiling oil in it, I hope." She closed her notebook with a snap and walked away. After a doubtful look at Emerson's darkening countenance, O'Connell followed her.

"Don't say a word," Emerson ordered.

"You got out of it very neatly," Ramses said.

"Yes, I did, didn't I?" Emerson fingered the cleft in his chin. "So there's no need to mention this to Peabody."

"No, sir," said Ramses and David in chorus.

Emerson hadn't finished with the tomb of Seti II. "Carter will need guards here too. And a locked gate."

Ramses was a trifle surprised that Carter had selected this particular tomb for his storage area. The second Seti was one of the confusing pharaohs, as his mother called them, a series of rulers of whom little was known except for their habit of shoving one another off the throne. Seti's mummy had been found in one of the royal caches; the tomb itself was rather nicely decorated, especially in the entrance corridor. Hauling boxes in and out wouldn't do the reliefs much good. The tomb had been open since antiquity, and Carter had cleared it back in 1902; Ramses couldn't help wondering how thorough a job he had done. The advantages of the site were clear, however; for one thing, there were no stairs to negotiate. The entrance was cut directly into the cliff face, and the first of the internal corridors sloped at a gentle angle instead of plunging steeply downward.

While Emerson brooded over the images of Maat on the entrance jambs, David and Ramses started walking back along the path. "It's quite a distance," David said somewhat wistfully. "Perhaps I'll be able to get a look at some of the objects while they are being transported here."

Ramses mentally damned Carter and Carnarvon. By rights he ought to have spared a few damns for his father as well; if Emerson hadn't lost his temper they might not have been banned from the tomb. But it wasn't fair to David, or to Cyrus, come to that, to hold them guilty by association with the Emersons. I wonder, he thought, if there is a way I could . . .

Turning back to the tomb, they were joined by Sethos. "I saw

Margaret heading from this direction," he said casually. "Has any-thing occurred?"

"Not really," Ramses said. "Where were you?"

"Lurking." Sethos blew his nose.

"Caught cold, have you?" Emerson inquired.

"Something lingering. But I do not anticipate boiling oil."

So he had been close enough to overhear the quotation (from *The Mikado,* if Ramses remembered correctly).

"You decided not to confront Margaret?" Ramses asked. He added softly, "Coward."

Sethos pretended not to hear him. "Anything interesting about this tomb?" he asked Emerson.

"Nothing that would interest you," said Emerson pointedly.

"Before long this uninspiring sepulchre will contain a great deal to interest a thief," Sethos replied, acknowledging the implication with a raised eyebrow. "Speaking as one who has had considerable experience, I'd rather try to rob this one than Tutankhamon's. Look at that nice wide doorway and the easy slope beyond. The objects will be conve-niently crated for shipping. Get a sufficient force together, snatch and run while some of your fellows hold off the guards, and hoist the crates straight up that slope to the top of the gebel. No need to cart the loot all the way back to the entrance."

"Good Gad," exclaimed Emerson.

"Just an idea," Sethos said. He buried his face in his handkerchief and let out a reverberating sneeze.

# CHAPTER NINE

WITH EMERSON OUT OF THE WAY WE GOT ON BETTER, THOUGH IF I
had been able to do so I would have shut the twins and Amira in the latter's doghouse and locked Gargery in his room. Egypt had revived the
old rascal; he had always considered himself to be in charge of the
household, and he and Fatima had had a number of run-ins about serving meals. He was at his most officious, puttering round the house from
kitchen to parlor, rearranging the decorations and offering unwanted
advice about how to prepare various dishes. However, by the time the
men returned demanding luncheon, matters were proceeding nicely and
I sat down with them to a cold collation of salads and sandwiches. They
were singularly reticent about their activities, but under interrogation
Ramses admitted they had encountered Kevin and Margaret.

"They have both accepted my invitation," I said. "Did they happen
to mention that they would be coming?"

"We talked of other matters," Ramses said, and took a very large bite
of his chicken sandwich.

He and David took the twins (and the dog) off to his house and promised to keep them there until the party officially began. Charla had been behaving suspiciously well (except for inadvertently pasting herself to a chair), and I anticipated a breakdown. Overnight reformation cannot be expected of a five-year-old. Emerson retreated to his study and Sethos to his room, with a few aspirin and a supply of fresh handkerchiefs.

At six o'clock everything was ready, and I inspected the house with a degree of complacency for which I believe I may be excused. I had managed to keep Fatima and Gargery from each other's throats, and bullied Emerson into his best suit. The table in the dining room was laid with my best crystal and my Limoges, the parlor was hung with greenery and paper chains, and the tree sparkled with candles.

"Let the festivities begin!" I cried.

"Hmph," said Emerson.

Sethos blew his nose.

We were to dine at eight, but some of our closer friends had been asked to come earlier, in order to watch the children open presents and stuff themselves with sweets. They (the children) would probably be sick later, but as I always say, occcasional excess is worth the consequences. Selim and Daoud were there, but Kadija had begged to be excused, since she did not enjoy large groups of strangers. At a quarter past six the Vandergelts arrived, and I was introduced to Sir William Portmanteau, Suzanne's grandfather.

Cyrus's description had been accurate. He might have sat for a portrait of Father Christmas, with his snowy beard and twinkling eyes. The benevolence of his expression as he watched the children beggars description.

"No pleasure equals that of having grandchildren gathered round one's knee," he declared. "Is that not so, Professor Emerson?"

"Quite," said Emerson, over Charla's shriek of delight. An arrow wobbled feebly in his direction and fell at his feet.

"Who . . ." I began. I thought I knew, though.

Ramses removed the bow from his daughter, explaining that it was only to be employed out of doors, and Charla fell on another package.

Their gifts for the adults had to be opened too; to do the twins credit, they took pleasure in giving as well as receiving, though perhaps not as much. Charla's little books were an enormous success. Daoud was quite taken by the engravings of Stonehenge and Buckingham Palace. Sir William chuckled over his collection of fashionable ladies, and admired David John's drawing of a pharaoh driving a chariot.

Before the children were carried off to bed, we sang a few carols, accompanied by Sennia at the pianoforte. Nefret had declared that she herself was out of practice, but she had done it, I felt sure, to give Sennia a chance to exhibit her talent. The dear girl managed the simple tunes quite nicely; the pride with which she played was pleasant to see. The children's sweet sopranos blended with the deeper voices, and Emerson's enthusiastic, off-key basso did not detract (much) from the general effect. Selim and Daoud and Nadji listened with smiling faces, and Sethos sneezed his way through "Good King Wenceslas." Sir William did not join in; he beat time with his fingers and chuckled. I began to understand why Cyrus's praise of the old gentleman had held a sour note. After a while the chuckles began to sound mechanical.

Charla insisted on kissing everyone good night. Sir William's benevolent smile cracked briefly when her cheek, smeared with the peppermint she had been sucking, stuck to his beard. But one could hardly blame him for that. He had behaved like a perfect gentleman thus far, acknowledging his introductions to Selim and Daoud correctly if without warmth. One could hardly blame him for that . . .

Once the children were out of the way, Fatima began clearing away the torn paper and scattered ribbons, and Emerson poured the whiskey.

"That went well," he declared, with the complacency of an individual who had had very little to do with its going well. "Who else is coming, Peabody?"

"Not as many as in other years."

"Hmmm, yes," said Emerson. "You didn't invite—"

"I asked only those who were not engaged elsewhere," I said, for I saw no reason to mention the names of "Carter's cronies," as Emerson called them.

"What about that bas—that fellow Montague? I trust you didn't—"

"No, Emerson, I did not."

Sir William looked up from his glass, which he seemed to be enjoying very much. "Is it Page Henley de Montague to whom you refer?"

"Yes," I said. "Are you acquainted with him?"

"Not well. We served on several committees together. Mr. Vandergelt mentioned him, with," he added, chuckling, "a certain degree of disparagement."

Our other guests began to arrive—Marjorie Fisher and Miss Buchanan from Luxor, Rex Engelbach, and finally, Kevin and Margaret Minton. They had come together, which surprised me until I caught Margaret's ironical eye. She was taking no chances on being waylaid again.

She was wearing what I took to be her best frock, of the same drab ash-brown as most of her other garments. A crimson scarf knotted loosely round her neck and a pair of small gold earrings were her only concessions to fashion. Compared with the other ladies present, in their emerald satins and blue silks, she looked like a governess. Even Miss Buchanan, who was noted for her sobriety of dress, had added a string of pearls and a tortoiseshell comb to her ensemble.

I managed to have a private word with Margaret before we went in to dinner.

"Do you dress badly on purpose?" I asked. "In your youth, as I recall, you kept up with the latest modes."

Her eyes glittered wickedly. "In my youth—and into my middle years—I was a fool. What is the purpose of decking oneself out in order to compete with silly women and attract foolish men?"

I was wearing scarlet, Emerson's favorite color, and the diamond earrings that had been his gift. Not one whit discomposed by her implicit criticism, I smiled and adjusted her scarf so that it framed her face more becomingly.

After much nagging I had agreed that Gargery should serve the wine, and I had instructed him to make certain it flowed freely. The Reader may question my motives for doing so. The Reader would be correct. *In vino veritas,* as the saying goes.

I got a little more *veritas* than I had bargained for. Margaret became more and more acerbic as the meal went on, and she and Kevin began sniping at each other. Rex Engelbach and Emerson got into a loud argument about Howard Carter, Emerson taking Carter's part out of sheer perversity. Jumana—very pretty in pale yellow—made a point of telling David that his copies of the Ay tomb paintings were the finest she had ever seen. Suzanne made a point of telling Jumana that she ought to find herself a nice Egyptian husband. And, during one of those unfortunate lulls in the conversation that sometimes occur even with us, Sir William asked Ramses whether Sennia was his illegitimate daughter.

He didn't use the word. "Under the blanket," accompanied by a wink and a chuckle, were the words he used.

The vulgar rumor had first been spread about when Ramses took the abandoned child under his wing and we proceeded to adopt her. In fact, she was, as I believe I have mentioned, the offspring of my despicable nephew Percy and an Egyptian prostitute; but those who are incapable of understanding nobility of character (I refer to Ramses) and love never believed the true story. I was sorry but not surprised to find that the lie was still in circulation. Malice is often stronger than truth.

Sennia's eyes filled with tears. She knew what he meant; she had been subjected to even more unkind insults when she first attended school in Cairo. Emerson choked on his wine and Ramses went white around the mouth, as he did when in a violent rage.

"She is my beloved adopted little sister," Ramses said, very quietly. "Cyrus, has Father told you of his theory that there is another unknown royal tomb in the Valley?"

It wasn't Emerson's theory; it was something Abdullah had told me. Cyrus, who had gone purple with indignation, took up his cue, and everyone began talking at once.

We got through the rest of the meal without incident. Sethos had excused himself from dinner, claiming that he did not want to inflict his cold on the other guests. It had reached a rather unpleasant stage, to judge by the number of times he used his handkerchief during the earlier part of the evening.

With my usual skill as a hostess, I kept the conversation centered on

Egyptology, knowing Emerson wouldn't permit a word on any other subject. I had to catch myself several times when people speculated on the splendid objects in the tomb chamber, and once or twice I saw Jumana flinch when someone stepped on her foot to remind her she wasn't supposed to have seen them. However, stories had spread, as they will, and Rex Engelbach was ready and willing to talk.

"Carter's excessive secrecy strikes me as unwarranted," he declared. "Granted, he cannot admit great numbers of people for fear of causing damage to the artifacts, but there is no reason why he can't describe them or distribute copies of Burton's photographs."

"They say that Carnarvon means to sell the photographs to the highest bidder," Cyrus said.

Rex was too wise to indulge in gossip, but his mere presence that evening indicated to me that he was not on the best of terms with Howard and his patron. His position was difficult. In theory he had authority over all archaeological activities in Upper Egypt, including the Valley of the Kings. However, the control exercised by the Department of Antiquities over foreign excavators and expeditions had always been lax, and Rex had neither the power nor the inclination to incite trouble. He could not prevent Carnarvon from monopolizing the photographs, but he could and did indicate his disapproval by describing certain of the objects.

"There is one chair—a throne, rather—that would take your breath away. Every inch of it is overlaid with gold foil and with inlaid decorative elements. On the back are figures in high relief of Tutankhamon and his queen. Their faces and bodies are formed of reddish-brown glass, their robes of silver, their wigs and other details of semiprecious stones . . ."

David leaned forward, his eyes alight. Even photographs, supposing Howard could be persuaded to share them, would not capture the glorious colors and gleam of gold of such treasures as the throne.

Howard was being selfish and unreasonable. Seeing David's rapt face, I determined that I would get him into that tomb somehow, by whatever means necessary.

Suzanne's grandfather had not spoiled our evening but he had cast a stone into the tranquil pool of seasonal goodwill. Cyrus took him away early. The old wretch had no idea that he had misbehaved; he bade us good night with perfect aplomb. Chuckling.

Our other guests, with the exception of Kevin and Margaret, did not remain long. As soon as they were out of the way, the rest of us began abusing Sir William. I permitted Sennia to stay up past her usual bed-time, because I wanted her to hear what we thought of such persons and their ideas. Kevin described Sir William with a few picturesque Irish in-sults and Daoud offered to carry him off and lock him up for a few days. Gargery, white hair bristling, declared his intention of challenging Sir William to a fistfight. This noble offer completed Sennia's cure; try-ing not to laugh (for that would have hurt her champion's feelings), she led Gargery off to his room.

"At least the old villain didn't get into the tomb," said Emerson with satisfaction. "He'd have bragged about it if he had."

"Not yet," I said. "How long is the old villain staying?"

"I didn't bother to ask," said Emerson.

"He leaves for Cairo on Boxing Day," said Nefret. "We won't have to entertain him again."

"We will have to encounter him at Cyrus's tomorrow," I said. "How-ever, there will be a good many people present and we ought to be able to avoid him."

Margaret had spoken very little. Having withdrawn to a quiet cor-ner, she was writing in her notebook. I did not object, since nothing newsworthy had occurred (Sir William's bigotry being, unfortunately, not unusual). I assumed she was making notes about the artifacts Rex had described.

"Will you sing more songs now?" Daoud asked. He loved music of all kinds and the pianoforte fascinated him.

"Nefret is looking tired," I said. "And Sennia has gone to bed. You don't play, do you, Margaret?"

"She plays very well," said a voice from the doorway. "But it is against her principles to demonstrate womanly talents."

Margaret's pen scraped across the page, and I said, "How long have you been standing there?"

"Quite some time. I was lurking, you see," Sethos explained. "I wanted to have a cheering word with Sennia before she went to bed. Well, Margaret? You wouldn't want to disappoint Daoud, would you?"

The look she transferred from Sethos to Daoud brought the latter to his feet. "It does not matter," Daoud said quickly. "I will go now."

And go he did, after hasty but heartfelt good wishes. Margaret closed her notebook. The crimson scarf hung limp round her neck, as if she had been tugging at it. "Are you ready, O'Connell?" she asked.

"Come, don't break up the party," Sethos exclaimed. "Have another whiskey."

"Well, now," said Kevin.

Margaret snatched her wrap. "Thank you for a delightful evening," she snapped, and stalked out of the room.

"Aren't you going to escort her back to the hotel?" I asked Kevin. He was in a mellow mood, as he always was after a lot of wine and a few whiskeys, and he was basking in the air of goodwill. His freckles glowed and so did his peeling nose.

"No need, no need, Mrs. E. The carriage we hired is waiting and I don't doubt she'll take it, leaving me stranded."

"Sufficient unto the day is the transportation thereof," said Sethos, taking the empty glass from Kevin's hand.

I turned to my son and discovered he had already left the room. He returned almost at once to report that Margaret had indeed got into a waiting carriage and driven off before he could offer his services as escort.

Nefret admitted she was tired—not surprising, after such a day—and Ramses went away with her. The rest of us settled down to what proved to be a very enjoyable time. Emerson insisted we sing, and rendered "Here we come a-wassailing" a cappella, very loudly and very off-key. Kevin sang several songs in a sweet tenor, and Sethos joined him in "The Cherry Tree Carol." We hailed the dawn of the day of the Savior's birth with a final chorus and went to the door with Kevin. He refused Emerson's offer to drive him to the river in the motorcar, declaring the fresh air would do him good. He strolled away, not *too* unsteadily, followed by our repeated farewells of "Happy Christmas," for on that day of all days it would have been churlish to remember Kevin's past offenses.

I will not deny that the whiskey may have had something to do with our state of mind.

Emerson seldom overindulges, but on the rare occasions when he does he is a perfect bear next morning, demanding sympathy and denying that he has taken too much to drink.

"Sethos has given me his bloody damned cold," he insisted.

"You haven't sneezed once," I retorted. "A cold shower and a few aspirin will put you right. Pull yourself together. The children are joining us for breakfast."

Deprived of the sympathy he did not deserve, Emerson followed my instructions, and by the time we were all gathered round the tree and the remaining presents, he was almost himself again. Sethos had pulled himself together too, though he winced whenever one of the children let out a shriek.

"I see your cold is much better," I said to him. "How is your head?"

"Fatima gave me aspirin," Sethos said, pressing his hand to his brow.

Over the past weeks we had received several parcels from England; it was these we had saved for Christmas morning, knowing that most of them would be for the twins. Everyone except dear Evelyn had long since given up on Emerson. He conjured up a smile when he opened her gift of a nice pair of gloves, and put them carefully aside. He had no others, since he kept losing them, and I did not suppose these would last any longer.

At my suggestion the grandparents and aunts and uncles and cousins had bought books for David John. I hoped they would hold him for a while, since children's books in English were difficult to obtain in Luxor, but I noticed that he already owned several of them, and that some others were far below his reading ability. However, as I said to David John, he must express proper appreciation and refrain from mentioning the duplications.

I always insisted that the twins write thank-you letters immediately upon receipt of gifts. It is the only proper way. And it provided a reason for them to sit down, at a table, on a chair, and curb their hilarity.

We all had a little rest, which some of us needed after the hilarity and Fatima's bountiful late breakfast. Then it was time to dress for Cyrus's soiree. Unfortunately Emerson and Selim had succeeded (or so they claimed) in getting the motorcar in running order. Fortunately there were too many of us to fit into it in comfort. Nefret and I and Fatima got into Cyrus's carriage. I did not want the motorcar preceding us, because of the dust, or following us, because of the possibility that Emerson and Selim had been overly optimistic about the steering apparatus, so I finally managed to persuade them to ride horseback. Selim rode magnificently and knew it, and Emerson was persuaded when I allowed him to wear riding kit instead of evening clothes, which he detests. They followed us, and I must say that they made an imposing escort.

We were among the last to arrive (thanks to the discussion regarding the motorcar). Cyrus's grand drawing room was filled with guests, all dressed in their best. The severe black and white of the gentlemen's evening suits was brightened by the ladies' gowns, in every shade from nile green to scarlet, and by the elegant robes of the Egyptian guests. Sir William stood by the buffet table, champagne glass in hand, chatting (and, I did not doubt, chuckling) with a gentleman who was a stranger to me. Probably a tourist; Cyrus always included a number of them in his invitations.

"I owe you an apology, Amelia," said Cyrus, observing the direction of my gaze. "Didn't get a chance to express myself adequately last night."

"Why should you apologize, Cyrus? It was not your fault."

"You didn't bring Sennia."

"I thought it better that she should not come."

"I'll make it up to her," Cyrus said fervently. "A late Christmas present, maybe. What would she like?"

"Only your goodwill, Cyrus dear. And she knows she has that."

We were joined at that point by Emerson. He was one of the few gentlemen not in evening kit, but honesty compels me to admit that he looks his best in less formal garments. He cut quite a handsome figure in boots and riding breeches and a well-tailored tweed coat; the eyes of many of the ladies dwelled admiringly upon him.

"I refuse to be polite to that bastard Portmanteau," he announced. "How much longer must we put up with him?"

"You needn't shout," I said, giving Emerson a little poke. "He is leaving tomorrow, I understand."

"No such luck," Cyrus said. "He's decided to stay on a few more days. But we won't see much of him; he's taking Suzanne to Abydos and Dendera. I think he's trying to persuade her to return to England with him."

"She can't do that," I said firmly. "Not without consulting me. I— we, that is—engaged her for the season."

"It would sure leave me in a pretty pickle," Cyrus said. "She never finished the drawings of Ay's reliefs. Not that they were much good. I don't suppose David—"

"Excuse me," I said. "Katherine is gesturing at me. I must circulate."

Cyrus had always been an excellent host, and Katherine added those little touches of elegance that only a wife can provide. Candles blazed in the elegant crystal chandeliers and sconces, potted plants provided quiet corners, and there were fresh flowers on each of the little tables scattered about. Several archaeological friends had come, though none of those from Metropolitan House. I deduced that they had refused Cyrus's invitation, as they had mine. The visiting tourists compensated, in numbers at least, for their absence. All of them wanted to hear about Tutankhamon, and as I made my way from group to group, I offered little tidbits of description—and tactfully avoided requests that I get them admitted to the tomb. The gentleman with whom Sir William had been conversing was particularly persistent. He was head of the board of some company or other, which, he seemed to feel, entitled him to special privileges.

After several glasses of champagne I decided I had better have something to eat. I made my way to the buffet table, where I found my brother-in-law.

"Allow me," he said, taking the plate from my hand. "What will it be? Foie gras, turkey, pickled oysters . . . Oh, of course. Cucumber sandwiches?"

Having indicated my selections, I allowed him to lead me to a table. "I have been chatting with Nadji," he said. "He seems a trifle low-spirited."

"You are becoming quite a kindly soul," I said.

"It's a dull crowd." Sethos leaned back. "Too many millionaires and their overdressed wives."

I did not reply, since my mouth was full. Surveying the glittering assemblage, I conceded his point. I was pleased to see that Ramses and Nefret had taken charge of Emerson, who was inclined, when unsupervised, to start arguments. Nefret looked absolutely stunning that night, her face aglow and her hair a crown of gold.

"I haven't seen Margaret," I said.

"Perhaps she had enough of us last night."

"But one would expect a dedicated journalist to attend, in the hope of picking up some bit of gossip." Kevin's carroty head moved through the crowd like a comet, and I identified several other guests as journalists. I can always spot them by the bulges in their coat pockets which indicate the presence of notebooks, and by their predatory looks. Messieurs Bradstreet of the *New York Times* and Bancroft of the *Daily Mail* were known to me personally (through no fault of mine).

A little before midnight Emerson came up to me. "Can we go now?" he demanded.

"If you like, my dear."

"I do like. There are too many damned journalists and not enough Egyptologists, and if I don't leave soon I will be impelled to tell Sir William what I think of him. Did you see the way he stared at Fatima, as if she were a servant who did not know her place?"

Emerson's threat could not be taken lightly. I slipped my arm through his. "Come and say good night to Cyrus and Katherine, then. I will see if the others are ready to go."

Fatima was more than ready. She was rather shy in company, and had come only because she did not want to offend Cyrus. She had been well looked after that evening, though, by Sethos and by Nefret and Ramses. The latter pair decided to come with us, and so did David, but Sethos declared he would stay on for a bit. Selim was having a splendid time, rolling his eyes at dazzled ladies and addressing them in an exaggerated accent, so I left him to it. The ladies appeared to be enjoying the performance.

As soon as we were seated in the carriage, Fatima fell asleep, leaning against Nefret's shoulder. "She works too hard," Nefret said softly. "We ought to get more help for her."

"I have offered, Nefret, to no avail. She likes to be in charge."

"We might at least keep the twins from bothering her so much. I know she adores them, but they can be very tiring."

"You could do with more help yourself," I said. "It is high time the children began their formal education."

There was no response from Nefret. Her eyes were closed and her head drooped.

We spent Boxing Day recovering from the ones that had preceded it. There was a general, though unexpressed, consensus that much as we had enjoyed the holiday season, we were relieved it was over, and with no worse disasters than a scorched tree.

"No worse thus far," I said. "I cannot conceive, Emerson, what mad urge prompted you to give Charla a bow and arrows."

Emerson had retreated to his study, whither I had followed. "Cannot a man have a little peace and quiet to get on with his neglected work?" he demanded. "I gave up several days—willingly and without complaint, Peabody—to your nefarious schemes. Now leave me be."

He picked up a pen and began writing at great speed. I sat down on the corner of his desk.

"You have misspelled artifact and stratification," I said.

"Curse it!" Emerson looked round for some object at which to throw his pen. I took it from him, to prevent further ink stains on the furniture.

"Since it was you who gave the deadly object to Charla, it is your responsibility to see it is not misused."

Emerson's shoulders sagged and his keen blue eyes took on a haunted look. "I can't take it away from her. I can't, Peabody."

"I know. It would be cruel and improper to take back a gift. What I propose is that you retain possession of the objects and allow her to use them only under your supervision."

"Me?" Emerson demanded, neglecting grammar in his consternation. "I don't know a cursed thing about archery. Nefret's the one. She was once very good at it."

"Then why don't you ask her?"

Grumbling but admitting his responsibility, Emerson went in search of Nefret. The dear girl at once agreed to the scheme (which I had discussed with her earlier), and we all went into the desert behind the house to set up the butts (bales of hay from the stable with targets painted by David). Charla was so pleased at being the object of our attention that she obeyed her mother's instructions faithfully and even agreed to let David John have his turn. It gave her no little satisfaction, I believe, when he proved to be less adept.

In the afternoon we distributed the Christmas boxes, most of which contained money. A few of the villagers dropped in, on the chance that they might be included. We handed out sweets to the children among them, and I caught Emerson dispensing baksheesh to young Azmi. I was on the veranda at the time, waiting for tea.

"For what services are you rewarding him?" I demanded. "I told you, Emerson, that you must not encourage a child to spy and sneak."

"The lad is learning a useful lesson," said Sethos, who had been an amused listener. "That he can earn more from sneaking and spying than from carrying water jars."

Since I could not in honesty deny this, I sniffed and picked up the newspaper I had laid aside.

"Reading a newspaper?" Sethos inquired. "Good Lord, Amelia. What has come over you?"

"Bloody waste of time," Emerson said, seating himself and taking out his pipe. "Isn't tea ready?"

"Shortly. I was just having a glance at the social column. I expect most of the honorables and sirs and lords will be descending upon Luxor before long."

"Is there any other news?" Sethos asked.

"Rioting in the Delta and the attempted assassination of the Minister of Public Works," I said, forgetting that I had "just" glanced at the social column.

Waxing impatient for his tea, Emerson got up and went into the house to encourage Fatima. Leaning forward, Sethos said softly, "You are still expecting some dramatic action from . . . them, aren't you? Don't worry your pretty little head about it, my dear. We've been left in peace, as they promised."

I flung the newspaper aside. "Something is bound to happen to someone, otherwise there would be no point to the business. I feel as if I were waiting for a bomb to go off."

"If it does, you won't learn about it from a day-old newspaper," said Sethos.

He was right about that. I learned of it next morning, from, of all people, Kevin O'Connell.

We had gone back to work in the West Valley. Emerson was fired up about a new theory, that the undecorated tomb number 25 had been meant for Akhenaton. He told us all about it at breakfast.

"Akhenaton did not transfer his residence to Amarna until year five of his reign. He would have started to excavate his tomb by then, in Thebes. Where else but in the West Valley, where his father was buried? It was never finished because he began, and completed, another tomb at Amarna."

"It makes sense, Father," said Ramses politely. "But there is no evidence."

"I am going to find it," Emerson declared, tossing his napkin onto the table. "I gave number 25 a cursory examination last year; this time I intend to examine every wall surface and every scrap with a magnifying glass."

"Good luck," said Sethos, accepting another cup of coffee from Fatima.

"Aren't you coming?" Emerson demanded.

"Oh, I suppose I may as well. As soon as I've finished this excellent coffee."

David had promised Cyrus he would continue copying the reliefs in the tomb of Ay, so after Sethos had dawdled over his coffee we all set out on horseback. An extremely unfortunate incident then occurred. An increasingly loud roar and a series of hoots made the horses start. Looking back, I saw a motorcar coming up behind us at considerable speed, carts and donkeys scattering before it.

We managed to get out of its way in time, though Emerson would have been seriously inconvenienced had not Ramses caught hold of the bridle of his horse and pulled it aside. The motorcar passed us in a cloud of dust and pebbles. Next to the chauffeur sat Howard, holding on to his hat. In the tonneau were Harry Burton—who gave us a cheery wave with the hand that was not holding his hat; Mr. Lucas, the chemist; and another gentleman whom I recognized as Arthur Mace, one of the Metropolitan Museum staff who had worked at Lisht in Lower Egypt. He was too preoccupied with holding on to his hat to acknowledge us, though I felt sure he would have done so otherwise. A pleasant, courteous man, he had had a good deal of experience working with fragile materials, and fully agreed with me on the superior usefulness of melted paraffin. The Metropolitan had certainly got its hand in.

Emerson's language is really not to be repeated. It took all my eloquence to prevent him from galloping back to the house and going in pursuit of Howard in our motorcar.

"You will never catch him up now," I insisted.

"He did it deliberately, in order to insult me," Emerson raged.

"If he is behaving so childishly, you need not descend to his level."

"Bah," said Emerson, eyes narrowed and jaw set.

I wondered if I could detach a bit of our motorcar and hide it.

After brushing off the sand the wheels of Howard's car had sprayed on us, we continued on our way. Even at that early hour the road to the main valley had begun to fill with tourists; after we turned aside toward the West Valley, blessed quiet descended, except for the muttering of

Emerson. As always, the West Valley cast its spell. A great amphitheater walled by cliffs carved into fantastic formations by wind and water, it is a very silent place, unmatched for rugged grandeur. The sun rose over the eastern cliffs as we rode along, bringing a blush of pale gold to the rock. We and our horses might have been the only living creatures on earth.

Our working area was several miles from the entrance. When we arrived, we found that Cyrus and his crew had got there just before us.

Catching Cyrus's arm in a firm grip, Emerson immediately launched into a bitter tirade, accusing Howard of daring to drive his own motorcar along a public road.

"Well, now," said Cyrus, when Emerson ran out of breath. "I reckon there's nothing we can do about it, is there? Shall we start work?"

"What? Oh." Emerson rubbed his chin. "You want David, I suppose. The rest of you gather round. I have a plan . . ."

With a wink and a nod at me, David descended into the torrid depths of Ay's tomb, accompanied by several of the workmen carrying torches. Emerson delivered a brief lecture on Tomb 25 and set the men to work clearing the stairs. In a single season sand and blowing debris had partially refilled them. I was given the task of resifting the debris we had removed the year before.

This is not the most absorbing of chores, especially when it is a repetition of work one has done before. My attention wandered, and at increasingly frequent intervals I rose to stretch cramped limbs. Thus it was that I was the first to see the boy Azmi coming full-tilt along the rough path. He was mounted on a donkey, which he encouraged to run by means of shouts and—until I advanced toward him—whacks of a stick.

He would have swerved round me had not the donkey decided to stop. No doubt it recognized a defender. I caught Azmi by the neck of his robe. "You know we do not permit an animal to be beaten," I said sternly. "Even if we do not see you, we know."

"You did see me," Azmi remarked. He scratched his side, captured a flea, and squashed it. "But I will not do it again, Sitt Hakim."

He tried to pull away from me. I held on. "What are you doing here? Why have you come?"

"To speak to the Father of Curses. I have news."

"Speak to me first."

Our discussion had attracted attention. Sensing potential drama, the men began drifting toward us, and Emerson hurried to my side.

"What is it?" he demanded of the boy.

"The Sitt orders that I should tell her first," said Azmi, basking in the attention.

"Er—tell us both," said Emerson, abandoning any hope of a private conversation with his juvenile informer. David must have been told that something interesting was happening; he emerged from the tomb, and joined the rest of the audience.

Azmi's little brown face opened in a grin. He was too young to have suffered from the dental problems that affect so many Egyptians; his teeth shone white as pearls. He spoke in a squeaky whisper. "They are taking the treasures from the tomb. Today. Soon. Now!"

"Make up your mind," Ramses said.

"It is of no concern to me," said Emerson. It was one of his more un-convincing lies. Undaunted, Azmi held out a slim brown hand, and after a sidelong glance at me, Emerson dropped a few coins into his palm.

"Be off with you," he grunted. "Back to work, everyone."

"Nonsense," I said. "How can any of us concentrate on work now? Especially David; this may be his best and only chance of getting a glimpse of the artifacts."

"And mine," Cyrus cried. "Let's go!"

We overruled Emerson's objections, which he had counted on our doing, and were soon on our way, trailed by Azmi, who held up his empty hands and grinned at me whenever I looked in his direction. He was a rather prepossessing lad, and I couldn't blame him for having no principles. To the very poor, morality is a luxury. He must be doing well, if he had the wherewithal to hire a donkey.

Ramses kept me company as we rode. Nefret, a far better horse-woman than I, had forged ahead with Cyrus and David.

"Mr. Burton must have finished the preliminary photographs," I said. "Surely Howard wouldn't move anything until the entire contents of the chamber had been recorded."

"Even Father admits, when he isn't in a temper, that Carter is a responsible excavator," Ramses replied. "I don't doubt he is going about it in the proper way."

"I wonder which objects he will remove first."

"He'll do it in order," Ramses said. "From one end of the chamber to the other, leaving the larger, more difficult pieces until last. I don't envy him the job."

He might not, but his father did. However, looking on the bright side (as I always endeavor to do), perhaps it was just as well that the task had not fallen to Emerson. Carter had assembled a staff unparalleled in its skill. It was unlikely that the Metropolitan Museum or any other institution would have been so accommodating to us. They counted on a share of the treasure, and Emerson would never have agreed to that. In addition, Emerson would have dragged every member of the family into the business. The job would take years, if I was any judge, and that would put a halt to David's independent career and to my plans for Ramses and Nefret.

There is a silver lining to every cloud, as I always say.

The news of Howard's intention must have got about, for the tourists were out in force and the area near the tomb was infested with journalists. The latter individuals must not have found Howard helpful, for they converged on us, whipping out their notebooks and asking what we knew.

"No more than you, I fancy," I replied. "That Mr. Carter intends to begin removing the first of the objects today. They will be carried to the tomb of Seti II, where they will be packed for eventual shipment and, if necessary, stabilized by Mr. Lucas and Mr. Mace. Many are in fragile condition."

They wrote all this down, as if it had been the word of the Prophet, and Mr. Bradstreet asked me to elaborate. "It is a complex subject, but I will make it as simple as possible," I replied good-humoredly. "When air is introduced into a hitherto sealed tomb, all substances except metal and pottery are affected. Plaster may crack and fall off, paint may flake, fabric may rot. It is sometimes necessary to apply chemicals—or, as I have always preferred, melted paraffin wax—to hold loose pieces in place and preserve the original design."

"What the devil do you think you are doing?" Emerson whispered, directly into my left ear.

"Why should I not oblige these amiable gentlemen?" I asked. "They have every right to the facts. This is not Lord Carnarvon's tomb; it belongs to Egypt and to the world!"

A somewhat ironic cheer greeted this statement, and Mr. Bradstreet said with a grin, "You've changed your tune, haven't you, Mrs. Emerson? First time I've ever heard you say the press had a right to anything. Couldn't be sour grapes, could it?"

"If the press chooses to misrepresent my remarks, it cannot be surprised that I dislike being quoted," I said severely.

He was about to apologize, I believe, when a buzz and a bustle around the tomb entrance drew all eyes in that direction. The gentlemen of the press abandoned me, shoving and pushing and aiming their cameras. A squad of soldiers took up position by the barrier. Then Howard came into view. His hat was tipped to one side, his mustache carefully brushed; in one hand he held his stick, in the other a cigarette holder.

"Back!" he shouted, brandishing his stick in military style. "Stand back, everyone."

From the entrance, carried on a wooden stretcher to which it was bound by strips of bandage, emerged the first object—the beautiful painted chest with scenes of the king in his chariot. Shouts of delight came from the spectators; the clicking of cameras rattled like hail. David, beside me, stood mesmerized and mute.

"Come farther along the path," I said, taking his arm. "You can get a better view from there."

We were the first to move; other spectators trooped after the bearers, trying to get a closer look at the lovely thing. A few actually reached out, trying to touch it, and were only prevented from doing so by the soldiers who surrounded the bearers.

David followed the procession all the way to the storage tomb, staring and stumbling and running into people. I was in perfect sympathy with him. Nothing like that chest had ever been seen before.

When he rejoined me he was pale with excitement. "Your description didn't do it justice," he gasped. "It couldn't. Good Lord, Aunt Amelia, I would give my right hand to be allowed to paint it!"

"Without a right hand you wouldn't be able to," I said, for I always think a little touch of humor helps excited persons to settle down. It had the desired effect on David. He took my arm.

"I beg your pardon, Aunt Amelia. I ought not have left you in the midst of this jostling crowd."

"Quite all right, dear boy," I said. "I had no trouble in fending for myself. I never do. Shall we go back? Howard may intend to bring out something else."

"I don't think I want to see anything else," David said softly. "Not today. I couldn't take it in."

"Then we will go home, my dear."

"You do understand?"

"Naturally. Your artist's soul has been transported. You require peace and quiet to contemplate the full wonder of what you have seen. And," I added, "perhaps a whiskey and soda."

Most of the spectators had pelted back to the tomb, but Kevin O'Connell was lying in wait for us. "What's the idea of giving out all that information to me rivals, Mrs. E.?" he demanded.

"Don't be silly, Kevin," I replied. "I didn't tell them anything that wasn't public knowledge. You were writing it all down too, I observed. I was surprised not to see Miss Minton."

"She didn't turn up today," Kevin said, falling in step with us. "Come to think of it, I haven't laid eyes on her since the night of your party."

. . .

"We should never have allowed her to go alone," I exclaimed.

Inquiries, which I had immediately set in train, confirmed Kevin's statement. No one had set eyes on Miss Minton since Christmas Eve. The night clerk, rousted out of his home, declared she had not returned to the Winter Palace that night. He had thought nothing of it. If a foreign lady decided to sleep elsewhere, it was none of his business.

Kevin had returned to the house with the rest of us and waited until the reports came in.

"It was my responsibility," he said, eyes cast down. Then he took another longish sip of his whiskey and soda and brightened. "But, Mrs. E., I don't see why you should suppose something has happened to her. Minton is always going off on her own, hoping to steal a march on the rest of us. She was perfectly sober when she left here and she was not alone. What has the carriage driver to say?"

"We have not been able to locate him," Emerson said. He and I were pacing up and down the length of the drawing room, avoiding each other with the skill of long practice.

Obviously we could not explain to Kevin why we did not believe Margaret had left of her own free will. None of the boatmen recalled having taken her across the river, so she must have been abducted while still on the West Bank. The carriage driver had vanished as well. Selim, who knew everyone on this side of the river, had gone at once to the fellow's house, only to discover that he had never returned home.

As I crossed paths with Emerson, he said out of the corner of his mouth, "Get rid of him, Peabody."

Kevin heard him, as did everyone else in the drawing room. Placing his empty glass on the table, he rose with great dignity. "I can take a hint, Professor."

"Never known you to do so before," Emerson retorted.

Kevin took himself off, meaning, I supposed, to pursue his own inquiries. If Margaret was on the track of an interesting story, Kevin would be on *her* track.

We knew better, of course. David and Ramses had gone off to search the riverbank and locate the few boatmen we had not been able to question thus far. Sethos was with them. He had been the first to propose we search for Margaret.

"So much for the promises of our adversaries," I said bitterly. "We relaxed our guard, and now they have struck."

"O'Connell may have it right," Emerson muttered. "Perhaps she learned something from us that night that sent her haring off in pursuit of an exclusive."

"Nonsense. She had nothing with her except the clothes she was wearing and a small evening bag. The driver's disappearance is highly significant. He was in cahoots with the kidnappers—or he was murdered to prevent him from talking."

"Do sit down, Mother," Nefret begged, as Emerson and I swerved round each other. "You are wearing yourself out. If the people you suspect have abducted Margaret, they won't harm her. This is only their way of ensuring that we remain silent."

She went herself to the sideboard and poured a soupçon of whiskey. I took the glass and sank into a chair.

"We would remain silent in any case, since we do not know what they plan," I said. "However, vain regrets and vague surmises are of no use to us now. Let us remain calm and consider what we do know."

"Not much," said Emerson.

"For one thing, we can now be certain that our adversaries are aware of Sethos's true identity. Had they not known Margaret was his wife, they would not have taken her."

"He was in considerable distress," Nefret said. "There were actually tears in his eyes." Her own eyes were soft with sympathy, blue as turquoise.

"A pity he didn't demonstrate his feelings for her before it was too late," Emerson said.

"Let us hope and pray it is not too late," I said.

David and Ramses returned to report that they had discovered no trace of Margaret or the driver. That was good news, in a negative sense; I had been haunted by images of a limp body washed up on the shore. The carriage, which had been hired from a firm located in Luxor, was found abandoned some distance from the ferry landing.

"It seems we have come to a dead end," I said. "Where is Sethos?"

"He went off by himself, saying he had an idea he meant to pursue." Ramses declined his father's offer of whiskey, saying he would wait for tea. "It occurred to me that he might intend to offer an exchange of hostages. Himself for Margaret."

"It is the least he can do," Emerson grunted. "Good Gad, any man who gave a curse about his wife would do the same."

"He knows how to communicate with them," I said. "Assuming, that is, they can still be reached through the address he once had. Oh dear. I can't see that an exchange would leave us any better off."

Ramses put a comforting hand on my shoulder. "I don't believe there is any cause for concern, Mother. She'll be released as soon as the abductors no longer need her."

The passage of time and a sip or two of whiskey had restored my reasoning powers to their normal efficiency. "Does this event suggest, perhaps, that that time is near at hand?" I asked.

"I wondered about that," Ramses admitted. "But if such is the case, there's not a bloody thing we can do about it."

I put a warning finger to my lips. "I hear the children coming. David, dear, you look very careworn, and you have not had a chance to meditate on the wonders of the painted box. If you would like to retire, I am sure Fatima will bring you a cup of tea and a biscuit."

"I'll wait until we hear from Sethos, if you don't mind," David said. "I can't really concentrate on aesthetics at the moment. Don't worry, Aunt Amelia, I am sure there is no reason to fear for her safety."

If one more person tells me that I will swear, I thought. How could he know? How could any of us know?

The children and the dog burst in. We put the dog out, and Fatima served tea. She had prepared a number of delicacies, as she always did when she believed we were in need of comfort. As I had promised I would, I dispatched a note to Cyrus, informing him that as yet we had no news. After that there was nothing to do but wait.

The chatter of the dear children proved a temporary distraction. As I had expected, several days of excessive virtue had taken their toll on both; Charla knocked over the chessboard David John had set up in the hope of finding an opponent, and David John kicked her. They fell upon each other. The dog began to howl. I was attempting to separate the combatants when there was a tap on the door.

"Is it safe to come in?" Sethos inquired.

"Get hold of the dog," I gasped, taking Charla in a firm grip.

"She's already got hold of me," said Sethos. "What seems to be the trouble?"

Charla stopped struggling as soon as I got my arms round her; to do her credit, she never kicked or bit any of the family except her brother. David John, sobbing with rage and/or remorse, had subsided into the arms of his father. The dog stopped howling and began to whine. She never bit anyone either; she had only seized Sethos by the arm, leaving a large slimy spot on his sleeve.

The children were sent off to bed and the dog admonished. "Any news?" I asked Sethos.

"No. Thank you, Fatima, I don't believe I care for tea. May I . . . ?"

"Yes, yes," said Emerson. "Help yourself. And Peabody, if she would care for another."

"I believe I will, now that you mention it."

"You look worried," said Sethos, handing me a brimming glass. "I didn't know you were so fond of Margaret. She treated you rather shabbily, after all."

"How can I blame her for behaving as I might have done under similar circumstances? Of course I am fond of the cursed woman."

"I assure you, Amelia," Sethos said earnestly, "that there is no cause for concern."

"Bloody hell and damnation!" I shouted.

A united gasp shivered through the air, and Fatima dropped a cup.

"Peabody!" Emerson said in shocked surprise.

"I beg your pardon." I took a restorative sip of whiskey and drew a deep, calming breath. "Fatima, stop wringing your hands, it was my fault. But I weary of meaningless reassurance. How the devil—excuse me—do you know there is no cause for concern? Why aren't you worried?"

"What makes you suppose I am not?" Sethos asked. He sank heavily into a chair, and now that I got a good look at him I saw that his appearance did suggest a certain degree of distraction. Hair windblown, mustache drooping, garments wrinkled, he was the image of a concerned spouse.

"I was attempting to reassure you," he said, his eyes lowered. "We have as yet no evidence that Margaret is in the hands of my enemies. Even if she is, they have no reason to offer her harm."

"Your confidence in their goodwill is not borne out by their actions," I exclaimed. "They have broken their word to leave us in peace."

"Perhaps they suspect we have broken our word," Sethos said.

"Have you?"

"No."

Her face drawn with sympathy, Fatima thrust a plate of sugar biscuits at him. Sugar biscuits do not really go well with whiskey, but he took one.

"Let us discuss this sensibly," Emerson said, taking out his pipe. "You"—he gestured at his brother—"you say you have done nothing to prompt such a reaction. Has anyone else?"

"You're on the wrong track, Father," Ramses said. Emerson blinked at his uncharacteristic lack of tact, and Ramses said, "I beg your pardon. But look at it this way. Supposing we had received a sudden revelation, which God knows we haven't, what would we have done about it?"

"Informed the authorities," I said.

"How?" He didn't wait for an answer. "By telegraph or in person, isn't that right? Most probably the latter. Telegrams may become lost in the bureaucratic muddle or be intercepted. No; we'd have gone straight to Cairo, to Thomas Russell or the high commissioner. They know that hasn't happened. We are under surveillance still. We always have been. For all we know, someone close to us is passing on information about our activities."

It was a damning and convincing summary. While we digested it, Sethos raised a haggard face. "Are you accusing me of betraying my own wife?"

"He doesn't mean you," I said. "Strangers in our midst . . . Nadji or Suzanne? But which?"

## From Manuscript H

Nefret sat at her dressing table brushing her hair. The dress she meant to wear lay across the bed. It was one of Ramses's favorites, a pale blue sprinkled with small white flowers and green leaves, but to him she was even more beautiful in her clinging silk slip, her white shoulders and little feet bare.

"You're looking absolutely marvelous these days," he said, capturing a stray lock of hair and winding it round his finger. "I like that dress. What's the occasion?"

"I felt like cheering myself up. And Mother."

"Women are lucky. We men haven't such easy means of cheering ourselves up."

"It's your own fault for following fashion so slavishly. Go and tell David it's time for dinner, will you? He's been brooding for hours."

There was no answer to Ramses's knock. After a second, louder knock he opened the door. The room was unoccupied. A drawing pad lay open on the writing table; David had started a sketch of the painted chest. Incomplete as it was, it had David's inimitable touch.

While Ramses was admiring it, the houseman came in with an armful of fresh towels.

"Where's Mr. David?" Ramses asked.

"I do not know. He told me to give you this," he said, as he handed over a folded sheet of paper.

Ramses read the brief message and swore under his breath. "When did he leave?"

"Just now, Brother of Demons."

Ramses hurried back to his room.

"What—" Nefret began, her eyes widening.

"Read this." He handed her the note.

She read it aloud. " 'Have gone for a walk. Won't be long. Don't worry.' What does he mean, don't worry? It isn't like David to go off like this."

"No, it isn't. I'm going after him." He buckled on the belt that held his knife.

"Not alone!" Nefret got up and came to him.

"I must leave at once. He's already several minutes ahead of me."

"I'm going with you."

"No." He took her by the shoulders. "Not this time. My darling, I'm only going to catch him up and remind him this is not a good time to be wandering about in the dark."

He was over the sill and out the window before she could reply. He had a last glimpse of her anxious face and parted lips before he turned the corner of the house.

Ramses swung by the stable and found Jamad asleep and the horses all in their stalls. So David was on foot. He was at least five minutes behind David, and if David had gone toward Gurneh or the western cliffs, he'd already be out of sight. If he had headed toward the riverbank, meaning to cross over to Luxor, there was still a chance of catching him up. He started down the road, running.

He had thought of several innocent explanations for David's behavior, including the one he had given. It was understandable that he might feel the need to be alone; the family en masse or individually could be wearing.

His straining eyes caught sight of a form moving along the road some distance ahead. He didn't need to see the man's face to make an identification. Since his war injury, David limped when he moved too fast.

So much for the first of the innocent explanations. Ramses told himself that David must have a good reason for going off this way, but he decided not to stop him. The main thing was to keep him in sight. Wandering round the streets of Luxor at night, for whatever reason, was to invite trouble.

Ramses slowed his pace and tried to figure out his next move. So far David hadn't seen him, but if he followed by boat he would be as conspicuous as a camel caravan. There wasn't much traffic on the river at this hour. Most of the tourists had retired to their hotels.

Keeping in the shadow of one of the vessels pulled up on the bank, he watched David negotiate with a boatman and climb aboard. Instead of taking a seat, he stood looking back along the road. Ramses was forced to the only viable means of pursuit. He slid into the water. A few long strokes took him up to the side of the boat as it got under way.

It was not the most comfortable way to cross the river. His head was under water a good deal of the time, and his wet clothes clung clammily to his body. Now and then he heard the boatman swearing. The fellow had noticed the boat wasn't answering as readily as usual, but it didn't occur to him that he had an extra passenger.

When they reached the other side David jumped out without waiting for the gangplank. He splashed through the shallows toward the bank. Ramses waited until he had climbed it before he pulled himself out of the water and pushed his wet hair out of his eyes. They met the stupefied eyes of the boatman. His mouth dropped open.

"Quiet," Ramses whispered. "Don't speak. I owe you baksheesh, Ali Ibrahim. Tomorrow."

The word of an Emerson was good all along the river. The man nodded dumbly. Ramses squeezed the water from the bottoms of his trouser legs and climbed the stairs to the street.

Unpleasant as the trip had been for Ramses, it had convinced David he had not been followed. Ramses attracted a lot of curious looks as he dripped and splashed along the pavement, but David didn't look back. He moved like a man who knew exactly where he was going, until he passed the Winter Palace and reached a quieter section of the road. Then he stopped and looked round.

There were only a few houses nearby, on the north side of the road. Ramses had dropped flat when David halted, there being no other place of concealment he could reach. He felt the water on his clothes mixing with the dust.

David went to the door of one of the houses—a rather imposing structure several stories high, with a flight of steps leading to a pair of carved columns that flanked the entrance. Ramses jumped up. Mud dripped off him. The hell with this, he thought. I'm going to confront him, ask him what he thinks he's doing.

He got as far as the top of the stairs. Arms clamped round his body. He twisted, freeing one arm and striking out. His fist smashed into a surface as unyielding as stone, and other arms gripped him. Someone let out a string of obscene Arabic epithets, and someone else offered a rude suggestion in the same language. A pair of hands closed round his throat. Then a voice called out a peremptory command. "Stop!"

He recognized the voice. It was that, as much as the stranglehold on his throat, that ended his resistance. Unseen hands pushed him into the house and slammed the door. The interior was dark, but he made out curving walls and a shimmer of reflection from what must be a mirror before he was hastily blindfolded. Half dragging, half pulling, they got him to an inner room and shoved him in. Sprawled on the floor, he heard a muttered colloquy outside the closed door.

They hadn't tied his hands. He pulled off the blindfold—a filthy rag that smelled of sweat—and discovered that the groping hands had relieved him of his knife. The door opened. A man entered carrying a lamp, which he put down on a table. The room was small and scantily furnished, with a low couch and a few chairs and tables. It had only one window, small and high in the wall.

"Are you hurt?" David asked anxiously.

Ramses got slowly to his feet. He was caked with dirt from chest to feet, and his throat hurt. His arm moved without conscious volition, delivering a hard, backhanded blow to David's face. David staggered back, his hand over his mouth. Blood dripped between his fingers.

"It was you," Ramses said. "All along, it was you."

# CHAPTER TEN

WE WERE IN THE DRAWING ROOM WAITING FOR DINNER TO BE AN-
nounced when Nefret came in.

"Where are David and Ramses?" I asked. "Dinner is almost ready."

"Gone out." Nefret brushed a loosened lock of hair back from her
face.

I suppose we were all a little on edge—or perhaps it was something
in her voice that made Sethos look up with a frown and Emerson get to
his feet.

"At this hour?" I asked. "What has happened?"

Nefret took a folded piece of paper from her bodice and handed it to
me. "Nothing," she said. "At least—I don't know, Mother. I couldn't
stop him, he moved too quickly. Out the window and off at a run. I
hadn't finished dressing . . ."

"Calm yourself, my dear," I said, handing Emerson the note. "I presume 'he' refers to Ramses, David already having departed?"

"Yes."

"He says he has gone for a walk," Emerson said. "Unusual, but not alarming. Nefret, my dear, sit down and let me get you a glass of—of something."

Sethos, the last to read the message, started to speak and then closed his mouth. Watching him, I said, "Emerson is right, Nefret. Agitation is bad for you, and I am certain you have no reason for concern."

For a moment I thought Nefret would swear, as I had done on hearing that phrase. Waving away the glass Emerson offered her, she took a deep breath and said, "I would rather have sherry, if you don't mind, Father."

"Oh," said Emerson. "Oh. Of course." He handed me the whiskey and served her as she had requested.

"Did you happen to see which way Ramses went?" I asked, determinedly casual.

"Not really." She was trying hard to keep her composure, but after a sip of sherry she burst out, "Why would David steal out without a word to us? He must have known we would worry about him. Ramses said he only meant to find David and bring him back, but he took his knife, and he wouldn't wait for me or ask you to help him search, and those devils have taken Margaret, and they're out there, watching us, and—and you tell me I have no reason for concern!"

"I'll go look for them," Emerson exclaimed.

"Where?" Nefret demanded. "They could be anywhere from Gurneh to the river by now. Hell and damnation! I should have followed Ramses, in my bare feet and half-dressed!"

Her eyes filled with tears.

"Nefret, don't." Sethos got up from his chair and came to her. "Believe me, there is no cause . . . All right, all right, I won't say it. I don't know what's happened to Ramses and David, but I'm sure they'll be back soon. Margaret . . ." He hesitated.

A tear slid down Nefret's cheek. She is one of those women who can cry beautifully, with no distortion of her face or reddening of her eyes. She raised those eyes, brimming and blue, to Sethos. "Oh, hell," he said. "Margaret isn't missing. I know precisely where she is, and I assure you she is unharmed. Furious, but unharmed."

A thunderstruck silence followed this statement. Emerson was the first to recover, and his response was typical of Emerson—a hard blow that sent Sethos sprawling.

"So," Emerson said in a voice like a lion's roar. "It was you. All along, it was you."

## From Manuscript H

"No," David said, his voice blurred by the blood dripping from his nose. He passed his sleeve across it. "No, not all along. Ramses—"

"Sorry I can't offer you a handkerchief. Mine is somewhat unsanitary." Bloodying David's nose had got some of the outrage out of his system, but his voice shook.

David fumbled in a pocket and found his own. "I don't blame you for being angry with me. If you'd just listen—"

"I'll listen. I haven't much choice, have I? Fighting my way out of here wouldn't seem to be a sensible option."

"You look like hell. Sit down, why don't you?"

He went to the door and spoke to someone outside. The door opened a few inches; a hand pushed an earthenware container inside. Now conscious of aching muscles and sore spots that would soon be bruises, Ramses lowered himself onto the narrow cot and accepted a drink of water. David sat down on the floor, legs crossed, and offered Ramses a cigarette. He was tempted to refuse what was obviously meant as a peace offering, but that would have been childish. Incredulity had replaced his anger; David looked just as he always had, his well-cut features concerned, his soft brown eyes anxious. His best friend, the man he trusted above all others . . .

"Well?" he said, after David had lit the cigarette for him.

"I'll tell you everything."

"That would be nice."

David flinched. "I'd rather you hit me than use that tone of voice. It's not what you think, Ramses. I knew nothing about this business until I arrived in Cairo. You told me a little, but we didn't have time to talk at length; there was always someone around. And you were always around, you never left me alone for a minute. As I learned later, other people were waiting for a chance to talk to me in private, before I left Cairo. You wondered why they bothered to carry Gargery off. They hoped we would separate in order to search for him—which we did. As soon as you were out of sight, one of them approached me. D'you remember the man you knew as Bashir?"

"One of the gang of radicals we infiltrated during the war? I thought he had been rounded up along with the other revolutionaries."

"He was. That was his nom de guerre; his real name is Mohammed Fehmi, and he comes from a well-to-do family. After the war, when he'd served his term they let him out, thanks in large part to his father's influence. He's now a respectable member of society, employed by one of the ministries. To make a long story short, which he had to do since he hadn't much time, he told me flat-out that he and his party are planning a coup. A bloodless coup. They're fed up with Fuad and his devious schemes; they want to replace him with someone who is sympathetic to their aspirations and who will abide by the constitution."

Ramses's lip curled expressively. "I know what you're thinking," David said. "But I had no reason not to believe him, Ramses. He insisted that they had harmed no one, that they meant no harm to anyone. I agreed to keep silent, at least for the time being. At that point I hadn't got the full story from you."

"You got it when we talked that night."

David nodded. "What you told me confirmed Bashir's claims. He frankly admitted that a few of their people had got the wind up after Sethos stole their precious document, and had gone a little overboard trying to retrieve it. Since then they have confined themselves to keeping a close watch on you and the family.

"I wanted to tell you, Ramses, I really did. But—well, I'm not as naive as you think. Bashir had offered the stupid donkey a tasty handful of carrots, but he might be hiding a stick behind his back. I needed to know more about their intentions, and the best way of doing that was to keep on good terms with them—let them believe I was with them wholeheartedly."

You are, Ramses thought, noticing that David was avoiding his eyes—with them, if not wholeheartedly. You believed Bashir because you wanted to believe in a bloodless coup that would realize your fondest hopes for your country, support of a cause you've believed in and fought for all your life.

It wouldn't be bloodless, though. Coups seldom were. There were always a few who joined in for the sick pleasure of violence.

Ramses knew what it was like to be torn between conflicting loyalties. He'd had to deceive his family, even Nefret, when he was working undercover during the Great War. He had hated the deception, his superiors, and himself, as David must be doing now.

"So what have you decided?" he asked.

Sensitive to every nuance of his friend's voice and expression, David reacted to Ramses's milder tone with a direct look and a tentative smile.

"I decided tonight, when I heard about Margaret, that I might have been more naive than I thought. Bashir had given me his word that no action at all would be taken. So I came here to demand an explanation. They had given me the address in case I needed to contact them."

"What have they done with Margaret?" Ramses asked, accepting another cigarette.

"They deny having taken her."

"Do you believe that?"

"I don't know what I believe." David passed his hand over his face. "Except that I may have made the worst mistake of my life. What are we going to do?"

"I don't suppose your chums mean to turn me loose with profound apologies?"

"You would report this, wouldn't you? Warn the authorities?"

He wouldn't lie to David. What would be the point? "Yes," he said.

"I knew you'd say that. I'll get you out of here, Ramses, I swear. I never meant this to happen."

"I know. Never mind that now. I've played the fool a few times myself. Perhaps you had better have a chat with the lads and find out what they have in mind—for both of us."

"They've no reason not to trust me," David said slowly. "I objected to them manhandling you, but they wouldn't hold that against me. I haven't had a chance to ask many questions." He smiled wryly and got to his feet. "Just as well; I might have said the wrong thing. I'll report as soon as I can."

He was out the door before Ramses could respond. There was no need for a response or a handshake or any other acknowledgment; they had known each other too long and too well. David hadn't forgiven himself, but he had put guilt aside until he could make amends for his mistake.

He had left the packet of cigarettes and the jar of water. Ramses helped himself to another drink, rinsed his hands and face, and made an inspection of his prison. It hadn't been designed as such, though there was only one door, and the single window was barred—a customary precaution against thieves. Someone had occupied it recently, and briefly, to judge by the paucity of personal belongings lying about.

Which didn't tell him much. One thing was certain, though. They couldn't afford to turn him loose. He knew where their headquarters was located. He and David would have to find a way of escaping. If they couldn't outwit a few ordinary thugs they didn't deserve the reputations they had earned, but they'd have to get Margaret away as well, supposing she was here and not in another of their lairs. And time was passing. He brushed dried mud off the face of his watch and found, as he had expected, that it had not survived its watery journey. The unmoving hands accused him. Nefret would worry. He'd caused her too much worry.

Some might have accused him of naïveté for believing in David's change of heart. They would be wrong. David couldn't have misled him, even if he had wanted to. He knew his friend too well. "We," David had said. "What are we going to do?"

They had been three adventurers together, David and Nefret and he, young and stupid and foolhardy. As a girl Nefret had been as reckless as they; she'd given him a few bad times too. He remembered the time she had blackmailed them into taking her along when they went to one of the worst parts of Cairo in pursuit of a valuable manuscript. They had barely made it out unharmed—with the manuscript. David might have got his throat cut that night if Nefret hadn't acted, decisively and instantly, while he stood frozen. That bond had never been broken.

When David came back, Ramses was pacing up and down the small room. Before he could speak David said loudly, "I brought you something to eat. Sit down and keep your hands in sight. If you give us any trouble we'll have to tie you up."

"I won't make trouble." Ramses went to the bed and sat down.

The door, which had been slightly ajar, closed. David handed him a plate. Ramses studied his dinner without enthusiasm. Fuul, the popular dish consisting of mashed beans, and a chunk of bread. No utensils had been supplied. He was accustomed to eating Arab-style, though, so he dipped his fingers into the mess and forced a bite down.

"You'll be let go in a few days," David said, sitting down next to him. "Unharmed. I made that a condition of my continued cooperation. Once they've accomplished their goal, there won't be any need to hold you."

He lowered his voice gradually as he spoke. Ramses took the hint. "How many days?" he asked softly.

"Two, three at the most. Margaret's not here. When I insisted, they let me search the house."

"They must be keeping her somewhere else. If we can take one of them prisoner, he may be persuaded to tell us where."

Despite his urgent need to return to his wife, Ramses's spirits had lifted. Having David on his side was as good as an army—better, in a sense. David was his balance wheel, the sensible member of the group, as he proceeded to demonstrate.

"At the risk of sounding callous, we can't worry about Margaret now. It will be hard enough getting ourselves away, without additional heroics. Here. I found your knife."

Something pressed against his side and he shifted position slightly, so that it was concealed under his thigh. He hadn't located any spyholes in the walls, but the keyhole was big and old-fashioned.

"We'll have to wait until most of them have gone beddy-by," David went on. "There will be two men on guard. Bashir has already left. I agreed to stay here. In fact, I refused to leave when they said I could. A disingenuous offer, wasn't it?"

"A test, perhaps."

"I thought so. The door is barred as well as locked, and they aren't careless enough to trust me with the key. I may be able to pick the lock. If not, you'll have to break the door down."

"I can hardly wait." Ramses rubbed his sore shoulder. "What time is it?"

"Almost eleven. In another hour the lads should be tucked in."

Ramses groaned. "Damn. Nefret must be getting more frantic by the minute."

"To say nothing of the parents," David said. "Maybe Aunt Amelia will appear, parasol in hand." ·

"Don't try to cheer me up," Ramses muttered. He took another mouthful of the disgusting food. It was cold as well as tasteless. "There's no way they could have traced us. I made sure—clever me—that no one followed me."

"I'd better go and put on a convincing show of cooperation." David held out his hand. "They told me not to leave the dish."

"Afraid I'll smash it and use the shards to carve a hole in the door? Here, you're welcome to the rest."

David took the plate and went out without speaking again. They would work together, and fight together if necessary, like the well-oiled machine they had become.

The key turned with a click. There was nothing to do now but wait.

Emerson stood over his brother with fists clenched and brow thunderous.

"Remember the code," Sethos said. He had prudently remained supine. "Mustn't hit a man when he's down."

"Get up then!"

"I'd rather not, if you don't mind."

The door opened and Fatima put her head in. "Dinner is—" Seeing Sethos flat on the floor she broke off and ran to him. "He is sick again?"

"No, I hit him," Emerson said between clenched teeth. "And I'll do it again if he so much as blinks."

"He will not blink," Fatima cried. "Do not hit him again."

"No, we want him conscious so he can answer questions," I said.

Keeping a wary eye on Emerson, Sethos sat up, rubbing his chin. "You needn't interrogate me, Amelia," he said indistinctly. "I am prepared to speak freely, insofar as my injuries allow. They say whiskey is good for a sore jaw."

Emerson snarled. "Give it to him," I said impatiently. "And let me add, Sethos, that frivolity is distinctly out of place. What have you done with Margaret?"

For of course, Reader, I had put two and two together. On the night of the party Sethos had gone out of his way to infuriate Margaret and induce Kevin to remain. I had thought nothing of it at the time, nor could I blame myself. Hindsight is always more useful than observation. And there was another thing I hadn't noticed at the time.

"Daoud!" I cried. "Is Daoud involved in this?"

Fatima, who had immediately supplied Sethos with whiskey, let out a little squeal of protest.

"He was ready and willing," Sethos said. "Didn't you tell him you wished you could abduct Margaret again?"

"Peabody!" Emerson exclaimed. "Did you?"

"Curse it," I said. "I did say something of the sort. But it was . . . it was an expression of regret, not an order."

"You shouldn't expect Daoud to make such distinctions," Sethos said. " 'Who will free me from this turbulent priest?' was good enough for the minions of Edward II."

"What does bloody Edward II have to do with this?" Emerson demanded. "And stop smirking!"

"I beg your pardon." Sethos's smirk vanished into the limbo of lost

smiles. "Daoud did harbor a few doubts. You may have noticed he has
kept out of your way the past few days. You mustn't blame him, he
thought he was doing as you wished."

"I don't blame *him*," I said. "Or the driver, who, I do not doubt,
obeyed Daoud's orders to stay in hiding. Where did he take her? Not to
his house, Kadija would have let me know."

"We decided, Daoud and I, that we couldn't risk that," Sethos said.
"Margaret resides at present with one of Daoud's innumerable kinsmen. He's deaf as a post and somewhat feeble-witted, and his wife is a
sour old beldam who is at odds with every other woman in the village.
She has been well paid to look after Margaret, however, so I believe my
dear wife has every possible comfort."

"Don't you know?" I asked in horror. "Haven't you been to see her?"

"Well, you see I had a plan," Sethos explained, leaning comfortably
against the wall. "It occurred to me that Margaret might be in need of
wooing again. Though she would never admit it, she has a fondness for
romance. After you pointed out that she might reasonably resent my
failure to do something dashing, such as having her carried off—"

"Are you blaming this on me?" I demanded.

"Not at all, Amelia dear. You made a sensible suggestion, which I duly
followed. I intended to stage a daring rescue, sword in hand—supposing
I could get hold of one—and carry her away from her captors."

"Good Gad!" Emerson exclaimed. "Are you telling us that Margaret's abduction has nothing to do with the—the other business?"

"That is correct," Sethos said. "I had to tell you, in order to relieve
Nefret's mind. It is possible that David got wind of my impulsive gesture and set out, like a knight of old, to free the captive princess."

"It is possible," Nefret said hopefully. "David has kin in Gurneh,
and they all love and trust him."

"I'll go and find them," Emerson said, jumping up.

"And free poor Margaret," Nefret said, with an indignant look at
Sethos.

"Dinner is served," said Fatima.

I took hold of my head with both hands, for it felt as if it were bursting with confusion and conjecture.

"Wait, Emerson," I said. "We must discuss this."

"Dinner is served," Fatima insisted. "What shall I tell Maaman?"

It was necessary for someone to keep her head. They were all about to rush off on a hypothetical quest, while Maaman wept into the soup and Sethos . . . I was not finished with Sethos.

"We may as well dine," I said. "No, listen to me, Nefret. Ramses and David may already be on their way home. Premature action will only confuse the situation."

As usual, mine was the last word. We seated ourselves, and Fatima served the soup. Nefret took one sip and put her spoon down.

"Is it not good?" Fatima asked.

"It's fine. I'm just not hungry." Nefret met my inquiring gaze and smiled faintly. "No, Mother, I'm not having one of my premonitions. If I were, I wouldn't be sitting here. He isn't in imminent danger. I only want to see him. To be sure."

"I understand, my dear," I said sympathetically. "And we will take action soon. First, however, a few matters require clarification."

I waited until Fatima had removed the soup plates and served the fish course. The delay was meant to get her out of the room, but it had another effect, which I had, of course, intended. Sethos seemed to have lost his appetite. He stared fixedly at his fish, which stared back at him with blank white eyes, until I addressed him.

"You got us off the track, with your customary skill, by your long-winded story about Margaret. I don't doubt it was the truth. You never lie when you can be easily caught out. However, it was not the whole truth, was it? Everything else you have told us, from the first, was a fabrication. There is only one logical way of accounting for all our misadventures. You arranged them. Kindly do not waste my time by denying it. It was you, all along."

"I thought so," Emerson growled. "By the Almighty, I knew it!"

It was not his black scowl but the disappointment and distress on Nefret's face that broke down Sethos's defenses. "It's a fair cop," he said with a sigh. "I'll talk. The truth, the whole truth, and nothing but the truth."

"Start from the beginning," I ordered. "And go on until you have reached the end."

• • •

"The famous message is a fraud. Gibberish. The man from whom I purportedly stole it is in our pay. He is also in the pay of the opposition, and for all I know, in the pay of a dozen other people. If you wondered how they got on my trail so quickly—as you ought to have done—that's how. He told them. And fingered me, as he had been instructed to do.

"Our people were on the spot too. Everybody following everybody else. The so-called attempt on my life at the railroad station was set up. My unfortunate colleague broke a leg when I shoved him off the platform, but the train had already stopped, and they fished him out alive. From that point on the only people who were after me, and you, were the opposition. I led them a merry dance, as I had been ordered to do. The reason, as Amelia has undoubtedly deduced, was to discover who they were—not the hired thugs, but the people who are running the show. Sooner or later, if their underlings failed, one or more of them would be forced to take a hand. So we reasoned, at any rate.

"I suppose it was inevitable that I should come down with malaria, after all that dashing about. I hadn't intended to throw myself on your mercy, but I didn't have much choice; and it had become evident that they would go after you in any case. In a way it was to our advantage, because it focused the hunt. My new instructions ordered me to sit tight and wait."

He paused to take a sip of water.

"Wonderful," Emerson snarled. "While you were sitting tight, they came after us, and poor old Gargery."

"That wasn't part of the plan," Sethos insisted. "I don't know why they made off with him, but he wasn't injured. If you look back, you will admit that none of the family has been hurt—only individuals like the holy man, whom they took for me."

He looked surreptitiously at his watch, and I saw him frown. "As I said, the message is a fake. We know what they're planning, and steps have been taken to prevent it. The only reason we've held off is that we're hoping to get a line on the higher-ups before we act."

"What are they planning?" I asked.

Sethos hesitated, but only briefly. "I may as well tell you, since I've spilled the rest of the beans. They're after Feisal of Iraq. He will be deposed and replaced by Sayid Talib, who wants a republic—so he claims, at any rate—and the end of the British Mandate. The British Commissioner will be expelled, and so will your friend Miss Bell. She is under the illusion that the Iraqis all adore her, but many of them resent the influence of a woman, a foreigner, and a heretic over their king. They don't think much of Feisal either, and the dear lady is partially responsible for the contempt in which he is held. Every time she marches into the palace as if she owned the place, his stock goes down."

He drank again, more deeply. "So now you have it," he said. "The plot, the whole plot, and nothing but the plot."

## FROM MANUSCRIPT H

Waiting was hell. He walked up and down the room, methodically working some of the kinks out of sore muscles, and fighting a useless, senseless desire to do something now, this instant, that would get him back to his wife. He could have sworn at least three hours had passed before he finally heard a scratching sound. He sprinted for the door.

"David?" he breathed into the keyhole.

"Here."

"How's it going?"

"Give me a few minutes."

Picking locks was one of the useful skills they had learned during the war. David didn't have the necessary tools, though, and the process wasn't as easy as sensational novels suggested. Ramses got his knife from under the mattress, slipped it into the sheath, and went back to the door. The scratching and clicking went on till he couldn't stand it any longer.

"I'll force it," he whispered. "Get out of the way."

"It's only been sixty seconds," David said calmly. "Control your impetuosity. That's always been your worst fault. I think . . . Got it."

The door swung open, and for the first time he saw the hallway down which he had been hustled. Cobwebs hung from the ceiling and dust lay thick on the floor, scuffed by footprints. On the floor lay the body of a man wearing a faded galabeeyah.

"I had to put him out," David said softly. "Don't even think about it, Ramses, we aren't hanging around any longer than we have to. There's another one at the front door. This way."

David was reading his mind, as he always did. And he was right, as he always was.

This part of the house was the servants' quarters. A door at the far end of the passage opened onto the salon, which was in the European style of the last century. Crumbling strips of bas-relief framed dusty mirrors and the faded remains of painted panels. Fallen plaster crunched under their feet. Moonlight filtered through cracks in the shutters.

"What about the other doors?" Ramses whispered.

"Chained, bolted, barred, and barricaded. Trust me, this is our best chance."

He stopped in front of a pair of ornate double doors. "Let me go first," he whispered, and eased one of them open. The rusted hinges let out a groan. David slid through the gap. Ramses moved forward and looked out into the entrance hall. A curved staircase led up to the first floor. A single lamp burned low. The man stationed at the front door wore European clothing, trousers and shirt and boots. He had been asleep, but the squeaking hinge had roused him. His eyes glinted in the lamplight.

This was the trickiest part of the whole business. Recognizing David, the fellow might not let out a yell, but he would certainly say something, if only, "What the hell are you doing here?" And he wouldn't whisper. David had just a few seconds in which to silence him, and he couldn't risk the sound of a struggle. Ramses stood poised, his hand on his knife, ready to move as soon as David did.

David leaped, knocking the guard flat on the floor. They rolled back and forth, the guard trying to free himself, David trying to keep his hand over the fellow's mouth. Ramses stood over them, waiting for his chance. The grappling bodies writhed and twisted. He was afraid of hitting the wrong man.

Then the guard got one arm loose and struck. David let out a grunt of pain and fell onto his back, with the other man astride him.

"What are you waiting for?" David gasped.

The guard's back was a temptingly vulnerable target, but Ramses couldn't bring himself to kill, not even then. He brought the hilt of his knife down on the bare black head. It was heavy enough to stun the fellow, and Ramses finished the job with a series of hard, methodical blows. Doubled over and breathing unevenly, David unfastened the chain, which rattled as it fell loose, and drew the bolts. A voice from the head of the staircase called out, demanding to know what was going on.

The door wouldn't open. The key wasn't in the lock. Ramses turned the unconscious man onto his back and started investigating his pockets. Then he saw the key, hanging on a string round the fellow's neck. A hard tug snapped the string. He forced the key into the lock and turned it.

Footsteps sounded on the stairs. David flung the door open and they bolted out. The time for caution had passed, speed was their only hope now. The pursuit was underway. David stumbled, and Ramses caught him round the waist, pulling him forward. They reached the street and turned right.

There was no one in sight, not even a cart they could hide behind. Heavy footsteps pounded after them. Ahead, too far ahead, Ramses saw the lights of the Winter Palace. Panting and leaning on each other, they ran on.

The first order of business, I decided, was to find Margaret. In fact, it was the only action we could take, since we had no idea what had become of the boys (as I would always think of them). They had not turned up when we were ready to leave; I instructed Fatima that if and when they did, she should tell them where we had gone and order them to remain at the house.

Nefret had changed out of her flimsy frock and evening slippers and I had assumed trousers and coat—and, of course, my belt of tools and parasol. There was no way of knowing what we might encounter. When we got to the stable Emerson had seen to it that the horses were saddled and ready.

The hour was late, the village of Gurneh dark and slumbering. The house we sought showed no signs of life. Emerson assured us it was the right place; he had identified it from Sethos's description of the owner.

We dismounted, and Sethos spoke for the first time since he had finished his story. "I don't suppose you would consider letting me go in first? I could snatch Margaret up and—"

Emerson called him a bad name, and I said coldly, "Your effrontery passes all bounds. Go ahead, Emerson, wake the poor old soul."

It was not the old man who came to the door, but his wife, and her reception of us was in keeping with her reputation. Brandishing a stick, she began shouting and swearing. Even the sight of Emerson did not daunt her.

"We are not thieves," he bellowed. "We mean you no harm. Curse it! Be quiet, woman, and heed the Father of Curses."

He snatched the stick from her hand and took hold of her. She went on struggling and screaming until I stepped forward, parasol in hand.

"Be still," I said sternly. "Or I will use my magic to turn you into a goat."

People can believe the most absurd things. My parasol was known and dreaded by some of the more superstitious Egyptians. Fortunately the old lady was one of them.

She led us, without further violence, to the room where Margaret was confined. Either she had not been asleep or the dispute had wakened her; she was on her feet, brandishing a jar which must have contained a beverage of some sort. I had deemed it proper to be the first person to enter. For a moment I thought she would heave the jar at me.

She thought better of it when she beheld Emerson, looming behind me. Words had never failed Margaret; they did not do so now.

"So you have decided to show your face at last!" she exclaimed.

"This time you have gone too far, Mrs. Emerson. I will blazon your perfidy across the front page of every newspaper in the world!"

"Well put," I said appreciatively. "However, in this case your accusation is unwarranted. Make yourself comfortable and we will—"

"Mother," Nefret interrupted. Her voice was peremptory, even, one might say, critical. Ramses and David had not been here, that was evident.

"I will be as expeditious as possible," I promised.

Margaret put the jug down and folded her arms. She was wearing the frock, now crumpled and sweat-stained, that she had worn to our party. It was an act of defiance; several other garments were hung on hooks or draped over chairs. The sight of them made me blink, for they were the sort of thing one finds in the bazaars, designed for tourists—sewn with beads and covered with gold and silver braid. Sethos must have supplied them, but no doubt Margaret had taken them for another of my comments on her unattractive attire, and resented them accordingly.

A quick survey of the chamber assured me that the old beldam had earned her pay. The room was clean and adequately, if not luxuriously, furnished. There was a basket of figs and grapes on the table, and the means of ablution had been supplied.

"It was not I who gave the orders for your abduction," I began.

"The carriage driver had been ordered to stop along the road," Margaret said, her eyes flashing. "When he did, Daoud climbed in and took hold of me. Whom else would he obey but you? Don't lie to me."

"I never lie." (Unless, I added mentally, it is absolutely necessary.) "Daoud did what he believed I would approve, but he was manipulated by another person."

I stepped away from the door. There was a little scuffle outside; then Emerson appeared, holding his brother by the collar. He shoved him into the room. "Here is the perpetrator," he said.

Margaret stared. "You?" she exclaimed.

Seeing no way out (for Emerson blocked the doorway) Sethos smiled in an ingratiating manner. "My intentions—" he began.

"Damn your intentions!" Margaret shouted. "Please don't repeat that fantastic tale of being pursued by enemies. I didn't believe it when Amelia told it me, and I don't believe it now. You didn't abduct me to keep me safe!"

"No," Sethos said. "I did it . . . I did it because . . ."

For once his glib tongue failed him. Looking from him to Margaret, I said, "He had planned to stage a daring rescue, Margaret."

Margaret's face was a study. "Rescue? From that decrepit old man and his octogenarian wife?"

"Oh, I'd have arranged it more dramatically," Sethos said, perking up. The signs were encouraging; she hadn't thrown anything at him or called him names.

Neither of them seemed to know what to say next.

"Get your things together, Margaret," I said.

She picked up her evening bag, shot a scornful look at the embroidered robes, and strode out of the room without looking at Sethos.

Matters were progressing nicely on that front. I only wished I could deal as easily with the others.


FROM MANUSCRIPT H

Safely surrounded by bright lights and mobs of people, Ramses collapsed onto the steps of the hotel and fought for breath. At last he managed to get out a few words.

"Are you all right?"

David nodded. "You?"

"Yes. I wonder . . . why they didn't . . . fire at us."

"I don't know." David wiped his sweating face with his sleeve. "D'you want something to drink?"

"No time." Ramses got to his feet. "We've got to inform the police."

"I thought you were anxious to get back to Nefret."

"I am, but they'll get—"

"Away," David finished. "It can't be helped. By the time we get to the zabtiyeh and convince the man on duty we have a legitimate complaint, and round up enough men, they'll have cleared out."

His reasoning was irrefutable. The police wouldn't be in any hurry to act; they might insist on getting authority from Aziz, who would have to be dragged out of bed. It wouldn't take the gang long to gather their scanty belongings and decamp.

"What's the time?" Ramses asked.

"Half after midnight. Let's go."

Not many people crossed the river at that hour, but there were a number of boatman about, hoping to entice tourists into a moonlight sail or pick up a late-leaving resident of the west bank. They headed toward Ramses and David, quarrelling over who had the right to this fare; but the first to reach them, pushing frailer bodies aside, was Daoud's son Sabir. He caught David in a crushing grip.

"Here you are, you are safe, alhamdullilah!"

David freed himself, laughing, and Sabir fell on Ramses. Ramses was made aware of bruises he hadn't noticed till then. Though Sabir was not as tall as his father, he had Daoud's large frame, and arms toughened by operating oars and sails.

"Yes, God be praised," he said, once he had detached himself from Sabir's fond embrace. "Were you looking for us?"

"Yes, yes, they sent me to wait. Come quickly. Nur Misur weeps and the Father of Curses swears, and the Sitt Hakim is putting bullets in her gun, and—"

"I hate to think what else," Ramses said. "We must hurry, then."

Sabir's was one of the few vessels that boasted an outboard motor. They got across in record time, and found Selim waiting with horses. He had seen them approaching, and his shouts had brought others of the men. They had to endure more loving embraces and cries of praise to Allah—with which Ramses was inclined to agree. Call it God, call it luck, call it Fate, he was perfectly willing to thank something.

"How did you know to expect us?" he asked Selim, as Risha nuzzled his shoulder.

"We did not know. We hoped," Selim said simply. "When the family found you had not gone to Gurneh, they sent Sabir and me to ask the boatmen whether anyone had taken you across. We have been waiting."

Selim, who loved drama, wanted to arrange a procession and was with some difficulty persuaded to have the procession follow instead of preceding them. Torches flaring, voices raised in song and praise, the whole lot ran along behind. David rode with Selim, at a canter, but Ramses let Risha out. Now that he was almost there, he could hardly wait to see her.

The house was lit from one end to the other. She came running to meet him, holding out her arms. He brought Risha to a halt and met her halfway.

"Now tell us," Selim urged. "Tell us all your adventure."

No one could possibly think of going to bed. The return of the lost had revived all spirits, even those of Daoud. We had stopped at his house on the way back from Gurneh, to tell him we knew all about it and that we did not blame him.

Kadija was not so forgiving. "So that is why you have been pretending to be sick. Daoud, you great fool . . ."

When she heard about the boys having gone missing she left off berating Daoud and said she would come with him to the house. Hoping against hope that the wanderers had returned, we left them to follow (with, I expected, a pot of Kadija's famous green ointment).

Having discovered that our hopes had not been fulfilled, I at once took steps, sending Daoud and Selim to gather our people and begin inquiries. It was Sabir who located the boatman who had taken the boys across. (He had added that the Brother of Demons had not paid for his passage, and that money was owed.)

"What are we waiting for?" Emerson demanded, after Sabir reported this. "They are somewhere in Luxor. I will—"

"Search the entire town, house by house?" I interrupted. "The boatman lost sight of them after they climbed the embankment."

My rational arguments had no effect on Emerson, who was storming up and down the veranda knocking over tables and annoying the cat. It was Nefret, perhaps the only one who could have done so, who dissuaded him. "We don't want to lose you too, Father. Give them a little more time."

She wouldn't have been so calm if one of her premonitions had gripped her. I would never forget the frantic girl who had begged for our belief and help when Ramses was in the hands of his worst enemy. She was the first to sense their coming. She ran out the door, and a few moments later we heard the shouts and saw the blazing torches. It is impossible to describe our feelings, but the sensitive Reader will have no difficulty in imagining them.

## FROM MANUSCRIPT H

David was suffering the reaction Ramses had feared. The loving embraces and exclamations of relief had been like scratching a bleeding wound. Lips tight and brow furrowed, he stared at his folded hands and did not respond to Selim. He was leaving it to Ramses.

The pandemonium following their arrival had given Ramses no opportunity to plan what he would say. Fatima kept running in and out with platters of food, Kadija smeared both of them with her famous green ointment, and everyone talked at the top of their lungs. His arm round his wife, savoring safety and her presence, Ramses postponed his explanation by asking about Margaret. Seeing her sitting quietly in a corner was one less weight on his conscience.

"It seems," said his mother, "that her disappearance had nothing to do with the—the other business. A certain individual took it upon himself to carry her off, for reasons of his own. She was never in danger. Let that suffice for the time being. We are eager to hear your story."

Sethos, sitting some distance away from his wife, stared off into space with a look of innocence that didn't deceive Ramses for a moment. Bastard, he thought. If it hadn't been for you . . .

The story could not be put off any longer. He hoped to get through the first part of it as quickly as possible, with as few details as possible. "Not long ago the conspirators got in touch with David, who cleverly pretended to be sympathetic to their cause—"

"No, Ramses." David raised his drooping head. "I won't have you make excuses for me. I willingly cooperated with them. I didn't tell Ramses or anyone else. I betrayed your trust."

A stir of surprise ran through the listeners. Ramses said quickly, "They had given him their word they would take no steps against the family and our friends. Margaret's disappearance made him think their word could not be trusted. He went to Luxor tonight to demand an explanation. I followed, and was fool enough to let myself be caught. I'd still be a prisoner if it weren't for David. He risked his life to get me away."

As Ramses might have expected, his mother was the first to break the astonished silence. Rising, she went to David and put her arm round his bowed shoulders. "As he has done innumerable times before. I think I understand, David. Do not reproach yourself. You are not the only person present who has committed an error of judgment. To err is human, to forgive—"

"For God's sake, Peabody, spare us the poetry," Emerson exclaimed. "Er—David, my boy, what about a whiskey and soda?"

His eyes moist, David accepted the glass Emerson pressed into his hand.

"Sir," he began.

"Never mind," Emerson said hastily. "Now let us hear the details, eh? You look as if you've been in a scrap."

"It was a bit dodgy at times," Ramses said. His father could only stand so much sentiment. "David had to pick the lock of the room in which I was confined, and knock out the guard outside the door—all that without making a noise that would awaken the rest of the fellows. We had another encounter at the front door, where there was another man standing guard. He took David for one of his own long enough for David to tackle him and bring him down. Between the two of us we put him out of commission, but we had made a certain amount of racket, and by the time we got out the door, the rest of them were in hot pursuit. I don't think I've ever run so fast in my life. When we reached the Winter Palace we knew we had made it. Sabir was looking for us, and . . . You know the rest."

His father leaned forward. "The place is near the Winter Palace? Where exactly?"

Ramses explained. "We should have gone directly to the police, I suppose, but—"

"No point in that," said Emerson, once more in charge. "The birds would have flown. But we had better do so at once."

"That will take hours," his wife said. "It can wait until morning and so can everything else."

Like Ramses, she had seen that David was on the verge of collapse from emotional as well as physical strain. She took him firmly by the arm. "Come along, dear boy. A nice warm glass of milk will send you off to sleep directly."

There would be "a soupçon of laudanum" in the milk, Ramses thought. Nefret didn't offer him milk, but she refused to let him get in bed until he had washed off Kadija's green ointment. It was undeniably therapeutic, but the stains were hard to get out.

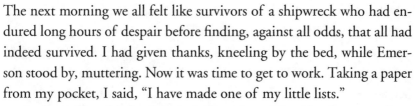

The next morning we all felt like survivors of a shipwreck who had endured long hours of despair before finding, against all odds, that all had indeed survived. I had given thanks, kneeling by the bed, while Emerson stood by, muttering. Now it was time to get to work. Taking a paper from my pocket, I said, "I have made one of my little lists."

Smiles suffused every face, including that of David, who was still inclined to mope. "Well, Peabody," said Emerson good-humoredly, "what is the first item to be considered?"

"Informing Inspector Aziz and requesting him to search the suspected premises."

"Be damned to that," said Emerson, giving his boiled egg a hard smack. "I intend to inspect the cursed premises myself. You may come along if you like."

Naturally I had intended to do so. A woman's eye, I always say, is keener than that of a man. "After that," I continued, "we must have a council of war."

Urged by Fatima, David had made a good start on his breakfast. Now he put down his fork. "I haven't told you what I learned about the conspiracy, Aunt Amelia. You didn't give me time last night."

I raised an admonitory finger. "Everything in order, David. 'Quiet calm deliberation will untangle every knot.' At least I hope it will."

Ramses and Nefret sat side by side, holding hands under the table. "I am coming to Luxor too," Nefret announced, in a tone that brooked no argument. She didn't mean to let him out of her sight.

Margaret was wearing one of my day dresses, a nice little frock of eau de Nil, whose lace trim and skillful cut became her well. After she had removed her horrible dress I told Fatima to cut it up for dusters.

"May I go to the hotel?" she asked meekly.

"No," I said. "We will pack your things and bring them back with us. I want you to attend our council of war. You," I went on, fixing Sethos with a stern look, "will come with us. And come back with us."

"Yes, Amelia," Sethos said meekly.

Ordinarily his ready acquiescence and that of Margaret would have struck me as highly suspicious. I thought they would both do as they were told, but I meant to keep a close eye on my brother-in-law. Just in case.

We had no difficulty in finding the suspected, or cursed, house. It was one of a number of expensive villas that had been built during the extravagance of the prewar period. Rather than waste time, I had dispatched a message to Inspector Aziz, requesting that he meet us there. We were a sufficient force in ourselves, even supposing we encountered opposition. It did not seem likely that we would. Like several others, this house had a derelict air, as if it had been long unoccupied. The flower beds were overgrown and untended, the shuttered windows broken.

Emerson marched up the steps and kicked the door open. A strong smell of mold and decay met us—but that was all. A quick search made it clear that the birds had indeed flown, leaving behind rotting food, a few discarded garments, and certain other evidences of their disinterest in elementary sanitation. Having made certain that there was no danger of an ambush, we divided forces for a more detailed search, examining every scrap of paper and piece of cloth. We were engaged in this when

Inspector Aziz arrived. His hail brought us all to the entrance hall, where he stood with folded arms and a critical expression.

"Your message was not very informative, Mrs. Emerson," he said sternly. "Why did you break into this house?"

"We are not guilty of breaking and entering, only of entering," said Emerson. "The door was not locked."

"Don't tease, Emerson," I said.

Ramses and David had come here searching for Margaret, I explained, and went on to tell the rest of it. As he listened, Aziz's expression changed from sternness to one of gloomy resignation.

"I have become accustomed to your habits, Mrs. Emerson, so I accept the fact that I won't get any more out of you. You ought to have reported this immediately."

"That would have meant getting you out of bed in the middle of the night, Inspector. And for no purpose. The miscreants took to their heels as soon as Ramses and David made good their escape."

"Who were they?" Aziz demanded.

"That is what we are endeavoring to ascertain. Do you happen to know who owns this house?"

"No, but I will find out. Is he responsible for this?"

"I doubt it," Ramses said. "The house was empty, so they simply moved in."

We left Aziz to carry out his own search. He was a conscientious man, and a good man; I regretted having to deceive him, but it was absolutely necessary.

We stopped by the hotel long enough to pack a suitcase for Margaret. The men left this to me, except for Margaret's notes and papers, which Emerson gathered into a bundle. I intended to have a close look at them before I handed them over.

When we reached the house we found Sennia and Gargery on the veranda. Both were bristling with indignation. Sennia ran to Ramses and threw her arms round him.

"Fatima told me! Why wasn't I told before? I would have gone and found you."

"That is dear of you," Ramses said, hugging her back. "But you couldn't have helped, Sennia. No one knew where we were."

"I would have taken the Great Cat of Re to follow your scent," said Sennia.

I looked at the cat, who was sprawled across the settee sound asleep. He was taking up as much room as he could, his plumy tail extended and his fat paws outstretched. Sennia's conviction, that one day he would prove to be Ramses's salvation, did not seem likely to be fulfilled.

"Fatima shouldn't have worried you," said David, who was being embraced in his turn.

"Someone else would have told her if Fatima hadn't done so," I said. "As you see, Sennia, everything has turned out all right."

Before we gathered for our council of war I remembered another duty I had overlooked. I penned a brief note to Cyrus, informing him of Margaret's safe return. I then invited everyone to join me in the parlor, where Kareem had placed chairs facing the large table I intended to use as a desk. Seating myself behind it, I arranged my papers and opened the meeting.

For the benefit of Selim and Daoud, who had not been present, I first described the results of our search of the house.

"I had hoped the miscreants might have overlooked something that would give us a clue as to their present whereabouts," I went on. "Unfortunately these few scraps were all that remained, and they contain no helpful information.

"We are somewhat further along, however. We know the nature of the conspiracy—to overthrow King Feisal and end the British—"

David committed the unusual discourtesy of interrupting me. Eyes widening, he exclaimed, "Feisal? It is Fuad who will be forced to abdicate. Zaghlul will be made—"

"What?" I cried. "That is not—"

"I knew someone was lying," Emerson growled. "By heaven—"

"Not me!" Sethos exclaimed. "I swear by—"

"Stop!" I said, raising my voice to be heard over the general outcry. "All of you, be quiet. Someone has certainly misled us, but let us not jump to conclusions. It might have been David's informants."

"Why would Bashir lie to me?" David demanded. "He doesn't give a fig for Iraq or Feisal; he is dedicated to the cause of Egyptian nationalism."

"He's a damn fool if he believes he can carry out such a scheme," Sethos said vehemently.

"He's right," Margaret said.

She was the last person I would have expected to come to his defense. Sethos looked at her in open-mouthed surprise. Coloring slightly, she went on, "It is much more likely that the target is Iraq. The political situation there is unstable, and the stakes are higher. Oil is a valuable commodity."

"Thank you," Sethos said, recovering. "I admit that I haven't an unblemished reputation for veracity, but Margaret has, with her customary acuity, lent support to my story. What have I to gain by lying?"

"I can't think of anything offhand," I admitted.

"That doesn't prove a damned thing," said Emerson, with a critical look at his brother. "His reasons often pass the bounds of logical ratiocination. However . . . innocent until proven guilty."

I consulted my list and then flung it down. "Good Gad," I said. "Instead of being further along, we are in even deeper confusion. The only positive thing to come out of this is that our adversaries have not broken their word. Margaret's abduction was not arranged by them, and Ramses and David—er—"

"Got what they deserved," said Ramses. "Rushing in where angels fear to tread. I don't know that we can count on their forbearance henceforth, however."

"A point to be considered," I agreed. "It would be helpful if we could be certain who 'they' are."

We stared at one another with a wild surmise, as Cortez had done on a peak in Darién. But these were wilder waters than the broad Pacific.

"Perhaps," said Daoud hesitantly, "there are many of them."

"Good for you, Daoud," said Sethos. "I wouldn't for a moment doubt David's word, but that group can't have anything to do with my lot or I would have been told about it."

"Two separate conspiracies?" Ramses demanded. "That's a bit much, even for us."

"Let us go on that assumption, to begin with." I took out a blank sheet of paper and headed it "Things to Be Done."

"Bashir," I said. "He is the only one whose name is known. We must hunt him down."

"I don't believe he's dangerous," Ramses said. "He was always an ineffectual sort of fellow, a follower rather than a leader. His lads didn't even fire at us. All the same, I suppose the authorities should be warned about him."

"Sir Thomas Russell is the man," I said, writing. "We can safely leave the matter in his efficient hands. How much time do we have, David?"

"They told me they would hold Ramses for two or three days. I assumed that that too was a lie; the time would have been extended, day by day. But now . . ." He shrugged helplessly.

"They may move their schedule up," I agreed. "We dare not delay. Someone must go to Cairo at once. I am the obvious—"

"Not you," said several people simultaneously.

"And not David," Ramses said. He smiled at his friend. "He is burning to make a full confession, but I'm not going to allow that. We'll keep him out of this if we can. I'm the obvious person, Mother. Russell trusts me."

"Very well," I said. "Now as for the other conspiracy—"

Fatima came running in. "Mr. Vandergelt is here," she announced. "And—"

She was pushed rudely aside by Sir William Portmanteau. Father Christmas was gone; hair and beard bristling, eyes wild, face livid, he reminded me irresistibly of the drawings of the enraged Nome King in Mr. Baum's charming books.

"Where is she?" he demanded. "What have you done with her? You and your native henchmen . . ." He started toward Daoud, who backed off in alarm. In his estimation Sir William had gone mad, and madmen, as everyone knew, could not be assaulted since they were protected by God.

"Sorry about this, Amelia," said Cyrus, trying to restrain his guest. "I couldn't stop him. He's kind of upset."

"So I see. Sit down and be quiet, Sir William!"

I did not shout; I employed the tone of voice I have learned to use on recalcitrant persons. Sir William of course did as I ordered. He was seriously out of breath anyhow.

"I take it you are referring to Suzanne," I continued. "Don't tell me she has gone missing."

Emerson groaned. "No, don't tell us. Not another one!"

Nefret's gentle touch and professional firmness succeeded in calming Sir William. She stood by him, her fingers on his pulse, while Cyrus explained.

Suzanne had returned from Abydos with her grandfather the previous evening. No one disturbed her that morning, since she had appeared to be very tired. When one of the maidservants finally ventured into her room she found no sign of its occupant. No one took alarm at first; it was some time before a search of the house and grounds determined that the girl was not on the premises.

"And she's not the only one," Cyrus said. "Nadji's gone too."

The name roused Sir William from his quiescent state. Pulling his hand from that of Nefret, he cried passionately, "He has carried her off against her will!"

"What for?" Emerson asked in bewilderment.

"For ransom! Or," Sir William groaned, "for . . . for a reason I dare not contemplate. You know how these people are! Lusting after white women . . ."

"Balderdash!" Emerson shouted, his face almost as red as that of Sir William. "You evil-minded old—"

"Now, Emerson," I said. "We don't need two infuriated men shouting at each other."

"She would never have left me of her own accord, without so much as a note of explanation," Sir William insisted. "We were going back to England together, she and I."

Nefret pushed him back into the chair from which he was struggling to rise. "You will have a seizure or a heart attack if you go on this way," she said firmly. "That won't help Suzanne, will it?"

I had never doubted that Sir William cared deeply for his grand-daughter. It did him no credit, really, since he regarded her as part of himself—his property, so to speak—and he had no interest in anything other than himself and his property. Nefret's appeal had the effect of calming him, and a sip or two of brandy, supplied by Emerson, was also helpful. Directed by me, Cyrus was able to continue his explanation.

"Cat searched her room and determined that she had packed a suitcase—toilet articles, jewelry, and a few clothes. How she left the house and the grounds unobserved we don't know. The gateman hadn't seen her."

"What about Nadji?" I asked.

"Same thing," Cyrus said, glancing at Sir William. "Clothes and personal belongings taken, no one saw him leave. We looked everywhere, questioned the boatmen and the local folks; then Sir William got it into his head that they—she—must have come to you."

The solution was clear. I did not propose it since it would have inflamed Sir William even further.

"Take him back to the Castle and keep him there," I said to Cyrus. "He is only in the way. We will investigate, and inform you immediately if we learn anything."

After they had gone Daoud said urgently, "Sitt Hakim, I did not do it."

"I know that, Daoud. The explanation is—"

"Obvious," Sethos interrupted. His eyes glittered like silver. "We asked who among us could be reporting to our adversaries. Those two are the only strangers in our midst. I have always had my doubts about the young woman; she is French, and France has interests in Syria."

"I can't believe that frivolous girl is an agent of French intelligence," Nefret exclaimed.

"The intelligence service loves to employ pretty young women," Sethos said darkly.

"She's not much of an artist, that's sure," muttered Emerson. "Her portfolio impressed Peabody, but someone else might have done the paintings for her."

"One could make an equally damning case against Nadji," David said. "He is an Egyptian and an intellectual, just the sort to be attracted by the nationalist cause. He might have arranged the attack on himself to allay suspicion."

"They both took themselves off last night," Ramses added. "Shortly after David and I escaped. Coincidence?"

Emerson tugged at his hair. "They can't be working together!"

"Why not?" Ramses inquired. "Suzanne can't have got away from the Castle unobserved without help. She is not noticeably athletic, and according to Katherine, she was burdened with a suitcase. A strong young man could hoist her up onto the wall and help her down."

Sethos nodded thoughtfully. "There are several places around the perimeter where the wall could be climbed by an agile man."

"You would know," growled Emerson.

"Quite," said Sethos agreeably. "But the fact that they presumably left together strengthens my hypothesis. They are and have been working as a team. I told you a number of different groups are involved in the plot."

"You told us a good many things," I said. That supercilious smile of his was extremely exasperating. "Are you sure you haven't omitted any information that might forestall additional near disasters? If you had admitted abducting Margaret, David wouldn't have gone to Luxor and Ramses wouldn't have followed him. It was thanks to the mercy of God and their own abilities that they escaped unscathed. No thanks to you!"

"I deserve that, I suppose," Sethos admitted. "But be fair, Amelia; had I but known David was mixed up in a plot of his own I would have acted differently."

"So you say," Emerson remarked, scowling at his brother. "Have you anything to add?"

"No," Sethos said, with every appearance of sincerity. "I give you my word."

# CHAPTER ELEVEN

FROM MANUSCRIPT H

HE HAD KNOWN NEFRET WOULD INSIST ON GOING WITH HIM TO CAIRO. He didn't argue. He knew that look of hers.

Sethos tried to talk them out of it. "You're wasting your time, Ramses. Bashir's lot can't pull this off. I wouldn't be surprised if Russell weren't already aware of their scheme. It's a matter for the CID, and he keeps a close eye on local dissidents."

"We can't take anything for granted," Nefret said. "Hadn't you better notify Mr. Smith of the latest developments?"

"I told you, we know all about it."

"Including the purported role of Suzanne and Nadji?" Ramses asked.

The faintest flicker in those pale eyes was the only sign of uncertainty.

"They haven't left Luxor," Sethos said. "Nor will they. Selim is watching the railroad station and Sabir is in touch with the boatmen. We'll find them. That's my job, and it's a good deal more important than arresting a few feeble revolutionaries. However," he added, "you might want to speak with our Mr. Smith. Tell him I'm close to accomplishing our original goal."

"Smith, and you, can get on without me," Ramses said brusquely.

"Dear me, what a negative attitude." After a moment Sethos said, without any trace of humor, "Keep your eyes open. If they are aware of your arrival, they may try to stop you from reaching Russell. Unlikely that they could succeed, but still . . ."

"Don't worry," said Nefret, taking Ramses's arm. "I'll be there to protect him."

They made it to the station with time to spare. Daoud went along to see them off, as was his custom, and the three of them joined Selim in a final scan of the departing passengers. None matched the appearance of the missing couple.

Seated across from his wife in the dining car at a table for two, Ramses felt a sense of unreality. The motion of the train didn't detract from the pleasant ambience—soft lights, white linen on the table, assiduous service. He couldn't remember the last time they had dined alone, just the two of them, with not a familiar face in sight and no prospect of seeing one until they reached Cairo. Almost twelve hours with no responsibilities and no interruptions—the prospect was dazzling.

As she often did, Nefret read his mind. "I feel as if we were eloping," she said.

"So do I. It's wonderful."

He took the hand she held out and raised it to his lips, indifferent to the hovering waiter. "I've given you so many bad hours, Nefret. Why do you put up with me?"

"On the whole, your virtues outweigh your vices," she said with that enchanting chuckle of hers. "And I've given *you* a few bad hours. D'you remember the time I talked you and David into letting me go after the Book of the Dead with you?"

"I was thinking about it last night, as a matter of fact. And of the time you marched into a room with a murderer and let him take you hostage."

"Were you making a list of my misdeeds?"

"Balancing them against mine." He let go her hand, and the waiter offered menus.

"Such as the time . . ."

Some people might consider reminiscences of near death and catastrophe unsuitable for dinner conversation, but it had all been so long ago—the follies and foibles of their youth. They could even talk about the hardest years, when mutual stubbornness and misunderstanding had kept them apart. It had taken Nefret a long time to stop blaming herself for that. Guilt, as his mother often remarked, is a wasteful emotion; forgive yourself and go on to do better. As was the case with most of his mother's aphorisms, you wanted to swear when she uttered the banal words with that bland assurance of hers, but they had a way of sinking in.

He didn't think of them again that night—nor, to judge by her behavior, did Nefret. At one point Ramses heard himself murmur, "Wonderful things," as Howard Carter had done under quite different circumstances. Nefret's laughter was the sweetest sound he had heard for years.

Neither of them woke until the train had stopped in Cairo. "Back to the real world," Ramses said.

"Curse it," Nefret agreed with a smile. "Let's get it over. Straight to Russell's office?"

Ramses consulted his watch. "It's still early. He won't be there for a while. We may as well have a leisurely breakfast."

They had it on the terrace of Shepheard's. It wasn't Ramses's favorite place in Cairo, but staying there had become a habit, and they could always count on getting a room if they had to stay over. The sunlight was dulled by the inevitable and omniprescent dust kicked up by hooves of animals and feet of humans and wheels of vehicles. Across the way the green gardens of the Ezbekieh were reminders of other youthful escapades. There was hardly a part of Cairo that was free of such memories, but this one was a favorite of Nefret's.

"D'you remember—" she began.

"Yes, and I'd rather not be reminded of it."

She went on remorselessly, "—that horrid girl who lured you into the gardens late at night? You never did admit whether she kissed you before she fainted dead away and you had to carry her out in your arms."

"I was only sixteen," Ramses protested.

"Did she?"

"Yes." He grinned. "It was quite a kiss, too. Or would have been, if we hadn't been interrupted by a would-be assassin."

"They do keep turning up," Nefret said, laughing.

"You enjoyed that, didn't you? You enjoyed all of it."

"Well, not all of it. The memories are better than the actuality. But . . . there's something about Cairo."

They sat in silence for a while, taking it all in—Cairo.

"He should be there by now," Ramses said, rising. "Finish your coffee. I'll telephone."

He came back to report that Russell hadn't yet arrived, but was expected shortly. "He'll see me."

"I should bloody well hope so," said Nefret. "Let's walk, shall we? It isn't far—round the gardens and straight down the Sharia Mohammed Ali."

"Are you sure?"

She slipped her arm through his. "If we see Bashir, I'll slap his face."

"He's far, far away by now," Ramses said. "He was never the stuff of which heroes are made."

They had almost reached the Bab el Khalk and the administration building when a passing man jostled Nefret. Ramses turned on him with a sharp reprimand, and saw, between the turban and the overlarge beard, a pair of frightened eyes. Bashir caught at his arm. "Run away," he gasped. "They are watching to see if you come here. Run—"

Ramses heard the crack of a rifle. He threw himself on Nefret, pushing her down behind a cart filled with sugarcane. Another shot sprayed green fragments across the street. Pedestrians scattered, screaming. In the middle of the pavement Bashir lay sprawled in a spreading pool of blood.

Children always know when something is amiss, no matter how normally the adults around them try to behave. Charla made a scene when she learned her parents had gone off without a word of farewell. My lecture had no effect; it was, I admit, somewhat half-hearted, since my mind was on other things. It required the combined efforts of David, Emerson, and Sennia to console her. A certain amount of bribery was also necessary—a handful of sweets, a visit to the stable, and an uproarious game of tag, with all of them participating.

David John felt their absence as keenly as did his sister, and I sometimes wished he would express his misgivings as openly as she. Temper tantrums were violent but soon over, whereas David John had a tendency to brood. After we had settled Charla I went looking for him.

He was not in his playroom with Elia or in the kitchen with Fatima. He was not with Amira. Eventually I located him in the drawing room, curled up in a chair with a book in his hand.

"One of your Christmas gifts?" I asked.

"No," said David John. "It is not one of my Christmas gifts. I have read them all."

Not until he held it up did I see the cover of the volume. The scene depicted a flimsily clad female clasped tightly in the arms of a male person wearing Bedouin robes. "Good Gad," I cried. "I have told you over and over, David John, you are not to take books from the shelves here."

"It was not on the shelf, Grandmama. I found it lying on the table, and since I had nothing else to read . . ."

The book was the popular romance I had lent Margaret. It *had* been lying on the table; I had never got round to putting it away.

I repressed an impulse to snatch it away from the child. He had not disobeyed me—not literally. "Do you find it interesting?" I asked, observing with regret that he had read a good half of the cursed thing.

"Quite," said David John. "There are a few parts I don't understand, though. Perhaps, Grandmama, you could explain what the lady means when she says—"

"No," I said quickly. "I fear I cannot allow you to finish the book, David John. I ought not have left it lying about."

"But the lady is in deep distress," David John protested. "I want to know how the book ends."

"It has a happy ending." I removed the book from his hands.

"Someone comes to rescue her from the cruel sheikh?"

"Er—yes." In this case, prevarication was absolutely necessary. Trying to explain that the sheikh was not really evil just because he had— And that the distressed lady didn't really mind that he had . . .

Out of the question.

"Why don't you write an ending to the story?" I suggested.

"Hmmm." David John considered this, his blue eyes pensive. "I have not attempted fiction as yet. It would be a challenge."

"A challenge indeed. I am sure you will be up to it. While you are doing that I will try to find you something else to read."

I got him settled, with freshly sharpened pencils and a pile of paper, and then went to my study to put the book safely away. Before I did so, I leafed through the beginning pages, hoping the contents were not as bad as I remembered.

They might have been worse. There was a good deal of panting and burning eyes and passionate glances, but, thank heaven, no anatomical references. David John could not have made much of it. I had to admit the confounded thing had a certain fascination for the vulgar, of whom there are a great number. It was not surprising that it had been the most popular book of the year.

A book that might be found on any bookshelf.

No, I thought. Ridiculous.

It would do no harm to try.

I had made my own copy of the mystery message. Taking it from the desk drawer, I got to work.


"There you are," said Emerson. "I have been looking—"

I started and let out a little shriek. "Don't creep up on me like that!"

"I was not creeping," said Emerson indignantly. "I was looking—"

"Look at this, then." I thrust the paper on which I had been writing at him.

Emerson's noble brow furrowed as he read. He looked as disheveled as I had ever seen him, his hair on end, his shirt hanging out of his trousers. An hour with Charla could have that effect.

"What is this nonsense?" he demanded.

"It is not nonsense. It is the mystery message. I have solved the cipher!"

" 'On the first day of the first month the Bull will die. The Judge will die. The Eagle will . . .' Die?"

"I hadn't quite finished." Referring again to the original numbers, I began turning the pages of *Desert Passion*.

"Yes," I said. "Die."

Emerson was not easily convinced. He had to check the first few words for himself before he admitted I was on the right, the only possible, track.

"Do you understand what this means?" I demanded, as Emerson contemplated the lurid cover of *Desert Passion* with raised eyebrows. "We were wrong, we were all wrong, about the nature of the conspiracy. It is assassination they plan. The cold-blooded murder of three people!"

"The Bull," Emerson muttered. "Oh, good Gad. Lord Allenby! He is known as the Bull to enemies and supporters alike. There are dozens of judges . . ."

"The Judge must be King Fuad. His name is derived from that Arabic word."

"Yes, yes." Emerson fingered the cleft in his chin. "I ought to have seen that. I am having a hard time taking this in, Peabody. Wait, though. The eagle is one of the Hashemite symbols. Feisal of Iraq?"

"I would assume so."

"Apparently," said Emerson, "these absurd pseudonyms were agreed upon in advance, leaving only the time of the attack to be determined in the final message. Let us have a chat with my brother."

We found Sethos on the veranda, being waited upon by Fatima and fawned upon by the Great Cat of Re. The cat had taken an unaccountable fancy to him. I should have known that was a bad sign.

"That child," Sethos declared, rubbing his back, "is the most formidable opponent I have ever encountered. Her idea of tagging someone is to run headlong into him. Margaret nobly offered to take charge of her after she—"

"The message is not a fake, nor gibberish," I said, for in my opinion time was of the essence. "I have deciphered it."

I handed him the paper. As he read it, his eyes narrowed to slits. "I don't believe it," he said flatly.

"Are you accusing Peabody of inventing this?" Emerson demanded.

"No. She wouldn't . . ." He broke off, biting his lip.

"Oh, yes, she would, if she had a good reason for doing so."

"Thank you, my dear," I said, much gratified.

"But she didn't," Emerson went on. "I have verified her deductions— not," he added hastily, "that it was necessary. There can be no question about it. You lied—again."

Margaret appeared at the door of the veranda. She looked windblown and disheveled, but there was color in her cheeks, and she was smiling. The smile didn't last.

"Lied?" she repeated, looking from Emerson to Sethos. "What did he lie about this time?"

"It was not a lie," Sethos said vehemently. "The story I told you was true. There must be some mistake."

"No mistake," said Emerson, arms folded and brow dark. "You knew all along the message was not gibberish. You knew that three lives were at hazard."

"Imminently," I added. "Today is the twenty-ninth of December. The first day of the first month must refer to the first day of the new year. We have less than three days in which to warn the victims. It will take until tomorrow to reach Cairo by train, even longer by other means of transport. We cannot risk sending a telegram. What could we say that would be forceful enough to command immediate attention but would not warn the assassins, should it be intercepted by one of them?"

"What's this all about?" Margaret demanded.

Sethos had tried several times to speak. It was odd to see him automatically continue to stroke the purring cat, while his normally impassive countenance expressed a series of conflicting emotions. Now he burst out, "Nefret. Nefret and Ramses. I warned them to watch out for Bashir and his lot, but if this is true, the consequences could be deadly, for it is not only he whom they have to fear. They must be told."

"An aeroplane," I cried. "You commandeered one before."

"No chance," Sethos muttered. "I might be able to pull it off, but I would have to go in person."

"You aren't going anywhere," said Emerson. "Peabody, send for Daoud."

Sethos did not take kindly to being locked up. He continued to protest as Daoud led him off to his room, with instructions not to leave him alone for a moment. He was in a state of considerable agitation.

"Or putting it on," said Emerson. "The man is a consummate actor."

"He is very fond of Nefret," I said. Glancing at Margaret, who had been a silent witness to the proceedings, I added, "In a platonic way, of course. Like a loving uncle."

"I haven't asked what this is all about," Margaret began.

"Yes, you have. Twice. I cannot explain, even if I were sure I could trust you to refrain from journalistic speculation. I hope we will not be forced to lock you up too."

"I haven't enough to go on," Margaret admitted. "Just tell me one thing. He kept insisting that he had passed on to you what 'they' had told him. I have a good idea as to who 'they' are. Could he have been telling the truth?"

It mattered to her. She hadn't taken out her notebook and her hands kept twisting together.

"That is what we intend to ascertain," I said.

## From Manuscript H

"He risked his life to warn us," Ramses said. "And I called him a coward."

Seated behind his desk, Russell gestured to an aide. "Coffee," he ordered. "Unless you'd rather have something stronger?"

Ramses shook his head. Nefret dabbed at a bleeding scratch on one cheek. "Something alcoholic," she said calmly. "To disinfect this. Cairo streets are filthy."

The police had arrived with commendable promptness. Russell's men were trained to respond quickly to sounds of gunfire, especially so close to their headquarters. They had not found the shooter, though. He had abandoned the rifle in the alleyway from which he had fired and melted into the crowd.

Russell was not the sort of man to waste time in sentiment. "Let's go over this again. You are telling me that there are two different conspiracies, one in Egypt and one in Iraq? That both aim at the bloodless overthrow of the governments? Then who murdered Bashir? One of his lieutenants who disagreed with his pacifist notions?"

Ramses couldn't blame him for sounding a note of cynicism. "Someone disagreed with him," he said. "Vehemently. Their intention was to prevent us from exposing the plot to you."

"Why the devil should they bother?" Russell demanded. "It's not much of a plot, is it? And it hasn't the chance of a snowball in hell . . ." He ran his hand over his chin. "Excuse me, Mrs. Emerson."

"You have expressed my sentiments exactly," Nefret said. "Bashir's murder casts the whole story in doubt."

"You say you heard it from Todros."

Russell's voice was studiously noncommittal. He had never quite got over his suspicions of David. Ramses said, "As I told you, Mr. Todros pretended to be in sympathy with Bashir in order to win his confidence. I do not doubt his sincerity or his accuracy. The plot against Feisal came from another source entirely. I confess I can't explain this development. However, there is someone who may be able to shed light on the situation."

"Oh, Lord." Russell's mustache drooped. "Not that bas— Not him. Those people in intelligence think they are above the law. He won't talk to me."

"He'll talk to me." Ramses rose. "Let's go, Nefret."

"I'll supply you with an escort," Russell said. "And I strongly suggest that you get out of Cairo as soon as you can."

Emerson was almost as difficult to deal with as was Sethos. Had he possessed an aeroplane or a winged horse, he would have set off at once. There was nothing we could do but wait for the evening express. Earlier trains were locals, which arrived in Cairo no sooner.

I did not point out the obvious, since he knew it as well as I. Ramses and Nefret had arrived in Cairo that morning. If an attack was to be made upon them, it might already have occurred.

They had promised to telegraph after they spoke with Thomas Russell. I sent Hassan to the telegraph office to make sure a message would be sent on the moment it arrived. The long day wore on with no news, and Emerson's control finally cracked.

"I don't think I can face tea with the children," he muttered.

"You must. They must not suspect anything is amiss. We cannot leave for several more hours. Go and tidy up."

"Damned if I will."

I had not the heart to insist. He had planted himself at the door of the veranda whence he could watch the road that led to the river.

I went to see Sethos. I had to wake Daoud, who was asleep across the threshold; as he explained, his prisoner was not inclined to conversation, so he had been bored. Sethos was sitting on the edge of the bed, staring down at his folded hands. He looked up with a haggard face. "Any news?"

"I will inform you at once if we hear. If we do not . . . Emerson and I are leaving for Cairo shortly."

"Let me go with you."

"Emerson would never permit that, and I must say I share his doubts."

"I can resolve them if I am allowed to have a few words with Smith. Please, Amelia!"

"I will have a few words to say to—"

Sethos leaped up. "Is that Emerson's voice?"

There was no mistaking it. I ran with winged feet to the veranda. Emerson had ripped open a telegram and was waving it like a banner.

"It's all right, Peabody. They are all right. They are coming home!"

"God be praised," Daoud exclaimed.

Sethos snatched the telegram from Emerson before I could do so. He was considerate enough to read it aloud. " 'All is well. Stay in Luxor. Taking train tonight.' "

"Ramses's telegraphic style is beginning to resemble Emerson's," I said, too relieved to scold Sethos. "Only nine words."

"Ten," said Sethos. "He added 'Love.' "


Needless to say, we were all on hand to meet the train next morning—all of us except Sethos. "Ramses may or may not have obtained information that may or may not clear Sethos of deliberately misleading us" was Emerson's comment. "He will be confined until we know, one way or the other."

As we had hoped, Ramses and Nefret were on the train. After the first cries of welcome and fond embraces were over, Ramses hoisted Charla onto his shoulder and I said to Nefret, "How did you get that cut on your cheek? Have you any other injuries? Has Ramses?"

"No, Mother." She put her arm round me. "I'll explain later. If ever there was a time for one of your councils of war, this is it. We have a great deal to tell you."

"And we," I began, "have . . . Good Gad. Who is that?"

In fact I knew perfectly well who it was. Pointed nose, narrowed eyes, thin mouth . . . None other than Bracegirdle-Boisdragon, alias Mr. Smith.

The thin lips stretched into Smith's best effort at a smile. Removing his hat, he said, "Good morning, Mrs. Emerson."

"Good morning be damned," Emerson exclaimed. "What are you doing here?"

"He came with us," Ramses said. "At my insistence."

"I came," said Mr. Smith, "because I owe you an explanation."

"Damn right," said Emerson.

"Damn right," shouted Charla.

"Emerson, please!" I said.

Anticipating the need for a council of war, I had instructed Fatima to move the furniture in the parlor accordingly. When Mr. Smith saw my arrangements he murmured, "Very efficient, Mrs. Emerson. Where am I to sit?"

I indicated a chair. The others took their places. Smith studied their faces with polite interest. "I take it that everyone present has a right to be here?" he asked, staring pointedly at Margaret.

"They do," I said, in a tone that allowed no debate. "There is one more witness to come. Daoud, will you bring him here?"

Sethos entered with his head held high and his features impassive. He had the air of an accused criminal expecting a harsh sentence. The sight of his chief brought an exclamation of surprise from him.

"You? Here?"

"Don't stutter," I said. "Mr. Smith, the first order of business concerns our mutual friend here. He told us that the so-called secret message was no more than a string of meaningless numbers. That was an untruth. Yesterday I broke the code and read the message."

"Mother, you didn't," Ramses exclaimed. "That is—how?"

"I found the right book," I said, with a little cough. "Purely by accident. We will discuss that at another time. What I want to know from Mr. Smith is who misled whom?"

"Ah, I see," Smith said. "Our friend's veracity is in question. He had no business telling you that much, but since he did I may as well clear him. He told you what he believed to be the truth."

Margaret's rigid form relaxed and she let out a long sigh. Sethos glanced at her and then looked away. "Thank you," he said ironically. "Now, sir, perhaps you will explain why *you* lied to *me*?"

"You know the rules," Smith said. "You were told what you needed to know. Nothing more."

"The devil with your bloody rules," growled Emerson. "I need to know everything—who was plotting against whom and why and wherefore. And if you mention the bloody Official Secrets Act I may lose my temper."

"Heaven forbid," said Smith piously. "Very well. I am prepared to break certain rules in order to set your minds at ease—and prevent you from stirring up trouble."

"Proceed," I said, taking pen in hand. Smith started to object, but wisely decided not to.

"There was only one conspiracy," he began. "Bashir's group and the malcontents in Iraq were part of the same plot, though neither group was aware of the other, or of the real aim of the people behind the affair. Both had been infiltrated by men who meant to use them to attain their own ends—professional killers, trained in the techniques of assassination. Poor fool that he was, Bashir meant no harm to anyone. These people and their bloodless coups . . . Really, they oughtn't be let loose without a chaperon.

"When Ramses and his wife suddenly decided to go to Cairo, the assassins took alarm. They knew the message was not a fraud and they feared he was about to expose the real conspiracy. They were tracking you two from the moment you arrived, and you made no effort to elude pursuit. Breakfasting in full view of the world on the terrace at Shepheard's! Somehow or other—we may never know how—Bashir got wind of their intentions and tried to warn you. He was a martyr, if you like," Smith concluded, with a nod at Ramses.

We paid Bashir the tribute of a moment of respectful silence. He had repented of his errors in judgment and possibly saved the lives of Ramses and Nefret. Then Emerson said, "Three murders. Why?"

"Is it not *cui bono* a rule of criminal investigation?" Smith asked. "Who profits? Ask yourself what would have happened had these crimes been committed."

His air of superiority was grating. Ramses, who disliked him any-how, said, "Egypt and Iraq would have dissolved into chaos. Britain would be forced to intervene. Possibly a full-fledged military interven-tion and the reestablishment of a formal mandate."

"Quite right," said Smith, with a gracious nod. "And who would have profited from that?"

"The jingoists and imperialists in Britain," I suggested. "There has always been a vociferous majority who believe the European powers have the right, if not the duty, to rule over those they consider to be their inferiors."

"And who else?"

It was, surprisingly, Sethos, who lost his temper. "The jingoists aren't the cause, they are the means used by the real instigators. Behind them are the people who expect to make money from British control. Oil in Iraq, cotton and foodstuffs in Egypt. And cheap labor in both countries. The financiers, the leaders of industry. The shadowy group I spoke of. Shadowy because they will never be held to account. In the end it all comes down to money. That's all they care about; they are in-different to the lives they affect and the deaths for which they are ulti-mately responsible."

Smith appeared somewhat put out. Sethos had anticipated his speech and delivered it with a passion he could never have matched.

"Essentially, that is the case," he said, propping his long chin on his folded hands.

"Then these people will never be brought to justice," I said.

"Never. Nor even identified. They don't give direct orders; they con-fer and hold committee meetings and drop veiled hints."

" 'Who will free me from this turbulent priest?' " I murmured.

"Not even as direct as that, Mrs. Emerson," Smith said. "But the message is clear to their subordinates, and so it goes down the chain of command, until it reaches the individuals who direct the actual opera-tions. Even supposing we could trace the initial instigators, we couldn't hold them accountable. They would express horror and dismay and deny that they so much as hinted at such a thing."

"It's a damned depressing picture," said Emerson, chewing on his pipe.

"I find it so," said Smith; and I saw a trace of emotion flicker across that masklike face. "All we can do is forestall, if possible, the deadly results and perhaps identify a few of the minor criminals. At least we've got a line on two of them. Malraux and Farid."

"I am so sorry," I said, with a somewhat hypocritical air of regret. "But I'm afraid you haven't. Suzanne and Nadji have nothing to do with this."

"Then why did they run off?" Emerson demanded. "Run . . . Oh, no. No." He clapped his hand to his brow. "Don't tell me this is another of your—your—"

"Precisely," I said. "They ran off—to be married. Suzanne did her best to win her grandfather over to the idea without actually asking his permission. She was afraid to risk that, but she hoped being with Nadji and other worthy Egyptians, seeing our fond relations with them would soften his prejudices. It was, as I could have told her, a forlorn hope. When he insisted on her returning to England with him, she felt she had no other choice but to elope with her lover."

Ramses closed his mouth, swallowed strenuously, and said in a very gentle voice, "Would you mind explaining, Mother, how you arrived at this remarkable deduction? Are you going to claim you knew all along those two were in love?"

"As your father has indicated, I enjoy a certain reputation for settling romantic affairs," I said modestly. "The complete indifference those two displayed toward each other was highly significant. They went to considerable lengths to ensure we would hire them both: Nadji for his unquestioned competence, and Suzanne because of the portfolio he had prepared for her. Who else would have conspired in that deception? You may have found your artist in Nadji, Cyrus."

"Good," Cyrus said, staring.

"Then where are they?" Nefret asked. "Why haven't we been able to find a trace of them?"

"They have gone to earth with one of Nadji's friends on the West Bank, I expect," I said. "You believed he had none? But he was in the habit of visiting a certain coffeeshop in Luxor. He made acquaintances there."

Emerson, who was familiar with my methods, hid a smile behind his big hand, on the pretense of fiddling with his pipe. Smith, who *ought* to have been familiar with them, eyed me askance.

"Forgive me, Mrs. Emerson, but all this is hindsight. And as yet unverified."

I couldn't help feeling a little sorry for him. He had tried so hard, and he so wanted to punish someone. However, truth must out, whatever the consequences. And I resented his implication.

"It shouldn't be difficult to verify," I said. "The habitués of the coffeeshop in question will talk freely if we assure them we want only to assist the lovers. Ramses should be the one to carry out that mission, I think. The word of the Brother of Demons is as good as another man's oath."

"One of Daoud's aphorisms," Emerson explained to Smith.

"Thank you," said Smith, baring his teeth. "You will not object, I hope, if I remain in Luxor until they are apprehended?"

"Suit yourself," I said. "However, it seems to me you would be more usefully employed in Cairo or Baghdad. Can you be absolutely certain your men are in a position to prevent the assassinations?"

"I wouldn't count on it," said Sethos. "There has been, shall we say, a certain confusion of communications on various levels."

Smith did not miss the implicit accusation. "Then you had better go yourself. The Baghdad flight—"

"No. I've done my last job for the Department."

"Come now," Smith exclaimed. "I understand why you might feel a certain degree of—er—resentment, but you're an old hand, you know it was necessary."

"Too old a hand," Sethos said quietly. "I am submitting my resignation, as of now, in the presence of these witnesses." He turned to Margaret, who was listening with parted lips. "I have said that before, but this time I mean it. Amelia won't let me squirm out of it this time."

Margaret jumped up and ran out of the room.

"Excuse me," said Sethos. He followed her.

As a rule I would never intrude on intimate moments, but I wanted to make certain that I could check this little item off my list. Peeking round the door, I saw that they were locked in a close embrace.

I tiptoed away.

"I believe that covers everything," said Mr. Smith. He appeared more than ready to go.

"If it was not Suzanne and Nadji who spied on us and reported on our activities, who was it?" Nefret asked. "We've run out of suspects, Mother."

"That wretched boy, of course. Azmi."

"What?" Emerson cried.

"I told you, Emerson, that you ought not have taught him to spy and sneak. Observing that he was in your confidence, 'they' approached him and offered him money to report to them. One cannot really blame him, since he did not suspect there was any danger to us. I will have to take him in hand. He is a clever child, and it may be not too late to instill in him a moral sensibility."

"If anyone can do it, you can," said Mr. Smith. "Good day, Mrs. Emerson."

I think he meant it as a compliment.


"Well, Peabody," said Emerson, "it seems that you are not about to add another scalp to your belt."

Stretched out on the bed, hands under his head, he watched me give my hair its one hundred strokes. It had been a long day, but I do not neglect such things.

"That is a very ugly metaphor, Emerson."

"Another notch to your gun?" Emerson suggested. "Another villain safely in custody?"

Nadji and Suzanne had been found, just where I had said they would be—at the home of one of the young customers of the coffeeshop. They had gone through a marriage ceremony conducted by the local imam. To be on the safe side, I hustled them across to Luxor and served as witness while Father Bennett married them again. It was a purely symbolic gesture, since (as the good father piteously pointed out) they had gone through none of the preliminary formalities. I promised we would take care of these, and that he could marry them again afterward.

"We have become spoiled, I fear," Emerson went on. "There is something satisfactory about ending a case with the arrest or the burial of the villain."

"Do not despair, my dear. There may yet be a villain to be arrested."

Emerson sat up. "Who? Please tell me it is Sir William Portmanteau."

"I wish I could. Whether he is complicit or not, he is the sort of man Smith meant when he spoke of shadowy forces, men without conscience. We cannot have him arrested, but cheer up! He will receive a painful blow when I tell him about Suzanne and Nadji."

"Perhaps he will have a fatal stroke," Emerson said hopefully. "Serve him right. Who, then? Curse it, I don't like fighting shadows, I want to get my hands on a flesh-and-blood villain."

He was so downcast, I was tempted to admit him to my confidence. However, I decided not to. Though I was fairly certain of my deductions, it would have been unkind to raise his hopes and then be forced to destroy them. Instead I offered consolation of another nature. It proved to be acceptable.


Consulting my list of Things to Be Done at breakfast, I was able to cross out several items. Sethos and Margaret had been dealt with, at least for the time being. With two such domineering personalities, further upheavals were likely, but I could not worry about that. The situation of Nadji and Suzanne was well on the way to a satisfactory conclusion, with only one more step to be taken. I am not in the habit of leaving unpleasant tasks to others, so I set out for the Castle immediately after breakfast.

Cyrus came running out to greet me. "What the dickens have you been doing?" he demanded. "You left me stuck with that old villain Portmanteau, and he's been driving me crazy. Even Cat is fed up with him, and you know she's not easily upset."

"I will deal with him forthwith," I said, brushing dust off my trousers. "Tell him I want to see him."

He was some time in responding, and when he came into the drawing room I observed that he had been comforting himself with brandy. Katherine was with me; having learned of my arrival, she could hardly wait to complain about her unwelcome guest. "He is no gentleman, Amelia, he ignored my hints that he should go to the hotel, and his language. . . !"

Sir Wiliam's appearance caused her to break off. He had abandoned any pretense of gentility. Red-faced and unkempt, he wasted no time in being offensive.

"Well, Mrs. Emerson, what have you to report? You promised me—"

"I know where they are," I said, raising my voice over his. "They are safe and very happy."

If the last word reached Sir William's ears, it never penetrated as far as his brain. "Where is she? Why didn't you fetch her here? By God, when I get hold of that girl—"

"You no longer have any authority over her," I said. "She is a married woman."

Katherine gasped. "Those two? Married?"

"Well, that's nice," Cyrus said.

Sir William's face went from red to purple and he was gobbling like a turkey cock. I watched him with, I regret to admit, more curiosity than compassion, until his breathing became so labored that he was forced to stop talking. I shoved him into a chair.

"I would recommend brandy but for the fact that you appear to have taken too much already. I would take you to see Suzanne but for the fact that you would only abuse her and her husband. The die is cast, Sir William, and you can't do a cursed thing about it. Your only recourse is to get yourself out of this house, across the river, and on to Cairo as expeditiously as possible. Perhaps (it does not seem likely, but all things are possible), perhaps in time you will come to your senses and attempt to reestablish friendly relations with your granddaughter."

"Never!" Sir William wheezed. "No kin of mine. Out of my will. Not a penny!"

"I will have the servants pack his bags," Katherine said. She hurried out.

"And I," said Cyrus, his eyes twinkling, "beg to differ with you, Amelia. A little more brandy, or perhaps a great deal of brandy, is just what he needs."

With the departure of our dear ones imminent, we found ourselves in a whirl of social activity. Selim and Daoud put on a splendid fantasia, and we celebrated New Year's Eve in the American style, with a glittering ball at the Castle. Cyrus had brought a musical ensemble all the way from Cairo. After a vigorous waltz with Emerson I needed to catch my breath, so I joined Katherine at one of the tables. She gave a guilty start when she saw me, and then burst out laughing.

"Caught in the act," she said, indicating her heaped plate. "But on the whole I have been good, Amelia."

"An occasional indulgence never hurt anyone," I said. "You do seem much stronger and healthier, Katherine."

"And wiser, I hope. Cyrus tells me this is the time to make resolutions for the new year . . ."

Her eyes moved to a couple whirling past—Nadji and Suzanne, whose healths we had all drunk in Cyrus's best champagne. They were to work with Cyrus for the remainder of the season, Nadji as staff artist, and Suzanne as Jumana's assistant.

"Seeing Sir William's appalling behavior," Katherine resumed, "made me realize that I had not overcome my own prejudices. It was like a caricature of my worst attitudes. Look at those two—blissfully happy—and I would once have said their marriage was doomed from the start."

"They will have difficulties to overcome," I admitted. "Including the differences in their religions. However, marriage is always a chancy business, Katherine. I have known individuals who appeared perfectly suited, by family background, religion, and nationality, who were thoroughly miserable."

"So you believe in taking the chance?"

"Certainly. What is life without some risk?"

She laughed and cut off another another bit of frosted cake. "That is my resolution, then. To take a few risks, and let others take theirs."

"Ah," I said. "Excuse me, Katherine. I have just remembered something I must do."

Jumana was dancing with Sethos, who was, in my opinion, holding her too tightly. She did not seem to mind. When the waltz ended, I asked if I might have a few minutes of her time.

"The next is Ramses's," she said, glancing at her dance card.

"He can wait. This cannot, it has gone on too long. You do care for Bertie, and not only as a friend. Don't deny it. Why won't you marry him?"

Jumana went white and then bright red. "How did you know?" she gasped.

"Detecting romantic attachments is one of my talents," I replied. "Why won't you?"

She looked me straight in the eye. "It would break his mother's heart. She has been good to me. I will not go where I am not wanted."

"Pride," I said, shaking my head. "It is cold comfort when one is unhappy, Jumana. Why not take a chance? Who knows, you might be pleasantly surprised."

Ramses turned up to claim his dance; I handed Jumana over to him with a comfortable feeling that matters were proceeding nicely. I took the additional precaution of saying a few words to Bertie, and sure enough, by the end of the evening we had another pair of lovers to toast. Cyrus's look of pride and pleasure was very nice to see, and so was Katherine's maternal embrace. The engaged couple appeared to be somewhat stupefied. But they would get over it.

All in all, it was a thoroughly satisfactory evening. The final touch was delivered in the form of a telegram, which we found waiting on our return home. Mr. Smith was as brief as Emerson would have been, but much more original. "The wrong has failed, the right prevailed. Happy New Year."

I had always suspected the man had the rudiments of a sense of humor.

Our own family gatherings were made more poignant by the knowledge that they were for the last time. The last game of chess (lost by David), the last little books of Charla's, to be delivered to the grandparents in England, the last of Fatima's magnificent teas, the last visits to the Valley of the Kings.

David couldn't stay away from the Valley. He took his drawing materials with him, and watched the removal of each item with yearning eyes. The crowds around the tomb had become a real nuisance, and I would have felt sorry for Howard had he not behaved so badly. Yet one could hardly blame the sightseers. The clearance had proceeded apace. Item after astonishing item had been taken along the path to the tomb of Seti II. Howard had made some concession to the visitors by allowing the artifacts to be carried uncovered.

After we had returned to the house following one such visit, Ramses sought me out. "There is a matter I've been wanting to discuss with you, Mother."

"I can guess what it is."

"Can you?"

"My dear, one is always *en rapport* with those one loves. You are thinking of David, wishing you could gain him entry to Tutankhamon's tomb. I have racked my brains for a means of doing so, but to no avail. I even lowered myself by writing to Howard, in a friendly manner, inviting him to tea. Don't tell your father."

"He would say, as do I, that you were wasting your time," said Sethos, emerging from the house. He had the smug, self-satisfied look of a cat who has cream on its whiskers. I deduced he had been with Margaret. Settling himself comfortably in a chair, he steepled his fingers and peered owlishly at me. "What did you do that for?"

I explained. "Ah," said Sethos. "Very nice. You were willing to humiliate yourself in order to help David. I trust you didn't ask Carter directly?"

"Good Gad, no. I would have worked up to that gradually. Ah well, I did my best."

"Quite," said Sethos. "Is tea ready?"

He made something of a pig of himself, pretending to squabble with Charla over the iced biscuits. Afterward he and Margaret went across to Luxor, to dine à deux at the hotel.

"I'll keep her out of mischief," he assured me, twirling his mustache.

"Not if I encounter O'Donnell," said Margaret. "He has got ahead of me, and I won't let him rub it in."

Next day was the last. David, Sennia, and Gargery were to catch the train the day after, on the start of their long journey home. We had invited our closest friends to tea that afternoon, to say good-bye. When I asked how they wanted to spend the morning, Sennia voted for a final visit to King Tut, as she had taken to calling him. David's eager face expressed his sentiments, and Gargery took it for granted that he would come along. Even Emerson condescended to join the party. He had given up on the motorcar for the time being. The part I had removed, with Nefret's assistance, proved to be essential to its operation.

Margaret was the last to join us in the stable, where the horses were being saddled. She had added a bright scarf and a selection of silver bracelets to her khaki trouser suit, and I detected a trace of artificial coloring on her cheeks. "Where is—er—Anthony?" I asked.

"Gone off on his own. Which am I to ride?"

"This donkey," said Emerson, hoisting her unceremoniously onto the saddle.

"I prefer a horse to a donkey," Margaret said with a mutinous look.

"I will keep you company," I promised. "You and I and Gargery and Sennia. Won't that be nice?"

After a somewhat dusty ride, we found the donkey park crowded with animals, sand carts, and two-horse carriages. We had made an early start, knowing the crush would increase as the day went on.

We arrived just in time to see a spectacular object carried out of the tomb—the glorious gilded throne Rex Engelbach had described. Mr. Mace walked beside it, his face furrowed with the anxious look of a father watching his child's first steps. I assumed that he had taken preliminary steps to stabilize some of the ornamentation, but still it was a touchy operation, and when he came back from the conservation tomb, smiling with relief, I called out a hearty congratulation.

A lull ensued before the next artifact appeared. There was a great deal of activity, however; importunate persons argued with the guards, trying to get past them, and people ran in and out with messages, including several telegrams. Tourists photographed every moving object; journalists wandered up and down, looking for someone to interview. One of them recognized Sennia and would have interrogated her—heaven knows what about—had Emerson not intervened.

I had brought refreshments, and was about to gather my group and retire for a quick luncheon when the appearance of Howard roused a great stir in the watchers. Ignoring the questions shouted at him by various persons, he stood with hands on hips, looking round. Nothing ventured, nothing gained, I thought, and waved my parasol in greeting.

No one was more astonished than I when Howard gestured me to approach, rather in the manner of a potentate condescending to a petitioner. Deciding that I was in no position to resent this, I made my way past the guards and joined Howard. He showed the strains of the past days; there were deep lines in his face and his eyes were shadowed.

"It seems to be going well," I said in a friendly manner.

"Yes, quite. No problems thus far. Er—is Mr. Todros with you?"

"As a matter of fact, he is," I said, attempting to conceal my astonishment.

"I have been instructed—I have decided—to allow him to make a drawing of one of the artifacts."

Taking it for granted that (or not giving a curse whether) he had been included in Howard's gesture, Emerson had followed after me. "Which one?" he instantly demanded.

Howard glanced at the paper he was twisting between his fingers. It appeared to be a telegram.

"Whichever he likes." With a flash of temper, he added, "But not in the tomb!"

"Of course not," I said. "You are busy there. The storage tomb."

Like Emerson, I realized we must seize time by the fetlock before Howard could change his mind.

"Yes," he said grudgingly. Taking a pencil from his pocket, he scribbled on the back of the telegram. "Give this to Lucas. And tell Todros I will hold him accountable for any damage!"

I gave Emerson a little poke to prevent him from expressing his indignation, and took the note from Howard's reluctant hand.

"Hurry," I exclaimed, as we retreated in haste. "Where is David?"

We had to battle our way through a horde of journalists; they were so hungry for news that they pounced on anyone who had spoken with Howard. Emerson told them to go to the devil and I told them Howard was about to give a press conference, whereupon they squatted like a pack of hungry jackals round the mouth of a rabbit hole. I led my group away. When we were at a safe distance I broke the news to David. The look in the dear boy's eyes would have brought tears to my own, had I been a sentimenal person.

"You have your drawing materials with you, I believe?" I asked.

"Yes. Yes, but—"

"What else do you need?" Nefret asked. "I'll go to the house and fetch it."

"Paints and brushes . . ."

"I understand. Will you come with me, Margaret?"

Margaret at once agreed. She appeared as pleased and excited as everyone else.

The rest of us went at once to the tomb of Seti II. The open area in front of the entrance was a scene of what appeared to be utter chaos; objects being treated lay on tables and trestles, boards for constructing packing cases leaned against the walls, paper and packing materials were strewn about. Inside the tomb, whose gate stood open, one could see half a dozen wooden cases and several working areas. Even from the outside the smell of acetone, collodion, and other chemicals was strong.

Lucas was not surprised to see us. He shook hands all round and read the note from Carter. "I wondered when Carter would get over his pique," he said. "As you can see, we are in something of a turmoil here, but I am happy to oblige. Are you interested in any particular item, Mr. Todros?"

David's eyes were fixed on it—the painted chest. It rested on a table several yards down the corridor. Lucas frowned. "The exterior only, I presume? The contents are in terrible condition and Mace hasn't started on them yet. I would rather not move it."

"I quite agree. I observe you have employed paraffin wax on the exterior," I said, craning my neck to see better.

"The wood had begun to shrink and the painted gesso to come loose," Lucas said. "We had to take immediate steps."

"There is nothing like paraffin wax," I said.

"It has done the job, and even enhanced the colors."

"We will leave you to get on with your work, then," I said, adding that someone would be coming by later with David's painting materials. David did not acknowledge our farewells. Seated on a campstool, he had already begun to sketch, and was lost in his own world.

"I hope he can finish today," I said to Emerson. "There is something decidedly odd about this. Howard's pique is still firmly in place. He received orders from someone to let David work."

"Lacau, perhaps?" Ramses suggested.

Emerson snorted. "Carter snubs and ignores the Antiquities Department. There is only one person from whom he takes orders."

"Lord Carnarvon," I agreed. "However, his compliance is equally inexplicable."

We reached the end of the wadi and turned into the main path, where whom should we behold but Sethos, sitting on a rock and smoking a cigarette.

"Where have you been?" I asked.

"Hither and yon. Is it time for luncheon? Sennia has informed me that she is ravenous."

We collected Sennia and Gargery and found a nice empty tomb. Seated in a circle round the picnic basket, we let Sennia explore the contents and hand them out.

"Where's Margaret?" Sethos asked, accepting a cheese sandwich.

"She and Nefret have gone back to the house to fetch David's painting materials," I said. "Howard has given him permission to copy one of the artifacts for the *ILN*."

"Has he indeed?"

"I think we should go home after luncheon," Sennia announced. "Gargery looks tired."

"What?" Gargery straightened and got a firmer grip on the sandwich that had been about to fall from his hand. "Tired? Me?"

"I want to wait until Nefret returns," I said. "That will be a while. Why don't you and Gargery go back with Emerson, or perhaps Ramses."

"I will escort them," Sethos said, foraging in the basket. "What do you recommend, Sennia, tomato or chicken?"

Upon her advice, he selected the chicken and settled back to eat it.

"There is still brown dye behind your ear," I said, out of the corner of my mouth.

Sethos grinned and went on eating.

The three of them went off after luncheon, and Ramses, Emerson, and I waited for Nefret. I was not the only one who had deduced the explanation for Howard's volte-face.

"Which one was he?" Ramses asked.

"The very ragged messenger with the very rude vocabulary, I think. You know his tendency to overplay a role."

"Good Gad," Emerson exclaimed. "You mean he . . . Sethos was the . . . How the devil did he counterfeit a telegram from Lord Carnarvon?"

"As he will no doubt say, he has his methods. I don't think he wants David to know. David's principles are so rigid he might feel Howard had been taken unfair advantage of."

"He was," said Emerson, a pleased grin spreading across his face. "Excellent! I must commend my dear, dear brother. For once he has put his questionable talents to good use. And the best of it is," he went on, "Carter will find out in due course that he has been deceived—when it's too late for him to do anything about it!"

He burst into a peal of hearty laughter, in which he was joined by Ramses. I confess I let out a little chuckle of my own.

We had resigned ourselves to a long wait, but were pleasantly surprised when Nefret turned up a good half hour before we could reasonably expect her. She was accompanied by Selim, carrying David's easel and paints.

"How quick you were," I exclaimed, hastening to meet them. "I trust you did not tire the poor horses."

"No," said Selim. He mumbled something.

"I beg your pardon, Selim?" I said. "Speak up."

"We drove the motorcar," Selim bellowed.

Emerson let out a cry of delight. "What a fine day this is turning out to be! You repaired it, Selim?"

"Yes," said Selim, studiously avoiding looking at Nefret, who was carefully not looking at me.

"Go along, Selim," I said. "Mr. Lucas is expecting you."

He went off at a run.

"I'm sorry, Mother," Nefret whispered to me. "I thought the emergency excused the betrayal."

"You were correct," I said with a sigh. "Into every life a little rain must fall."

Naturally Emerson insisted on driving home in the motorcar. That left the rest of us to deal with the horses and several reluctant donkeys. We left David's Asfur for him. He would not stop until the last of the light had faded.

Dusk was well advanced and our other guests had assembled before Asfur came, at a walk, with David cradling a covered box as tenderly as if it were a baby. He handed it down to Ramses and Jamad led Asfur away. When David lifted the lid, a universal cry of admiration arose—except from David, whose cry was one of woe. "It's smudged—here and here—it was wet, I couldn't wait for it to dry . . . Damn!"

"It can be repaired," I said. "Or copied again. David, it is splendid! You have captured the colors and the vivacity of the scene as no one else could."

"Darn right," Cyrus exclaimed. "Congratulations, my boy. *The Illustrated London News* will be delighted."

David looked up from his inspection of the painting. "I cannot offer

it to the *ILN*, sir. Not without Mr. Carter's explicit permission. I looked
for him before I left, to thank him—"

"Damnation," said Emerson.

"Sir?"

"Er . . . never mind. Go on."

"Unfortunately he had already left for the day," David said.

"Ah," I said. "We will thank him for you, David. Er—you don't
need his permission to sell it to the *ILN*, you know. His and Carnarvon's legal rights are questionable."

"Oh, I wouldn't do it unless he said it was all right," David exclaimed. A smile of utter bliss transformed his face. "The important
thing is that I could do it. That I have it. I wouldn't lower myself by attempting to make money from such a marvelous task."

"It's a damn good thing David is leaving tomorrow," said Emerson,
after our guests had left and David had gone to his room to finish packing. "He'd be determined to call on Carter personally. Confound the
boy's confounded principles!"

"What matters to him is the work itself," Sethos said. "He has that
and will always have it."

"Yes," said Emerson. "Quite. Er—well done. What do you say to another whiskey and soda?"


We saw them off early next morning, amid tears and laughter and as-
surances that we would soon meet again. David carried the box containing his painting as if it were made of glass.

"Be good," I said, giving him a final embrace.

"I've got off much easier than I deserved, Aunt Amelia."

"You got precisely what you deserved, David. Our fondest love and a
wish come true, and, perhaps, a little lesson to be pondered."

"I will," David said earnestly. "You may count on that."

When we gathered for tea later that day, Emerson grumbled, "The
house is too quiet. I miss that child." I gave him a little poke and he said
hastily, "But I have you, my darlings, to console me."

"I presume that isn't meant for me," Sethos said. "Margaret and I will be taking our departure before long, but I expect you will endure that loss manfully."

"He was talking to us," Charla said emphatically. "Come and play archery, Grandpapa."

"Or chess," said David John.

Caught between Scylla and Charybdis, Emerson decided on archery. He and Charla went off together, and while David John was setting up the chessboard I said to Sethos, "Now that you have retired, what are your plans?"

"I am going to try my hand at writing thrillers. David John has promised to collaborate."

David John, who had his eye on Sethos as an opponent, took the bait. "Would you like to see the ending I wrote for the book Grandmama would not let me finish reading?"

"Nothing would please me more," Sethos declared with heartfelt sincerity. Anything was better than losing another game of chess to a five-year-old.

David John ran off to get his manuscript. "Not that I mean to sound inhospitable," I said, "but have you settled on a date for your departure?"

"That depends on you, Amelia."

"I cannot imagine what you mean."

"No? You've been watching the road and snatching at every message that has been delivered. I think I know what you're up to, and I wouldn't want to miss it."

"Good Gad," I said, in some confusion.

"Good Gad," Sethos exclaimed, taking the manuscript David John handed him and scanning the first page.

I had indeed been waiting for a message. The delay was beginning to wear on me. What the devil could the man be waiting for?

The long-expected letter arrived that afternoon, by messenger. We were on the veranda when I read it, and I was unable to repress a cry of triumph.

"Aha! As I suspected!"

Emerson was somewhat wroth when I explained. However, the prospect of action was sufficient to distract him from what he was pleased to term my confounded reticence. We made plans to leave shortly after dinner, taking the path that led over the plateau to the Valley of the Kings. The moon was bright, and we all knew every step of the way. Since Margaret did not, she was persuaded to remain at home.

When we reached the top of the gebel above Deir el Bahri, I cautioned everyone to move quietly and refrain from speaking. We had not gone far before I heard the sounds I had expected: low-pitched voices and the ill-tempered grumble of several camels. Avoiding the dark forms that had gathered round the rim of the cliffs above the Valley, I summoned my allies to my side.

"We cannot wait until they begin lifting the packing cases," I whispered. "We must stop them now, before damage is done to the artifacts."

We had arrived in the nick of time, thanks to my informant. A burst of sound and a blaze of flame was followed by loud outcries from the wadi below.

"Now!" I cried. Brandishing my parasol, I dashed at the group of villains.

It was a brisk but brief encounter. Caught off-guard, the thieves had been on the point of descending into the wadi when we fell upon them. Realizing that my supporters had the situation well in hand, I went in pursuit of a man who was creeping away among the ridges of the uneven terrain.

"It is no use, Sir Malcolm," I cried. "You are fairly caught. Stand up and face your punishment like a man."

The arrival of Sethos put an end to any idea of resistance Sir Malcolm might have entertained. We escorted him back to what had been the scene of battle. The would-be thieves huddled on the ground, watched over by Ramses. Among them were Aguil and Deib ibn Simsah.

"Any damage?" I called to Emerson, who had descended the cliff and was inspecting the tomb.

"A largish hole some yards down the wadi. Well done, you fellows," Emerson added in Arabic.

He came back up, climbing like a mountain goat. The thieves had proceeded along the lines Sethos had proposed. One group had fallen upon the guards in front of the tomb of Seti II, after setting off an explosion to distract them. The guards had been warned and were ready for them. We, atop the cliff, had taken care of the party waiting with ropes and camels to carry the loot away.

Sir Malcolm seated himself on the ground. He had lost his wig; his head, bare as an egg, glimmered in the starlight. I stood over him with parasol raised, while his servant crouched at his feet.

"Caught red-handed," Emerson exclaimed in satisfaction.

"Doing what?" Sir Malcolm was not an easy man to intimidate. He had had time to catch his breath and invent an excuse. "I came here for the same reason you did, Professor. I suspected an attempt would be made to rob the tomb."

"That's a lie!" Emerson cried.

"Prove it."

"I can," I said, holding Emerson back. "Mr. Gabra?"

Sir Malcolm's servant rose to his feet. "May I present Lieutenant Gabra of the Luxor police," I said. "He is here with the permission of his chief, Inspector Aziz, and he was present, though unseen, during every conversation you held with Aguil and Deib. Being men of little wit and no morals, they were willing to go on working for you even though you were responsible for the death of their brother."

Sir Malcolm's face was as white as his bald head. "His death was an accident," he cried. "The fool ignored my instructions."

"Ah," I said in satisfaction. "You have admitted that much."

Gabra spoke for the first time. He was still wearing his patched galabeeyah, but his bearing had changed, so that he now looked like the upstanding, competent man he really was.

"That is what he told Deib and Aguil," he said. "The bomb was a practice run, as you say; Farhat was supposed to take it to a safe distance and set it off, to prove he knew how. He did not know how."

"Negligent manslaughter," I said musingly.

"You cannot charge me with that," Sir Malcolm muttered. Despite the cool of the night, sweat was running down his face. "Farhat was an arrogant fool."

"Perhaps I cannot," I admitted with regret. "But there is enough evidence to charge you with an attempt to steal the treasures of Tutankhamon. Take him away with the others, Lieutenant, and congratulations on a job well done."

"He'll talk or bribe his way out of it," Sethos said. Half-reclining in an easy chair, legs stretched out, he raised his glass in a general salute.

"I fear so," said Emerson. "He's a rich titled Englishman and Gabra is, in the eyes of the idiot administration, 'only' a native."

"Do you mean I can't print this?" Margaret asked.

"He would sue you for every penny you own," said her husband lazily. "I can't afford it."

"We may take satisfaction in the fact that Sir Malcolm has been thoroughly humiliated," I said. "The word will get round. I doubt he will have the temerity to show his face in Egypt soon again."

"If he does, I will give him the thrashing he deserves," grunted Emerson. He turned his scowl on his brother. "Speaking of thrashings, I am inclined to give you one. Why did you tell us that rigmarole?"

"I had to tell you something," said Sethos, stroking his mustache like a stage villain.

Emerson snarled. "Do not try my temper, I beg. I am willing to accept that you were acting under orders and that you had been misled about the nature of the conspiracy, but if you thought the code was a fake, why did you let Ramses waste days trying to decipher it? Why bring it here at all?"

"That was only an excuse," I said. "He came to us because he was ill and alone and afraid."

My words fell like stones into a sudden silence. Margaret caught her breath, and Emerson's sapphirine eyes softened. Sethos bowed his head and looked down at his clasped hands, a slight flush staining his cheeks.

"Why be ashamed to admit it?" I demanded. "Anyone would do the same—yes, Emerson, even you."

"But I wouldn't admit it either," Emerson muttered. "Leave the man alone, Peabody."

"One more thing," I said, taking out my list. The paper was somewhat worn with frequent handling, and almost all the items were crossed out. "The man in the suk."

"What man?" Ramses asked.

"Had you forgotten? I had not. The nice man who gave Charla money the day she eloped with Ali. You," I said, pointing at my brother-in-law, "were there, watching the hotel—watching for a sight of us. Your family."

Sethos raised his head and threw up his hands. "You've won, Amelia. My humiliation is complete. Yes, I felt a contemptible need to see you, to know all was well with you. When Charla came dancing out with that useless suffragi I followed them."

"Giving her enough money to make herself sick with sweets was one of your little jokes, I suppose," Ramses said. There was no accusation in his voice, only a touch of amusement.

"I knew she wouldn't be sick. I did it because . . . because I wanted to."

Like his humiliation, my revenge was complete. He was finally, thoroughly reformed! I decided he had suffered enough, so I changed the subject.

"What are your plans?" I asked.

"Back to England and Home, accompanied by Beauty," said Sethos, with a nod at his wife, who rolled her eyes and grinned. "I will humble myself to my daughter and learn to know my grandson. We will be leaving shortly. Contain your grief, I beg."

"And I," said Margaret, "will see to it that he does as he has promised. But I'll be back in time to see Carter open the burial chamber. I am determined to get a story out of this, somehow!"

"The house seems very empty with everyone gone," Emerson said with a sigh.

It was a perfect opening, but neither Ramses nor Nefret had the courage to take advantage of it. As usual, the chore was left up to me.

"I have been looking in the newspaper," I said. "There are several nice houses to let in Roda and Maadi."

Emerson sat up with a start. "What?"

"You have decided, haven't you?" I prodded Ramses.

"Yes. Father, we—"

"Then you had better get at the task of finding the right house. You will want to be settled in before April."

Ramses ran his hand through his tumbled curls. "You know. You knew!"

"Of course. I am very happy for you, my dears."

"What—" Emerson is always a little slow to catch on, but this was something he had been yearning for. "What? Nefret is . . . You are . . ."

"Yes, Father." Nefret knelt by his chair and took his hand. "Please say that you are happy too."

His face working, Emerson carried her hand to his lips.

The child was a girl. I had spoken with Abdullah about it the previous night.

"Well, Peabody," said Emerson, "I hope you are pleased with yourself."

I was, rather. We had retired to our room after several celebratory whiskey and sodas (Nefret had a nice glass of warm milk) and fond good nights. I sat down at the dressing table and began taking the pins out of my hair. Emerson, already shirtless, sat down in a chair and removed his right shoe.

"You are, aren't you?" Emerson demanded. "I can see your face. You are smirking. When did you know? Why didn't you tell me?"

"I have known for some time. There are certain indications . . . But it was their little secret, Emerson."

"That has never stopped you before."

I turned my head to look at him. Slowly and carefully Emerson removed his other shoe, weighed it in his hand, and threw it, with perfect aim, at a rather ugly lamp.

"Why, Emerson," I exclaimed. "What is the matter?"

Emerson rose to his feet. "This entire season," he said, in a voice like a distant rumble of thunder, "you have deceived me, worked behind my back, left me out of your confidence. I have had enough, Peabody! I will endure no more!"

"But, Emerson—"

"Not another word!" Emerson shouted. He crossed the room in a single bound and snatched me up into his arms.

"Well!" I said, when I had got my breath back. "I have been waiting months for you to do that. Have you concluded that I am not breakable?"

"I have concluded," said Emerson, carrying me toward the bed, "that you are immortal. Age cannot wither . . . nor time decay your infinite variety."

"Poetry, Emerson!" I cried.

"Shakespeare," said Emerson proudly. "I know another poem, Peabody."

"May I hear it?"

"'It little profits that an idle king . . . matched with an aging wife . . .'"

I put the pillow over his face. After a short interval he broke off to say breathlessly, "You did not allow me to finish, Peabody. How does it go? 'Tis not too late to seek a newer world.' Shall we get the *Amelia* back on the river and go sailing again? 'Push off, and sitting well in order smite the sounding furrows?'"

"'It may be we shall touch the Happy Isles,'" I went on dreamily.

"And see the great Abdullah, whom we knew."

"You are making a dreadful hash of Tennyson, Emerson."

"It's the thought that counts, Peabody. 'One equal temper of heroic hearts,' that's what we are. We will strive and seek and find, and never yield."

# AFTERWORD

Apparently Mrs. Emerson felt that the quotation from one of her favorite poets served as a fitting conclusion to this volume of her journals—or perhaps she believed other writers would describe subsequent happenings which did not affect her family directly. Many thousands of words have been written about the events surrounding the discovery of Tutankhamon's tomb. The accounts differ in a number of ways, some significant, some not. One would suppose that the most accurate would be that of Howard Carter himself; yet, as recent investigation has proved, he was not entirely candid. Some of the so-called eyewitness accounts were written after the event and are therefore contaminated by inaccurate memory. The editor feels she owes it to the Reader to point out certain of these discrepancies.

The well-known story, that Carnarvon told Carter in the summer of 1922 that he had decided not to finance any further excavations in the Valley, and that he was persuaded into one more season by Carter's offer to pay for the work himself, rests on hearsay—the statement of Charles Breasted, son of the famous American Egyptologist. Charles

Breasted claimed that he heard the story from Carter. Carter himself never mentioned it. The ill-conceived intervention of Emerson makes even better sense, and it is understandable that neither Carter nor Carnarvon would admit it.

The day-by-day events leading up to the great moment when Carter gazed into the gold-filled outer room of the tomb have been well documented, and agree in general with Mrs. Emerson's description. What Carter actually said on that momentous occasion, in response to Carnarvon's eager question, is in some doubt. "Wonderful things" has become the official version, recorded by Carter himself. According to an account written by Carnarvon a few days afterward, Carter said, "There are some marvelous things here." In my opinion Mrs. Emerson's version—that at first Carter was too thunderstruck to speak at all— makes better sense in psychological terms.

The most damaging accusation made against Carter and Carnarvon is that they entered and explored the tomb in secret, before the official opening. Other evidence, aside from Mrs. Emerson's own account, gives credence to this charge. According to her, the illicit entry took place on the evening of the twenty-sixth of November, and not, as some have suggested, a day or two later. Her version seems more reasonable to me. The excavators' appetite had been whetted by what they saw through the small aperture, and as Mrs. Emerson admits, only men of iron could have waited any longer. Furthermore, the chief inspector, Rex Engelbach, was due to visit the tomb the following day, and any disturbance that occurred afterward might have been noted by him. The accusation that objects were removed from the tomb by Carter and Carnarvon is unproven; however, the private collections of both men contained articles that may well have belonged to the young king. The interested Reader may find the evidence pro and con in the numerous volumes on the tomb. The encounter with an irate Emerson explains Carnarvon's subsequent animosity against the Emerson family, and his refusal to let them participate.

The burial chamber was not officially opened until February 17 of the next year. The Emersons are not mentioned in the list of notables present on that occasion. In April Lord Carnarvon passed away from an infected and neglected mosquito bite. His death brought the story of the curse into full flower, despite the fact that his health had always been poor. Sensible persons pointed out that the so-called curse inscription in Tutankhamon's tomb was a journalistic fabrication, and that most of the persons directly involved in the work on the tomb lived to reasonable old ages, including Carter himself; but as Mrs. Emerson might say, common sense is no match for superstition. Obviously she succeeded in keeping the story of Emerson's curses quiet; but it would be interesting to learn how the Father of Curses reacted to Carnarvon's being struck down. He was a sensible man, so let us hope he did not take the matter to heart.

It took Howard Carter eight years to finish clearing the tomb of Tutankhamon. Only the sarcophagus, the outermost coffin, and the mummy of the king were left in place, where they remain today. The years were difficult for Carter. A number of writers have mentioned his autocratic behavior and tactlessness, which eventually led to a head-on confrontation with the Egyptian authorities. He was temporarily expelled from the tomb, but was later allowed to resume the clearance. The end results were devastating for foreign expeditions. The regulations regarding partage were tightened and the contents of the tomb were taken by the Cairo Museum.

One must make allowances for Carter. His was an onerous task, made more difficult by demands from all sides. As Emerson himself admitted, few excavators could have carried out the job as well.

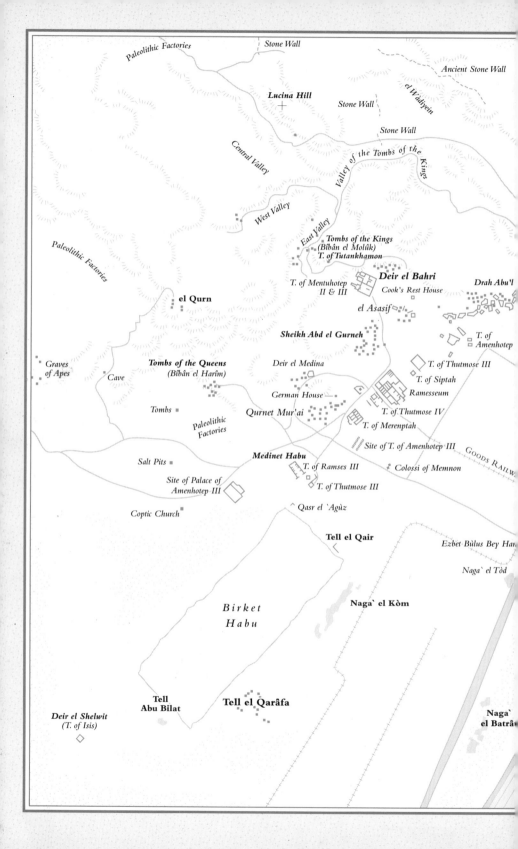